PJ G_r

A Lifetime of

Vengeance

A McKinney Brothers Novel
Book 1

PD House Books

Copyright © 2006 by P. J. Grondin

Second Edition

Published by P.D. House Holdings, LLC.

Library of Congress Control Number: 2010901629

vww.pjgrondin.com

3N 978-1-7370004-2-6

Dedication

This work is dedicated to my parents, Nicholas and Patricia Grondin, and my wife's parents, Alan and Mary Fleming. They taught us what we needed to know and how to figure out the rest.

Acknowledgements

To my dear wife, Debbie, for encouraging me to finish when I could have given up. To my children for putting up with my stressful moments. To my sister, Cathie, for her technical proofing and practical suggestions. To my friends who read excerpts of the manuscript and told me, "Hey, this isn't too bad." You all gave me the incentive to keep going. Thank you.

The second edition is the result of many hours of reviewing and revising the text to make the story flow better. This edition is more enjoyable to read. The story remains unchanged.

A Lifetime of

Vengeance

PROLOGUE

1961

William Hammerick built the vault in the early part of 1961 at the height of tensions between the United States and the Soviet Union. The Cubans were establishing closer political ties to the Communists in Moscow and fear of nuclear attack permeated the atmosphere of casual conversations all across America. "Duck and cover" was being taught as a defense against the horrors of exposure to radioactivity should a nuclear attack actually occur. The silly sounding public service commercials were played on all three networks. "Duck...and cover..."

Hammerick, third generation orange grower from rural Apopka, Florida didn't buy that "duck and cover" junk. That's why he took matters into his own hands.

It had been nearly sixteen years since the United States dropped "the bomb" on two Japanese cities and the horrifying pictures of the disfigured bodies and the living dead, the results of those attacks, still invaded his mind. He remembered the news accounts which said many people were vaporized along with everything around them. *They could have ducked and covered all they wanted to and they still would've been turned into little more than radioactive dust. Those were small bombs back then. Now they're big...megatons! They can destroy whole cities. And the radioactive dust will even reach out into the country. If they bomb the defense plant in Orlando, we'd still get the fallout.* He was determined to protect his wife and himself from that fate. That's why William Hammerick had to do something drastic.

In the middle of his orange grove off of Kelley Park Drive, he constructed a twelve foot by twelve foot vault. The vault was buried. Only about a foot of the vault was above ground. It had a six-and-a-half foot high ceiling and was constructed of two inch galvanized steel, welded at the seams. It had a massive door with a padlock and rubber seals to prevent air from getting into the vault. Ventilation ducts ran out of the vault in four directions. Each duct had dampers for securing the air inlets. There was also a pressurized air supply which would bleed air into the vault for about ninety-six hours. He thought that in the event of radioactive fallout, that would be adequate time for the decay of the radioactive dust...at least enough to allow opening of the vents to breathe outside air. He'd read some books about the effects of the bomb and the resulting radioactive cloud. He figured that with natural air movement and the settling out of radioactive particles, the normal air would be fit to breathe in two days and that would give him a two day cushion of compressed air.

In addition to all the mechanics of the design, Mr. Hammerick stocked the vault with enough canned food, dry goods, and water for up to two months. Also included in the plan were two relatively comfortable cots, blankets, pillows, sheets, a portable toilet, other toiletries, extra clothes, and a first aid kit. The vault was some 700 yards off of the main road and only 300 yards from their house which was located in front of the grove. Several huge camphor trees with long flowing Spanish moss stood in front of the house, partially hiding it from the sparse traffic on Kelley Park Drive.

Only a handful of their closest friends knew anything about the vault. The few who did know thought old William Hammerick had lost his mind. "The government would never allow a nuclear war to get started after what we know about the power of these bombs. They'd lose all that power and money. Their lavish lives would be destroyed," they'd said.

But William Hammerick didn't take any chances or spare any expense. He built the vault and felt secure knowing that it was there if he and his wife needed it.

1984

When they first looked into buying the grove, they'd noticed the overgrown trail that led to the center of the grove. When the oldest brother asked where the trail led, the real estate agent, Jimmy Pitman, said that it led to an old storage bin that wasn't used anymore. That got his curiosity up and he wanted to know more about it. Jimmy Pitman shrugged his shoulders and gave a head motion to follow him. The four made their way down the trail, deep into the grove, pushing through brush, spider webs, and dead bushes. Finally, they came upon an inclined path that went down at about a 30 degree angle to the steel, padlocked door of the vault. Part of the sandy wall alongside the inclined path had collapsed, but they could still access the door with little effort.

The real estate agent turned to the brothers, "There it is. As you can see, it isn't much to look at. The steel is deteriorated pretty badly. No one's been in there in years."

The padlock on the vault's door was coated with rust and was caked with dirt and old spider webs. A thick coat of rust also covered the visible parts of the heavy door. Indeed, no entry had been made to the vault in many years.

"How big is the storage area inside?" the oldest asked. His younger brothers could see his mind working overtime. They knew that some "brilliant" idea was cooking up there. Jimmy Pitman scratched his head, shrugged his shoulders, raised an eyebrow, shrugged his shoulders again and admitted that he didn't know. The elder brother looked directly at him and said, "Well let's find out, shall we?"

With a blank stare and a moment's hesitation, Jimmy, in his southern drawl said, "Yes sir. I'll have to call the owner and see if she still has a key. I know that the agency didn't get one."

"Then let's get to it. We'll wait here if you don't mind." It was a statement, not a request for permission.

"That'll be fine." Jimmy turned and trekked off towards the house to try to get the vault key from old Mrs. Hammerick, grumbling as he went, "These hippy punks don't have two nickels to rub together. Why am I wastin' my time?"

***

Jimmy Pitman was very happy with his commission on the sale of the grove to the brothers. Mrs. Gertrude Hammerick was happy to see that the new owners of the property were going to continue the orange grove business. Since her husband's death two years before, she'd had to depend on the processing company to handle the maintenance of the grove. She was tired of the hassle and, at 72, had no desire to continue her husband's business. He'd left her a significant fortune and she wanted to move to a cooler climate. She had already bought a new home in Sapphire Valley, North Carolina and another just outside of Wilmington. "After all, it's only money," she had told the new grove owners at the closing. Mrs. Hammerick wished the boys good luck and with that, boarded a flight to Asheville, North Carolina, and her new home in the foothills of the Blue Ridge Mountains.

1986

Mrs. Hammerick was enjoying her new home in North Carolina and the brothers were in business. The grove was producing quite well. The three brothers were splitting a good profit from the grove; twenty-five percent for each one of them and twenty-five percent for their parents. Their new venture into indoor foliage was starting to pay off as well. Since Apopka, Florida is the indoor foliage capital of the world, their business in that area was a natural. The combination of the grove and the greenhouses earned each brother in excess of $80,000 per year; a good income by most standards. But that was small potatoes compared to their real business.

The vault was cleaned up, refurbished with a new electric service, an emergency generator, and a septic system. A dehumidifying system was installed to keep the moisture level and the vault deterioration level to a minimum. A new electronic lock system was also installed along with other security measures. Additional landscaping was added to obscure the entry to the vault and the brothers made a new, out of the way path to the vault door.

When the work was complete, the interior of the vault looked like a military command center. The outside looked like nothing at all. An intercom system allowed communication between the vault, the greenhouses, the nursery warehouse, and the main house. The recording system could only be deactivated by use of a five digit code at the vault's entrance. The code was known only to the brothers and was changed on a monthly basis. The only time the recording system was purposely deactivated was at night when the delivery van brought the usual twenty bales of marijuana to the vault for storage or when the dope left the vault, two to five bales at a time. The security measures were expensive, but the brothers were able to split $250,000.00 on average each month. When you take home over $80,000.00 in cash each month, not only can you afford the elaborate security, it is essential.

The brothers didn't expect to end up in the illegal drug trade. It developed over a number of years. Pat, the oldest brother, was shorter than most of his classmates at 5'7". He had sandy brown hair that hung over his ears and the start of a thin mustache. His blue eyes were his most striking natural feature. Coupled with his smile, most girls at school thought that he was cute in a safe kind of way.

One feature that he'd acquired while working in a nursery outside of Apopka was a scar just below the left side of his mouth. While hammering a nail into a rafter board on a greenhouse, the hammer missed the head and caused the nail to ricochet into Pat's jaw. The nail stuck about an inch into the skin along his jaw bone. There was no permanent damage, but over the years the scar turned white. Pat had a habit of rubbing the scar with the middle finger of his right hand whenever he was concentrating on an idea or simply daydreaming.

He never tried to play the tough guy like many of his male classmates. At Apopka High School he'd been involved in many extra-curricular activities. He played basketball and baseball and was in the choir. He'd wanted to go on to college and was hoping to get a baseball scholarship, but that never happened. He'd maintained decent grades, A's and B's, throughout his school career. He was well liked and considered a leader among his classmates. He always smiled and joked with people and made friends easily. He was built well enough because he worked out to keep in shape for baseball season.

During his junior year, he and a few of his teammates met after practice at one of the boy's house. One of his friends pulled out a small bag of grass from his dresser, rolled a joint, and offered it to the group. Pat was scared to try it at first, but after his friends passed the joint around and none of them went insane, Pat caved in and tried it. Once he got home, he thought to himself *what's the big deal? Nothing happened. I thought that this was supposed to be fun?* He went for weeks without trying it again, but eventually did go back to his teammate's house where they all indulged in the evil weed once again. This time Pat got *the buzz*. The pot-induced laughing went on so long and hard that his voice was hoarse afterwards. That was the beginning for Pat. He started buying the stuff himself. Soon he found that he needed a job to get money to buy it.

It wasn't long before he realized that he could get free stash if he sold small quantities to his friends. Then he introduced his middle brother, Joe, to the joys of smoking grass. Joe was taller than Pat. At 5'11" he was the tallest of the three McKinney brothers. He was a muscular guy with large biceps and a six pack stomach. He worked out a lot and planned to join the Marine Corps ROTC program when he completed high school. He was just a year behind Pat in school. Joe was more intense than Pat. When he worked out, he would block out everything from his mind and concentrate on lifting. His face would turn red and contorted to the point that anyone watching him would swear he was having a heart attack. But he could adapt to social situations as well. He smiled when conversation was light, but was intense when the topic was serious.

Pat and Joe could pass for twins, though Joe's facial features were harder than Pat's. His jaw was square with a cleft in the middle and his neck was wide where it met his shoulders. Joe had darker, shorter hair than Pat and his eyes were slightly more gray than blue. The girls were attracted to his good looks and confident manner. He was also an excellent student. He paid attention to the details of any situation.

When Joe found out that Pat was smoking grass, he was initially infuriated. Only after Pat talked to him about it several times did he conclude that it wasn't as bad as the authorities were advertising. He finally tried the weed after Pat's repeated attempts to get Joe to try it. Like Pat, the first time was a real letdown. Nothing happened. But eventually he caught the buzz and took up the habit. It took the edge off of his serious manner. Pat felt that was a good thing. He always said that Joe was too serious. Joe didn't agree. He found himself missing details in his papers at school. His grades slipped a bit over time but not significantly. He too got roped into peddling to close friends. Joe was much more secretive about his dealings. He wanted as few people as possible knowing that he was indulging.

Finally, the youngest, Mike, learned what they were doing and wanted to see what it was like. Mike was carefree, compared to his older brothers. He wasn't a real serious student though he maintained a decent 3.1 grade point average. He was more interested in hanging around with friends and playing Atari, the newest rage in video games. He wanted to learn how to write computer programs so that he could develop video games but he was too busy playing them to learn about creating them. Getting high fit right in with his personality at the time. His hair was nearly to his shoulders even when he was an eighth grader.

Their parents were not pleased back then. They used to ask Mike why he wasn't more like his brothers. He'd just shrug his shoulders and give them the 'I don't know look.' Mike was a pretty big kid at 5'10" and weighed in at 215 pounds. He was strong. He could take either of his brothers at arm wrestling even though Pat and Joe worked out. Mike was tough, too. Pat and Joe used to use Mike as a punching bag. They said it was to toughen him up. By Mike's junior year in high school, they could no longer get away with that. Mike would grab Pat or Joe and get them in a bear hug. He'd make them cry uncle before he released the crushing hold on them.

The brothers were pretty much All-American teens when they were introduced to the world of drugs. They all graduated from smoking casually, to smoking heavily, to having to deal to support their habit. It wasn't an addiction, per se, but it was a bad habit, and a tough one to break. Before Pat graduated from high school, he was dealing five pounds of the stuff per week. His younger brothers wanted in on the 'business' and soon, it was growing on its own. Before they knew what was happening, they were dealing serious weight. They had little time for social lives and no time for college, baseball, the Marine Corps, or developing video games.

On the up side, they were starting to accumulate some serious cash. By the time Mike had graduated from high school in 1983, the brothers were having a hard time hiding the fact that they were making far more money than their Dad. That's when they realized that they had to make some changes in their lives. They had to find a way to clean their money, make it look like a legitimate business. They'd worked in a family-owned nursery so they knew a little about the nursery business. They also knew that orange groves were big business in central Florida. That's when they bought a medium-sized nursery, the Hammerick grove and the vault.

Chapter 1

October 1988

The vault had been a well-guarded secret for several years. The brothers, Pat, Joe and Mike McKinney, were doing well in their legal and illegal business ventures with no interruption and little cause for any real concern. Most of their business associates were both professional and discreet. But Pat, the oldest brother, was becoming concerned. It had been their policy from the beginning to keep everyone away from the vault to prevent even the temptation of theft by a business associate. He warned the other two that things were going too well and that they were letting their guard down. He even went so far as to recommend shutting down the operation for about one year and to reevaluate their business associates. Too many people were getting to know about their real business. They each had weapons that they could use to defend themselves and their property, but they all agreed that if they had to use guns, their troubles would only be starting.

Mike, the carefree brother, thought that his big brother's fears were unfounded. He and Joe were confident that business could continue as usual. They even talked about expanding the business. They were so unconcerned that they were taking associates to the nursery warehouse in front of the grove to load bales that they'd sold. Early on, they'd agreed that the vault, the nursery, and the warehouse were off limits for drug transactions. But over time, these rules were loosened and all but forgotten. Now even Pat was doing business in a way that was contrary to their original agreement. The use of the warehouse for loading and unloading bales of grass became commonplace and the vault was a natural location for money exchanges due to its seclusion. He was getting worried despite how smooth operations were going.

Pat, Joe and Mike were also skimming the bales; taking small quantities of grass out of the bales before shipping them to their customers. To compensate for the loss of weight, they would spray the bales with a mist of water or drop in a handful of sand. A few sprays into each bale added the weight back from the skimmed weed. That seemed to be a fool proof solution until one of their customers found out about the ruse. About this same time, they decided to raise prices for their illegal product. The combination of the watered down grass and raised prices didn't sit well with a few of their customers. Word spread quickly that the McKinneys were cheating. Joe called Pat one evening in mid-October. It was right before Mike's wedding to his girlfriend, Julie. He said that he'd been feeling guilty about their dope business. He recommended that they shut down the business and get out. They'd made a small fortune and had no real need to continue.

Pat told Joe that he'd been feeling the same way. He'd been doing some soul-searching. What he found he didn't like. Pat said that he even thought about talking to a priest but decided against it. He said that he'd rather talk to God directly instead. Pat and Joe made a pact. They were getting out as soon as their current holdings were sold out. That would be a little over a week. When they told Mike, he was angry at first, but Pat explained that he knew a friend that could invest their money. With the nursery and the grove, they'd be set for life. Mike confided that he'd been feeling guilty, too. He agreed that it was as good a time as any to get out. Pat was relieved, but still concerned. They still had a sizable amount of grass to sell. Pat grew more nervous with each passing day.

Pat's concerns escalated when he was confronted by a friend, Brian Purcer. Brian was a skinny guy, weighing about 140 pounds soaking wet. He had a huge head of frizzy hair. He was the only white kid with an afro that any of his friends had ever seen. He was also an up and coming rock musician who bought the occasional bag of dope from Pat. He wasn't in the dope trade. He was a casual user and a good friend of Pat. He'd just bought some weed from Pat that was so wet from being sprayed down that it wouldn't stay lit. The level headed Brian came unglued and unleashed a serious berating of Pat and his business practices. He told Pat that word on the street was that he and his brothers were going to be taught a lesson about ripping people off. Pat's worst fears were soon realized, and the family business was now in jeopardy.

November 1988

Jamie Watkins, Donnie Lee Lester, Bobby Acquino, and Randy Farley were sitting in the ABC Liquor Lounge on State Route 436, in Apopka, Florida. They were celebrating. They'd just been released from custody at the Orange County jail. Their alleged crime was the rape and murder of a young lady named Julie McKinney. Julie was the new bride of Mike McKinney. They'd been married just over two weeks. The four had allegedly broken into the house of Mike and Julie McKinney and attacked the young woman when she arrived home from grocery shopping. Part of the attack was videotaped by the attackers. The Orange County Sheriff's Department had found that tape but it had disappeared from the evidence room at the Sheriff's Office. Within a few days of the arrests, the case was dropped. That tape was the only key piece of evidence and it was gone.

The beers were flowing, shots were slammed, and the laughter was loud and rowdy. They'd also forged a new partnership; they'd put the McKinney brothers out of business. They were excited about the prospect of making a ton of money. Their previous suppliers were gone, run out of town. They'd turned-tail and run-scared. The McKinneys dealt strictly in grass. Those days were over. No more limits on who they could talk with and what they could sell.

"I told y'all them McKinney boys would haul ass outta here!" That was Jamie talking, more like yelling, about how the McKinneys couldn't take the heat. Jamie Watkins was originally from Garland, Texas, a suburb of Dallas. He was a stocky young man. He had a freckled face and light red hair which made him appear younger than his 24 years, but when he talked he sounded anything but youthful. He always wanted to be the center of attention. He did this by talking louder than everyone around him, no matter what the situation. In the ABC Lounge, he was nearly yelling over the music and crowd noise.

"They saw us comin' and decided it was time to get back up north where it's safe for pussies like them. Back to momma's tit. Hidin' under her skirt. They couldn't stand the southern heat."

Loud laughter sprinkled in as Jamie went on with his monologue about the wimp, Yankee McKinneys. He called them about every name in the book and even made up some new ones.

They were all pretty well polluted. Each joined in Jamie's berating of the brothers. The only one who seemed a bit reserved was Bobby Acquino. He felt miserable about what they'd done but he dared not voice that view in the middle of this drunken party. Bobby lost the only true friend he had when events started to unfold. He was sorry that he didn't have the guts to stop it. He simply went along with the madness.

Bobby was Puerto Rican by birth but his parents moved the family to Florida when he was a young child. Bobby still had the dark olive skin of his ancestry and he had very dark hair and eyes to match. He spoke with a slight Puerto Rican accent that he'd acquired from his parents. He was raised Roman Catholic and still prayed before every meal and before bed each night. He prayed every day that the madness would stop but then he turned around and continued his association with his current friends, this band of thieves.

Donnie Lee and Bobby were best friends now. They seemed to stick together the most out of these four. Donnie Lee was a Florida boy through and through. He was born and raised in the rural south in Zellwood, Florida. His parents worked for Zellwin Farms which grew corn in an area known as the muck farms. He was a big man at 230 pounds and 6'2". He kept his light brown hair shaved close to his head and looked as if he couldn't grow a hair on his face, which kept him looking younger than his age. Donnie Lee, like Bobby, also felt guilty about what happened to Julie McKinney. But he was less concerned about guilt and more concerned about getting rich. He didn't want to follow in his dad's footsteps on the farms. That was exceptionally hard, dirty work and he wanted nothing to do with it.

Donnie Lee was the first to suggest that they should change the arrangement that they had with the McKinneys. He knew that they were skimming dope off of every bale. That was the first string pulled that caused the unraveling of a tightly wound package; an arrangement that was working well for a number of years. It started out small and ended up making them all quite a bit of money. They were willing to overlook the skimming. Then they found out the McKinneys were adding weight by spraying the bales. The moisture added nearly half a pound to each bale and added another $300 per bale to the McKinneys' already good take. Within days, the close business arrangement fell apart. Friendship was replaced by accusations, anger and hate.

That's when they took matters into their own hands. That's when they raped and beat Mike McKinney's wife of only two weeks and left her for dead. The McKinneys and all of central Florida were stunned. After several weeks, charges were filed against Jamie, Donnie Lee, Bobby and Randy and subsequently dropped. Evidence disappeared. The Sheriff's office said they couldn't make the charge stick with no physical evidence tying the four to the scene.

That was the last straw. The McKinneys left central Florida. Before they left for good, they had a meeting at the vault. They put together a long range plan. It sounded good on paper but who would remember the details over the next seven years? Then Mike said he couldn't follow through with the plan. He couldn't do it and wouldn't be a party to it. He was defeated before they even had a chance to get started. But Pat and Joe were determined. It would take years, but it was worth the wait. They shook hands, hugged and went their separate ways to prepare.

Less than ten miles away, Jamie, Donnie Lee, Bobby,

and Randy hoisted more beer to their victory. They thought they'd won the war. They didn't realize that it was just the first battle.

Chapter 2

June 1995

Donnie Lee Lester and Roberto "Bobby" Acquino were drinking at the ABC Liquor Lounge in Plymouth, Florida. They were talking about what success they'd had over the last six years in their partnership.

The nursery they owned had nothing to do with the day to day operation of growing, packaging, and selling plants, but it was an excellent front for their real business; importing Columbian marijuana and Peruvian cocaine. Donnie Lee and Bobby, along with their other partner, Jamie Watkins, had built up quite a trade with each partner pulling down over half a million dollars a year for the last three years.

Donnie Lee was a tall, stocky, southern man, with a drawl that accentuated the fact that he'd lived in rural Florida all his life. It wasn't that he liked living in Florida. He just hadn't been anywhere else. Donnie Lee wasn't particularly bright either. He nearly flunked out of high school and barely received the minimum number of credits to graduate with his class. He'd joined the Army, but was released with a less than honorable discharge for drug abuse. Even that was generous, because he was caught, red-handed, selling cocaine to an undercover Army investigator.

He was cool under pressure, though. Years ago, when the partners were first getting started in the illegal drug trade, he was driving south on Route 441 towards Orlando in his 1977 Ford LTD. With ten pounds of Columbian grass in the trunk, he was being very cautious. Then he decided to pass a slow-driving elderly woman. He'd been cursing her for the last half mile when he made his move. Just then a white Cadillac ripped along the side of Donnie Lee's LTD and literally rammed it into the ditch along the west side of the road. Neither driver was hurt, but both were shaken up a bit. Apparently, the driver of the Cadillac, a tall, skinny guy in a business suit had more to hide than Donnie Lee. He'd rushed over to see if Donnie was alright. When he got to the LTD, Donnie noticed that the man was very nervous and didn't want to hang around for the Highway Patrol to arrive. The guy handed Donnie Lee five hundred dollars, handed him a business card and assured Donnie that if he called him in a few days he would reward him further...if the local police never found out about this incident. Still in a daze, Donnie agreed. With that, the man literally ran back to his damaged Cadillac, got in and drove off just as another car stopped to see what was going on.

Donnie Lee remained cool under questioning from everyone that stopped. He told the same story about how a drunk kid in a white, beat up Dodge Dart had rammed him, didn't even stop, made an illegal u-turn on 441 and took off without even looking his way to see if he was hurt, dead or whatever. During the incident, Donnie Lee never even glanced toward the trunk of the battered LTD. It remained closed through the entire ordeal and nobody asked him to look inside. Finally, the police report was complete. The officers were off in search of a '67 or '68 white Dodge Dart with a battered right front panel, being driven by a young, long haired, white kid.

Donnie Lee's car was not in drivable condition so he had it towed to a garage on Washington Street in Ocoee. The garage was owned by Wilbur Lester, Donnie Lee's older brother. It would be an easy matter for Donnie Lee to remove the stashed weed from the trunk while at his brother's garage. That was Donnie Lee Lester's first brush with the law during the illegal activity of transporting drugs for resale.

That little accident turned out to be a favorable stroke of luck for the partners. The tall, skinny guy was Jason Roberts. He was very generous to the partnership once the parties understood the nature of each other's businesses. When Donnie Lee called Mr. Roberts after the accident, he invited Donnie Lee to his home for dinner. Donnie Lee wasn't familiar with the area where Mr. Roberts lived. After driving down Markham Woods Road in Lake Mary towards Sanford for about ten minutes, he came to the entrance of an exclusive subdivision. From the road, you couldn't see a single home.

Donnie Lee stopped at the guard house and gave the guard the required information and was allowed to drive on. Another few minutes, after driving past homes that had to be owned by wealthy lawyers, doctors, and business tycoons, he came to the address on Wild Cherry Court. He pulled up to the gate at the foot of the driveway and spoke into the intercom. The guard at the other end of the intercom was polite, but serious. He assured Donnie Lee that he was expected and requested some identification. After displaying his driver's license to the camera, the gate opened and Donnie Lee followed the driveway back to the house. When he saw Mr. Robert's home, he was awe-struck. It was the largest home he'd ever seen; like something off of the TV shows Dallas or Dynasty.

Donnie Lee was seated in Mr. Robert's office, looking from wall to wall, taking in all the expensive woodwork, cabinets, artifacts, and books. Everything was elegant and expensive. Mr. Roberts spoke and broke Donnie Lee's trance. He explained that he'd done some checking up on him and his partners. He explained to Donnie Lee that he knew they were dealing drugs, what kind of drugs, and how much they were selling. He went on to explain that they were clean as far as investigation by the local police, county sheriff, or local drug task force.

"To anyone who cares," he explained, "you guys are just a bunch of average citizens. I'd like for you guys to work for me. I think you'd be a good fit for my organization. I'll make sure that, if you join with me, you'll immediately more than double your income."

Donnie Lee was astonished. He couldn't believe that anyone could dredge up this much accurate information on the partners' activities. *If this man could dig up this much information, certainly the police could, too, couldn't they?*

Mr. Roberts continued and explained that it was his business to know who did what in the drug trade in the area. "I am the major supplier of Peruvian Cocaine in central Florida. If anyone else tries to break into the market, they come through me or they're out of business, permanently. Understand?"

He was willing to show Donnie Lee and his partners how to really make money; how to launder it; how to keep the law enforcement people off their back; how to keep competition to a minimum. He gave Donnie Lee the details and told him to discuss it with the partners. With that, Donnie Lee thanked Mr. Roberts for his hospitality and left the house, dazzled by what he had just seen and heard.

After explaining the deal to Jamie and Bobby, he could almost predict their responses. Jamie Watkins, the brash, outspoken red-head, was thrilled with the prospect of making millions of dollars. Bobby was not so pleased. He felt that this was a little bit of a jump for the three. Later, when Jamie left the room, Bobby expressed his fear that this would send Jamie's ego into the stratosphere. He'd be blabbing his hotshot mouth all over town. Donnie Lee assured him that it wouldn't happen. Mr. Roberts would impress upon Jamie that his brazen personality would have to be toned down.

"Believe me. Mr. Roberts will take care of Jamie's mouth. We won't have anything to worry about."

So a mutually beneficial business arrangement developed.

Sitting at a table at the ABC Lounge on Route 436 in Apopka, Donnie Lee and Bobby toasted Jason Roberts and his bad driving habits. In the few years of their association with Mr. Roberts, they'd gone from small time fifty pounds of pot per week to being major players in the central Florida drug trade. They had to develop security measures, pay for protection from some local law enforcement officials, realign their nursery business as a cover and keep close tabs on who got to know their names and faces. Their homes were small fortresses, nothing as fancy as their mentor's, but nice, fenced-in, and electronically secure homes of between 3500 to 4500 square feet, in exclusive central Florida neighborhoods.

The partners met for a drink on a pretty regular basis. Donnie Lee, in his faded jeans, denim short-sleeve shirt and cowboy boots was asking Bobby what he did with all his money, besides buying expensive toys like four wheel drive trucks, a new swimming pool, a Jacuzzi, a bar, and a boat. Bobby's hand went to the bridge of his nose and rubbed the slight knot from where it had been broken as a youngster. He replied that he actually gave a good amount to charitable organizations and the church; all in cash, all anonymously. He wasn't comfortable talking about his religious beliefs with most people mainly because he was afraid of spending an eternity in hell. He feared that he was heading down that road and his only hope was a bedside confession. It really tugged at his conscience. After what they'd done to Mike's wife, though he never touched her personally, he hadn't stopped the brutality either. Donnie Lee frowned but then his frown turned to a smile. He knew that Bobby was religious. He was afraid that one day Bobby's conscience would get the best of him. Would he turn himself in just to try to relieve the mental anguish caused by his feelings of guilt?

Bobby Acquino had just a very slight touch of his father's accent. At five-feet, nine inches tall, he was the tallest member in his family. His brother was in prison for armed robbery and assault with a deadly weapon. His sister was a freshman at the University of South Florida in Tampa.

Bobby felt guilty about starting the partnership's current business with money stolen from the McKinneys. Mike McKinney was Bobby's closest friend. They'd been friends through high school and got along well until things fell apart. Bobby knew that what they did to Mike's young bride would land him in hell and he prayed every day to be forgiven. He also knew that Mike had been destroyed by their betrayal. Mike sobbed in front of Bobby, "How could you...?" That's all that Mike could choke out before he was consumed by grief. They never spoke again. But Pat and Joe had more to say. Pat had screamed in Bobby's face, "You know, you, Donnie Lee, Jamie, and Randy will pay for this. I don't know when, and you won't see it coming, but you will pay." And with that, Pat and Joe helped Mike McKinney walk away.

"What are you day-dreaming about?" The question broke Bobby out of his momentary trance.

He looked at Donnie Lee and asked him, "Do you ever wish that you could turn back the clock, travel back in time and fix what we did? Mike was our friend."

The words made Donnie Lee shiver. "Look, Bobby, they were our friends, but they weren't perfect either. They were ripping us off or don't you remember that?"

"Don't try to pass this off on them! They were our friends, and we betrayed them. Look, let's change the subject. This is making me sick. We could've been in business with Mike and done just as well as we're doing now. Plus we wouldn't have Jamie as a partner. We'd be better off without him. Sure, we've got money. We've got money because we suckered someone who trusted us. We're rich but I have a hard time looking myself in the mirror at times."

"With that mug, I'd have a rough time lookin' in the mirror, too!" Jamie Watkins always liked to make a grand entrance. His Texas accent coupled with a back-country Florida drawl, mixed with a plug of chewing tobacco, resulted in a conglomeration of barely discernible growls.

"Is our Bobby feelin' sorry for hisself again? He must be worried 'bout ole Mikey McKenzie and his brothers...or whatever their names' was. Look, Bobby, forget those jerks. They got the rash and we got the cash."

Jamie's smile was broad and he was having a grand time poking fun at Bobby. He knew how to get Bobby's goat almost instantly. Donnie Lee could see Bobby's face redden and figured he'd better step in before the two got into a knuckle-buster right there in the bar.

He got off his stool at the bar and said calmly, "Cool it, Jamie." He stepped between the two and told Jamie he'd buy him a drink.

"Lay it on me, brutha!" Jamie exclaimed and Donnie Lee

ordered a round of whiskey and waters. This kept Jamie quiet for almost one minute. Jamie started bragging about his new four-wheel-drive truck and how he'd gone to the clay pits to try it out. He described the hills and valleys that his new toy conquered and how it could do almost anything. The other partners were not impressed. They knew Jamie's habit of stretching the truth. When he finished bragging about his new truck, he spotted a couple of young women sitting at a table by themselves.

Jamie turned to his partners and said, "See you boys later. It's party time."

Before Jamie left the bar, Donnie Lee reminded him that there was a business meeting in the morning at 9:30 at the nursery.

"I'll be there. Don't worry about me."

Donnie Lee grabbed him by the arm just as Jamie turned to walk away, and with a serious look said, "Jamie, I'm not kidding with you. This meeting is important. We got some serious business to take care of."

"Alright already. I hear you." With an annoyed expression, Jamie left the bar to chase skirts.

Bobby looked at Jamie as he left and shook his head in disgust. He made it clear that he didn't like Jamie. He didn't like his loud, obnoxious mouth, his rude manner, and he didn't like the way he conducted his deals for the partnership.

Bobby turned to Donnie Lee and asked, "Why don't we dump Jamie? He's gonna get us busted with his big mouth. The last thing we need is him telling all these chicks our business."

Donnie Lee knew that Bobby was right. He said, "Bobby, you and I both know that most of what Jamie says is bullshit. Those babes wouldn't know where the bullshit starts or ends."

Even as the words left his mouth he knew that Jamie was becoming a liability. He was running his mouth too much to too many people. Maybe he'd talk to Mr. Roberts about it after the meeting tomorrow. For right now, it could wait.

Chapter 3

It was 9:30 PM when Karen Grimes heard the front door of the apartment shut. She was already furious and ready for a battle. The normally tanned and smooth complexion on her face was beet-red with anger. It had been a particularly long day at work, and so far, since she'd arrived home, things hadn't changed. Nothing was going right. She'd prepared a fabulous dinner for her husband, Bill, and he didn't show up to share it. It used to bother her when Bill would be late or not call. She would always imagine the worst; a fight or an accident. Now she knew that it was just Bill. He was always scheming. He always had a plan to get rich. Those plans always involved robbery, drugs, or both.

William Harvard Grimes was never satisfied working for a living. For a while, he was able to get by on his good looks. He was a strong, handsome young man with blondish-red hair and light brown eyes. He walked with a swagger that exuded confidence. He always wanted to have more than the next guy. He wasn't smart enough to make things happen, though. The smartest thing about him was his middle name. He'd say to his friends in a half-joking manner, "I'm really a genius. That's why my folks named me Harvard. They figured that I'd be going there someday."

Bill finished high school only because his girlfriend, Karen Ann Farrar, did most of his homework for him. If she didn't do it, it didn't get done. So Bill got by with marginal grades and got his diploma. Then he went from one dead end job to another working for minimum wage. He rarely lasted more than six months at one company. He was a dreamer without a means to carry out those dreams. He always bragged about the things he was going to do when he got rich.

That's what hooked Karen, the high school cheerleading

squad captain and homecoming queen. She looked like a model, tall and thin with shoulder length blond hair. She was infatuated with Bill. She figured that anyone with such a clear vision of the future must have a good head on his shoulders. He was always talking about traveling to far-away places and seeing things that country girls from rural Central Florida had no chance to see. She'd never been out of the state and she had very little prospect of ever doing so. Her imagination was stimulated by Bill's talk of trips to exotic places. So Bill was her chance to actually see the world. He was her ticket out of the rural country existence she lived day to day.

Over the years, living with Bill, she'd come to realize that Bill was all talk. All her efforts to change him were failing and she knew that their five-year-long marriage was all but over. She couldn't change Bill; she couldn't make him smarter; couldn't get him to follow through on his plans. Even as crazy as they were, illegal and dangerous, Karen wished that Bill would do them just so he would follow through on something. It pained Karen to realize that she would be leaving her husband soon. It scared her because she'd never been with any other man but Bill. It was a frightening thought to her to meet, much less date, another man, but right now, she was not thinking about anyone else. She was enraged. She'd gone to the trouble to fix this meal to try to set the evening on the right course and it had just followed the rest of the dismal day. Karen was not a woman to be calmed now. She had a chip on her shoulder as large as a ten story building, and it was about to fall on Bill.

"Where the hell have you been? I've been waiting all night for you to call or come home! Dinner's been done for almost three hours and now it's ruined! Why didn't you leave a note or call or something?"

Bill could see that he was in a no-win situation. Karen was red in the face she was so angry. He knew that when she was like this, there was little reason to say anything. But he was going to try anyway.

"Baby, I've been working on a deal. I've got the details worked out, and I can finish it up by this Saturday. We'll be making some real cash and some real stash on this one, I promise you."

Bill started to move towards Karen to embrace her and try to settle her down. Years ago, it would have worked, but these days there was no smooth-talking his way out of tough arguments like this one. Karen was beyond being consoled; she'd been through it too many times before.

"Bill, just drop the 'big deal' line," she hollered, almost hurting her throat. "Forget it! There is no 'big deal!' Even if there was, at this point, I don't want any part of it. If you can't even get home in time for dinner, I don't care about any 'deals.' Do you understand? I don't care. I'm fed up with your big dreams! You never follow through on anything! You and your friends sit around and get drunk and stoned and never accomplish a thing! I'm sick of it! If you don't get your shit together, I'm leaving and I'm not coming back."

Bill just listened. She'd said all this before. She was just mad. He'd screwed up, and he probably deserved to be tongue-lashed. But this deal was important to him. He'd show her. He'd follow through on this one.

"Listen to me, baby. I'm real serious about this one. I just got done talking to Jamie Watkins and he said..."

That sent Karen through the roof. She was already steamed, but to think that Bill was talking to Jamie Watkins really topped things off.

"You what? You're dealing with that low life piece-of-shit? How could you even think about doing that? Don't you have any conscience? That guy screwed your best friend! He raped and killed his sister-in-law. He ripped him off for thousands of dollars, or don't you remember?"

Karen's words were hitting a nerve in Bill. He did remember, all too well. But that was years ago and they hadn't heard from their once close friend, Pat McKinney, since then. Besides, Jamie dealt the best stuff in town and Bill could get the stuff up front, no cash. He wouldn't have to put out a nickel of his own cash to get thousands of dollars' worth of pot and cocaine to sell. It would put him in with the big time dealers. He wasn't sure how Jamie could afford to do it, but he was glad to have a chance to prove to Karen that he really could make it in the big time. He'd buy her whatever she wanted. Right now all he wanted was for her to believe in him. Bill knew that Karen was losing faith in him and he wanted to prove to her that he could succeed. *She's got her shit together but I'm gonna show her I can do it, too.*

The sound of dishes being literally thrown into the sink woke him up out of his momentary trance. Karen was clearing the table and launching the dishes in the general direction of the sink and counter. Broken glass, food, drinks, silverware, pots and pans, all the remnants of what could have been a romantic dinner, or at least a civil one, were scattered across the kitchen. Karen was acting crazy now. What was left on the dining room table was scooped up inside the table cloth which Karen was using like a hobo's sack. She picked up the four corners of the cloth cover, brought them together in one motion, and tightened the contents into a ball. What was now a little sack of napkins, some food scraps, spilled gravy, a trivet, and other odds-and-ends, was pitched in the direction of the waste basket. Without looking at Bill, she walked into the bedroom and closed the door. Bill tried to follow, but when he got to the door, it was locked. It wasn't a real big trick to trip the lock of one of the cheap apartment doors, but Bill figured he'd better leave Karen alone until she cooled off. He'd had enough experiences with these fights to know when enough was enough. He heard the shower in the master bedroom come on and so Bill thought that the soothing water of the shower would cool her off. *She's not thinking straight now. Later, she'll calm down and understand.*

Bill went to the spare bedroom where his gun cabinet stood. He opened the cabinet and took out his Colt AN1911 45 caliber pistol. He'd bought it from Karen's brother Steve. Steve had been in the Navy and had access to the weapons locker on base where he was stationed. He'd managed to steal one of the standard Navy hand guns and sold it to Bill for drug money. Bill paid a mere $50.00 for the classic piece. He knew he'd never be able to sell it to an honest gun collector but he had no intention of ever selling this gun anyway. Bill field stripped the gun and cleaned it, making sure all the parts were immaculate. He reassembled the parts and ran the piece through a few dry runs, cocking, firing then re-cocking the slide. Satisfied with his job, smiling to himself, he loaded a full clip into the chamber, made sure the safety was on, and stuck the colt in his pants at the small of his back.

He'd seen this on Magnum, P.I. and he'd found that this actually was the most comfortable way to carry it without a holster. Just then he heard the door to the master bedroom open. He expected Karen to call to him and talk things out. Then he heard her footsteps heading for the front door. Without a word, Karen Grimes was out the door and heading down the stairs of the second-floor apartment. Bill had the urge to chase after her, but he thought better of it. He now realized that she was as mad as he'd ever seen her. It might be a few days before things were back to normal.

He'd just have to ride it out.

He heard the screech of tires outside the apartment window, then a horn blast. He looked out just in time to see Karen pull away, and the truck that had apparently gotten in her way, pulled into the parking spot next to the one Karen had vacated. It was Jamie Watkins.

**

Karen was still fuming when she pulled her Chevy Camero into the drive at her parent's house. She turned off the engine and sat thinking about Bill's various schemes. He never seemed to have a thought about honest work. His old friend Pat McKinney had noticed it early in their friendship. She remembered Pat telling her that there may come a time when she would have to go it alone, that Bill was just too far out there to settle down to an honest living. *He just doesn't want to grow up.* Pat had told her this just before he left Orlando. She remembered smiling at Patrick and saying, 'Sure, you can say that. You've already made your mark. When did you ever make an honest living?' She remembered Pat's reply, 'I'm starting right now.' She couldn't believe it when she'd heard that Pat had joined the

Navy. She knew he had made some major cash over the years and thought that he had it stashed somewhere. It didn't make sense that he would join the military. She wondered if maybe he'd lost it all gambling or something like that, but that wasn't Pat. He was pretty frugal when it came to spending his money. He never drove an expensive car, never flashed money around and never talked business in a public place. No, Pat hadn't lost his fortune. He was just hiding it somewhere.

She wondered where Pat was now and wished he were here with her. He knew how to talk to Bill and bring him down to earth when he was on one of his dream schemes. Pat was also a big dreamer, with one very big difference from Bill. He seemed to know when a dream was just that; a dream. He also knew when a dream was within reach.

Karen realized that her marriage was over. She said quietly to herself and the evening stars, "I'm leaving him."

The words came out with surprising ease. Her thoughts flowed smoothly and Karen Grimes was certain that the events of this evening were the last straw.

***

Jamie Watkins bounded up the stairs and walked right into Karen and Bill's apartment without knocking. Bill was somewhat surprised to see him display so much brass, but he knew he shouldn't be. He'd seen Jamie be obnoxious and rude many times before. He also knew that Jamie would do whatever he wanted to do, no matter who was trying to stop him. When someone said something about Texas, Bill thought of Jamie. If everything was big in Texas, Bill thought, Jamie's mouth and ego were all Texan.

Jamie, without any greeting asked, "Are you ready ta do this?"

Bill was suddenly chilled to the bone. He wanted to make this deal to prove to Karen that he was serious, but he was scared. Here, standing in front of him was his opportunity to actually do something for a change. He was hedging a little, and Jamie could tell.

"Come on man, snap out of it. Are ya in or not? I got

people chompin' at the bit to take up this deal. I won't do it for everybody. Are ya in or are ya too chicken?"

That last line pushed Bill over the edge. He wasn't going to let Jamie Watkins make him out to be a chicken. He knew that if he backed out now, Jamie would blab it all over town. He'd be the laughing stock of central Florida. Jamie would make sure of it.

"Let's do it." Bill surprised even himself. He was committed now. He'd verbally agreed to make the deal.

"All right! You follow me to my place in Ocoee. Don't get lost either. I'll make sure I don't leave ya in the dust. Y'all need a place to keep this stuff that even Karen can't find. Ya don't want anybody to get hold of it except you. Do ya have a place in mind?"

Bill didn't have to think about this. He would be putting it in a storage area above the closet in the spare bedroom. He'd already checked it out and figured that it would be ideal for twenty-five pounds of marijuana and a pound of cocaine. "Don't worry about me, Jamie. I've got it all figured out. It'll be outta here before the end of the week."

"All right partner, let's roll. We got work to do."

Chapter 4

Diane McKinney was hurrying around the house trying to get everything ready for her husband's arrival home. She had received her call a few minutes before from the wife's group ombudsman letting her know that the USS *Alabama* was to dock at 9:00 AM this morning. Even though she'd been expecting the ship to come in around this date, she was still bubbling with excitement. After all, it had been eighty-two straight days since she'd laid eyes on her husband. Eighty-two straight days since they'd spoken to each other; or touched...

Diane broke out of her trance and realized that she'd been daydreaming about having sex with Patrick. She longed to feel him wrap his arms around her, to hold her, to stroke her hair, to be inside her. *It has been a long time.*

Being a Navy submariner's wife was difficult. The long periods of separation were bad enough, but the submariner's wife had other burdens. All those tasks normally delegated to a husband, like cutting the grass, handling the finances, taking out the trash, fixing plumbing and electrical problems had to be handled. She had to be a self-starter, aggressive, self-assured and clever. Some wives couldn't handle the long separations. Some didn't have the self-confidence to do the additional tasks that a wife with an absentee husband needed. Others couldn't stand the loneliness that comes, night after night, not knowing where your husband was in the world. Still others simply got bored and turned to the local singles bars for excitement. Some turned into alcoholics. Others simply packed up their belongings and went home to their parents' house and started over. Some wives were still teenagers and had never been away from home. Now they were in a strange city, with strange people, with tremendous responsibilities, and these young girls just didn't have the skills to handle it.

Diane Hart McKinney was different than most. She was Pat's height at 5'7", and had beautiful light brown hair which hung around her shoulders. She usually kept her slightly wavy hair back in a ponytail. Her skin was light and smooth and her eyes were to the green side of gray. She was 110 pounds light with perky 'C' cup breasts. But her smile was her brightest feature; captivating and genuine. She'd been living away from home for several years when she'd met Patrick. They worked together in a department store for several months. Pat had always been attracted to her but never worked up the nerve to ask her out on a date. It was several years later, when Patrick came home on leave and called Diane for a date that sparks started to fly.

They were both twenty-five years old when they went to see "On Golden Pond" for their first date. As they entered the theater, they looked around and noticed that they were the only people that didn't have gray hair. They were the youngest couple in the audience. It wasn't a bad movie, it just moved a little slow for a couple of twenty-five-year-olds.

When Patrick dropped Diane off at her apartment, he nervously went to kiss her and missed her lips, kissing her on the chin. They were both like a couple of high school kids, on a first date, getting a first kiss. They both laughed. Patrick had said, "Let's try that again," and they did. Three months later, Patrick McKinney asked Diane Hart to marry him.

Patrick explained the hardships of being a Navy wife to Diane. He knew the added responsibilities and long separations would be tough on her but he also knew she could handle it. She had the advantage of living on her own for a few years so she knew how to handle money, fix meals, juggle a hectic schedule, and be alone when you really would rather have company. Patrick knew that, if she got into a situation that she couldn't handle alone, she was smart enough to get help from the wives' support group.

So on February 11, 1990, they married. Diane Hart McKinney was thrust into the world of the U.S. Navy. Diane never really knew where her husband was when the USS *Alabama* was out to sea. She never knew how long he was going to be gone for sure and she could only guess when he would return. She only knew that the ship was coming home when she got that long awaited call from another member of the wives' support group. Even then she remained skeptical until she saw the great ship coming up the Cumberland River.

It wouldn't be much longer. It was now 6:37 AM. The kids had to be dressed and fed. There was laundry to start, the breakfast dishes would have to be loaded into the dishwasher, and beds made before she and the children could leave for the base. She wanted everything to be perfect when Patrick arrived home. Diane remembered that the car needed gas. That was fine, though, because she had to get a six-pack of "Bud Light" on her way to the base. Even though it was illegal to have an open beer in a moving vehicle on base, Patrick always wanted Diane to have a cold one ready for him in the car when he left the ship. She remembered him saying, "A cold beer always tastes best when you get off the 'pig' boat after a patrol and you drink it in defiance of their bullshit rules. After all, I deserve a break from this shit." Diane couldn't argue, even if she felt that he could wait another ten minutes until they were safely off the base and in the comfort of their own home. He probably was right; he probably did deserve it after spending eighty-two days under the water in a hollow steel tube with one hundred and fifty other guys, most of whom Pat said he didn't particularly like.

Diane got their son, Sean, up and told him that she had a surprise for him later that day. When six-year-old Sean asked what it was, Diane said, "You'll just have to wait. I think you're going to like this surprise a lot."

Diane didn't realize just how bright her smile was and Sean was a very perceptive child. Right away he guessed what was happening. With a burst of energy and excitement, Sean yelled, "Daddy's coming home today, isn't he! I can tell, Mom! He is, isn't he?" Diane was overcome as tears of happiness and surprise welled up in her eyes.

"Yes, son, your daddy is coming home today. So let's get

going, we have lots to do before he gets here. We have to get your sister up, eat breakfast, get dressed in our best clothes, get daddy's welcome home present wrapped and get gas on the way to the base."

"Mom, does Dad have to go back out on the submarine again?" Sean missed his dad whenever he was gone to sea. He would cry every time Pat would leave for a patrol and he would sulk for days after the ship left port. There were several instances when Pat was home that he was just going to the store or the library, and he would come home to find Sean red-eyed from crying. Sean was certain that Daddy was going to the submarine and didn't even say good-bye to him before he left. Diane couldn't convince him that his father was just going to the store and would be back in a few minutes.

"No, Son. Dad's not going back out on the submarine ever again. Let's go wake up your sister. Dad's boat will be pulling up to the dock in less than two hours and we don't want to be late. Don't fight and don't fool around so we can get there on time."

"Yes, Mom," came the response. Diane looked at the clock and realized that she and the children had to get moving. There were so many things to do and not much time to do them in. "Let's see. What's next..." She started doing the few dishes by hand and methodically completed each task on her list of "things to do today."

Chapter 5

It was a pretty good crowd for a Thursday night. Most of the tables at the Rock Alliance, Orlando's hottest new nightclub, were still full and the crowd had really gotten into the live rock and roll. Brian Purcer and the Hot Licks' three-hour set had drained them. They were done for the night. Now it was time to relax.

Brian, with his dark, wild black hair, blue jeans and dark blue Led Zeppelin tee shirt, sat at a table with his drummer, Rick Wessler. They talked about how well the set had gone and pointed to different women as they walked by, commenting on various attributes of the ladies. The band was right on; the riffs were smooth as silk; the vocals clear; and Brian's guitar playing was like magic. His screaming Stratocaster had really wailed for him tonight. It was as if it were a part of him. The crowd's response told him that his assessment of the show was correct. Young men and women, and some kids, were coming up to Brian and asking for his autograph! He couldn't believe it. This was only the band's tenth live gig and there was already talk of cutting an album. An agent from Atlantic Records had approached Brian and told him to contact his office early next week so they could talk about the band. He wanted to know the band's history and musical background. He told Brian that he and his band could use the company's Orlando studio for a few hours just for talking to him. The agent left his card and told Brian before he left that drinks for the band were on his tab. He told Brian that he'd already arranged everything with the bartender, so don't even offer to pay.

Brian looked around for a few minutes. He wanted to see if Bill and Karen Grimes had shown. They said that they would, but Brian knew not to depend too much on them. They'd promised things before, and had never come through. Brian was pretty sure who was to blame for the broken promises. He'd always felt that Karen was too good for Bill.

Karen had class, good looks, brains, and a body that turned heads. Bill was handsome, but was dumber than dirt. He talked a good line, Brian knew, but that was it. He didn't see them anywhere, so he assumed that Bill had screwed up again.

Rick had been watching Brian and wondered what was on his mind. He ran his hand up his forehead and brushed his shoulder length, sandy blond hair back away from his face. Rick had known Brian for a few years now. He and Brian played together with many different musicians. Over the years, they'd looked for a good bass player and keyboardist to fill out the band but it took quite a while to find just the right mix. He helped Brian pick the other band members so that he had the best possible meshing of musicians and personalities. The result was one hot band with Brian writing and playing lead guitar. Usually vocals are the focal point of a band but not so with the Hot Licks. Brian's guitar undoubtedly was the main attraction.

"What are you thinking about?"

Brian was taken aback for a moment as he considered Rick's query. He had to shake his head once to clear out the cobwebs and focus on the question.

"Karen." The single name answer said it all. Rick knew that Brian was hooked on a fish; one that he couldn't reel in.

"Brian, it's just starting to look as if we're going to get a big break. I know you think Bill's a jerk and Karen is some kind of goddess, but we have other things to worry about right now. Don't take this the wrong way pal, but you need to forget about her and concentrate on the next few weeks. It could mean the difference between making the big time or not. Besides, there's plenty of fish out there. How about that chick, Ginny? Remember the one that was at our session a month or so back? You two seemed to hit it off."

The conversation was interrupted by three very young, giggling girls who couldn't have been over seventeen. They walked up to Brian and asked for his autograph in a shy kind of voice. They said how much they enjoyed the show and asked where the band was playing next. Brian told them and the girls said they'd be there. Then they giggled and left.

Brian calmly looked at his drummer and said in a casual voice, "Thanks Rick, but shut up and butt out." He gave Rick a sly smile, letting him know that he was only partially serious. "I know what's at stake. I'll handle it. Look, I appreciate what you're trying to do, really I do. I'm okay. Really."

"Okay, man. I'll back off. Do you need a refill? I'm headed to the bar."

"Thanks, man, but I'm outta here. I've gotta work tomorrow. We're not stars yet, my man. What time do you want to meet tomorrow night? Show starts at 9:00. I don't get off work until 6:00."

Brian's job was a drag. Working for the Orlando Sentinel in the mail room just wasn't a career enhancing position. The long hours of work and the crappy early morning shift coupled with the bands weekend gigs were starting to wear him down. He longed for the day when he could call his boss and tell him their eight-year-long employer/employee relationship was over. The developments for the band over the last month gave him hope that it was possible for him to say good-bye to the dead end job. He was going to be embarking on a career. He was through with "jobs."

"6:30, then. I'll see you backstage."

Rick and Brian shook hands and Rick turned towards the bar. Brian watched Rick blend into the crowd, then turned towards the door. He got as far as the last row of tables when he saw 21-year-old Ginny Parks sitting with Danny Vallero. Ginny was from Ohio and was going to the University of Central Florida. She was a real looker, with tan skin and very light brown hair that hung down to just above her shoulders where the tips curled up slightly towards her neck. It was parted just to the left of center. She wore very little makeup. Her blouse was light blue with spaghetti straps that showed off her tan shoulders. She had on small gold hoop earrings that shimmered with the flashing lights in the bar. His eyes were drawn to Ginny's ample breasts as he approached the table.

Danny saw Brian first and shouted, "Hey Brian, how are ya doing? Great set tonight! You guys were cooking. Ginny and I were just talking about how you guys ought to get an agent and try to cut an album. Sit down. I'll buy you a beer."

Brian looked away from Ginny and said, "Thanks, Danny, but I've got to work in the morning, so I can't stick around."

Brian didn't like Danny one bit. He thought that Danny was a loud-mouthed jerk who didn't know when to shut up. He hated his Boston accent; hated his dark, handsome complexion and even more; hated the way Danny treated women. Brian had always been taught to treat women with respect. Women were creatures to be coddled, pampered, and cared for in a special way. Danny, on the other hand, saw women as objectives, one-night conquests, beings to be used and discarded.

Brian hated Danny for those reasons and many others. He hated Danny because he knew that Danny had never worked an honest day in his life. His income was derived from swindling, selling drugs, and bumming off his conquests with a never-fulfilled promise of repayment. Brian's hatred of Danny was intensified now, seeing him trying to impress Ginny Parks with his supposed friendship with the star of an up and coming rock band.

"Hello, Ginny."

Brian's greeting of Ginny surprised Danny, and before she could return his gesture, Danny butted in and asked, "You two know each other? Small world. Why didn't you tell me, Ginny? Brian and I go way back. We used to do some business together. Sit down and have a drink with us, Brian. We can talk and catch up on a few things. Maybe I can set you up with a few good connections to give your career a boost."

It was all Brian could do to restrain his anger. He knew Danny had absolutely no ties to the music world and had no way of helping his career. And the only business they did together was through an old mutual friend, Pat McKinney. Brian knew that Danny was merely trying to impress Ginny, and it seemed to be working. Ginny smiled at everything Danny said. Brian thought that she was hooked on Danny, and he was afraid for her. He ignored Danny's last statement, turned to Ginny and asked if she would like a ride home. Brian knew this would rattle Danny's cage a little, but he really didn't care. All he wanted to do now was get her away from this jerk and keep her from becoming a notch in Danny's belt.

She smiled at Brian and said thanks, but that she had her car here and would stay a while. She added that she'd enjoyed the set tonight. She had heard Brian's band before during a group practice a little over a month ago. She was with her roommate, Sharon, who'd been dating Brian's drummer, Rick, at the time. Rick invited her and Ginny to one of their practice sessions. That's how Ginny got to know the hottest new guitarist in central Florida. After the practice was over, Brian and Ginny talked and talked. They'd hit it off well and Ginny really wanted to get to know Brian better. She figured that she had little chance to form a relationship with Brian, though, because he had very little free time with practices and work. He'd gotten her phone number and promised to call her, but never did. She figured he'd forgotten her by now.

Brian looked longingly at Ginny but felt there was no use pushing the issue further. He was tired. His thoughts briefly drifted to Karen Grimes and the tough situation she was in. He didn't want to see another smart, beautiful woman fall into a similar situation.

"It's nice to see you again, Ginny. Don't stay too late. By the way, do you have classes tomorrow? We have another set here tomorrow night and I'd like you to be my guest."

With that, Danny interrupted. "We're going out to dinner tomorrow night. But maybe after dinner, we'll both stop in."

It wasn't what Brian had in mind, so he let it go without further comment.

"Well, good night then."

Brian headed towards the door. He was surprised when Ginny got up and stepped in front of him. She lightly held his arm and kissed him on the cheek and said, "Call me. It really was a great set tonight." She looked Brian right in the eyes and smiled.

Brian made one last attempt to get her away from Danny. "Are you sure you don't want to leave right now? We can pick up your car tomorrow."

"I'm sorry, Brian, but I really can't. Call me, though. Do you still have my number?"

Brian nodded. "Good night, Ginny."

As Brian continued on towards the door, he was sorry too. He was sorry that he couldn't think of some way to convince Ginny to come with him to get her away from Danny. He'd tried his best, but now there were other things to think about, like sleep. Brian Purcer, the up-and-coming rock star had to transform himself into Brian Purcer the mail room worker; and it was getting harder and harder to do.

Chapter 6

Joe McKinney walked out of the personnel office at the Camp Lejeune Marine base in North Carolina. As he walked down the hall to the front door of the building, he passed the historic display of swords.

They'd been used by the US Marine Corps from their inception on November 10, 1775, when a small military unit called the Continental Marines was created, to current day. He admired the craftsmanship that must have been used to create such fine weapons so long ago. He'd been attached to the II Marine Expeditionary Force. Joe's ability to quickly learn how to use small arms had caught the attention of his superiors early in his career. He mastered many of the standard and special weapons used by the Corps and became an instructor in their care and use. Joe mentally reviewed the procedure for disassembly, cleaning, inspection and reassembly of the M16 in the display case. He imagined himself shouldering the weapon from a wooded area and firing on a group of enemies. He could vividly see the faces of the enemies as they writhed in pain. They weren't communist insurgents or Islamic Jihad. They were former friends from central Florida.

This brought a wicked smile to Joe's face when a voice from behind him said, "Sergeant McKinney, I understand that this is your last day on active duty."

Joe turned to see Major Griggs, his first instructor when he moved to Camp Lejeune after leaving boot camp at Parris Island. Griggs was in his late thirties, with salt and pepper hair, though not much of that showed. The creases on his shirt looked sharp enough to cut a finger. He was starched and pressed. He was fit as any man on the base. "Yes Sir, it is."

"There's always a place in the corps for you, son, if you

decide that civilian life isn't for you. All you have to do is call. Plus you've got a stint of reserve time to do, so don't be surprised if Uncle Sam comes calling for your services. You know our Commander in Chief is itching to take out that quack in Iraq."

That statement made Joe think a little. *Better tuck that information away in the old brain, just in case.* He knew that the Corps could call on him in a time of crisis, or any time that they deemed that there was a crisis, but he thought that the chances were remote that he'd be in uniform again. Only time would tell.

"I understand, sir. If called, I'll be happy to serve my country." And Joe meant it. He just hoped that it wouldn't interfere with the business at hand. There was this small matter of revenge that needed to be addressed back home.

Over the last two years, Sergeant Joseph McKinney's job had been to train the special operations unit of the II Marine Expeditionary Force. These Marines are the first men into the field to do whatever it takes to clear the way for the main units during any military maneuvers. It was their responsibility to make sure that the opposing force strength, positions, firepower, and readiness were assessed merely by sneaking in under dark of night, planting listening devices, taking pictures, whatever was necessary to ensure that the best intelligence was gathered and usable to the tacticians. The reason Joe was selected for this position was because he was good at it. He was better than good. He was so good that his superiors were looking at ways to keep him in the service. He was a good Marine and they wanted him to remain an enlisted Marine. There was the old saying, once a Marine, always a Marine. But that was a brotherhood more than a legal commitment. You covered your brothers' backs at all times, whether in or out of uniform. There was no secret code, you just did it.

Joe was in his dress blues for his last day of active duty. His dark brown hair was freshly cut to Marine Corps specs, his shoes were polished to a super-high gloss spit shine. He was leaving the United States Marine Corps under honorable conditions. In fact, his commanding officer, during his discharge interview, specifically requested that he consider re-enlistment for the sole purpose of continuing to train special forces units with the added benefit of a command promotion to Staff Sergeant. That was a rarity in peacetime, especially since Joe had only served during a single live armed confrontation. He'd been in the special force II Marines that made the initial reconnaissance mission into Iraq prior to the massive air strikes of Desert Storm. Joe's sniper skills were proven when they'd encountered Iraqi Army patrols. He was able to silence the patrols and allow his team to complete their surveillance. Their successful mission proved to be pivotal in the success of the initial air strikes around Baghdad.

Joe walked out to the parking lot after leaving his final interview. The sun was bright. There was not a cloud in the sky at Camp Lejeune. It was a perfect day. There was no one there to greet him, only the open road back to his home in Orlando, Florida. He'd already set up an apartment in the Pine Hills area on the west side of town. He was anxious to get started on his new life. It was going to be exciting. He had some old business that needed to be addressed. There were scores to be settled.

***

It was a magnificent sight to behold. The 560-foot Ohio Class submarine, the USS *Alabama*, was maneuvering its way next to the pier at King's Bay Naval Station. Sailors quickly walked back and forth on the missile deck of the great ship preparing to cast mooring lines to the waiting sailors on the pier. Two tug boats were aiding the process, pushing the sub from the starboard side of the ship so that the port side was facing the pier. The lines were tied to cleats on the ship on one end and would be secured to pylons on the pier.

Petty Officer Patrick McKinney could feel the goose bumps on his arms as he relayed the information to the control room that the first line was over. That meant that the ship was officially docked. He could hear the cheers all the way up in the conning tower from the open control room hatch. His last deterrent patrol was over. He was only hours away from the end of one career and the beginning of a new one.

Heading forward through the ship, McKinney's smile grew broader and brighter. Everyone he passed could tell he was getting out of the United States Navy. He had one last stop before he left the ship to see his family. Down in the berthing compartment, Petty Officer William "Hatch" Hatcher was stuffing his seabag with clothes, magazines, and some other things that, to McKinney looked like junk. But Patrick didn't question Hatch about hauling junk off the boat. Pat also noticed the beautifully polished knives, three of them, still lying on Hatch's bunk. You could see your face in the highly polished eight-inch blades and Pat knew that they were sharp enough to shave with.

William Hatcher, from north of Moniac, Georgia was a piece of work. At 6'1" and 185 pounds, he looked like a farm hand, lean and lanky, no fat but not muscle bound like a bodybuilder. He had brown curly hair and dark eyes. His skin was dark like a deep tan. Pat suspected that one of his parents was African-American but Hatch never talked about family. He lived on the southern edge of the Okefenokee Swamp, a little over an hour's drive from King's Bay. An electronics technician by rate, he had other special skills that are not normally associated with submariners. He was an expert marksman with any small arms weapon that the Navy had in its arsenal and was particularly adept producing and using hand crafted weapons. Large hunting knives were a specialty. He'd made many knives for several members of the crew and was popular with many of the "lunatic fringe," the guys seemingly on the edge of reality (the submarine force had more than its fair share).

"Hey, Pat! Shipping out for good today, huh?" Hatch was glad that Pat took the time to see him before he left the ship.

"Yeah. I had to come down and see you first. Thanks for helping me out. I owe you. There are some things that I'm gonna need pretty soon, so I'll be looking you up."

"Sure, no problem."

"I've got your number and address packed away."

Except for the knives, Hatch was through stuffing his duffel bag and grasped Patrick's hand. "Listen, when you get settled into your new place in Florida, look me up. Maybe you can come up for a couple days and we can play war and squeeze off a few rounds. You know, kill some imaginary bad guys. Maybe even do some fishing. You know the swamp's got tons of different varieties of fish."

Patrick smiled. "Sounds good, Hatch. I still have a lot to learn and not much time to learn it in. And I'm not talking about fishing."

Patrick's glance went back to the knives on Hatch's bunk. He stared at the shiny blades and fell into a trance. He began to rub the scar on his chin as he was thinking of all of the different so-called "friends" that had betrayed him and his family. The names were ringing in his brain, torturing him as his trance grew deeper. Jamie Watkins, Randy Farley, Danny Vallero, Donnie Lee Lester, Roberto Acquino. His deep hatred was evident in the expression on his face and he had every intention of not just getting even, but getting ahead. With some people, time heals old wounds. With Pat, time only rubbed salt in them. Hours alone in a bunk on a submarine tends to give a man too much time to think...and plan.

Patrick shook his head to clear his mind, thanked Hatch again and headed for the pier.

***

Diane smiled brightly and gave her husband a huge hug and kiss, then backed away. "What do you mean, you're done? Don't you have duty tomorrow?"

"Nope. I'm really done. All I have to do tomorrow is come in and check out. This is it, babe. Take one last look at everything around you as you drive by because you won't be seeing it anymore. We're history, as far as the Navy's concerned."

It finally dawned on Diane that they were really leaving Kings Bay, Georgia. She couldn't believe it. Sean did all the talking on the way to the car. He seemed to be trying to tell his dad everything that had happened while he was out to sea. Anna looked pretty as a flower in her new, rose colored dress that Diane had made just for this occasion. She tried to get a few words in but to no avail. Pat listened intently and tried to take in every word. He loved his son and had missed his wild imagination. He was holding his daughter on the way to their car and kissed her on the cheek several times. She seemed to have grown a year in the last three months. He swore to himself that he would never leave his children or his wife again.

When they finally got to the parking lot, Patrick told them, "Take one more look at the sub, because you won't see it anymore, ever." *Thank God, only once more for me.* With that, Patrick and Diane loaded the kids in the car and started the engine. Before the car was in gear, Diane handed Patrick a cold Bud Light. As Patrick took his first drink, Diane reached over and put her hand on his crotch and whispered in his ear, "This Bud's for you." Patrick nearly choked on his beer.

***

Mike McKinney finished off his third beer of the morning. At 9:30 AM, it was still early, even for him to chug down this much beer. The sun blazed brightly enough through the open curtain to hurt his bloodshot eyes. He woke up with a hangover and the only thing he could think of was getting something to drink. He knew if he didn't get a drink his hangover would last for the entire day. He'd thought about his love, Julie, but that only made him want to drink more. She was gone and that was that. There was no bringing her back. *How could those bastards have taken her from me? Why didn't I stay with her?* He had to get something stronger so he went to the liquor cabinet in his Spanish style home and looked for something, anything with alcohol. There was nothing there. He sat down on the love seat, put his hands between his legs and started to cry. He cried for a few minutes then stopped. He wiped his nose on the front of his tee shirt, laid down and fell asleep.

He immediately started to dream about a beautiful woman in a bright white dress. She was holding out her hands to Mike. Her face was pale white but silky smooth. She was smiling and her teeth were bright white and perfect. She was calling to him but he couldn't make out her words. At first it sounded soothing like a lullaby. The sounds were not words but a sweet melody. Then her face started to contort into a sad appearance. She looked like she was saying help me. She was repeating "help me, help me" and her face changed from sadness to fear. Then he saw several hands reach up over her mouth and cover it. A hood was thrown over her head and ropes were being tied around her. A single hand tugged on a length of rope that hung to her side and she began to fall away from him. He reached for her but he couldn't reach her in time. She continued to fall away, getting smaller as she fell into an abyss. He screamed, "No!" His own scream woke him. He looked around and figured that he must have fallen off of the love seat during his restless sleep. He was staring at the front of the love seat from the floor. He was sweating and his hair was matted. He'd had another nightmare. They were getting more vivid. He didn't know what that meant and he sure wasn't sharing this with any shrink. The last thing he needed was to get some quack head doctor telling him what all this means. He already knew. And he was sure he would never get any better. Nothing could bring Julie back. *I can't keep doing this.*

Mike picked himself up off the floor and headed for the bathroom. He figured that he had to go out and get some booze so he could make it through the day. That seemed to be his only escape. He drank until he passed out. If he drank heavy enough, he wouldn't dream too much. But if fell asleep too soon, he'd have a dream that would rip the scars off of his mental wounds. He had no idea how to break the cycle without going insane. Of course, maybe he was already there. He wanted to go back to Florida to see his family; Mom and Dad, Pat and Joe. But they'd think he was soft. He couldn't handle it. They'd try to tell him that he could break out of his—what had Pat called it—his funk. *This is one hell of a funked up funk*, Mike thought to himself and smiled at his little joke. Then he went back to thinking about Julie. He could see her beautiful eyes looking back at him. Then his mind faded and he couldn't focus on her clearly. Again he decided he needed a drink. Then he decided he needed a shower before he went out in public. He headed towards the bathroom and found himself standing in front of the mirror. He hated what he saw. His beard had a full three days growth. His eyes were sunken from lack of sleep, too much alcohol, and not enough food. He was killing himself, slowly but surely. Seven years ago, he weighed 215 pounds, had a full head of hair, and hardly an ounce of fat on his body. He was 5'10" tall and could hold his own in an arm wrestling match with either of his brothers. Now he was 5'9", weighed 150 pounds soaking wet and could barely lift his arms over his head to put on a tee shirt. His hair was gray, thinning and his skin was wrinkled with age spots all over, like a seventy year old man.

He showered and shaved, cutting his chin in the process. He brushed his teeth for the first time in days. He managed to find a clean pair of pants and a shirt that wasn't in too bad shape. He had a maid service come in once every two weeks to dig him out of the mess he accumulated. They cleaned the house from top to bottom, did the dishes and the laundry. They used to feed and care for his cat, but they'd long ago convinced him that he shouldn't have animals. He couldn't take care of them and his cleaning service couldn't come in more frequently and make sure that they were still fed. They were sure that Mike would have been dead long ago if they weren't there to help him. And they were probably right.

Pat and Joe called often to check on him. They really wished that they could help him, but they had lives back in Florida now that they were both out of the service. Mike was proud of them both. They had strong character and could withstand adversity. He'd wished many times that he could be like them. But it wasn't in the cards. He was far less stable. Now he was the weakest of the three, both physically and mentally. He couldn't handle the stress when things got a little dicey. He just wanted to run away. Pat had told him once that he'd felt the same way. He said the only thing Mike had to do was overcome the urge to run once and he'd have that fear conquered. He never found out if that were true. He could never get up the nerve to hold his ground. That's why he moved to Las Vegas. He had to get away from his old life and all the old faces. Pat and Joe moved away, too but that was to get away to regroup. Mike ran away in fear never to return. He was a coward and he knew it. *I need a drink.*

Chapter 7

Brian couldn't sleep. His thoughts kept going back to the Rock Alliance and Ginny Parks. He was angry at himself for allowing Ginny to stay with that son-of-a-bitch, Danny. But what else could he have done? Danny had out-charmed him and Ginny wanted to be there. *If she winds up broken-hearted, it's her own fault. She's a big girl. I guess she can handle it.* Then his mind wandered to Karen Grimes and her low-life husband, Bill. He shook his head, trying to clear his mind of women troubles.

The ritual beer and two bong hits of Columbian red bud didn't seem to be working this evening. Usually, after a long day at the Orlando Sentinel, or after a particularly long gig or jam session, a Bud Light and a couple hits off the bong did the trick; more effective than valium. But with women on his mind, Brian was doomed to a near-sleepless night. He needed his sleep this weekend. With two more nights to play at the "Rock" and two more ten-hour days at the Sentinel he didn't need the aggravation of a sleepless night, especially over two women with whom he wasn't even personally involved.

He got out of bed and fixed up another bowl of red bud. He spotted the stack of mail on the television. *Maybe looking through the mail will clear my head.* There was the usual junk mail, the electric bill, and a letter with the return address of King's Bay, Georgia. Puzzled, Brian decided to open this one first. He didn't even know where King's Bay, Georgia was, or that it even existed for that matter. He ripped open the flap on the envelope and pulled out what seemed to be three full pages, with beautiful print, on heavy tan paper. As he read through the opening lines, he couldn't believe what he was reading. Pat McKinney was alive and well, and married, and had two kids. He was moving back to Florida, starting his own business. How long had it been since he'd seen Pat...almost seven years? Well, six at least. Things sure had changed for him. Brian continued to read the letter:

I've made a few minor changes in my life since the last time we talked. When was that? 1988? Sure doesn't seem that long. I remember you jamming down at that old house that I was renting in Longwood when the neighbors came over complaining. We talked them into staying and listening and they started partying with us until past midnight. Anyway, my wife Diane, and I bought a house in Dunnellon and hope to move in by the end of May. We'd love to have you up for a housewarming dinner when we get settled. I'll be down in the Orlando area about May 12th to take care of some business so I'll look you up then. I heard that your band is really starting to take off. Sounds like beating on that 'Strat' for all these years might actually pay off. Be seeing you soon. Patrick

Brian thought for a moment. *How did he know about the band? He hasn't been around here for ages. Maybe he's been in touch with Bill and Karen. He always was close to them. Pat was always full of surprises.*

With those thoughts, Brian yawned. He tossed the rest of the mail into a pile on the television. His last coherent thoughts were *Why do I even have a television? I never use it. It is a good place to stack mail, though. I guess I'll keep it.*

***

Pat McKinney's right index finger was rubbing the scar on his chin as he tried to relax. The flight was three hours long but it allowed him a chance to rest and to get his mind off of the task at hand, at least for a while. It was one thing planning and talking about killing another human being. Actually following through with such a plan was a whole different matter. You didn't get the death penalty for thinking about it, at least not in this country. This was something he was looking forward to, and if he kept thinking about it, he might not actually do it. All he had to do on this trip was scout out the house that Joe had set up for their first hit then head for Moniac, Georgia to meet Hatch.

Diane had been really upset about not being able

accompany Pat on the trip. She'd argued that it was her house too. Why did Patrick have to go alone? Her parents could take care of the kids. Besides, it was only going to be three days and they'd be back in Ohio, getting ready to drive back down to Florida. But Patrick insisted that he come alone. There was no need to spend the extra money on two plane tickets when only one of them was needed. Pat had said that it was just a small problem with the house that needed inspection by the purchaser and a set of initials so that the loan processing could be completed. The mortgage company said it could be done by mail, but it would hold up the closing by some two weeks. Patrick said that he could walk the paperwork through the rest of the way. This would allow them to move right in when they arrived in Dunnellon.

Now he was relaxing in his coach seat, trying to sleep. The plane was full, the crowd consisting mostly of businessmen. He would touch down in Orlando in an hour and forty minutes according to the pilot. He went over the plan in his mind. Rent a car; drive to Moniac, Georgia to hook up with Hatch. Drive back to near Dunnellon and spend the night. The next morning, take care of the problem with the house. Later that night, take care of Danny Vallero. After that, visit with old friends and new neighbors. *Sounds good on paper,* he thought.

Pat started to think of just who he would like to visit when he dozed off. An electronic tone woke him. Next he heard the Captain's voice which advised passengers to fasten their seatbelts and prepare for landing at Orlando International Airport. *Wow. That was a quick flight.* It was the second best sleep he'd gotten since being off the ship less than a week ago. The best sleep was the first night that he was in his own bed, with Diane. He had just performed the most strenuous activity since the previous time he'd come in from sea. Making love had a way of relaxing a man. *There must be some chemical release in a man's body which causes drowsiness after a long night of sex.* He didn't have time to dwell on that thought. A young, blonde flight attendant came by and reminded him to put his seat to a full, upright position. Patrick did this without comment and prepared for a landing in the vacation capital of the world; Orlando, Florida.

Chapter 8

Bill Grimes stared at the open trash bag. He'd never seen so much Columbian pot at one time. And to top it off, it was his. He ran his fingers through the grain and felt the dry, coarse texture of the dope. His nose was filled with the sweet aroma of the powerful weed. Now he was in the big time. *Bill Grimes; major player in the central Florida marijuana trade.* Karen would finally be impressed with him and she'd fall back in love with him. She couldn't say he never followed through on anything now.

Bill grabbed some rolling papers and found one of the biggest, resin-filled buds that he could find and began to twist up a joint. He broke up the bud onto a tray and pulled the stems from the fine weed. As he sifted the seeds out of the bud, he thought back to the instructions that Jamie Watkins had given to him. Bill had two weeks to get the money back to Jamie. That was it; two weeks, and no more. He didn't have to ask what would happen if he went past the two week deadline without payment. He knew that Jamie was a ruthless bastard and one way or another, he'd have his money. Jamie would have his own mother's fingers broken if she was late on payment. *Why am I dealing with a bastard like Jamie?* Well, it was too late to worry about that. The deed was done. It was time to hustle. He lit the joint that he held between his lips and began dialing the phone.

***

Outside the town of Apopka, some twenty miles to the northeast of Orlando, Al Michaels' phone rang. Al had just come in from fixing a broken sprinkler line in the number three greenhouse and he wasn't in a good mood. The water line had severed and had been pumping water directly into a philodendron bed for the last six hours. The break was located just upstream from the controlling solenoid valve so there was no way to isolate the leak. He had to kill the power to the well pump's motor. That had to be done manually. Al had just gone up to the greenhouses for a final inspection after dinner and to lock the doors for the night when he discovered the watery mess. A whole bed of Philodendron had been washed out and was now scattered throughout the greenhouse. The water from the break had been flowing freely. The entire 100 foot by 24 foot greenhouse was a muddy mess.

Al shut off the pump and made the repairs on the PVC water line. The muddy mess on the floor would have to wait until morning. It was just too much to worry about now. He'd already sent his employees home and he didn't want to try to call them back in at this late hour. It could wait. Besides, the peat moss would dry some overnight and would be easier to handle in the morning.

Al had been in the nursery business since he graduated from high school. He started out in a partnership with his mom and dad, but his dad had taken ill with cancer and couldn't work the business once he started with chemotherapy. He was able to give Al advice but was physically unable to help in the day to day tasks. Then Al's mom was involved in an auto accident. She died in the hospital after holding on for several days. Al's dad gave up trying to fight the cancer and died two months after his wife. At the very vulnerable age of eighteen Al was left alone to run a business and a household. He married young but was divorced within six months. His young bride couldn't stand him working all the long hours and felt neglected. That was a number of years back now. He was able to survive the tragedy and was stronger for it. He was 6'2" tall, and weighed a trim 195 pounds. He let his dark, wavy hair grow to his shoulders. He had rough, workman's hands from working twelve hour days in the greenhouses.

He always wore blue jeans and tee shirts. His work clothes were stained with peat moss, fertilizer, and other remnants of the business. He had a clean set of blue jeans that he wore when he went out on the town, which was almost never.

Al picked up the phone and asked, not too politely, "Yeah, who is it?"

"Hey, Al, this is Bill. What's up?"

"My greenhouses are flooded. I'm filthy, wet, and tired. That's what's up," Al barked into the phone. He wasn't in the mood for Bill Grimes tonight. He really didn't care too much for Bill and he didn't spare words on him. "What do you want, Bill?"

"Sorry to catch you at a bad time, man. Sounds like you could use some good news. I thought you might like to check out some red-bud. I just got it and it's real good. The pounds are real fluffy too. I can get some coke, too. I don't have it on me but it's easy enough to get hold of. I can have that here in an hour or so. Interested?"

Al thought about it for a few seconds. He'd wanted to get some good weed for some time. He also knew his buddy, Mitch, would want some if the dope really turned out to be good quality. Al wasn't into coke anymore, but Mitch would probably take some coke, too.

"I'll tell you what, Bill, I'll call Mitch and see what he needs and call you back in a few minutes. We'll probably get some, I'll let you know. How much are we talking about, cash-wise?"

Bill hadn't thought about this for very long and he wasn't sure what price a pound should go for. He thought for a minute. He was paying eleven hundred dollars a pound for the dope. So he figured he should charge at least $1500 per pound. On the coke, he was paying one thousand dollars an ounce, so fourteen hundred didn't seem unreasonable. He spoke into the phone after the long pause, "The redbud goes for $1500 a pound and the coke for $1400 for an ounce. Those are good prices, the best you'll find in this area."

Al thought for a few seconds. Not too bad, if the quality was good.

"Okay, Bill. I'll call you right back." With that, Al hung up and thought for a few minutes. The deal sounded good. He was dealing with Bill Grimes, though, and that was scary. His thoughts drifted for a few minutes. *What a strange night. First, the greenhouse disaster, now, he was buying dope from an idiot. What else could happen?* As soon as the thought hit him, he looked for some wood to knock on. Weird occurrences always happened in three's, didn't they? And he'd only experienced two.

***

At the other end of the line, Bill thought *This is going to be easy. This stuff sells itself. All you have to do is call people, and they beat a path to your door.* He hadn't actually sold anything yet. He'd merely had someone say that they were interested. But to Bill, that was evidence enough that he'd hit the big-time. He picked up the phone and dialed again.

Chapter 9

The area north of Moniac, Georgia, the southeastern-most point of the Okefenokee National Wildlife Refuge, was a beautiful place in early June. Folks in this area called it 'the swamp.' The Spanish moss hung down from the huge cypress trees like veils adorning a bride on her wedding day. The early morning sunlight made an eerie scene as the seemingly random rays of light streamed through the tree branches. A mist rose from the swampy waters. The odor in the air was a mixture of dead fish and musky decaying plants. The bugs were terrible and came in clouds. Mosquitoes seemed to be the size of small birds and some the insects were unidentifiable. Their bodies looked like a combination of several cross-breeding experiments; something out of a sci-fi movie. Maybe they were from outer space, Pat McKinney thought as he walked with Hatch along the dock to the storage shed across the swampy channel from the main "house."

The main house was a beautiful, three-bedroom log cabin. Pat was somewhat surprised to see that Hatch lived in such a remote area with no other homes nearby. He'd just have to wonder, though, because Hatch was the kind of guy that you didn't ask personal questions. Patrick had tried once, but he got a polite, but direct, "It really ain't none of your business." There wasn't anything menacing or nasty about his reply, but it had some finality to it. Pat didn't want to push it.

Once at the shed, Hatch moved some steel sheets that were rusting terribly and exposed a locked cabinet. The cabinet was made of heavy steel, painted haze gray, like the equipment on a submarine. *What a coincidence*, Pat thought to himself. He watched as Hatch unlocked the cabinet, opened the three foot by five foot door and exposed other locked doors. The interior of the cabinet was broken into several more locked compartments. Hatch unlocked the two foot by five foot compartment first.

Pat's eyes grew wide as he realized that the steel case must have been four feet deep. All he could see inside the steel case were gun barrels. He couldn't tell what kinds of guns were in the case, but he could see by the size of the barrel openings that there was a combination of shotguns and rifles of various sizes. Hatch then opened one of the smaller compartments and exposed numerous automatic weapons. Another compartment contained dozens of hand guns. Patrick was dazzled. He expected to see several guns to choose from, but he didn't expect to see an arsenal of this size. On previous visits to Moniac, during off crews, or weekend duty days off, he and Hatch would come here to shoot. Hatch only kept about a dozen guns in his log cabin. Patrick was duly impressed by those few guns back then. But seeing this, he could hardly hold his jaw up. Hatch could wage his own small war with this equipment. Much of it was military grade.

Hatch reached into the cabinet and pulled out an Iver Johnson AMAC Sniper Rifle. The powerful gun looked as if it had just been polished and been in a store glass showcase. He made sure the safety was on and pulled the action back, inspected it to make sure no rounds were chambered and handed it to Patrick.

Pat repeated the sequence that Hatch had just performed. One thing Pat had learned from Hatch was that no matter who told you a weapon was unloaded, the only way to be sure was to check it yourself.

Pat had seen a friend of his killed by an 'unloaded' gun. He was at a party when a seventeen year old kid brought out one of his dad's guns. It was a Winchester 30-06. He started showing off, tossing it around like a soldier in a drill team. A couple of the girls at the party told him to stop fooling around with it, but he said "What's the matter, it's not loaded." He then threw it to one of his buddies who began pointing it at people around the room saying, "pow, pow." He didn't pull the trigger as he did this though. He went to hand the gun to another friend, barrel first. When his friend grabbed the barrel the hairpin trigger was pulled by accident. The striking pin was released, striking the chambered round. The report was deafening and the projectile entered the teen's chest cavity. As the bullet passed through his body it severed the sixteen year olds' spinal cord. The young boy died instantly. The gasps and horrified looks on the young kids in the room haunted Pat to this day.

Pat gave the weapon one final look. When he looked up, Hatch had already pulled out a box of shells and a Hecklar and Koch 9MM pistol. After going through the same routine with the 9MM, Pat said "This should be everything for awhile. I'll drop you a line in a few weeks and let you know what's going on for my future needs. Did you get the wire receipt?"

"Yeah, Pat. Everything is done for now. Thanks for the bonus too. You don't have to put extra in there, ya know. I'm doing fine without it. My retirement's already taken care of. My folks left me a small fortune plus all this beautiful land." He smiled as he said it realizing that they were standing in the middle of swampland.

Pat was surprised by this revelation. Hatch had never talked about his personal life with anyone on the boat before. Pat thought Hatch was poor, and that he spent all his money collecting guns and fishing equipment. When they got back to the log cabin, Pat disassembled the rifle and packed it into the hard plastic carrying case. It was quite compact and fit nicely into Pat's 26" American Tourister suitcase. He covered it with some clothes. The pistol went into a smaller suitcase along with all the ammunition. His short trip to Moniac, Georgia was a success. Now for the long drive to Dade City, Florida.

It was just before 10:00 AM when Pat thanked Hatch. He'd be visiting William 'Hatch' Hatcher again. He needed good quality military grade hardware for his 'missions'. He was glad that it would be real convenient for him to obtain what he needed with a relatively short drive to beautiful Moniac, Georgia.

***

Diane McKinney loved her new home. Their furniture had

arrived in May, fourteen days late. It was pretty hard to believe that a move from King's Bay, Georgia to Dunnellon, Florida would take almost three weeks. But they got settled in and, after Diane rearranged the furniture for several weeks, they felt at home. It was now early June and Diane was still thrilled with her new home. The children had already picked out their rooms and started making plans where they would put their books, games, puzzles, coloring books, stuffed animals, and other toys.

Sean's room had to be painted a different color. He took exception to the light green paint. He said. "I want dark blue like my old room."

Diane agreed. It did need a little work.

Anna Marie, however, loved her room just the way it was. The pink paint on two walls matched the other two walls of pink designed wallpaper beautifully. They also matched most of little Anna's dresses. She loved pink. The white trim and intricate ceiling molding gave the room a rich appearance. Anna told her mom, "I love my new room." Her mom was quick to acknowledge that. She had enough work to do without repainting every room in the house.

The master bedroom was a massive room with two walk-in closets. The bedroom was decorated in light blue with a texture patterned ceiling and beautiful, soft, light blue carpeting. Patrick and Diane's king-sized bed and bedroom set would look small in this room. *No more knocking knees on the bed's corner posts*, Diane thought as she surveyed the room.

The master bath was the size of a small bedroom and had a shower with separate two-man garden tub, a double-sink vanity, and a walk-in linen closet. It was impressive and done in a rose color theme.

The final indoor feature was Patrick's favorite; a large office with oak book shelves, oak window trim, and a large oak desk. The family of the elderly couple who had lived there told Patrick and Diane that the movers would have had to dismantle the doorway to get the desk out of the room, so they decided to leave it there as a house-warming present. Pat couldn't believe it since they had already sold them the house at an embarrassingly low price. He'd made a fuss over the desk when they looked at the house, but made no inferences to wanting it. It was quite a surprise to them when it was still in the house after the closing.

The way the sale came about was the former owners had died in close succession to one another. Their children, all of whom lived out of state, wanted a quick sale. They were also a very Christian family and when they met Patrick and Diane, they liked the McKinneys so well, they'd said, "God wanted the McKinneys to have this home."

So an offer was made and no counter was offered. The McKinneys became the proud owners of a home that would have retailed for nearly $125,000. So when the actual sales price of $85,999 was contracted, the McKinney's net worth took a large jump. Several realtors approached Patrick about buying the home almost immediately after closing, but Pat said no. He was certain that he wanted to live the rest of his life in this home. He also knew Diane would have killed him for even entertaining the thought.

This house was everything that the McKinneys wanted. There were plenty of rooms. There were so many rooms, in fact, that the McKinneys didn't have enough furniture to fill them all. Diane looked around the house for a moment and thought to herself *This is my home*.

Patrick was busy looking at the garage. He'd never had a garage before. Down in Georgia all they had was a carport and a small locked storage room. Many houses in Florida had carports but this house was exceptional; 3200 square feet of beauty. He fell in love with it the first time he'd laid eyes on it. The beautiful white brick exterior; luxurious landscaping; circular driveway were all superb.

As he stared at the wall where he planned to hang his tool collection, he began to daydream. Through the imaginary cross-hairs of a powerful rifle, he imagined a perfect view of Danny Vallero's forehead. He held the rifle steady, slowly put pressure on the trigger, then...

"Honey, what would you like for dinner?"

Diane startled him and he jumped. There was a bead of sweat on his forehead and it took him a second or two to orient himself.

"Oh, honey, you scared the hell out of me. I was sitting here thinking of a dream that I had back on the sub."

The lie came out smooth as silk and so he continued to tell Diane about the real dream that he did have while sleeping on the USS *Alabama*.

"I was in the escape trunk just after we got under way. The trunk is supposed to be closed but we were having a problem with grounds or something in the trunk. The Captain authorized the hatch to be opened while another electrician and I looked for the problem. While we were up there we heard the ballast tank vent valves open with a loud whoosh which meant the sub was diving with the hatch open. I tried like hell to close that hatch. Then I heard the lower hatch close. I was trapped outside the ship as it began to submerge. I climbed up higher in the trunk to get more leverage on the hatch, but I still couldn't get the hatch to shut. Seawater was starting to come over the edge of the escape trunk, and I was being forced down into the trunk by the water."

"Oh my God. What happened next?" Diane was caught up in the story. Patrick could see he'd headed off a bad situation.

"I woke up. The guy in the bunk next to mine woke up and asked me what was going on. I was clutching my bunk light, kicking the ceiling to my bunk, thinking that it was the escape trunk hatch. The guy, Dell Johnson, said I was making a hell of a racket. I skinned my knuckle pretty bad during that dream. It's still scarred, see?"

Pat showed her the real scar he'd received during the dream. It wasn't a bad scar, but it did add credence to the true story.

Diane was impressed. She asked, "Do you still have this dream? I mean have you ever had other dreams like this before?"

"Sometimes...most of my dreams are "X" rated, and you're the star."

Diane blushed, then added, "you're sick", as she put her

arms around her husband.

Pat thought to himself, *Boy, that was close. I'll have to watch myself. I've got to put this out of my mind.*

"Now, Mr. McKinney, what do you want for dinner? Or do I have to send you up to the escape trunk to work?"

"No Ma'am, Captain, Ma'am." Patrick gave one of his mock snappy salutes. "We should go out to eat. We really don't have anything in the house. Let's go out, then go shopping right afterwards. Have you got a shopping list put together?"

"I've got plenty of lists, buddy, and you're at the top of most of them."

They laughed, then hugged, and went arm-in-arm into their fabulous, new home.

Chapter 10

Danny Vallero stared down the barrel of the Browning 357 magnum pointed directly between his dark, brown eyes. He couldn't think of anything except what the next few seconds, maybe the last of his young life, might bring. He'd never felt fear like this before.

He knew what fear was because he'd been in tight spots in his nineteen previous years. When he was seven years old his step father punished Danny with his belt. Victor Vallero, in a rage over his son's theft of $20.00 from his mother's purse, drew his belt off slowly, trying to calm down. He knew if he hit Danny just then, he would probably beat him to death. Victor watched Danny's eyes as he doubled the leather strap over and backed him into a corner. He wanted to make sure Danny got the message. Theft was wrong and Danny would soon know it. He got the beating, and though it was severe, he apparently didn't get the message.

Early one summer evening as the sun was setting when he was seventeen, he took a drive down I-95 south of Boston. He'd borrowed Victor's 1968 GTO without his step father's knowledge. This was one hot car, now in more ways than one, and Danny was too cool for words. It had a 400 cubic inch V-8, four on the floor Hurst transmission. It was orange with flame decals on the front end so no one could miss it. It was one mean machine. He and two friends were going to New York City to find some babes and party. The "Goat," as the GTO was fondly called, would make the babe pickup easier than normal, which, for Danny, meant it would be a breeze. He was already somewhat of a stud and a minor legend around his Boston neighborhood. He had $530.00 in his pocket. His friends had just under $200.00 between them. Danny always seemed to have cash, good dope and therefore many friends to entertain. They were going to get a hotel room and party.

Driving in heavy traffic at 80 miles per hour on Interstate 95 is usually not too much trouble. You're passing some, but not all the traffic and anyone driving under 70 mph was just in the way. As Danny cruised up behind one of these "slow-pokes," he hit the brake pedal to slow down, but the pedal went to the floor. The "Goat" didn't even flinch. The brake fluid had leaked out and was strewn along several miles of highway. Fear raced through Danny's body. His brain was scrambled. Panic overcame his friends as the "Goat" rapidly closed on the car in front of them. They felt the jolt as the GTO's bumper struck the rear bumper of the Mercedes just enough to slow the "Goat" down and give the Mercedes a little boost. At 75 mph, the driver of the Mercedes must have been petrified.

Danny quickly got his wits about him and realized what he had to do. He was able to match speed with the traffic flow and slowly ease his step-dad's valuable car between the traffic in the right two lanes and onto the shoulder. Still going 60 mph, he took his foot off the accelerator and let the big V-8 slow the beast down until he could manually apply the emergency brake and stop the car. A few seconds passed before the three let out a collective sigh of relief.

The fear subsided until Danny remembered he had to face Victor. Victor had beaten him nearly unconscious over lesser offenses, how would he react to this? He thought about abandoning the car and hitching back to Boston. He could claim someone had stolen the car. Then he resigned himself to the fact that he was going to have to face Victor. Surely he'd take a beating for this. But if he lied and Victor found out about it, he'd be dead for sure.

And Victor did beat him...broke his jaw, blackened both his eyes, and would have continued if not for his mother's intervention. But Danny lived through it.

The fear that Danny felt at age seven and again at seventeen was like a French kiss compared to the terror he was experiencing now. His heart was pounding so hard he felt it in his ears. The sweat was pouring off his forehead and his throat was dry and tight, so tight he couldn't utter the least protest. He hadn't learned his lesson at Victor's hand with the belt or by his fists. He hadn't learned when he was beaten nearly to death for taking his step-dad's expensive sports car. Now it seemed too late for him to learn as the barrel of the Browning seemed to be burning a hole in his head. He wished he'd learned that stealing was wrong, especially stealing from drug dealers. But how was he to know that the brown paper bag filled with twenties, fifties, and one hundred dollar bills was the property of Celio Barardi?

Barardi, with his slicked back, greasy hair and black eyes was a small time dealer in the big scheme of things in Boston. He had only six men working for him in drugs, prostitution and numbers. These trades brought him well over a million dollars a year but that also had to keep his men paid. In 1970 that was one hell of an income, but still small potatoes compared to the big guys.

Danny had seen one of Barardi's men place the bag filled with cash in the wooden crate at Curio's, the abandoned fish packing warehouse by the wharf. Danny played around there often when he was younger. As a young teenager he would bring his easier conquests there. He'd set up a mattress in the loft area of the warehouse with relatively clean sheets, because he hated dirt. There was even running water close by so he and his "date" could wash afterwards.

Sometimes Danny would go there to be alone and think. It was on one of those 'thinking' occasions that he'd seen one of Barardi's men nail a crate shut with only two nails. It had been left for delivery in the morning but Danny made the pickup himself before the owners could get there. The man who was supposed to watch the stash was busy relieving himself outside when Danny had made his move.

He was so cool. He snuck down from his loft, un-nailed the crate, grabbed the bag of cash, put the lid back on the crate without nails, and quickly but quietly made a clean getaway. It was so smooth, so easy. Just like in the movies. Local kid makes big time heist of unmarked drug money. It seemed all too easy.

And it was all too easy. Especially when a nineteen year old punk who had never made more than $250.00 per week in his life started flashing money around like a Hollywood Film Agent and dressed up like a pimp. It didn't take Celio Barardi long to figure out who had his money and that's when Danny found himself here at the end of the gun.

"You stupid punk," the voice behind the gun grumbled. It was the kind of grumble you'd expect to hear from a mob figure. Barardi wanted to take care of this one himself to send a message to anyone else who knew about this little charade. You didn't mess with Celio Barardi.

"I don't take kindly to punks stealing my property," Barardi said. "Where's the rest of it? If there's enough left, I might let you live, maybe just some broken ribs and legs. It's better than what you're gonna get now."

Danny's throat was still dry as a bone. He managed to think some relatively straight thoughts. *If I tell him where the money is, I'm dead.* He tried to clear the frog in his throat and said in a quivering almost inaudible tone, "I...I can take you to it. It's not far from here."

The voice grumbled back, "How stupid do you think I am? Tell me where it is or I'll blow you away right here and now. I'm tired of wastin' my breath."

Again Danny quivered as a chill ran the whole length of his spine. "I'm...I'm too...too nervous to...tell you. I...can show...you real easy."

"Too late kid, times up." Danny's whole body shook and his eyes widened in horror as the hammer on the big .357 was drawn back by Barardi's finger pressure on the trigger. Then he heard Barardi say, "Good-bye punk."

"AAAAH!"

The scream was blood-curdling, horrifying. Ginny was sure the neighbors could hear it. She was startled and didn't know what to do. Danny's restlessness had awakened her a few minutes earlier. He'd been talking in his sleep. It was something the likes of which she'd never heard before.

Ginny Parks, the 21-year-old nursing student at the

University of Central Florida in Orlando, met Danny the night before at the Rock Alliance. The Rock Alliance in Orlando was featuring a hot new band called Brian Purcer and the Hot Licks. A few months back, Ginny had met Brian Purcer, the lead guitarist and founder of the band so she wanted to hear him play. She'd done all her required labs and needed a break from the stress of the full load of scheduled classes. She and her roommate, Sharon, decided it was time for some stress relief.

She was immediately attracted to Danny's dark Italian eyes, dark silky hair and close trimmed beard. She was further charmed by his quick wit, flair for extravagance and his strong New England accent which was a rarity in central Florida. He was quite a switch from the immature school boys at UCF or the local "country boys" from Oviedo where she shared a two-bedroom rented house.

Ginny's roommate was a real party girl. She liked to stay out late and it wasn't unusual for her to be gone for several days at a time. Ginny said she didn't mind but deep down it bothered her that her roommate was gone so much. She knew what Sharon was doing, and that was troubling enough, but Ginny didn't like being alone overnight in their house. It was out in the "boonies" and that was frightening. She enjoyed getting out occasionally, but not like Sharon. Ginny didn't sleep around though she did have an occasional fling.

Her on-again off-again boyfriend back home in Avon, Ohio didn't like this arrangement one bit. He was trying to force the issue of marriage, her quitting school and moving back home, but it wasn't working. She wanted no part of it and his attempts only made a bigger gap between them. They both knew it was coming apart and Ginny felt it was all for the better. Her boyfriend, on the other hand, didn't want to face the fact that their relationship was going the route of many high school sweetheart romances. Once distance cooled off the heat, there was no real substance to hold the thin bond intact. They still kept in touch, but the letters were coming less frequently and their content was less substantive, unless they were downright hostile.

Now she found herself in uncharted territory. She was in

a strange bed with...Danny...*what was his last name?* He was screaming at the top of his lungs, obviously in great fear, sweating profusely. He was mumbling "Don't shoot me, please don't shoot me, I'll take you to it. No...no...please no." Then, "AAAAH!"

"Danny, Danny, wake up, please wake up!"

Danny shot up like a rocket to a sitting position, eyes wide open, staring ahead, sweat rolling off his olive skinned body. He was so tense that his skin was taut. A blood vessel on his left temple throbbed as the blood raced through the vein.

He looked over at Ginny and could see the confusion mixed with fear all over her face. He started to slow his breathing as he regained consciousness and realized he was no longer in front of the gun barrel he'd escaped some twelve years ago. He'd had this nightmare several times a month ever since then. It was one thing he felt he never would totally erase from his past. He'd managed to get away from the old neighborhood, his old buddies, most of whom were dead or in prison. But somehow he knew, Celio Barardi would continue to haunt him, maybe for the rest of his life.

Danny saw the fear in Ginny's eyes and the expression on her face; like a young, frightened child, lost in a crowded shopping mall, not knowing if her parents would ever find her. He took a deep breath. He said to the frightened young woman, "What a nightmare! I'm sorry you had to witness that." As Danny soothed Ginny's fears, he reached over and put his arms around her and slowly stroked her hair, pulling her head to his shoulder.

"You were talking in your sleep. Some of the things you said...the way you were saying them..." She started to cry in long sobs, tears streaming down her cheeks to Danny's shoulder. The whole episode pushed her over the edge. Between the pressures of school, living over 800 miles from her parents, being in an unfamiliar house, in an unfamiliar bed, with a guy she hardly knew, and he was having a bad dream...no, a major nightmare, she just couldn't hold it back. The tears were flowing faster now and Ginny began to shake; chills running down her spine.

He had to think for a minute before he spoke. *What is this girl's name? Where did I meet her?* Then he started to remember. It had been his third girl in the last week, so he wanted to be sure he had her name right. *The Rock. That's right. Jenny, I think. She knows Brian. I'll have to remember that.* Softly, and still stroking her hair, Danny said, "Take it easy, baby. It's okay now, it's over." He continued to stroke her hair and held her very gently; he knew how to smooth things over with women. You just have to tell them what they want to hear.

Ginny was starting to calm down now. Her tears were slowing. Her breath was settling into a smooth pattern. Danny held her tighter and gently pulled her down on top of him as he eased back down onto the bed. He slowly stroked her shoulders, down her back and to her rear. He slowly worked the magic that made him a neighborhood legend. He started out slow and gentle. Within ten minutes, he was pushing hard and fast into her. Fifteen minutes later, she was near an orgasm, but Danny came first, rolled her off of him onto the bed and fell asleep.

Ginny began to quietly cry again. But that didn't stop her from finishing the job herself while she thought about Brian Purcer.

***

Al Michaels was a bit annoyed. He'd had a rough night last night with the pipe bursting in the greenhouse. Then he had to clean up the mess all day today. It was hot in the greenhouse during the day at about 105 degrees and it was hard work. He was tired and sore. He wasn't in the mood to sit on the phone trying to scare up customers for Bill Grimes' new venture. He had his own sources for weed and he really didn't like to handle cocaine. He decided to at least make an effort to move some of the dope to some friends. *What the hell? Maybe I can move enough that I can pick up some free stash.* It was late in the evening but he could make some calls and catch them as they were just getting home from the bars. Most of his close friends were in their late twenties to early thirties and didn't stay out all night like they used to when they were in their teens. Their bodies just couldn't handle the all-night parties and then get a productive day's work in the next day.

Al sat down at the breakfast nook in the kitchen and opened his personal phone directory. He punched out the seven digits of his first potential customer. The phone rang seven times and no answer. Al decided to go to the next name. Again he punched out a seven digit code. This time he got an answering machine. You don't leave these kinds of messages on an answering machine, so he hung up. By this time, Al was getting frustrated. He went on to the next name and went to pick up the phone. As he was reaching for the phone, it rang, startling him just a bit. He took a deep breath to regain his composure and answered.

"Hello?"

"Al, this is Brian."

The noise in the background was heavy metal and Al figured right away that Brian Purcer was between sets at the "Rock." He had intentions of going to see Brian and his band but hadn't had the time to get away from the day to day hassles of the greenhouses.

"Brian. What are you up to? How's the gig going?"

"Pretty well. When are you coming out to the 'Rock?' Tonight would be a good night. We've got two more sets to go. Besides, I wanted to tell you about an interesting letter that I got last night. It was from Pat McKinney!"

Brian was nearly hollering into the receiver and it was hurting Al's ears. Al shouted into the phone, "Hey Brian, you don't have to yell, I can hear you just fine."

"Sorry." Brian lowered his voice some, realizing that it wasn't necessary to yell because Al didn't have the background noise of loud, heavy metal rock-and-roll to compete with. "Anyway, when I got this letter from Pat, I thought I should get in touch with you and tell you what's going on with him. I can't believe what he's been up to. He was in the Navy for six years, man! He's moving to Dunnellon. He's started his own company. There's more. He's married, man! He's got kids! Can you believe it?" Brian paused before going on. "Besides, I thought you'd like to get out and relax a little. You've been working yourself to death lately, man. You're not getting any younger."

Al thought for a minute. It was Friday night and there was nothing pressing to get done tomorrow in the nursery except a daily tour to make sure all the automatic sprinklers were working properly. Besides, he hadn't been to a bar in ages. Since his divorce, he'd only been out on a date once. *A date? I'm thinking like a teenager.*

"Okay, Brian, you're right. After tonight I need a break. You should hear who called me. I'll tell you about it when I get there. It'll take me about forty-five minutes. I'll catch you at your next break."

"Great. I'll be looking for you."

"See you soon."

With that, Al hung up the phone again and headed for the bathroom to get ready for his first night on the town in a very long time. Brian was right. He needed a break from the daily grind of the business world. It was turning him into a mindless machine, thinking only of processing orders, planting schedules, worker problems, growing liability problems, due to certain pesticides, fungicides, etc. He caught himself in a daydream about the business and shook his head clear. *Boy, do I ever need a break. This is driving me nuts!* Al put on his good blue jeans. He was ready to party. It was going to be a good night.

Chapter 11

The night was cool for July in Florida. Seventy-three degrees with a breeze that was so slight, it was barely perceptible. A cold front had moved through earlier in the day and a heavy rain had fallen on the entire region. The roads were almost completely dry, as was normal in a central Florida shower. Only puddles in pot-holes or deep grooves in the road still contained evidence that there ever had been a major rain shower that evening. There was no moon as it was still slightly overcast and the night was very dark.

The four small block houses were situated on a cul-de-sac at the end of a street about two hundred yards long. The developer had gone bankrupt after completing these four and no other builders had come in yet to pick up where he'd left off. The houses were single story ranches with brick veneer across the front. The other three sides were cement block construction, which was common in central Florida. There was no basement or crawl space as each was built on a concrete slab. Each home had about 1200 square feet of living space with three bedrooms, one and a half baths, an eat-in kitchen, and a carport. The lots on which they sat were odd pie shapes, narrow at the street and wide at the back of each lot. The cul-de-sac and adjoining street had six more vacant lots, all overgrown with weeds and palmettos. The street opened up to Orange Blossom Trail, a four-lane state highway. Within half a mile in either direction there were several roads that connected this isolated area with the vast central Florida suburbia. A man could get lost in the crowd of traffic traveling these back roads within minutes and never be seen again.

Pat McKinney had time to think while he was sitting...waiting...staring out the window at the house across the round stretch of blacktop. He was making sure all the tasks that Diane had laid out for him over the phone earlier were complete. Pat found out that there was a shopping mall within thirteen miles of their house. *That's exciting. Now we know where to hang out when we are bored to death.* Pat also found the local library, the courthouse, the city hall, the state license bureau, a grocery store, and several strip malls. *Now we know where all our money will be going.*

He looked around the small bedroom where he was seated in a lawn chair, the only furniture in the house. There were curtains on all of the windows. The rooms in the house were all painted antique white. The house had absolutely no character. The doors and windows were trimmed on the inside by fake plastic trim that was meant to be used in house trailers. The doors were hollow, light weight interior style doors. They had no insulating qualities whatsoever. The door to the main bathroom had been punched through. Apparently, an angry husband wanted to get to his wife real bad. According to the absentee owner who lived in Tampa, the last tenants left in the middle of the night. He'd found out later that they'd gotten divorced but not before the man had assaulted the woman and put her in the hospital for several days. The McKinneys were able to rent the house for a song. Marleena Johnson, a prostitute, was hired to make the cash deal. She told the owner that she'd need the house for at least six months. Using the brother's money, she'd paid his first and last month's rent. She'd made the second month's rental payment a week in advance of the due date. She was now in the third month of the lease. Ms. Johnson was happy to make the $500 cash to secure the lease for Pat. She didn't even have to perform the normal professional services for the big payday.

The owner of the home was happy. If he'd ever visited, he would have wondered why the place had never been furnished. If all went according to plan, Pat's need for this house would be fulfilled and this would be his last night here.

Pat's concentration was broken for a moment. He saw some movement from the house across the street. Lights came on in the bathroom. There was a shadow in the clouded glass. The shadow moved around, but was staying in one general area. *Probably combing his greasy, dago hair. You better comb it now, you grease ball. You'll want to look good in your casket.*

The light went out. Pat scanned the house for other signs of movement. Then a light came on in the living room. Pat got his first good look at Danny Vallero in over six years. It had been that long ago that Danny walked away with over $50,000 of the brother's money.

Through the scope on the powerful RAP Model 500, Iver Johnson AMAC-1500 sniper rifle, he could see Danny as if he were standing ten feet in front of him. The scope cross-hairs were held steady as Pat followed Danny's movements past the door, then in front of the living room window. Pat simulated a couple of shots, mimicking pulling the trigger. *You've been killed three times since you walked into the living room, you cock-sucker. I can't wait until later tonight.* Then Pat saw another person enter the living room; the same young lady that stayed over with Danny. *Well, I'm a patient man. I've got all the time in the world. No sense rushing.*

***

Al Michaels walked through the front door of the "Rock" at about 11:45pm to the screaming of Brian Purcer's Fender Stratocaster. The crowd was responding as if this were a concert hall and not a local nightclub, clapping their hands along with the music and bouncing up and down. Al was amazed. He'd never seen a club rock like this.

The main bar was seventy-five feet from the club's front door directly in the back. A second, smaller bar was to his left. The stage was to Al's right. There was a large dance floor directly in front of the stage of light colored teak. Tables lined the dance floor. There was an area of the floor that was raised about three feet along two walls of the bar where two rows of tables were situated to provide a better view of the dance floor and stage. There were nearly a hundred people, mostly young women standing on the dance floor lined up at the stage like a concert hall. The crowd had their hands above their heads, clapping and swaying to the hard driving music. Brian and the band were hitting on all cylinders and Al could feel the raw energy coming from the stage.

He smiled to himself and walked over to the bar and ordered a rum and coke, then stood at the bar, scanned the crowd, and enjoyed the music. The bar was smoke-filled but not overpowering. There were fluorescent lights along the underside of the bar so that the bartenders could see what they were mixing and pouring. Beer signs hung on the walls and in front of the mirror behind the bar. The only other lights were from the band's stage lights, flashing red to pink to purple.

The crowd seemed very young to Al. He looked at a couple of girls that looked like they were still in high school. They were dressed in skimpy halters and mini-skirts or very thin tank tops. They all had the look of being too easy. For all he knew, maybe they were. He shook his head and thought to himself that he must be getting old. *I'm thinking like my dad.*

The song ended and the crowd erupted into loud applause, whistles, cheers, and screams. What a hot song. Al couldn't believe that quiet, skinny Brian Purcer was going to be a star. *Who would have thought?*

The band started into the next song and the crowd's screaming and cheering subsided. Again, Brian's guitar took control of the crowd, mesmerizing them into a rock and roll trance. Al noticed a man walking toward him out of the crowd. In the dimly lit bar, he couldn't see the man's face clearly as he made his way through the crowd. He was dressed in a light sports coat that fit loose on his frame. He was making a beeline straight to Al. As he approached, his face came into view. It was Randy Farley.

Al hadn't seen Randy in several years, and, in contrast to the young girls in the Rock, Randy looked old. Even in the darkness of the bar, Al could see that life had been tough on Randy. His eyes looked sunken into their sockets. Dark rings and baggy flesh hung under them. The lines in his face were etched deep. As he approached Al, he smiled, but Al could tell that this was a worn-down man.

With as much enthusiasm as he could muster, Randy shouted, "Al Michaels! How are you? I haven't seen you in two or three years at least. Where the hell have you been hiding?"

The questions were hitting the mark. Al had been so busy trying to make his business a success that he hadn't been out on the town in a long time. "I've been pretty busy, working the nursery. It doesn't leave much time for a social life. How have you been?"

Al looked at the strained face of Randy Farley. His response was calculated. "Well, I ran into a bit of bad luck. I got caught in a bust a couple of months ago and my trial is coming up pretty quick. My lawyer says I got a good chance to beat the charges but the whole deal has me down. I'm broke. I can't get a job that's worth a shit. As soon as the company I was working for found out about the charges, they trumped up some crap on me and fired me, the bastards. Since then, I've been on a down-hill ride into the shit pile. Other than that, I'm doing great." The attempt at a joke fell short of the mark.

Al wanted to change the subject. He really didn't want the problems of an old friend to ruin his first night out in years. Randy solved the problem for him.

"How about Brian? Isn't he sensational? And the rest of the band is great, too. I'm telling you, Al, he's on his way. The record companies are wooing him big-time. They're talking six digits just to sign him. Can you believe it? Skinny little Brian?"

"He always did have the talent," Al shouted over the music. "We knew that long ago. I figured that he'd be working at the Sentinel all his life, though. I really didn't think that he'd motivate himself enough to get a solid band together, much less land a recording contract. The band sounds great. They're hot."

"Well I'm glad to see that at least some of the old gang is doing well. I mean, I'm all fucked up, but you and Brian are on the move. Have you talked to anybody else lately?"

"No, I haven't, but I guess Brian heard from Pat McKinney the other day."

Randy's demeanor immediately changed when he heard Pat's name. Al noted this but went on.

"Pat wrote him a letter and said that he's moving to Dunnellon. He's started his own business, consulting firm working mainly for nuclear power plants. That's almost as amazing as Brian and his band. Who would have thought in their wildest dreams that Pat McKinney had enough brains left intact to even think about nuclear power? I haven't seen or heard from him in about seven years?"

The news about Pat McKinney changed the desperate look on Randy's face to something close to terror. Al could see that he'd struck a raw nerve. It was like Randy saw a ghost. Al had heard that Pat and his two brothers had problems with old friends, but he figured that seven years would heal any hard feelings. He was obviously wrong. From what Al remembered Randy used to be pretty good friends with Pat, but they'd had a falling out before Pat and his brothers left town. Al didn't know that Randy was involved in the rape and murder of Mike's wife, Julie. He did know that Randy had made a few deals with Jamie Watkins and he knew where the dope came from. It was part of the stolen stash from the McKinneys. Al thought that might be the reason for Randy's reaction.

"Are you okay?" Al was looking carefully at Randy who was still thinking about Al's revelation. What color he'd had left in his face was now drained, and Randy looked sickly.

Trying to regain his composure, he looked at Al and asked, "When did you say Brian heard from Pat?"

"He didn't say exactly. He just said 'the other day' so I'm guessing Tuesday or Wednesday. Why, did you want me to let him know you asked about him?"

The question was more to get a reaction from Randy rather than find out what Randy wanted. Randy's look was priceless. His quick, fearful glance at Al let him know for certain that there was definitely more to the Randy Farley - Patrick McKinney story. He wanted to know what it was but decided to not push it any farther.

For his part, Randy could feel his throat tighten. His anxiety was rising, his eyes widening in barely controlled fear. When he looked up at Al, he could see that Al was studying him with a curious look.

Randy said, "You don't have to. I haven't talked to Pat in years. He probably doesn't even remember me. Where'd you say he was moving to? Dunedin? Isn't that over by Tampa?"

"Dunnellon," Al said. "Yeah, northeast of Tampa. There are only a couple thousand people there. I was over that way a few years back. If you blink, you'll miss it."

Randy looked defeated once again. The news about Pat McKinney was one more thing for him to worry about. Al saw the total despair across Randy's face. He was definitely a man at the end of his rope.

Randy stared off into the crowd now. He spoke as if he were talking to the crowd, though Al knew it was directed at him. "Maybe after I get this monkey off my back, I'll be able to get a business going. Or maybe I can convince someone that I'm trustworthy enough to get a good job, get myself back on track. What do you think?"

Al was sure that Randy was a loser for life. He didn't believe Randy could get out of trouble and stay out. He was lost, and no one was going to find him.

With conviction he said, "Look, Randy, if Pat can straighten himself out, you can too. Don't be too hard on yourself. You've just had some bad breaks. You'll get it back together. Just keep trying. You'll get your second chance."

Even as he said it, he wondered how many second, third, and fourth chances Randy had used up. You usually don't get that screwed up from one simple mistake. It takes practice, and lots of it. It may start out with something as simple as a drug bust, but it can stop there if you learn your lesson. Randy just wasn't learning.

"Thanks, Al. Good to see you again. Don't be a stranger."

"Sure, Randy. Good luck with the trial."

Just as they turned away, the music stopped abruptly and the crowd again exploded into applause, whistles, screams, and cheers.

Brian stepped to the microphone, held his guitar over his

head and yelled, "Thank you!! Thank you all very much! We're going to take a twenty-minute break before our last set. Don't go away, there's more hot rock and roll coming your way!"

More screams and cheers from the crowd rang out as the band left the stage.

Chapter 12

Bill Grimes wasn't having much luck as a salesman. He was starting to get a little worried that he wouldn't be able to move the weed that was fronted to him, not by the deadline anyway. He'd made twelve calls and only three people were home. Only two of those expressed any interest in purchasing any significant quantities of the stuff. Bill began to doubt his own ability to do anything right. Maybe Karen was right when she said that he'd never amount to anything. Well, she hadn't said that exactly, but she might as well have said it. His thoughts of self-doubt were compounding, feeding upon themselves. The more he thought about his inadequacies, the more he began to believe in them. He went to the refrigerator and opened a beer and began to think about what his next move should be. Just then the phone rang, almost causing Bill to drop his beer.

"Bill, this is Phil Daniels. How are you doing?"

There was a pause as Bill tried to think. *Who is Phil Daniels?* The name sounded familiar, but he just couldn't place him. So Bill replied, "Fine. What can I do for you? *Who are you, 'cause I don't remember you,* is what he wanted to ask? He was trying to be cautious, but friendly, because he didn't want any unexpected guests to show up at his apartment right now with the huge amount of stash he had in the closet.

"You remember me, don't you? We used to hang around with Cindy Worthington, way back in high school. Remember, we went to the Boston concert at the Lakeland Civic Center with her and that other chick, the sleazy one, Sandy Essy. Remember we used to call her Sandy 'easy' because everyone was jumpin' her bones. What a show Boston put on that night. And what a slut Sandy was. She got hosed by three different guys that night. Just the kind of chick you want to bring home to momma, right?"

Bill remembered this guy now. He was a real freak back then. Bill hadn't remembered him that well because he'd been so drunk that he'd passed out during the warm-up band's set. Phil had helped carry Bill out of the concert hall. They weren't real sure that Bill would survive. Karen was his girlfriend back then. After Bill passed out, she'd latched on to a friend of Phil's for the rest of the show. Phil thought that Karen was going to go down on Buddy right in the civic center. As it turned out, she did on the way back to Orlando in the back of the van. Bill never found out about that. He was passed out all the way home. Boston did put on a good show, but Bill missed the entire thing. It was no wonder that he couldn't remember Phil very well.

"Yeah, Phil, I remember now. How are you doing? What can I do for you?" Bill was still being a little cautious. He had no idea why Phil Daniels would be calling him after all these years.

"Well, a mutual friend of ours said that I would be doing well to call you about some business matters. He mentioned that for a mere $12,500, I could get about ten big ones from you. You know, of the leafy variety. So how about if I come over and check it out."

Bill was amazed. He hadn't talked to this guy in over six years! Now, out of the blue, this guy was willing to put $12,500 into his hands.

"Sure, Phil. Do you know where I live?"

"Yeah. Jimmy Duke told me. I'll be over in a few minutes. I'm just around the corner."

"Okay, see you in a few."

When Bill hung the phone up, a thousand thoughts rushed through his head. What if this guy was working for the cops? What if this was all a set up? Where could I hide the stash? Should I get my gun and have it ready? After all these frantic questions raced through his head, he finally decided that it would be prudent to have his gun loaded and on his person. He took a sports coat out of the closet and laid it on the bed. He put his AN1911 .45 caliber pistol in its holster and put on the shoulder harness. He then donned the sports coat and checked himself in the mirror. Bill smoothed out some of the wrinkles on the coat and made sure that the weapon was not visible from all angles. He was ready. He looked at himself again in the mirror, sticking out his chest with pride. *Man, I even look like a successful dealer.* Just as he was making the last adjustments to his suit, the door-bell rang.

As Bill walked to the door, he thought to himself that maybe he should have checked out Phil's story with Jimmy Duke, their common friend. Bill had called Duke earlier that evening, and the Dukester wasn't interested. He didn't even let on that he knew anyone that was interested. It was a little late for a checkup call now. $12,500 was waiting at the door.

***

"Man, Brian, you guys are hot! I can't believe the crowd, man. The chicks are screaming like back when the Beatles were just coming into the big time."

Al Michaels's compliments were a little too much for Brian. He knew the crowd was into the songs, but like the Beatles? That's a stretch, he thought. "Thanks, man. It really feels good to hear the crowd getting into it like that. We play just that much better. The energy pumps us up. Our last set is going to be a short one, because of the time. We've been playing over on the normal sets because the crowd is really into it and we want to keep the energy level up. It's fantastic."

Just then a group of young girls came up to the table to ask for Brian's autograph. He obliged and received several kisses on the cheek for the trouble. After they left, Al looked at Brian in near amazement.

"You must be moppin' up on the pussy around this town. They're falling all over you; throwing themselves at you. How do you keep up with the pace?"

Al's question hit a nerve, and for the first time, Al saw that Brian Purcer had a temper. Even in the darkened bar, Brian's red face was visible. Brian dropped his eyes to the table before he shouted, "Al, I'm not handling it well! OK? I'm tired, I'm lonely, and I'm not getting pussy every night! I'm too fucking tired to even think about it! Even if I wanted to, the women I want to be with are always taken!" He began to think about Karen Grimes...then Ginny Parks. They were the loves of his life; at least in his mind. He wondered what they were doing tonight.

Al broke into his thoughts, "Brian, I'm sorry, man. I didn't know you were whipped like this, but I know the feeling."

He thought about his own workaholic lifestyle. He changed the subject to get Brian's mind away from the drudgery. "Are you getting' a recording contract soon? I mean, you could quit your job as soon as you sign and get a big paycheck."

Brian calmed down some. "Look, Al, sorry for the outburst. I'm just way out on the edge right now. I've been working overtime at the Sentinel and with the weekend gigs and all, I'm just wiped out. The only energy I get is from the crowds. They keep me going, man. I really get fired up on the stage." He paused and thought about Al's question. "We should know later in the week about the contract. We're discussing numbers right now. I have an agent and everything. Even the preliminary numbers look great, and our agent is working on some improvements to those. We'll be in the recording studios by the end of the month to cut an album. I'm hopin' anyway."

"Excellent! You guys are...how do they say it these days. . .Awesome, dude! Keep me in mind when you get to be famous."

Al was truly feeling good for Brian. If there ever was anyone who deserved to be a star with all the good things that go with it, Brian Purcer did. He was a selfless individual who would do anything for you; a genuine nice guy. Not many nice guys make it to the big time in this world. Brian was about to break out of that mold and go against the odds.

Just then, two figures approached. Al didn't know either one but Brian tensed visibly. Al noticed that Brian was not pleased to see these two.

"Brian! Great show tonight. We just got here to hear the last three songs. You were awesome!"

Brian mostly ignored Danny Vallero except to say thanks. He immediately turned his attention to Danny's date. For the second night in a row, Ginny Parks was at his side. That was unusual for Danny. He usually didn't like repeat dates. He especially didn't like to be seen in public with the same woman two nights in a row. It hurt his image. Brian figured that it was just to get under his skin.

"Hi, Ginny. How are you?"

"I'm fine. It's good to see you. Danny's right, you guys are terrific. Are you going back on soon?"

"In a few minutes." Pointing to Al, Brian said, "This is Al Michaels. He runs a nursery out in Apopka. Al, this is Ginny Parks, and this is Danny Vallero."

"Nice to meet you." Al could feel the chill in the air. Brian didn't have a whole lot more to say to Danny, but continued to make eye contact with Ginny. This meeting had all the ingredients for a bad scene.

Ginny seemed to be responding to Brian's stares. Finally, Danny said, "Let's go Ginny, Brian's got to get back up to play."

Ginny turned to Danny and coldly stated, "He has a few minutes, don't you Brian."

"Sure, we're not due back on stage for another five minutes. Stick around."

Brian's reply was directed at Ginny, no mistaking that. Al could tell that this might escalate quickly. Brian and Danny were playing mental tug of war and Ginny Parks was the rope. Brian pulled a chair out and told Ginny to sit for a while. She obliged, and now Danny was hot. He wasn't going to have anyone, not even a rising rock star show him up.

He glared at Brian and sternly stated to Ginny, "Let's go." That was all he said. The chill now turned to a deep freeze. Danny expected his women to obey his commands, so when Ginny said that she was talking, he screamed, "I said, let's go! I mean now!"

Brian and Al both jumped to their feet and told Danny to back off, that the lady wanted to stay a little while. A small crowd was circling the scene by now and Danny didn't want a scene. He looked down at Ginny and shouted, "That's it, bitch. Find your own way home."

Brian didn't like that a bit. No one calls a friend of his a bitch. As Danny turned, Brian leaped on him, drew his fist back and caught Danny's jaw on the right side. Danny felt the attack and turned to retaliate, but Brian was already being dragged back by Al and Rick Wessler, the band's drummer. He had just shown up on the scene to tell Brian that it was time to play. Rick and Al stood between the two combatants and told them both to cool it. Brian shook his shoulders and turned away. Danny couldn't let it pass without one last barb.

"That's not the end of it, Purcer. You hear me? This isn't over."

Al couldn't resist the temptation. "Bag it punk. Do yourself a favor and go take a cold shower."

Through all the rustling, Ginny Parks sat quietly. She didn't want to be with Danny anyway. She was hoping that Brian would give her a ride home since her ride was walking out the door of the "Rock" as she stared. Before Brian went back on stage, he talked to Ginny for a few minutes, mostly small talk. He offered her a ride home. Rick Wessler said, "Come on, lover boy. We gotta play if we're going to make a living at this."

They left Al and Ginny sitting at the table alone. Al's first night out in several years was an eventful one. He'd seen a different side of a close friend, one he liked. Finally, Brian Purcer had some fight in him. Al figured that he would need that spunk in the industry that he was about to enter.

He turned to Ginny Parks and talked for a few minutes, mostly about Brian. He asked how they met and the usual casual conversation that two near strangers have. Al could see that this woman would be good for Brian. Then the man himself raced out onto the stage, and a wailing Stratocaster took control of the crowd.

Chapter 13

Pat McKinney finished the tenth chapter in the spy thriller that he was reading to pass the time. He wasn't much interested in books until he went into the Navy and ended up on a submarine. There wasn't much else to do on a sub if all the work was done and you saw all the movies that were played. He decided that reading was the best way to pass the time; time that otherwise seemed to drag by painfully. So reading filled a big void, as it was doing now. He looked at his watch. 1:55 AM. He began to think about Diane and how he wished she were there with him in this empty house, furnished only with a cot, refrigerator, and coffee maker. He was drinking decaf because he didn't want his hands to shake on the "job." But Diane wouldn't understand why he was doing this. She didn't know enough about his past that she could see justification in this act. If she knew more about his past, maybe she wouldn't be with him. She would never know anyway, Patrick thought. She didn't have a "need to know," according to military jargon. Besides, all this happened before they met. This was unfinished business from a previous life. The circle would be closed after the plan was completed.

Patrick's mind drifted to another empty house, the one Danny Vallero used to live in. Pat went there to collect on just over $50,000.00 in drug money. When he arrived at the house, Danny and all of his belongings were gone. Pat told himself then that he should never have trusted Danny. He was a streetwise punk from Boston and he always seemed to have one scheme or another up his sleeve. The signs were right there in front of Pat's nose, but he refused to believe them. For all of his street smarts, Danny Vallero didn't know one thing; he should never have screwed with Pat McKinney.

Pat's attention was captured by the approaching lights of

a car. The 1985 Cadillac DeVille pulled up to the house across the cul-de-sac and stopped. The lights went off and the occupant got out. He went up to the front door. Pat could see by the actions of the person at the door, a dark-skinned man with dark clothes, that he was agitated. He rang the door bell several times then began pounding on the door. He looked back to the car momentarily and motioned to another person inside the car. They also got out of the car came up to the door beside the first man. They both looked around nervously. Once again the first man pounded on the door. They started talking to each other in loud, agitated voices. The second man appeared to be taking charge. Pat could hear the voices and could easily tell that they were not speaking English. *Spanish maybe*, he thought to himself. He could also tell that the two men were up to no good. One of the men left the front door and began looking in each of the windows around the front side of the house. Satisfied that there was no one home he motioned to the other man and they got back in the car.

Patrick watched intently and could see movement in the car. *What were these two greasers doing?* It was pretty clear that they were no fans of Danny and this concerned Pat. He came here with one thing in mind; that was to kill Danny. This was a complication he did not need. He already knew this was going to be a long night and this would only make it longer. *Why did these two clowns have to show up now?* He wondered what Danny had done to get these two spun up. He realized long ago that he wasn't the only person that Danny had double-crossed. He just didn't think that he'd run into any of them.

Pat decided to wait to see if the new arrivals would leave. He went back to reading his novel because he didn't have anything else to do to pass the time. The tension was mounting with each passing minute. It didn't help that the heroine in his novel was trapped in a seemingly inescapable situation.

He'd found himself trapped between the mob and the FBI in a no-win situation. Just when he thought that there was no escape...

He heard the engine start on the car across the street. He

peered out the window and saw the car back out of the drive and head towards US Route 17-92. Pat sat motionless for a few moments then breathed a sigh of relief. *I may get this done after all.* He sat back and began to relax once again, reading his novel. Even without the distractions, it was going to be a long, tension-filled night.

***

After leaving the Rock Alliance Danny Vallero drove up 17-92 towards his house. His altercation with Brian left him in a foul mood. He'd planned on spending the evening with Ginny again but Purcer had screwed that all up. *How could that skinny little punk mess up my evening?* He was talking to himself, getting himself pumped to take some action. He wouldn't do it tonight. Maybe he'd go back out and find another mark tonight. *Maybe a better looker than that bitch, Ginny. Who the hell does she think she is, embarrassing me like that? No chick does that and gets away with it.* He was so angry, concentrating on what he was going to do to get even, that he missed the turn into his neighborhood. He ended up stopping at the ABC Lounge on South Orange Blossom Trail for a night cap. He spent forty-five minutes in the lounge but no one there was up to his standards so he left and headed for home, still fuming about the scene at the Rock. He pulled into his drive at 2:20. He was very much awake and expected that he would be for quite awhile.

***

Pat could see the lights coming on and staying on in various rooms. He could see that things were being thrown around the house. This man was seething with anger. Pat didn't know or care why, but someone had pissed this dude off. No matter, Pat thought to himself. *He'll only be pissed off for a few more minutes.*

He looked through the scope of the powerful sniper rifle and adjusted his eyes for the most comfortable position. His rifle had been fitted with a fairly bulky silencer so that the noise of the report would be unrecognizable to the average person. He had a clear view into several rooms in the house across the cul-de-sac. His nerves were calm and the cross-hairs of the scope were steady as he acquired his target. The target was still moving frantically around the house from room to room. Finally, after about two more minutes of apparent raving, the target settled down in the easy chair in a direct line through the front screen door.

Pat placed the crosshairs on the bridge of the target's nose, took a deep breath and began to apply pressure to the trigger of the powerful rifle. The target jumped suddenly, slamming his fist onto the coffee table directly in front of him. Pat eased off the trigger, but maintained the gun's sights positioned on the target.

Again Danny settled back into the easy chair. Pat again leveled the scope cross-hairs on the top of the nose, took a deep breath and slowly squeezed the trigger.

The recoil of the powerful gun rocked Pat back several inches. The report was little more than a whisper of sound. Pat immediately smelled the cordite from the weapon.

Across the cul-de-sac, the projectile hit Danny's forehead about one inch above the bridge of the nose, slightly to the left of center, and ripped into his skull. As the projectile flattened, it ripped bigger and bigger portions of brain matter to shreds. The projectile then ripped the back of Danny's skull out and spread its contents into a messy pattern on the wall behind him. Pat looked through the scope and saw the body bounce to the floor after recoiling off the soft cushion of the easy chair. He saw the pattern of human guts on the wall, immediately became nauseous, and threw up his dinner beside him. He took several deep breaths then wiped his face clean with a paper towel. After a few moments to get his nerves under control he cleaned the mess from the floor and packed it in a bag.

Whatever Danny was angry about didn't matter now. He would never be angry again. Pat was certain that there was no life left in him. He calmly disassembled his Iver Johnson rifle, packed it into the suitcase, knelt to one knee, and prayed to God for forgiveness; a forgiveness that somehow he knew he would not receive.

He stopped for a moment and thought to himself. He

should feel better, relieved, or at least partially vindicated. He felt none of it. Instead he felt dread. The black cloud that was hanging over his head was still there, except now it was a darker shade of black. Maybe revenge wasn't the answer. Was there another way to even the score? No matter, the plan was in motion. There was no turning back. As he walked to the carport to put the suitcase in the trunk of the car, he knew for certain that he would see hell.

Chapter 14

Detective John 'Johnny' Poleirmo sat back in his unmarked car and tried to relax. He and Detective Ray Krebs had another five minutes before they and twenty other law enforcement officers were to storm a suspected crack house on Orlando's West side off of Church Street. The neighborhood was a run-down section of town within walking distance of an area that had become one of Orlando's hottest night spots: Church Street Station. The Orlando City Council was anxious to use its new power to board up, condemn, and tear down "known drug houses" within the city's boundaries. It was a powerful new law and was supposedly having positive results in other cities across the nation. The law was of no consequence to the two detectives waiting to perform one of the most dangerous maneuvers in law enforcement. They were going over the procedure in their minds, trying to make sure that they weren't forgetting details of the coordination and execution phase of the bust.

The surveillance over the past month had demonstrated a need for the bust. There had been almost five thousand dollars in crack sales to undercover informants over the last month. The men involved in the sales were not just street dealers. They were trying to move larger quantities of crack cocaine to other street dealers in an attempt to increase their income from the potent, addictive drug. Johnny and Ray hoped that they could put an end to this group's trade today.

Johnny looked at his watch which was synchronized with the other officers involved in the raid. *Four minutes to go. Four minutes! Has my watch stopped?* Johnny's thoughts were echoed out loud by Ray.

"Jesus! This seems like it's taking forever! I hate all this dead time before the move. Every time I'm on one of these things, it seems like the last few minutes drag on forever. Have you checked everything over?"

"Only a dozen times or so," Johnny replied. His response had an edge to it, letting Ray Krebs know that Johnny was not in the mood for small talk at this late juncture. It was nearing show-time and the senior detective did not want to be sidetracked by chitchat. A veteran of the Orange County Sheriff's Department for over twenty-two years, John Rolando Poleirmo had been involved in dozens of busts. Almost all had gone well, but every veteran cop seemed to have a story about one that had gone bad, and people got hurt. One of Johnny's best friends was gunned down in one of those 'busts-gone-bad.'

Johnny and his partner, Dick Randall, were the lead group through the front door of an apartment building where it was suspected that a group of Cubans were warehousing and selling large quantities of cocaine and heroin. Johnny kicked the door in and raced in with gun drawn, his partner Dick, right behind him. The Cubans had been alerted to the bust; the element of surprise, so important to a bust, was lost, and the Cubans were armed and ready. As soon as Johnny saw the drawn guns pointed at him, he yelled to his partner to get down, but it was too late. As Johnny laid out flat on the floor and rolled to cover, the Cubans opened fire. Four lead slugs ripped through Dick Randall's chest, piercing his heart and both lungs. The assault team returned fire and in the ensuing battle, two more team members were killed, three were wounded and all five Cubans were killed. An investigation into the incident cleared the officers of any wrong-doing, but it was never determined how the Cuban dealers were tipped off. That incident was always an extra burden on Johnny's mind while preparing to execute another bust.

Johnny's stomach was starting to churn. He could hear the growls from his stomach in the near silence of the unmarked detective's car. The tension was thick as his watch told him there were three minutes to go. In the back of his mind, he wished the signal, the words "green light", would not come over secure radio on the seat next to him. He knew that was a pipe dream. It would only be...what, two minutes, now. Let's get this over with! Come on, time.

He again went over the procedure in his mind. He and Ray would approach the front door behind the officers with the battering ram. They would have ten seconds once they left the car to get themselves positioned. At that moment, officers in cars around the perimeter would turn on the police car sirens full blast. That was the signal to ram the front and back doors down, enter the premises, and take control of the occupants. The idea of the sirens screaming is to throw the apartment occupants off guard for a split second and allow the assault team the gain quick entry. Once through the front door, they would immediately scan the room and determine what threat exists, and "neutralize" that threat. *Who comes up with these sterile terms for killing people? Neutralize. It's really blasting the hell out of them, scattering their guts all over the room. Neutralize. Right.*

One minute to go. Johnny suddenly felt nauseous. He took a few deep breaths and tried to relax a little as the "green light" time approached. *Now is not the time for this.* Rolling his window down just a few inches, Johnny tried to take in some fresh air, and calm his nerves. *I should have known this was going to happen, it does every time.* He finally gained control of his stomach, and looked at his watch. Thirty seconds. He counted backwards with each second; twenty-five, twenty-four...eighteen...Johnny looked down at the portable radio. The red pilot light shone brightly in the dark car, its LED core showing through the glass enclosure. Looking back to his watch: nine...eight...Johnny looked at Ray and asked, "Ready?"

"Ready as you can be in these...

Ray's response was cut short by the words "Green light" coming over the radio. Without another sound, Johnny and Ray exited the car, lightly closed their doors, and approached the apartment building quickly, but in near-total silence. They could see other officers' approach from different angles, all in black suits with POLICE in white letters across the chest, over the top of bullet-proof vests. Within eight seconds everyone was in position. Suddenly, the quiet night air was filled with wailing sirens, shouts of commands, and battering rams on the front and back entrances to the apartment. Within two seconds, Johnny and Ray were inside the front door, Johnny moving right and dropping to one knee, Ray to the left doing the same.

In the dining area to the right, just off the kitchen, two men and a woman were sitting across a table from one another, their eyes wide and their mouths open, jaws nearly to the table with a look of total surprise. They looked as if they had not even had the chance to move. One of the men had a crack pipe in one hand and a lighter in the other, still lit ready to light the piece of crack in the pipe. Seeing the guns drawn and leveled at them, the men and the woman did not move. From the rear entrance, other officers had entered, finding two more people in bedrooms and another passed out in the bathroom.

Ray Krebs was frozen at his position. His gun was pointed into the living room at three children sitting on a couch, watching television. His heart sank as he realized that the children were the victims of neglect. Their parents were too busy selling and doing crack to care for them. Ray looked at them to make sure they were not a threat. He slowly lowered his gun.

The assault team had cuffed the six adult occupants. They were being led out the front doorway which hung by one hinge, badly damaged by the battering ram, when Detective Krebs stopped the exodus. He demanded to know who the parents of the children were. When the woman who was sitting at the table answered that she was, Ray lunged at her and drew his fist back. He was stopped by several officers in the assault team and restrained. He still had fire in his eyes.

Johnny yelled, "Get that scum out of here before I puke!" He then turned to Ray. "Don't ever lose your professional demeanor on the job again. That's how people get themselves and their partners killed. Do you understand me?" Ray was still fuming, but Johnny shouted again, "Do you understand me?"

"Yeah, Johnny. I got it." By all indications, Ray was an excellent detective. He was not as experienced as Johnny but he appeared to have the right skills for the job. Johnny understood why vice cops become emotional seeing the innocent victims of these 'victimless' crimes. It was happening all too often all over the country.

"We'll take these kids down to the station and call Human Services. I think Jim Walters is on duty. He'll take care of them." Johnny did his best to reassure Ray, but he knew that these kids had very little chance to succeed in life. They had started out poor, and were dealt a bad hand in life by being born to a single, drug addicted mother whose only care in life was satisfying her addiction to crack cocaine. *What a waste of human flesh and bones*, Johnny thought to himself.

The evidence was gathered; several thousand dollars in crack, a small amount of marijuana, four hand guns, all with the serial numbers ground off, and a few hundred dollars in cash. It was not as much as they'd expected. It wouldn't break any bust records but it would put this house on the known drug house list. That meant that it would be boarded up and eventually razed.

That much cash and the kids were still starving. This crack is some powerful stuff for a mother to neglect her kids just to get high. Johnny just shook his head.

The actual bust had taken a total of twenty seconds. Add the ten second approach time and in half a minute, the team had secured the house and made the apprehensions. That might have been a record had any statistics been kept on such matters. The evidence gathering had taken about forty-five minutes so in less than one hour another crack house was out of business in Orlando. *A good night's work.* Johnny was very satisfied with the performance of the assault team and though the net from the bust was not as big as expected, he was certain that the evidence would hold up in court.

Back at the station, Ray came over to Johnny and suggested, "Why don't you go home, Johnny? I can finish up the paperwork." Ray seemed to want to make amends for his outbreak back at the apartment.

"All right, Ray. Let me call home and let Rachael know that I'm coming. I have to call her anyway, let her know I'm okay. She worries when I'm in on a bust."

Before Johnny could reach for the receiver, his phone

rang. He picked up the receiver, annoyed at this interruption.

"Poleirmo, Vice."

"Johnny, this is Al Porecwzski, homicide. Are you busy?"

Johnny wanted to say yes and just hang up, but he heard a little urgency in Al Porecwzski's voice. It was a rare occasion when someone from the homicide department called vice for their help. He liked most of the guys in homicide. Like Al Porecwzski, they were pretty good guys. Johnny had been in homicide four years ago but left for the vice squad at the urging of his captain, Frank Sterns. Sterns said that vice needed help in trying to stem the flow of crack into the central Florida area so they accepted transfers from all the other departments to upgrade vice. It was supposed to be a two-year stint, but as fate would have it, Johnny was doomed to vice maybe until he retired. That was a long way off.

"Yeah, Al, what's up?"

"You guys got a file on a punk named Danny Vallero?"

Johnny had to think for a minute. The name sounded familiar but he couldn't place it. "The name rings a bell, but I can't place him off the top of my head. Why, what's up with this kid?"

"Somebody took off the top of his head. Looks like an assassination with a high power rifle. He must have really pissed somebody off. We found dope in the house too, but not any great quantity, not enough to get hit over. This guy appears to be small potatoes. He must have stepped on some big toes though."

"Give me about ten minutes to finish some things up and I'll get back to you. Where can I reach you?"

Al gave Johnny the phone number. He wrote it down on a piece of scrap paper and stuffed it in his shirt pocket. "Okay, Al. I'll get back to you."

Poleirmo scratched his head then rubbed his face with both hands. He would look for anything Vice had on Danny Vallero after he called his wife to let her know he was okay and that he would be home late again. He picked up the phone and dialed. There was only one ring and a female voice said,

"Poleirmo's, Rachael speaking."

In a tired voice, Johnny said, "Hi, Baby. I've got good news, and I've got bad news…"

Chapter 15

The news of Danny Vallero's murder spread quickly. Channel 10 News treated it as a possible drug-related murder in a struggle over turf as did the Orlando Sentinel. The medium sized article took up two columns, approximately four inches long. Brian Purcer stood in the mail room digesting the article with great intensity. He couldn't believe it. He'd just had a fight with this guy about the time that the news story said that he was killed. How could that have happened so quickly after the scene at the bar? He thought that he might be a suspect, but he had several hundred witnesses to the fact that he was on stage at the time of the killing. Besides, the police had to know that Danny had made many enemies in his lifetime, several, in fact, at the Orange County Sheriff's Department.

He put the paper down and got back to his duties in the mail room. His mind still raced a mile a minute as he tried to put the thought of Danny Vallero's violent death out of his head.

***

Al Michaels sat eating his breakfast scanning the same story that Brian Purcer had read. He, too, was stunned. The timing was unbelievably close to the time of the argument at the "Rock." Had it not been for the timing, Al would have thought "good riddance" to himself and not given the story another thought. He'd just met the guy and already knew that he was no fan of Danny's. Even as he sat there contemplating the events surrounding Danny's death, he felt no remorse. Danny's demise is the world's gain, he thought. He thought about giving Brian Purcer a call to ask if he'd seen the article, but let the thought pass. He had to work. Besides, Brian worked at the Sentinel. Certainly he'd read the story by now. He'd call Brian later.

***

Ginny Parks was horrified. She read the story for the third time and still couldn't believe it. Could this have been my fault? Did Brian or his friend Al have anything to do with this? I hardly even knew this guy. Should I call the police? What should I do? She was frantic and her roommate Sharon noticed.

"What's up, Gin? You look scared shitless." She paused as Ginny read the story again. "What's wrong?"

Ginny turned to her friend and said, "You know that guy that I went out with the last couple of nights?"

"You mean the good looking guy from Boston? How could I forget that stud? What's the matter, did he dump you?"

Ginny's tears were welling up in her eyes as she tried to get the message across that it was much more serious than that. She simply handed the paper to Sharon, and pointed to the article with the heading, "Dealer killed in turf war." Sharon's expression went from dazed to amazed. Her jaw dropped to the table as she scanned the article, then went back over it with more intensity. She was in disbelief that her shy friend could end up in bed with a big-time dope dealer.

Finally she looked at Ginny, who was regaining her composure, and asked, "What the hell happened last night?"

Ginny told Sharon the whole story about her night at the "Rock," from arriving with Danny, to Danny's fight with Brian, to the ride home with Brian and their good-night kiss. She told her how glad she was to be away from Danny, because he was being an obnoxious pig, and how Brian was such a gentleman. Brian had asked her to go out next week, during the week so that it didn't interfere with the band's gig schedule and she agreed.

"Now this changes everything," she sobbed. "What should I do? I can't even think straight."

***

By Saturday afternoon, Jason Roberts had had enough bad news. He needed something to cheer him up. The demise of Danny Vallero was no big loss, financially or emotionally. Frankly he was surprised that it took so long for him to get himself killed. He was a loud mouthed punk who thought too much of himself. Like Jamie Watkins, he was trouble waiting to happen. Unlike

Jamie Watkins, he brought in a comparatively small income to the organization. Jason Roberts liked to know when things happened, how they happened, and why they happened. He didn't like not knowing why one of his people was "hit" and by all indications, this was a professional hit. He wanted answers and he wanted them soon.

Buddy Mahaffey, his body guard/secretary buzzed him. Buddy was brought into the organization by Phil Daniels. Phil and Buddy were friends in high school. Buddy liked to brawl in barrooms and got a reputation as one tough guy to handle. The Orange County Sheriff's Department didn't like to get calls from bars in Northeast Orange County when it involved Buddy. They knew they were in for a tough night just trying to get him under control. It was after one of these nights that Buddy found himself waking up in the Orange County Jail with a major hangover. Somehow, Phil Daniels had found out about his plight. Phil bailed him out, got the charges dropped, even though Buddy had put two guys in the hospital. Phil offered him a job as a bodyguard for a guy named Jason Roberts. The one condition of employment was that Buddy stay out of the bars, stay sober while on duty, which was twelve hours a day, and don't let anyone near Mr. Roberts that didn't have proper clearance.

Buddy had done his job well since signing on with Mr. Roberts and was earning $100,000 per year for his trouble. Buddy was sober, wealthy by some standards, and was staying out of trouble with the Orange County Sheriff's Department. Everyone was happy, especially the deputies who no longer had to wrestle with him on the weekends.

"Mr. Roberts, Phil Daniels to see you, sir."

"Send him through, Buddy," Jason Roberts said into the intercom.

Buddy turned to Phil and said, "Go on in, Phil. Did you see where Danny Vallero got wasted? What a shithead. You had to figure he'd get it sooner or later."

"Yeah, that might be one of the things Mr. R. wants to talk about. I hope I can take over some of his territory. I know some of the folks he was rippin' off. I'll let you know how it goes."

With that, Phil entered the massive office of Jason Roberts. No matter how many times he visited the office, he was awestruck. With all the book shelves filled with legal volumes, classics, and reference books, one would think Mr. Roberts was a lawyer. Jason Roberts was also an avid diver and collector of rare sea creatures. Some were stuffed, some were in aquariums. Others were on the walls in fabulous paintings. Jason Roberts loved the sea and all the beauty it held. Phil was especially impressed by the enlarged photos of underwater sea life. There were several on each wall of the office. But it was business time now.

"Good job hooking the Grimes kid, Phil. Do you think he'll work out over the long haul?"

"Yes sir. He'll do fine. The only potential problem may be his wife but she's teed at him right now and we're gonna make sure she stays that way. She'll be leaving him real soon for good. Neither one of them know it right now though. Sir, I'd like to run with this one. I know I can make a real dealer out of him and keep him in line." Phil wanted to move up in the organization and the only way to do it was to convince the main man that you could bring in the cash and protect the organization. He felt that Jamie Watkins was a liability at the latter.

"Jamie brought in this mark, Phil. It's his operation. I can't take that away from him. We can't be snaking our own people like that."

"Mr. Roberts, may I speak frankly? Jamie...well, he's gonna get...he's trouble waiting to happen. You know how he is. His big mouth is always drawing attention to himself and anyone he's around. I know he brings in a ton of bread to..."

Mr. Roberts held up his hand, indicating that he'd heard enough. Phil knew to stop at that point.

"I know what you think about Jamie. But he brings us over $1,000,000 a year and is constantly building on that. Can you match those numbers?"

Phil knew he couldn't, but he was no slouch either. His

numbers were growing at a faster rate than Jamie's. He knew this because he had access to the books. Phil hadn't been working for Mr. Roberts nearly as long as Jamie but already was bringing in over $600,000 each year, and he was hungry. He wanted more action.

"Sir, I'll show you what I can do and I'll also do it without sticking out like a sore thumb."

"Maybe it is time for a carpet call for Mr. Watkins. I've heard a few things about him recently that have disturbed me. In the meantime, keep your head up. You're doing a fine job and because you're doing such a fine job I've got something special for you. You've heard about this Danny Vallero thing?" Phil nodded. "We're going to have to make some adjustments. We don't know much about the hit yet. We want to make sure we recover as many of Danny's customers as possible. You worked with Danny some so I felt that you'd be able to handle it. Are you up to it?"

Phil eyes widened. He hadn't heard the term "hit" with regards to Danny's death. He thought that it was some punk that Danny was ripping off or some jealous husband whose wife Danny had screwed. The general feeling among the organization was that it was no loss.

He looked at his boss and said with absolute confidence, "Yes sir. I'll handle it. Is there anything else that needs attention in regards to the hit that you'd..." Again Mr. Roberts held up his hand and cut Phil off.

"It's being handled, Phil. You just concentrate on business. If you need help finding Danny's contacts, Donnie Lee Lester will assist. He's already been told to lend a hand if asked. Listen Phil, I know you're eager and that's good. But don't get too eager. That's when you start to get sloppy...and dangerous. We can't afford to lose good people."

As Phil rose, he said, "Yes sir. Thanks. You won't be disappointed."

"I know." Mr. Roberts enjoyed giving his guys the pat on the back when they deserved it. Phil Daniels was one who did. He'd come a long way in a short period of time, but he still had much to learn. Now he had to deal with one who knew too much and had the bad habit of showing it off in public. Jamie Watkins might bring in the bucks, but he was quickly becoming a liability. He needed to be calibrated. Mr. Roberts was a real technician when it came to calibrating.

The other thing on Jason's mind was about Danny Vallero's shooter. It was an exceptionally clean job. Rented house across the street for surveillance; high power rifle; bulls-eye shot to the center of the forehead from about 120 yards. Worse, his contacts in the Sheriff's department had no clues beyond some hair, and some partially digested food. No other leads. The renter was a known prostitute who was long gone from the area, according to her friends. The name on the lease was fictitious. Worse, it wasn't a turf war like the paper said. In a turf war, messages are passed warning of a takeover of territory. There were no messages. Nothing to indicate that a gang was moving in. No attempts to scare other dealers and only one dead body. Danny Vallero. No big loss. He'd have felt better if he'd have had Danny killed himself. But not knowing really bothered Jason Roberts. Who? Why? These were big questions, but they had no obvious answers.

Chapter 16

Joe McKinney looked out of the apartment window down into the parking lot, not looking at anything in particular. It was another hot, humid central Florida day. The sun gleaming off the pavement hurt his eyes and he had to squint to see clearly. The only blessings on days like today were air conditioning and swimming pools. He caught a glimpse of a young woman heading towards the pool in a tiny bikini with a towel, suntan lotion, and a can of some kind of cold drink. Lisa Goddard was her name. She worked at the Publix Grocery Store in the plaza down the street. At 21 years old, 105 pounds, tan, five feet-two inches tall, 35-22-36, she drew many stares; like the one Joe was giving her now. He'd never talked to her before but had thought many times about it. He'd thought about asking her out, but he didn't want to drag anyone into a relationship right now. At least not until this business with his brother, Patrick was finished. Trying to have an honest relationship with a woman was tough enough, but carrying excess baggage into it was like fighting a heavyweight contender with one hand tied behind your back.

Joe couldn't see how Patrick could handle the stress. Living two lives; one with a wife and two children and starting a new business; the other, an assassin, hiding every move from the family you love, from close friends, and from the law. Joe shook his head at the mere thought. He wondered if Patrick really was handling the stress as well as he appeared to be.

Finally, Lisa "the goddess" Goddard was out of his sight behind the privacy fence. Joe's thoughts turned towards what he would do if he were totally free to choose what he wanted to do. He had plenty of money. The money that they'd made in the dope trade was laundered and was now invested in legitimate holdings like stocks, bonds and some real estate. The blind trust where their money was invested produced over $395,000 per year. The principal was still growing. Joe's draw was $125,000 per year. Pat and Mike each drew an equal cut. It was totally clean money, taxed by all levels of government. The trust was being managed by an attorney that Pat knew. He was a former small-time customer of theirs. He now specialized in securities and exchange law. He showed the McKinneys some great things about money; like how it could be hidden, used as collateral, laundered, and kept squeaky clean, all without having the real owner's name attached. He helped the brothers make the right move to preserve their cash and make significant income in the process. So Joe didn't have to do an honest day's work for the rest of his life if he so chose. He did have a job to do, though.

The plan had gone well so far. The plan, which Pat and Joe wrote out years ago, was not written down anywhere now, but they both knew it by heart. The small details of each person's part of the plan were not known to each other. Only the outline and the timetable were important to be known by both of them. That way if one of the brothers was caught, the other was relatively safe. No specific details could be collaborated. Patrick knew more of the details than Joe, but he still insisted that Joe carry out his part independent from anything that Patrick did. The original plan had been burned in a fire in their orange grove, the ashes scattered and buried in the sandy floor.

Basically, Joe did the preliminary investigative work; followed subjects to get information on their habits and routines, note any deviations, and see if specific schedules existed. Danny Vallero was pretty easy even though he didn't have a regular job. He always went out in the evening on weekends and usually came home with his conquest for the night by 1:00 AM. About 30% of the time, he didn't score and came home alone. When he came home alone, he would pour himself a drink, shoot up his smack fix, and plug in a skin flick and pass out in front of his unlocked screen door after about twenty minutes. Sometime around 5:00 AM he would wake up, lock his front door, stagger to his bedroom, and pass out again. He was very consistent. Bingo. Joe's job was done. He passed this information to Pat along with the most current information on the other subjects. Pat's job was to pick the dates and times for the actual hits. Joe's was then to run interference. During the Vallero hit, Joe took a trip up to Leesburg, Florida and "accidentally" left one of Patrick's gas credit cards at the gas station, making sure the attendant got a good look at him. Joe and Patrick looked so much alike that it would be hard to tell them apart, especially in a court room. After getting gas, Joe drove up to Jacksonville and checked into the hotel, again using one of Patrick's credit cards. The shoot took place, but Patrick couldn't have done it. He was on his way to Jacksonville to attend a seminar on low level radioactive waste storage. Patrick did in fact attend that seminar. He just arrived at Jacksonville at 4:30 AM, not 11:30 PM like the hotel log said. But logs don't lie.

The next subject should be relatively easy, too, Joe thought to himself. Just as he was thinking this, he saw Patrick's Ford Taurus pull into the apartment complex parking lot. Patrick got out, grinned towards Joe in the window and made the ascent to the second story apartment.

***

Jamie Watkins was still fuming. He thought Mr. Roberts was way out of line calling him on the carpet like that. How much money had he brought in for this organization anyway? Millions over the years. "For over six years I've put my heart and soul into this organization, and this is the thanks that I get! I bet that Phil Daniels had something to do with this. He's been trying to fuck me over for quite a while now. Well, he'll get his own taste of this shit when I'm through."

Jamie was literally screaming at Donnie Lee Lester and Bobby Acquino. They were trying to look interested, but for the last three weeks, every time they'd seen Jamie, he was barking like this. Finally Bobby had had enough.

"Jamie, shut the hell up!"

Jamie stopped in mid-scream. Donnie Lee turned and stared at Bobby for a moment, then said jokingly, "Looks like its ten Hail Mary's for you, pal."

"That's not funny," Bobby retorted. "I'm sick of Jamie's

constant bitching and whining. He's got every expensive toy in the world and enough money to run a small country. He's whining because the guy that makes it possible tells him to keep his dick in his pants and his mouth shut before he gets us all killed or thrown in jail. I have a brother who's in prison and I don't plan on joining him." He turned to Jamie and yelled, "If you would think for a minute instead of constantly spouting off, you'd realize that Mr. Roberts is just trying to protect you from yourself." Bobby's voice became calm, but strained, "Mr. Roberts just wants you to get your head back on straight. You're a loose cannon, and he wants us to keep our shit together. You know that the Vallero thing rattled him a little. Just quiet down in public a little bit."

"Is that all, Bobby?" Jamie's voice oozed with sarcasm. "Well then, I guess I was just over-reacting. I should bow down and kiss ole Mr. Roberts right square in the middle of his Yankee ass. Well I'll tell both of you a piece of news; Jamie Watkins don't kiss no-one's ass! Not Mr. Roberts'! Not Phil Daniels'! And neither one of yours! So go fuck yourselves! Don't ever try to tell me what to do! Now get the fuck outta here!" Jamie waved his arms towards the door, his face red as a beet, and veins throbbing at his temples.

Donnie Lee and Bobby turned and walked out the door of Jamie's house in Ocoee and got into Donnie Lee's four-by-four pick-up. They looked at each other in amazement for a few moments. Donnie Lee then started his truck and pulled out of the long driveway. He didn't know what to think. His mind raced, trying to remember Jamie going berserk like that before. Jamie had done some nutty things. He'd cut his coke with anything he could to make extra cash. He'd taken on two women at once and bragged all over town about it. He'd even insulted Buddy Mahaffey to his face and lived to tell about it. He'd done a lot of crazy things, but Donnie had never seen him go so completely off the deep end like this. It scared him. After a couple of minutes all he could muster was, "Wow, is he ever out of control."

Bobby didn't reply. He just stared ahead at the road and

mentally replayed the whole incident. He had just made up his mind that he was going to leave the organization. The only trick was how to tell Mr. Roberts. Bobby had to devise a plan. You don't usually leave an organization like this. *That's what the McKinneys tried to do and look what happened.*

Chapter 17

Ginny Parks had enjoyed her summer break. Her trip to Ohio had gone well. Her ex-fiancé had a new girlfriend which made their brief encounter easy compared with what she'd expected. She was prepared for a knock-down drag-out fight with him over getting back together. The brief discussion, though somewhat awkward, was cordial, polite, and almost pleasant. They both knew it was over and level heads prevailed.

Now she was back in Florida looking forward to school and seeing Brian in concert. Brian's contract signing ceremony was early next week for his band "Brian Purcer and the Hot Licks." Brian wanted the name shortened to the "Hot Licks" but the record company representative said that was out of the question. "You are the band, Brian." The guys in the band had to agree, without Brian, they didn't have a chance at the big time. He wrote all of the songs, though Rick Wessler added his two cents' worth to the lyrics on occasion. But Brian put the arrangements together and made most of the improvements to the songs when things didn't fit together right.

Ginny and Brian had been dating for three weeks and were hitting it off well. The separation for Ginny's Ohio trip was painful for both of them, but they survived. Since the Danny Vallero episode, things seemed to be falling into place almost like clockwork. Ginny's total outlook on life was improved. It took about two weeks for her to completely get over Danny's death, but with Brian's help, she managed to gain some genuine perspective. She knew now that the shooting wasn't her fault and no one around her was involved. Brian had explained how he and Danny knew each other and just what kind of complete jerk Danny was; a doper, a womanizer, and a self-centered ass. Brian explained that Danny thought he was a powerful individual with influence over everyone he met, particularly women. He told her how much he loathed Danny and was not surprised or saddened when he was killed. He also assured her that he was not the only one who felt that way about Danny.

Ginny wasn't sure that she was completely in love with Brian, but she was certain that she could fall anytime. There were some exciting, but unknown things in Brian's immediate future. There was no doubt that Brian could be an extremely wealthy man, but she didn't know him well enough to know how it would affect him. He could leave her flat on the way to his first promotional tour which was rumored to be in about two months. Besides, he hadn't asked her to even be his steady girlfriend or even a close friend. She wasn't sure what she would say if he asked her to be his girl. Life on the road must be extremely difficult. What about school? What about my nursing career? Her mind raced. She broke out of her trance when she heard "Cripple Creek" by "The Band" on the classic rock station on the radio. *I must be crazy to even think about the possibility of going on the road. Brian is about to be a big time star. Will he even remember me after his tour?* Ginny's mind wandered again as Loggins and Messina belted out *Angry Eyes* over the FM airwaves. The phone rang.

She answered, "Hello."

"Hi, Ginny."

"Brian, how are you doing? I missed you."

"I missed you, too. How was your trip?" Brian was a bit nervous as he waited for the description of Ginny's trip to Ohio and to an encounter with her ex-boyfriend. He was encouraged by the fact that she came back to Florida. He feared that her ex would convince her to stay up north and get back together with him. This wouldn't do because Brian had decided that Ginny Parks was the girl for him. He wanted her all to himself. He was afraid that she might not want to get hung up on a guy that was on the verge of being a road whore. He didn't even know what was in store for his life on the road. How could he expect her to leave school and abandon a career that she didn't even have yet?

"It went just fine. I saw Tom at a bar in Avon. We talked for a few minutes. He has a new girlfriend and seems very content." Ginny hesitated then teased, "Why, were you worried that I wouldn't come back?"

Brian got very serious and simply said, "Yes, I was."

Ginny's heart began to beat very quickly and she smiled. She could feel herself falling for this guy like a ton of bricks.

"Brian, would you like to come over tonight? I'll fix dinner. How about lasagna? I'm not Italian, but my step-grandmother was. That's how she captured my Grand-dad's heart, through his stomach. Anyway, she gave my mom and me this great recipe and it only takes a few..."

Brian cut her off. "Ginny, I'd love to come over. I'll bring a bottle of wine and some Italian bread. I'll see you in a couple of hours."

Her heart beat even faster. "Okay. See you then. Bye." She smiled to herself and twirled her shoulder length hair like a sophomore in high school awaiting her first date.

"Bye, Ginny. Oh and Ginny, I'm glad you're back. I really missed you." The phones had a distinct pause before being placed back on their respective cradles. In that short instant, Ginny Parks had made up her mind. If Brian Purcer asked her, she would drop everything that she had worked on for the last few years and follow him to the ends of the earth.

Brian smiled at the receiver as he placed it back on the cradle. He was head over heels for Ginny. His confidence in his own abilities and his chances for success were growing. His love for Ginny Parks was growing faster.

**

"It looks like we're ready, Joe. You're confident that you'll be able to get the timing right on this one?" Patrick knew the answer. He just wanted to see if Joe was still in it for the duration. Since the Vallero hit, they both knew that the plan was real. There was no turning back.

"It'll be right. This one's easy. Don't get cocky, though." Joe didn't mind the test. He knew that Patrick had to be extremely cautious. They'd talked about getting even with these bastards for months before formulating the plan. The plan only took about five hours to put together but there were details that had changed over time. This was particularly true after Joe spent time in the Marines learning warfare tactics. This newly learned skill was particularly useful in making adjustments to the original plan. It would only take about a week before the plan was completed. Joe could finally see some light at the end of the tunnel. Once the plan was complete, he could get back to living his life the way he wanted. But for now, the plan had to be executed to perfection. It consumed all of his waking hours. He definitely had a future as a private investigator if he was so inclined.

Patrick nodded. "Okay, then. I'll talk to you in a few days." Pat stood, put his hand on Joe's shoulder and said, "You're doing a great job. It won't be long now, and we'll be free of this. The slate will be clean."

Joe continued to stare at the carpeting. "Pat, do you ever wish that Mike had stayed with us on this?" Mike McKinney had listened to the plan early on, when it was no more than idle talk. When the talk started to get serious, Mike declined to join in and advised Pat and Joe not to talk about it in front of him. It was obvious to his brothers that he had no stomach for getting even with the people who had wronged them. It was fine with Pat, but Joe seemed to take exception to Mike's bowing out. Joe asked him how he could let these scum get away with what they'd done. Mike just turned to his brother and said, "They aren't getting away with it. They will pay. They'll have to answer to God."

Mike was seriously out of it. Since his wife's murder, he was fully consumed by despair. Patrick could see that it wasn't in Mike's blood to get even. Some people break things in anger. Some plotted revenge. Still others handle it in a more personal and emotional way. Shortly after the details of the theft and the murder became known to the brothers, Mike sat down in front of Patrick and cried his eyes out.

"Mike never was with us on this, Joe. It's lucky for us that he isn't. He'd have broken down and run to the cops or his Priest by now."

"You're probably right. I just miss him. Maybe we can

go see him when this is done."

"Absolutely." With that, Pat McKinney gave Joe's shoulder a comforting squeeze and left, closing the door behind him. Joe remained staring at the carpet. He wished the plan was completed and cursed Jamie Watkins, Donnie Lee Lester, Bobby Acquino, Randy Farley, and Bill Grimes. He also cursed the soul of Danny Vallero.

Chapter 18

The man who called himself Radar arrived at Randy Farley's apartment, parked the rental car, and surveyed the area. Nothing seemed out of the ordinary. The dimly lit parking lot was nearly full of cars. Most of the apartments were dark at 11:30 PM on a Friday night. Randy's apartment had a single light shining from the kitchen window.

Radar donned his plastic gloves and picked up the bag containing two bottles of Jack Daniels. Randy wasn't home yet. *Everything's going according to plan so far.* He exited the car and walked up the flight of steps to the second story apartment and let himself in using the stolen apartment key. He entered the apartment, re-locked the door, and made his way into the living room.

The apartment was a mess. Beer cans, dirty glasses, empty booze bottles, cigarette ashes and butts were everywhere. The room had the stench of acrid, stale smoke and old beer. This place hadn't been cleaned in quite some time. Radar wasn't sure why, but he was surprised by Randy's total lack of class. He made his way down the hall past the bathroom and looked into the unused bedroom. Randy used it for junk and dirty clothes. *What a pig. This guy is really messed up.* Finally he made his way to the master bedroom. At least there were no dirty clothes lying around. He staked out the room: a king-sized bed, an old dresser with the mirror conveniently angled down towards the bed, and a night stand with a lamp on it. The dust on the dresser and night stand was thick. *If he brings women home, either he leaves the lights off until morning or they're too drunk to care.*

The closet had two louvered bi-fold doors. He opened the door on the left, stepped into the closet, and closed the doors. Through the louvers, he had a decent view of the bed and a good part of the room. He thought about relaxing. Based on his surveillance of Randy's standard routine, he had 45 minutes to an hour and a half before Randy would be home. He put the bottles of Jack Daniels on the floor next to him and closed his eyes to think about his next moves.

He began to think about why he was here in the first place. This guy and his buddies were killers. That wasn't the worst thing they did to her. They raped her and tortured her. Then his accomplices robbed the house. He remembered hearing that they'd made a home video of the incident up to the point where the cameraman couldn't take it anymore. According to news accounts of the incident, Randy's friend, Jamie Watkins, was taunting the brothers, letting them know in no uncertain terms that he was the one who was in charge of the heist. His three accomplices, Donnie Lee Lester, Bobby Acquino, and Randy Farley were just along for the money, laughing at Jamie's taunts. Donnie Lee and Bobby were friends of the family. Jamie was the one who'd actually done the killing. He'd looked right into the camera and said to the other three in his annoying, sarcastic, Texas accent, "Don't worry boys, them McKinney boys don't have the balls to come after us. And even if they do, we'll kill 'em. Those spineless pussies. They probably wear silky panties."

His mind came back to Randy's apartment. Randy had screwed with the McKinney family for the last time. His part in the rape and murder earned him the death sentence. No court or jury would have to worry about this one.

The sound of footsteps coming up the apartment steps caused him to frown; the sound of keys in the apartment door. If it was Randy, he was having trouble getting the key in the lock. Then he heard something that made him shiver. A female voice said, "What's the matter, Randy? Can't you get it in the hole?" She giggled. The woman with Randy was apparently drunk, and if Randy was having trouble getting into his own apartment, he was probably drunk, too. After a moment, the door was unlocked. Randy and his date almost fell into the apartment. They both giggled at this. They were both very drunk. The door was closed and the security chain was put in place.

In the closet, Radar's mind raced. *Keep calm. Think. This is not according to plan. Just sit tight and don't move. This will work out. Patience.* His breathing was controlled and even. He listened for Randy and his date as they moved around the apartment. As drunk as they appeared to be, he figured that they would be passed out within the hour. That was good. Hopefully his estimate would be accurate.

Randy was really putting the moves on his date fast. He tried to get her to lie on the couch but she wanted to get a drink first. Randy grabbed her by the arm and escorted her to the master bedroom and asked her to sit on the end of his bed. When she said she really wanted a drink, Randy got a bit more forceful with her. He lightly pushed her on the shoulders. She fell backwards onto the bed and Randy crawled on top of her. She started to protest, but he covered her mouth with his hand. Even as drunk as she was, she feared that she was about to be forcefully raped and she wasn't going to let that happen.

Randy spoke to her and said in a calm voice, "Mandy, I love you. Don't resist me. I'll take my hand away if you promise to be good." Randy slowly took his hand away.

"It's okay, Randy. I'll be good to you. But my name is Sandy." This seemed to irritate the drunken Randy. Still sitting on top of her, he ripped her blouse open exposing her silky Victoria's Secret bra. Then he broke the front clip of her bra. Her breasts were now exposed. He remained sitting on top of her. He grabbed her by one wrist with his left hand and covered her mouth again with his right. Watching from the closet Radar was getting angry at the way Randy was pushing this girl around. He imagined that this is the way he'd forced himself on other women. It was all he could do to keep from breaking out of the closet door and finishing Randy right in front of this girl. How would he explain it to her? Would she keep quiet about the incident? Could he trust her? Maybe this is what she wanted and she and Randy were just playing a sex game. Be cool he told himself.

He didn't have to wait long. Sandy took her fist and gave

Randy a right cross to the jaw. It wasn't a direct hit but it knocked him off her and he fell to the floor beside the bed. She jumped up and kicked him in the jaw then ran into the living room. It happened so fast that the startled, drunk Randy was stunned. The door to the apartment opened and closed almost before Randy could get to his feet. He stumbled towards the living room shouting, "Mandy, wait, I'm sorry. Mandy, give me another chance. I love you." But Sandy was already gone. Radar took a long, deep breath and thought to himself, *Thank you, Randy, for being such a smoothie with women. This makes things much easier.*

Randy stumbled back to his room and fell back onto his bed face up. Within ten minutes he was snoring loudly. Radar waited an additional ten minutes to make sure that Randy was in a deep sleep. For those entire twenty minutes, Randy didn't change positions. It was safe for Radar to get to work.

He picked up the bag of booze, grabbed a handful of Randy's cheap ties and made his way out of the closet. He threw the ties and booze on the bed and left the room to make sure that the front door was locked. When he returned to the bedroom, he went right to work.

Randy couldn't have been more cooperative. He was still snoring with his arms above his head, crossed at the wrists. His snoring was very loud and his breath reeked of alcohol. One of the ties was slipped slowly around his wrists, leaving the slip knot loose. The other end of the tie was secured to the headboard. He then moved to Randy's feet where he fitted his ankles with one tie each. He then tied his ankle ties to the bed. He was prepared to stuff another tie in his mouth if necessary, but Randy remained sound asleep. *Almost ready*. He opened both bottles of Jack Daniels and set them on the night stand. Then he pulled the slip knots tight around Randy's wrists and ankles. Randy finally stirred. His eyes opened as Radar sat on his chest. Randy started to say "what the f..." As he opened his mouth, the neck of a bottle of Jack Daniels slipped in. Radar put his knees on either side of Randy's head to keep it as still as possible. The Jack Daniels started to empty into Randy's mouth.

He struggled as his body tried to eject the bottle. Radar was gritting his teeth as he maintained pressure on the bottom of the bottle. As Randy's lungs struggled to get air, the contents of the bottle surged into his stomach and lungs, bubbling like a water cooler.

"Do you remember Julie McKinney, Randy," he asked through gritted teeth? "You remember, don't you? You helped kill her, and now it's payback time. I'm your judge, jury, and executioner. Don't worry, it'll be over soon. You won't have to stand trial for those nasty drug charges. You won't have to feel guilty anymore. You can join Danny Vallero in hell."

Randy's eyes grew wider. Randy's stomach heaved as his body rejected the alcohol intrusion and his body continued to convulse. He couldn't breathe, he couldn't do anything. Finally, his body relaxed and the contents of the bottle flowed out of the sides of his mouth. Randy's eyes remained wide open, stricken with fear even in death. Radar checked his jugular vein...no pulse. He checked for breathing...none. He waited another ten minutes to be sure. There was no movement from the body of Randy Farley.

He untied Randy's hands and feet. He left the other bottle on the night stand and went to the bathroom to check himself in the mirror. He smoothed his hair, straightened his clothes, and put the surgical gloves in his pocket. He took one last look at Randy Farley and left the apartment. He got into his car and headed for the Orange County Convention Center. There was a reception that he needed to attend. Even if he smelled like Jack Daniels, that was no problem. Everyone there would smell like some kind of alcohol. Besides, he was already checked into the seminar and he'd signed the attendance sheet. He'd been there all night. It was a great presentation on using computers to improve records handling for large corporations, like nuclear power plants or gun manufacturers.

Chapter 19

"Good morning, Baby. How'd you sleep without me?" Pat's voice was a welcome sound early in the morning.

"Not bad. I missed you though." Diane yawned into the receiver as she looked at the clock; 6:30 AM. She had to get up in fifteen minutes and get ready for another busy day. "How was your trip?"

"Okay. It's been pretty boring without you. You're going to have to come with me on one of these boondoggles. It would be fun. You could shop at one of the malls while I'm at these seminars. Then we could go to some tourist traps."

"And just what do we do with your lovely children?"

"We could ship them to their grandparents. Mom and Dad would love to see them. So would your parents. Or we could bring them along."

"No way, dear. I can suffer through parenthood right here without having us go broke. When does your seminar start?"

"We have to be in the conference room by 8:30. Registration starts at 8:00. Three hours of listening to boring facts about Nuclear Regulatory Commission regulations, a long lunch, three more hours about more boring regulations. It's really not much fun. I do get to meet all kinds of interesting women, though." Patrick loved to tease his wife. And she took it well.

"Bring them home with you. I'll introduce them to my new boyfriend. He's cute, and he's got a great body."

"I guess I'll just have to come home and kick his hillbilly ass. Or I could just show you who's the better lover." Pat paused to see if Diane would react. When she didn't he continued. "How are the kids doing?"

"Well, right now they're still asleep. Sean should be waking up any second now. Will you be coming straight home after the seminar?"

"I should be. I may have to talk to some prospective new clients but that is usually just an excuse to have a few drinks. I'm sure I won't be sticking around here for long. Honey, do you ever think that I went into the wrong profession? I mean, are you happy with me traveling and all? Am I screwing up by not being around the kids more?"

Diane thought for a few moments before answering. She'd recently been thinking about how much time Pat had been spending away from home. It wasn't like being on a submarine where he would leave and be gone for eighty to ninety days at a time, but it was becoming a regular thing. Diane had been feeling the additional strain because of the way the children were behaving. Sean was asking why Daddy had to be gone so much. He even asked if Dad was going back to the submarine. That question hit Diane a little hard. She had laughed at first, but when she thought a little longer about it, Sean's question really touched a nerve. If Sean was noticing his father's absence, surely their daughter was, too.

She was feeling a bit lonely herself, lately, but being a Navy submariner's wife gave her some pretty tough skin.

"Listen, Mister, you don't have time to worry about this kind of stuff. You've got a business to get going. After you hit the big time and hire some flunkies to run the business, then you can hang out around the house. Hey, if you're still worried about it when you get home, we'll talk about it then. Right now, you've got important information to absorb. Now get going!"

The mock order surprised Pat a little. He answered with just as much sarcasm, "Yes Sir...I mean Ma'am." Then in a more serious tone he said, "I'll see you tonight, Baby. Let's go out to eat tonight, someplace nice. Can we get a sitter?"

"We'll see. Just get home safely. I love you."

"I love you, too. See you tonight."

The click on the other end of the receiver put a lump in Patrick's throat. He loved this woman so much. He couldn't stand the thought of hurting her. He knew that if he continued with the plan, the possibility of being caught would become greater and greater. Hurting Diane, the most wonderful woman he'd ever met, would only be the beginning of his troubles, but to him it would be the most painful thing of all of the consequences he would ever have to face. The tension level was rising and there wasn't a thing he could do about it. The plan was in motion. The best thing he could do now was complete it and make sure that he didn't get caught. He also had to hope that he could live with the guilt for the rest of his life. He put the receiver down and rubbed his shoulders. They were tight, and there was tightness in his chest. He'd felt this tightness before, but it was becoming more noticeable with each passing day. *I should get a physical. This tension is killing me.* Patrick got up, straightened his tie, and headed down to the restaurant for breakfast and a good cup of coffee. Just what the doctor ordered.

That's the ticket. I'll relax, read the paper, and think of pleasant things.

As Patrick sat waiting on his breakfast, his mind wandered. He vividly saw Danny Vallero's head explode onto the wall in his living room. He smiled to himself and visibly lurched, as the scene made his stomach turn. He was startled when the waitress brought his order to the table.

"Are you all right sir?" she asked with genuine concern.

"Yes, I'm fine." he replied. "I was just thinking of my wife and how much I miss her. Why, was it that obvious?"

The young girl thought for a moment, puzzled. If he was thinking about his wife with that expression on his face, she was afraid for her. His look was rather sinister. Whatever he was thinking, it wasn't about blissful sex. She read an expression of him inflicting pain...and pleasure. "No sir. I thought you might have been choking or spilled your coffee or something." It was the best lie she could come up with off the top of her head.

"Thanks for asking," he looked at her name tag, "Judy."

Judy forced a smile and left. Patrick began to wonder about his ability to conceal the events that had already passed and, knowing that the plan was not complete, wondered if he could stop his conscience from torturing him. Then he wondered how his brother Joe was coping with this? It all seemed so easy when it was just words. They were justified in their actions weren't they? They'd been betrayed by their closest friends and that was all the justification that they needed. Or was it? Could they stand the feelings of guilt for an eternity? Again, Patrick visibly shivered, shook his head to clear the thoughts away, and began to eat his eggs and sausage. He looked at the paper and almost choked. "DRUG MURDER" headlines hit him in the face. He took a deep breath and read on. It was a story about crack dealers in the central city. Seven separate murders had been committed over the last three days involving gangs and their turf war. Patrick took another deep breath and finished his breakfast. He needed to calm down. *Just relax. Everything's going to be fine*. He wasn't doing a very good job at reassuring himself that all was going well. Relaxation was not one of those things that he took for granted these days. Tension, on the other hand, was something he could count on each and every day.

***

Steve Sortini didn't sleep a wink last night...or more accurately, this morning. He was down at the sheriff's department trying to explain why he broke into the apartment of a man he'd never met...a man who was now dead. Steve had given his statement six times to about eight different officers and his story was the same each time. For some reason, they didn't seem convinced. He cursed himself for letting Sandy talk him into beating up some guy he didn't even know. This was all Sandy's fault. She shouldn't have let this drunken asshole take her home. Hell, she even drove her car to his apartment. This guy was so screwed up he didn't even have a car. How could she get suckered by a bum like that? He swore that he'd get even with her when this was all cleared up.

He'd explained to the deputy sheriff that he had gone to the apartment to beat up this guy because he had tried to rape a friend of his, but he didn't have a chance. The guy was already dead when he arrived. Hell, why would he have called the cops if he had really killed the guy? "I'm not a rocket scientist, but

I'm no idiot either," he'd told them. The questions had gone on for several hours. When they finally finished questioning Steve, it was 6:12 AM. He would remember that for a long time. The numbers on the large digital clock in the hall outside the interrogation room were so bright that they hurt his eyes when he looked at them. He was tired and hungry. As he turned towards the door that led to the lobby, he saw Sandy coming out of one of the other interrogation rooms. He was angered and started to say something to her but he could see the fear in her eyes. He stopped, but the deputy behind him said to keep moving. Steve asked the deputy if he could talk to her for a moment, but he replied that it would have to be a little later and that she would be done in a few more minutes.

"Is she being charged with anything?" Steve's question displayed genuine concern.

The deputy replied that, no, she wasn't but they wanted to ask her a few more questions. After all, this guy was murdered, and she was the last one to see him alive. That is, the last one besides whoever did the killing.

"How do you know he was killed? Maybe he just drank himself to death. You know, alcohol poisoning."

"Save your breath, Steve. I can't discuss details with you. But I can tell you he was murdered. You can take that to the bank."

Steve took a deep breath. He sat in the lobby of the Orange County Sheriff's Department and waited for Sandy to finish her statement.

About a half hour passed when the door to the interrogation rooms opened. Sandy came out followed by a female deputy. She told Sandy that she was free to go. Sandy turned and saw Steve and stopped cold in her tracks. Tears streamed down her face and still standing there in fear, she started babbling, "I'm sorry, I'm so sorry. I didn't know. I didn't mean to get you involved in this. I didn't know."

Steve walked towards her, trying to calm her down. "It's okay. It's not your fault. How could you know that this guy was going to get himself killed?" He went over to her and put his arms around her in a loving way. He would have beaten Randy nearly to death if he'd had the chance. This kind of job was not foreign to Steve Sortini. He worked as a bouncer for many different bars since getting out of high school eight years earlier. He liked the work. At 6'4", 250 pounds and all muscle, head knocking was fun and he was good at it. He liked being around the ladies, too. Because of his good looks and size, they were attracted to him. He usually had his choice of women throughout the year. He rarely had a drought of sex. He thought that beating Randy's brains in for Sandy would net him a few good nights of sexual favors. Sandy was very attractive with a great body. As he held her close now, though, he wasn't thinking about sex, he was thinking about what had happened to that poor bastard...*What was his name? Randy. Randy Farley. That schmuck! He sure screwed my night up.*

Sandy was still whimpering, almost collapsing in his arms. She was exhausted. She'd almost been raped. Now she was nearly a suspect in the murder of a guy she'd just met that night at a bar. He was a complete jerk. She didn't even like the guy. But she could have been a suspect.

Sandy was afraid that Steve was gonna beat her to death for getting him involved, but here he was trying to comfort her. She glanced at the clock through glazed, teary, tired eyes. 6:45 AM. The bright numbers hurt her eyes, too. She wanted to go home and sleep. She wasn't sure she could, even if she tried. Her mind was still racing from the events of the evening.

"Let's go, Sandy. I'll buy you breakfast," Steve offered. She looked up at him with bloodshot eyes. He could see that she wasn't up for breakfast. "Forget that. Let's go to my place. I'll make sure you're not disturbed so you can sleep. Are you supposed to work today?" Sandy nodded her head without saying a word. "I'll call in for you from my apartment. You're in no shape to go to work. You can get some sleep and then we can try to figure this out. Sandy...this whole deal really pissed me off, but I know it's not your fault. Let's try to forget about it for now. We both need the rest."

Steve lead Sandy out to the parking lot when he realized

that his car was back at the apartment complex where Randy Farley was killed. He went back inside to ask for a ride, and a deputy was assigned.

***

It was an eerie feeling seeing the foggy parking lot at the Silver Star Road Apartments at 7:10 in the morning. The fog looked like something out of a horror show scene at a cemetery. What was even worse, the coroner was just getting Randy's body out of the apartment. Sandy, now in the passenger side of Steve's car, began to whimper and cry again. She began to mumble over and over..."I'm so sorry, I didn't mean to get you involved, I'm sorry..."

Francis Marie Berger was confused. Should she call the sheriff about the strange car that she'd seen at Randy Farley's apartment the other night or should she keep it to herself? It was a rental from National Car Rental Service. She knew because she saw the bumper sticker clearly with her binoculars. She saw the car from her balcony through the sliding glass door. She just wasn't sure that she needed the trouble. The last time she reported something odd at the complex, the sheriff had ignored her. They treated her badly. She wasn't just some nosy old snoot. She cared about the people, about her neighbors in the complex. They were her friends. At least she felt that they were. The phone book was already open to the right page. All she had to do was to look up the number again. This time when she picked up the receiver she would dial that number. *That poor Randy Farley. He was such a nice man. He always helped me when I had trouble with my apartment. He'd said to not tell the regular maintenance man because he didn't want to get us in trouble. Who would do such a horrible thing? Certainly not that nice girl that he'd had over. Whoever was in that car, he's the real killer. I've got to tell the sheriff!*

She'd finally convinced herself that it was the right thing to do. Call the sheriff and he'd know what to do. It was her duty as a good citizen to turn in criminals and that's exactly what that guy in the rental car was. She just knew it. So she dialed the number for the sheriff's department. When the dispatcher came on she said, "I'd like to speak to a detective about a murder."

Chapter 20

Bobby Acquino had a difficult time sleeping on this hot, muggy night. The windows in his large home were all open which allowed the sticky central Florida air to invade the entire house. The air conditioner was working but was turned off. He wanted to feel the heat and the moisture. He wanted to sweat. He had much weighing on his mind. The episode with Donnie Lee and Jamie was eating away at his insides, tearing at his gut. He had to get out of the organization.

He thought back on how he found himself in a partnership with Jamie in the first place and those thoughts didn't comfort him in the least. He'd already been to confession. He'd talked to Father Keifer at St. Francis of Assisi Catholic Church and told him of the terrible deed that he'd done to his best friend. He'd stolen from him and his family. He confessed that all the wealth that he now had was due to that one act against his closest friend. That friend wouldn't even talk to him when he'd tried to apologize to him. He'd told the old priest that he even tried to pay back the money that he'd stolen. He felt terrible and he'd been troubled by this ever since. And he'd witnessed a horrendous crime against his friend's wife but he didn't report it to the police because he was afraid.

Bobby didn't tell Father Keifer that it was drugs that he, Jamie, and Donnie Lee had stolen. He only said he had stolen. Bobby's grief was also the motivating factor for his anonymous contribution to the church in excess of $5000.00 each week. Bobby maintained a modest income for himself, $2000.00 a week, but preferred to keep his income and his charitable contributions a secret from his partners. He could already hear Jamie taunting him for being so generous. He knew that if Jamie found out about it and started in on him, they would come to blows.

Bobby wanted none of that. At this point he simply wanted out. Getting out was not going to be an easy task. He suspected that Danny Vallero might have been killed by one of Mr. Roberts' men. He knew that Mr. Roberts was not very fond of Danny, but who was? It was a toss-up as to who was the bigger asshole, Danny or Jamie. Maybe if he stayed with it long enough Mr. Roberts would take care of the problem for him. Jamie was next for sure, that is if Mr. Roberts was taking his problem children out of the picture. But Mr. Roberts seemed genuinely upset that Danny had been hit. It didn't appear that he was faking the grief he'd felt when he'd heard that Danny was dead. But maybe his concern had been more for the loss to his organization.

Bobby knew one thing for certain; the pressure of the organization, and the guilt he held inside for the betrayal of his friend, Mike, were chewing him up inside, and he wanted out. One question remained. How?

***

The attempt to reach his wife didn't go well. Karen Grimes told her mom to tell Bill that she wasn't there and that she'd be staying with a friend for a few weeks. Bill knew that Karen's mom was covering for her daughter. He threatened to come over to the house if she didn't let him talk to his wife. So she coaxed Karen to the phone.

"Listen, Baby, I miss you. Won't you please come home? I've got great news. I finally made it. I've got $9000 in my hand right now and there's more coming. We're gonna be rich, Baby!"

Bill's words were falling short of the mark. Karen had already made up her mind, and no amount of money could change that. Bill just didn't get it. This wasn't about money. This wasn't about love. It was about trust. She just couldn't trust her husband. She was suddenly afraid of and for him. He'd said that he had a lot of money on him and she knew her husband's mind. She knew he was already thinking of ways to keep some of the cash that was supposed to pay for the drugs. With this much money involved, the players were probably big time; bigger than Bill could handle anyway. Bill was so dense that he didn't even realize what he was getting himself into.

"Bill, don't try to call me again. It's over. I called a lawyer this morning. He will have the divorce papers in the mail to you by the end of the week. I'm sorry but I just can't take it anymore."

The phone went dead, then a dial tone. Bill just held the receiver to his ear. His high had just been crushed. This woman, the only woman he'd ever loved, was divorcing him. The excitement of hitting the big time was now obliterated. He was a shattered man. The receiver went back on the cradle and Bill Grimes went to the liquor cabinet, pulled out a bottle of Jim Beam, and proceeded to take healthy gulps straight. He sat down on the couch and finished the last quarter of a bottle. The results were predictable. The fact that there was only a quarter of a bottle left was the only thing that saved him from dying of alcohol poisoning. He would have one whale of a hangover in the morning though. From drug kingpin to abandoned, heart-broken, ex-husband in a matter of minutes. It's enough to get to most men who are legends in their own minds. And Bill was quite a legend.

***

Pat sat in the vault and looked around at all the equipment that they had installed years ago. This is where it had all begun for the McKinneys. The four walls looked exactly the same as when the vault was hot with activity. The shielded cameras were still functional and the security system worked fine, too. Patrick realized that they needed some adjustment; a little "preventive maintenance" as they said in the nuclear navy. The entire setup, including the link to the old house, was the same. The orange co-op had taken excellent care of the grove, the house, and the surrounding land. The nursery and warehouse had been leased to a local nurseryman who'd done a little renovation to the greenhouses and heating system, but all-in-all, the McKinneys' property looked exactly the same as when the brothers had left town.

Patrick had heard, second-hand, that Jamie and his cohorts were bragging about how they'd run the McKinneys out of town "with their tails between their legs." There were other comments as well. But Patrick gave them little or no credence.

As he sat in the vault, he began to relive the events that brought their business to a halt. How could he not have seen the feeding frenzy on the McKinney family coming? All of the perpetrators were supposedly their closest friends. Were they that poor at judging character that they could not choose honorable people as close associates? Or did the brothers just become so loose with their secrets that their friends saw a clear path to their fortune? After all, when opportunity knocks, one should answer the door. In this case, Patrick reasoned after all these years, that not only did opportunity knock, the McKinneys left the door wide open for anyone who knew their business to take what they wanted. Since being out of the drug business for a number of years, Pat had come to realize that there were no honorable people in this business. Drugs were illegal to possess, sell, take, conspire to distribute, etc. If you were in this business, you were not honorable. Your morals and character were suspect. No, they were not good judges of character because they themselves at that moment had no character. They were pushers, dope dealers. According to every drug education program in America, the McKinneys and everyone in their business were killing the youth of this country. After six years in the nuclear navy and his own school of hard knocks lessons, Patrick could see that these teachings probably had merit. He'd seen otherwise intelligent men ruin their lives by testing positive on urinalysis tests at a time in their lives when they should have known better. They had families to raise and provide for. They had every reason to not ruin their lives by illegal activities, even if it was only the use of a mind-altering substance. Hell, everyone he knew drank alcohol.

But alcohol was legal wasn't it? And that was the difference in the use of alcohol and other drugs. Marijuana was illegal. It didn't matter that the outward effects of marijuana were not as damaging, not as intoxicating, not as long lasting, as alcohol. It also didn't matter that there were no hangovers, and no substantial long term effects of marijuana that were known. It only mattered that marijuana was illegal and alcohol was not. Because of that simple fact, lives were ruined. His former life had been, well, criminal. He had no idea how many lives he'd ruined, or even if he'd ruined any. He only knew that he'd sold lots and lots of pot. He'd also made lots of money in the process. He tried to process all of these thoughts in his mind as logically as he could. He'd come to hate drugs. The industry that used his consulting firm did not tolerate drug use by its employees. They didn't tolerate drug use by their contractors either. But somehow he could justify killing the men who helped him get out of the drug trade.

He intended to tell his wife all of the details of his former life including the fact that they were wealthy. Patrick's financial holdings were fairly sizable, as were his brothers'. He had no real need to work, but had to continue building his business to keep up the front of a source of income.

If anything was on the right track, it was the consulting business. It was going well. Patrick McKinney got to know many contacts in the nuclear power industry. He got along well with almost everyone he met. There always seemed to be one jerk in every crowd but Pat didn't let that bother him. His knowledge of commercial nuclear reactor operations was impressive even though he'd never worked in a commercial facility. He learned all this by studying in his spare time on the sub. Pat had been pounding the turf for just a few months and he'd already picked up a number of clients and had a growing prospect list. He had to be careful or this was going to become a full time job. When the industry was young, in the early-to-mid 1970s, it was commonplace for a navy nuke to come out of the service, land a job at a power plant, enter the Senior Reactor Operator Program immediately and make big bucks with good bonuses. At that time, at the rate that the United States was building nuclear power plants, operators with good training and experience were in high demand. The Navy's Nuclear Power Program was an excellent pool of talent for the burgeoning commercial nuclear industry.

But when Petty Officer First Class Patrick McKinney was discharged, new commercial nuclear plants were a thing of the past. Only a handful of plants were still under construction and no new plants were ordered. Utilities weren't interested in taking the gamble on a new nuclear plant after the Three Mile Island meltdown. The costs were just too prohibitive: overpriced "quality grade" construction materials, overregulation by the federal government and over-taxation by state and local governments. All these factors were straining the utility industry when it came to nuclear power. The government had been taking money from each and every operating power plant in the nation to build a centralized spent fuel repository at Yucca Mountain in Nevada, but the money was being used to attempt to balance an out-of-control federal budget. Billions of dollars had been spent at Yucca, but billions more had been diverted to other programs that had nothing to do with nuclear waste disposal. Politicians were afraid to take action on a host of highly charged political problems dealing with low and high level radioactive waste. The issue of waste disposal alone was so controversial that no politician would talk of establishing even a new low level radioactive waste facility in their state, much less in their own district. And those were just a few of the power industry's problems. All those issues add up to 'no new nukes.'

So, all of that talent that had come out of the service in the 1970s and early 1980s had glutted the job market. Newly discharged nukes had to wait for a long time to enter the SRO Program. Pat saw that trend and decided to start a computer software consulting business. He'd learned that commercial plants had very little computer expertise and even fewer programs to track and monitor maintenance and operations activities. He'd put together a program that worked well for those two key areas of a power plant.

Not only did Pat have the computer skills, he had a special talent. He knew how to deal with people. When he talked to people, even in casual conversation, he made an impression. Not in a cocky way. In a way that made people feel good about themselves and those they were with. One day, one of his contacts remarked in an offhanded way that maybe Patrick should enter politics...maybe run for the Florida State House. In his usual politically correct style Pat remarked, "No way. There's too much dirt in that pit. It's like wrestling with a pig. You both get muddy but the pig likes it."

In fact, Patrick had thought about running for city council in Dunnellon. Their house was located in the city limits and he'd have enough time living in the city within the next year and a half to meet the minimum time requirements.

But right now getting his business up and running, even on a part time basis, was the only task he could handle with the extra added burden of taking care of his past problems. He certainly didn't need the added aggravation of a political career. The spotlight tended to be a bit bright on local politicians. That would only add to the tension that he already felt. In fact, his nerves were starting to show the signs of the added stress. His temper was getting short and he had very little patience, especially with his son, Sean. It seemed that no matter what his son did, it wasn't right. Even Sean brought it to his dad's attention that he didn't deserve the verbal abuse. And that's what brought Pat to the vault this evening.

Earlier in the evening, Patrick had yelled at his son at the dinner table for talking with his mouth full. He'd yelled so loud that Sean complained that his ears hurt. Diane jumped to his side and told Patrick to back off because his screaming wasn't helping. That only served to anger Patrick more. "You have no business correcting me in front of him," he'd hollered at his wife. "He won't listen to anything that I tell him now. It undermines my authority."

Diane was in no mood to hear this from Patrick. She'd practically raised these children alone while Pat was out to sea. Sean was a good kid. He didn't deserve what his father was giving him. The punishment didn't fit the crime.

"When you apologize to your son and stop acting like a two-year-old yourself, then we'll talk about 'undermining your authority!' I will not stand by while you brow-beat your children. They don't deserve it." She then turned to Sean who was looking down at his half empty plate, tears streaming down his face, and said, "Sean, apologize to your father for talking with your mouth full."

Sean looked up at Diane as if to ask, 'Do I have to?' She nodded towards Patrick. Then Sean, with his eyes still looking down said in a quiet voice, "Sorry Dad."

Patrick felt two inches tall. He knew that he'd gone overboard. Tears welled up in his eyes as he looked around the dinner table at his family and he said to all of them, "I'm so sorry to put you through this. Sean, I'm sorry for yelling at you. It isn't your fault. Dad's going through some rough things with his business."

Pat looked back down at the table, then back at Diane and said, "Please excuse me. I have to be alone for a while."

With that, Patrick left the table and walked towards the front door.

Diane asked him, "Where are you going?"

Pat didn't answer and continued towards the door.

Diane persisted. "I said where are you going? You can't just leave us like this. We have to talk. I know you're under some stress. But let's talk!"

Pat turned towards the door without a word, with only a blank stare on his face. She was still angry and grabbed his arm to try to turn him around but it didn't work. He continued to make his way towards the front door. As he reached for the knob, Diane gripped his biceps with both hands as forcefully as she could, trying to get him to face her. In the dining room, Sean and Anna were both starting to cry loudly, adding to Pat's anxiety. He stopped at the door with his hand on the knob and turned his head slightly to look at Diane's hands on his arm, then looked up to meet her eyes. The look in Pat's eyes was something that she'd never seen in her husband before. His eyes were not the cold, blue eyes that she knew. They stared through her like daggers. Her grip immediately loosened as she continued to study these angry, madly insane eyes. She suddenly had a chill and released his arm completely.

Pat opened the door, turned to his wife and said, "I won't be home tonight. I have to calm down a bit. I'm going to get a room. I promise that I'll be alone and it probably will be just for tonight. I should be home tomorrow. I love you and the kids but I need a short time alone to relax. Do you understand?"

All Diane could muster was a weak "No, I don't understand. I don't know what's going on here. I really don't know. I've never seen you like this. Are you going to be okay?"

"Yeah, I'm...I will be fine."

The door closed and Pat drove straight to the vault.

***

As Pat lay in the vault thinking about the events of earlier that evening, he wondered if he would be all right. If he'd really wanted to relax, this was not the place to do it. It was a continuous reminder of what some supposed friends did to him and his family many years ago. He could feel the stomach acid churn and it continued to build his hatred of the perpetrators. It was slowly but surely driving him insane. The longer he thought about Jamie, Donnie Lee, Bobby, Danny, Randy, and Bill, the more he was certain that the only key to his sanity was their demise. The plan was already in motion. It had to have closure.

Chapter 21

Detective Al Porecwzski had a bad feeling about the expanding case. Randy Farley's murder was gathering some steam as more and more facts started to come into the station. The coroner's report was due today. Forensics came up with some very peculiar facts. The Jack Daniels that was in Randy's body didn't make its way to his stomach. Most of it was in his lungs. It wasn't mixed with any stomach contents. So he hadn't suffocated on his own regurgitation. He did not die of alcohol poisoning. Rather, he'd drowned in Jack Daniels, plain and simple. One thing was apparent; he hadn't done this to himself. The back of his throat was cut and bleeding most likely from the bottle being shoved forcibly down his throat. His teeth were chipped where the neck of the bottle hit them. The neck of the empty bottle had his blood all over it.

All in all, the facts were pointing to a very brutal murder. The only thing that they didn't have yet was a suspect. Though many people didn't like Randy Farley, not many people hated him either. This Sandy Allison just wanted a fun night out. How she ended up with this loser was a different story. It always seemed to be that the low-life doggy guys were the ones who were the sweet talkers. But this sweet talker would soon be six feet under.

Now this new twist. Some nosey old broad from the complex had called the station with information on a rental car. No one else in the entire complex saw the car or heard anything unusual except her.

So Detective Porecwzski dialed the number for the rental car company to find out what he could. He had his scratch pad close at hand with the license number, make, and model of the car. He also read the rental car sticker as seen through Mrs.

Berger's binoculars. *This should be pretty routine*, Al thought to himself as he dialed the number. National had numerous rental car sites throughout the greater Orlando area. They were all linked by computer so someone in California could check on the status of a car in Kansas or anywhere else in the country for that matter.

"National Car Rental, Orlando International Airport Office. Steve Porter speaking. Can I interest you in a weekend special for $19.99?"

"Good morning Steve. This is Detective Porecwzski of the Orange County Sheriff's Department. I need some information on a person who rented a car from your agency, possibly in the last few days. The car was spotted in the vicinity of a crime scene and it would be helpful if you could provide the name, address, and phone number of the person or persons who rented the car. We can and will get a warrant, if necessary, to obtain your records."

The very direct tone of the detective made an impression on the young clerk. He was a bit intimidated by the more experienced man on the other end of the line. "Sir, I'd be glad to help you, but I think I'd better talk to my supervisor. Will you hold for a moment?"

"Sure, Son. No problem."

While the standard audio of National Car Rental Service ads filled the receiver, Detective Porecwzski thought about the odd circumstances of this crime. Why would a murderer use whiskey to basically drown his victim? He was already drunk as a skunk from the eye witness reports. Sandy Allison swore that he was nearly passed out when she ran out of the apartment. The first officers to respond noticed the red marks on his wrists where he'd been tied up while he was being assaulted. With him being that drunk it wasn't really necessary to be that strong of an individual to do that poor bastard in. Where had she said they were? The Rock Alliance. New heavy metal rock joint. Said that she'd seen him there several nights in a row. He'd told her that he was some hot-shot salesman from Jacksonville. What a loser. She'd figured that he was lying, but she just wanted to have a fun night out until he'd started to get pushy. He turned out to be another creep. Now he was a dead creep.

"Detective, this is Nick Brody, Shift Manager. What can I do for you?"

"Well, Nick, like I was telling Steve, your clerk, I'm with the Orange County Sheriff's Department and one of your agency's vehicles was seen at an apartment complex where a murder was committed. We just wanted to get an ID on the renter."

"Do you have any information which would verify that the car was one of ours, detective?"

"We have an eye witness that saw the National Car Rental bumper sticker on the bumper and also recorded the license plate number. It's Florida, number OC-45392, a white Dodge Acclaim with black wall tires and a dark interior. It was located in Pine Hills at The Silver Star Road Apartments between 11:00PM and 1:00 AM on Friday night and Saturday morning." Detective Porecwzski could hear the computer keyboard keys clicking over the receiver as the shift supervisor punched in the information.

"Here it is." Bingo! "The car was rented to a Mr. James Carlson, 23234 West Palmetto Boulevard, right here in Orlando. He used a credit card, Visa, number 4879-734-345-912, expiration date, November 2001. He carried State Farm Insurance and..."

"That's all I'll need for now, Mr. Brody. I don't mean to cut you off but we're in a hurry to catch up to this guy. Thanks again." The receiver went to the cradle before Mr. Brody could get in another word. Detective Porecwzski sat and thought for a moment. *That was much too easy. Something just doesn't add up here. This guy is leaving a trail. Well maybe he just isn't a real bright guy. But could he be leaving us this trail on purpose? Maybe he just didn't expect to be seen at the complex. After all Mrs. Berger was the only eyewitness. What a way to kill someone; drowning in whiskey. Almost like one of those country and western songs, drowning my sorrows in my whiskey bottle. But this murder had a rock and roll connection. The Rock*

Alliance. Something's familiar about that place. Recent history...think man! He turned to his partner and said, "Rich, get your stuff. We've got a house call to make."

***

Ginny was lying on the beach in the hot Florida sun with her bikini straps undone and at her side. Coated in lotion with a protection factor of 15, her skin glistened as it soaked up the rays. She wanted to look her absolute best when she saw Brian at the Rock tomorrow night. He was coming back from a gig at a bar in Gainesville. The place was supposed to be a combination hall and bar, the largest of its type in Florida. The Rock Hall of Fame is where thousands of students from the University of Florida go to unwind after long hours of intense study. Instead of unwinding most of the time they wind up getting plastered far beyond their capability to handle it. Brian Purcer and the Hot Licks was the hottest new band in the south and the crowds were supposed to overwhelm the place. Ginny warned Brian to stay away from the local female students saying "they're nothing but sluts and real trouble for you, Mr. Purcer." At first Brian had a confused look on his face. He didn't quite understand where Ginny was going with her comments.

Then a look of complete understanding came on his face. He was in love with Ginny and he could see that Ginny was falling for him. He had no idea just how in love Ginny was. She was now 100% certified in love with an up-and-coming rock star. She also knew that he was in love with her. They'd known each other for a short time, but the attraction was there. It just seemed right. He would be back tomorrow after a stop in Dunnellon. He wanted to visit an old friend of his, one he hadn't seen in some seven years. The guy was in the Navy for six years, which for some reason, absolutely amazed Brian. Ginny didn't know what was so amazing about being in the Navy, but what the heck. He would be home soon enough.

***

The knock at the front door startled Diane McKinney. She hadn't heard from Patrick for a day and a half and was worried sick about him. She didn't know whether he was sick, hurt, or worse. She didn't want to call the police because Patrick had said he'd be okay. Thoughts of something bad happening to her husband haunted her. These last two nights reminded her of the long periods of time that Patrick was away while on patrol. The days were not as bad because she kept busy with housework and errands.

She didn't have a clue as to who might be here at this hour of the morning, but a chill went down her spine when she thought, *Could it be the police? Is Patrick hurt?* When she looked through the peep hole, the distorted sight of the long-haired man on the other side of the door made her a little more nervous, and a bit frightened. What would this guy be looking for? Well, best to use caution. She left the security chain in place and opened the door only enough for the sound of her voice to travel through.

"Can I help you?" Her sheepish voice showed little confidence in any ability to defend herself from a would-be assailant. As soon as she heard her own words come out, she knew it.

"Yes. Is this the home of Patrick McKinney, ex-navy nuclear power guru?

"Yes it is. And you are...?"

"I'm Brian Purcer. Pat and I were buddies a few years back. He wrote to me and said to drop by some time. I was on my way back to Orlando from Gainesville and I thought I'd take him up on the invite. Is he home?"

"I'm sorry, but Pat isn't home right now. What did you say your name was again?" Diane was still talking through the slightly cracked open door.

"Brian. Brian Purcer. You must be Diane. Pat told me about you, Sean and Anna in a letter he'd sent to me some weeks ago. I was really surprised to see that he'd moved back to central Florida. I was really surprised about a lot of things, like you for instance. I didn't think Pat would ever get married, much less have kids." Brian's smooth manner was causing Diane to relax a bit. He continued. "I'll tell you what; tell Pat that I stopped by, sorry I missed him and all. Let me give you my phone number and he can call me when he gets home. Or better yet, I'll stay in town for the afternoon and I'll call back later.

"I'm not sure when he'll be back. He really didn't say what time or what day he'd be home. Why don't you leave your number and I'll tell him to give you a call. I'm sure he'll appreciate that you took the time to come by."

Brian could hear the pain in Diane's tiny voice. He wasn't sure how to read what he was hearing but there was a certain amount of loneliness behind the words. Had Pat been hurt? Was there something wrong in their marriage? He wanted to ask but he'd just met this woman. All he knew was that she was married to a friend that he hadn't seen in years. He felt for her even though he knew nothing about her except what Pat had written in his letter. *She is the most kind and compassionate woman that I've ever met. Considering what I've done in my lifetime, I know that there must be a very forgiving God, for he has blessed me beyond my dreams.* He decided to ask the question. Pat and he were best friends at one time. He felt as if it was his duty to help if he could. Brian took one long, deep breath. "Diane, I know we've just met, and I can't even see you, but you seem a bit unnerved. Is everything okay? I mean is Pat all right?"

The question totally disarmed her. It was as genuine as gold, she could tell. She closed the door, removed the security chain, and invited Brian Purcer, a total stranger, into the house to talk.

Over the next two hours, Diane McKinney learned more about her husband than she'd learned in the past seven years of their marriage. The story, as told by Brian Purcer, provided the answers to many of Diane's previously unanswered questions. The many sleepless nights, and the latest episode of him leaving without a trace and providing no means to locate or contact him. Diane was more worried now than she was before, though she didn't know why.

"Did Pat ever sell the nursery and grove?" Brian asked.

"Pardon me?"

"You know, the nursery. He grew foliage plants. And the

grove. Heck, I don't know what all kinds of fruit the grove had."

"What nursery? What Grove? I never heard anything about a nursery or a grove. What kind of grove? You mean he owned, or still owns a nursery and a grove? Where?" Diane's questions were not mock surprise. She had absolutely no idea that Pat had all of these things, and might still have them. That wasn't all. Brian Purcer, a man who had supposedly been his best friend for years, had just appeared and filled her in on facts that Pat should have told her. Pat had never mentioned his name before. The more that she sat and thought about the man she'd married, the more she realized that she really knew very little about him. The years that they'd been married were nearly flawless. Only since he was discharged from the Navy and started his business was there any marital discord. Diane had attributed all of that to the stress of starting a business from scratch. The side of her husband which was now revealed to her gave her cause for more concern. Worst of all, Diane could imagine her husband doing everything that Brian had said that he had actually done. Except that she'd just met him, she had no reason to doubt Brian's word. And if they were true, then who was the man she'd married? What happened to the money from these businesses? Was Brian Purcer typical of all of his past friends?

Pat hadn't told her much about his past. He'd always say in a joking manner that it "wasn't anything exciting" or "there's nothing to tell". And "you really don't want to know. I work for the CIA. If I tell you, I'll have to kill you." He'd commented one time that he "was a very dangerous man," then laughed as if he'd told a joke.

"You had no idea? How could you not know? I mean, he loved the grove. And he never talked about any of his old friends?"

"No." She shook her head slightly back and forth. Her eyes were starting to moisten. The tears were on the verge of flowing freely.

"Well, Pat always was a bit secretive when he wanted to be. But the grove? He had to have said something." Brian felt as if he'd known Diane for years. She was easy to talk to even now as the stress of the situation was eating at her very soul. But he was now sure that he had erred in telling this woman so much about her husband that she obviously didn't know. There was no taking the words back and he felt very uncomfortable. Why had Pat left so much of his life unknown to this woman? This was his wife for Christ's sake! He could tell by talking to her that she would never betray him. He was everything to her, and she to him, so why all of the blank pages? Just then, an eerie thought crossed his mind; the incident at the bar with Danny Vallero, followed by his murder—no his assassination. Pat had threatened revenge on Danny and others. *No. It can't be. Pat's too smart for that. He has a wife and family now. He has a great future with a new business and though Diane apparently doesn't know it, a small fortune.* He left out that part of his revelation of Pat McKinney. *He wouldn't risk all of this on scum like Danny Vallero, would he,* Brian thought to himself?

Diane was reading his face. "What is it, Brian? Is something wrong? Has Pat done something wrong?"

"No. It's nothing. I mean yes. Something is wrong. My best friend in the world screwed up. He's kept a beautiful, caring person, who loves him, in the dark about some important things. Look, I know you're worried about Pat, but from what I remember, he can handle himself. I've never seen him get into a situation that he couldn't figure a way out of. I'm sure he'll be home soon. Try not to worry. Okay?"

Brian got up and started towards the door. "I've really enjoyed meeting you and talking with you. I hope I didn't worry you or confuse you more."

"No. On the contrary, you've helped me understand my husband more now than ever. I know he'll be home soon. You're right, you know. He is sharp. That's why I married him."

"I can see why he married you. You're very special. When he gets back, tell him to call and we'll get together for dinner. It was a pleasure meeting you, Diane. Pat is a very lucky man. I'm sure that he realizes that."

"Thank you, Brian. It was nice to meet you, too. And

when Pat gets back...," her eyes started to well up again, "...make sure you come visit. Good luck with your music career. It sounds...exciting," she managed to choke out as she dabbed her eyes.

"Well, thanks again," Brian said as he made his way to the door. He hated to leave this woman in such a sad state, but he had other things to do himself.

He closed the door to his mini-van and headed out towards Orlando. Immediately his mind went back to the Vallero murder. *It couldn't have been. No way!* But the doubts continued to linger. Brian had an idea about where he might find one Patrick McKinney and his mind plotted a course on the Florida back roads to Kelly Park Drive in rural Apopka, Florida.

Chapter 22

West Palmetto Boulevard was in a neighborhood with homes that were in the $175,000 to $245,000 price range, by Detective Al Porecwzski's estimate. They were a nice mix of styles, none repeating each other. It was refreshing to drive through a nicely kept neighborhood for a change. The pleasant drive would soon give way to the unpleasant task of possibly arresting a man for murder, or at the very least, taking him in for questioning. There was some element of danger in this little excursion. They were, after all, questioning a potential murderer.

Detective Porecwzski pulled into the driveway of 23234 West Palmetto Boulevard and turned off the engine. It was a two-story Spanish style home with the classic orange tile roof. White stucco covered the walls of the home's exterior. As with all of the homes in the neighborhood, the yard's landscaping was exceptional. They took a moment to verify the address and looked for movement in the windows. They were in an unmarked car so they would not attract undue attention. But the moveable searchlight mounted on the side of the dark blue Chevrolet Caprice Classic was a dead giveaway. Al and Rich approached the house, rang the doorbell, and waited. They held their hands close to their holstered guns, continually scanning the surrounding area for anything suspicious. They could hear steady steps approach the door from the inside. The door opened and an attractive, slender woman with light auburn hair, in her mid-to-late forties stood in the doorway. "Yes, can I help you?"

Both men instinctively moved their hands away from their guns and relaxed a bit. Al spoke for the duo. "Yes ma'am. I'm Detective Al Porecwzski and this is my partner Richard James. We're looking for Mr. James Carlson. It seems that he rented a car..." The detective stopped in mid-sentence. He noticed the horrified look on the woman's face, her hand coming up to cover her open mouth. As her breath became shorter, it appeared to the two men that this woman was about to pass out. Al reached for her to attempt to support her. She shook loose of his grasp and regained her balance, placing her other hand against the door jamb.

A voice from inside the house called out, "Honey, who's at the door?" She still had not moved her hands and appeared to be stunned by the question, though neither man could possibly know why. The man inside came to the woman's side. "Honey...Honey, what is it?"

She took a long, deep breath before she spoke. Through a choked-up throat she said, "Sweetheart, these men are looking for Jimmy."

The twisted, pained expression which appeared on the man's face was quickly mixed with anger. "Is this some kind of sick joke? Who are you? Why are you doing this to us?"

"As I told your...wife, I assume, I'm Detective Al Porecwzski..."

"I don't give a damn who you are! If you want to see our son, you're about nine years too late. He was murdered in 1989. Why...How...What the hell is this all about? Why are you bothering us?"

"Maybe if we could come inside we can tell you what this is about. I really don't mean to impose. We truly are sorry for your loss but we need to verify some things. I promise it won't take but a moment." Al paused then continued as he watched the expression on the man's face. "We'll only take as much time as we need. We won't intrude further."

"Honey, is it okay?"

Mrs. Carlson nodded. The tears were very evident on her cheeks now. This inquiry had opened up some deep wounds and there was no way of knowing it beforehand.

***

It was a stroke of luck that the tenants of the brothers' house in front of the vault on Kelley Park Drive decided to move out just before Pat was discharged from the Navy. This way, Pat had a place of refuge to try to clear his head and work out the minor quirks of the plan. There was definitely solitude from the rigors of life on a submarine. No exams, no Naval Reactors Inspectors looking over your shoulder, no wife, no kids...*no love or caring, no home cooked meals, no one to rub my back or give good advice when needed. Boy do I need some now!* This was not an ideal place to be, particularly when you wanted to clear your head of troubles. After all, this is where all the troubles began. The ghost of Julie McKinney haunted the vault. Now the ghost of Danny Vallero was here, too. He was in a different section of the vault. Julie smiled down at Patrick saying *thank you for helping free me.* Danny was crying, begging forgiveness. None would be granted from Patrick. He only promised the ghost of Danny that he would be joined soon by at least four others; more if anyone tried to get in his way. His family would get revenge. Payment would be painful to those who'd betrayed them. He and Joe would see to it.

The monitors picked up an approaching vehicle. This was not a welcome sight to Pat. No one was supposed to know where he was, not even Joe. Maybe it was just some teenagers looking for a place to make out. Pat watched the car as it made its way between the orange trees towards the vault. It was a mini-van. That probably meant that it wouldn't be teenagers unless they were in their parents mini-van. He sat in silence as it made a slow approach through the trees. It was coming directly at the vault and stopped right behind Pat's car, blocking any escape route. Pat was basically trapped in the grove. If he had to get out for some reason, on foot was the only way.

Pat used the controls to zoom in on the driver's side door of the van as it cracked open slightly. There was only one person in the van, Pat could tell. The shape of a man with long hair exited. *It couldn't be! Brian Purcer! What the hell? How did he find me?* Pat went to the door of the vault, unlocked it and yelled, "Brian! What in God's name are you doing here? How'd you know I was here? How've you been?"

Pat's smile was bright and glowing for the first time in days. He took a few steps up the incline from the door of the vault to greet his old best friend; a friend whom he hadn't seen in over six years found him in a place where no one was supposed to be able to find him.

"Pat, what in the hell are you doing here? Are you nuts, man? This place is haunted. There is nothing here for you." Brian looked around at the grove then back at the vault. "I thought that you'd sold the place." He waved his hands around at their surroundings. Why didn't you sell it? It's gotta be eating you up to be here."

"What, no *Hey Pat, how are you?*" Pat's smile faded, seeing the look on Brian's face. Brian had the look of an angry father about to dispense punishment to a son who'd strayed to the wrong side of the line. The two stared at each other for what seemed like ten minutes. Friends who hadn't seen each other in over six years were thrown together in circumstances that neither fully understood. How could they carry on their friendship as if nothing had changed? Brian had just spilled his guts to the wife of this man, revealing things that Patrick had never told her. He also had a strong suspicion that Patrick might have been involved in the murder of Danny Vallero. After all, he had sworn that he would kill Danny and others before disappearing to the U.S. Navy. Could anyone hold their rage this long and unleash it on people who'd never suspect that their actions, committed almost seven years before, would bring about their death? Now how could Brian hold a normal conversation with his friend? Or exactly who was this man now?

The Pat McKinney that he'd known could never have committed murder. Had he changed so drastically? Maybe the rape and murder of his sister-in-law had driven him to this. Could he blame Pat? How would he feel if it had been his brother's wife? There were too many questions racing through his mind to simply say 'Hi, Pat. How's it going?'

Pat's mind raced as well. How did Brian know where he was? As he stared back at his friend, he had to figure out the purpose of this unexpected visit. Brian's presence was not unwelcomed. The timing could have been better, but Pat needed to talk with someone. There was a lot of time and distance between these friends. Could they just pick up where they left off and have it be like old times. Pat doubted it.

This *thing* was eating him up. Brian was right, the ghosts in the vault were there and they wouldn't let him rest. Maybe that's why he came here, to get the hate built up to a point of no return. That way he could finish the plan, driven by the ghosts of his sister-in-law and the ghosts of his enemies. They would drive him to finish the task at hand.

Brian broke the silence as he swatted a mosquito away from his ear. "I met Diane today."

Pat's expression changed from suspicion to confusion. "You mean Diane, my wife?"

"Yeah, you big dope. Diane, your wife, the woman who idolizes you."

"Where did you meet her? How did you know it was her?"

"You really have turned completely stupid over the years. You sent me an invitation to your house to meet your wife and kids. I took you up on it. Didn't think that I would, did you?"

"No, not really. How'd a rising rock star like you have time to visit a washed up, junk-head like myself? From what I hear, you don't have much time to spend fooling around anymore. You've got albums to cut, concerts to perform, and money to make. You're on your way to the top."

"Oh yeah. That's all it takes. Somebody hints that you might sign a contract and you're a multi-millionaire. You should try it. See my rock star type vehicle?" Brian pointed over his shoulder. "It's a six year old mini-van. But I'm so rich now, I think I'll get rid of it and get a five year old mini-van." They both smiled for the first time in their brief encounter. They both swung their arms at mosquitoes buzzing in their ears. "Are we just gonna stand out here in the Florida heat and let the mosquitoes carry us away, or are we gonna go inside Houston Control, here?"

"Come on in. I sure need the company."

The two men moved inside. Just as Brian had said, the mosquitoes were getting mean, swarming around the men's heads with bothersome buzzing as they flapped their wings in Brian and Patrick's ears.

"So how's Diane? I scored pretty well there, didn't I?"

"Except for the fact that she's married to an unappreciative, jerk-asshole, she's holding up okay. She misses that jerk pretty badly. She's worried about you, Pat. I don't think I helped your case any, either."

"What do you mean?"

"Let's just say that I assumed that she knew a lot more than she did." Brian let a long stare go on without any further comment.

Pat broke the silence this time. "Brian, what did you tell her?"

"Only that you owned a nursery and an orange grove. Wait, I just said grove. I don't think I told her what kind of grove. Man, why didn't you tell her about this stuff? You can't keep this kind of shit secret forever! Women pick up on this shit and use it against you for the rest of your life."

"Wait a minute. What do you know about women? Last I heard you were still celibate."

"Well, mister smart ass, I have a very rock-solid steady. You're gonna meet her very soon, if I can drag you out of this fortress." Brian's face turned serious again. "You have to go home, Pat. Diane is going crazy without you. Besides, you've got a lot of explaining to do. You can't keep secrets from your wife."

"From the sound of it, I don't have any more secrets. Before we leave this vault, you're going to fill me in on everything that you told her. You also have to tell me how in the hell you figured out that I was here! I didn't think anyone knew that we still had the place. It's in a blind trust, you know. Joe and I are the only owners in the trust. That sure makes it easy to control. Why am I still talking? Spill your guts, man."

For the next hour, Brian and Patrick talked about many things; Brian's conversation with Diane McKinney, old friendships, and old enemies. The conversation finally came around to Danny Vallero's murder. Brian didn't know quite how to bring it up, but Pat saved him the trouble.

"You know, Danny Vallero was gunned down the other day. Shot through the head. Couldn't have happened to a nicer guy, the bastard. I'd of done it myself if I'd had the chance. You know, since I didn't get the satisfaction, his ghost has been in here laughing at me. All of those assholes who screwed us are in here laughing at me, Mike, and Joe. Even the ones who aren't dead. It's like they're torturing me for not seeking revenge, laughing at me for being a chicken. I don't have the guts, they're saying."

"Man, we've gotta get you outta here. You're losing it. Why the hell didn't you sell this place years ago when you went in the Navy? It's no good for you now, man!"

"You're right, let's get outta here. I've got some major league explaining to do. I survived all those years dealing, all those years in the Navy, and I'm going to die at the hands of my wife."

"If she doesn't, you let me know, cause I'm gonna do it for her. You prick. She's the best fricking thing that ever happened to you. You go home and make her happy. She'll probably kill you before you have a chance. I'd hate to be in your shoes, man."

"I know. I screwed up big time." *More than you'll ever know my friend*, Pat thought to himself. "Brian, thanks for coming. I still can't believe you thought to drive all the way here just to find me."

"It's the least I could do, Pat."

Pat was sure that Brian Purcer was a believer. He believed that Pat didn't have the guts to pull off Danny's murder. That's what Pat hoped anyway.

***

Brian had doubts. He still wondered if Pat was the one who killed Danny. Brian was not as easily swayed as Pat thought. He would keep in touch with Pat and Diane. They both needed a friend. Brian hoped he could maintain both of their friendships. The new one would be pretty easy. It was the life-long friendship that he was worried about.

Brian pulled out first heading south on Kelly Park Drive. His minivan had just a little difficulty making the sandy road out of the grove before grabbing the asphalt of the two-lane road. His mind was troubled after the first encounter in over six years with his best friend, Pat McKinney. Pat had aged more than those six years. Even though he was outwardly cool, as he always was, Brian could see something behind Pat's eyes. Something in the way that Pat would stare, his gaze drifting off to some other place, told a story that Pat wanted to remain untold. Was Pat being straight with him when he'd said that he had no involvement in the Vallero killing? Or was it a lie, a diversion? Did Pat have the balls necessary to kill Danny Vallero and then look his best friend in the eye and say, "I had nothing to do with it?" He hadn't said that, really. He'd avoided that confrontation altogether by asking the question first. If Brian had asked him directly, could he have lied? Would he lie if Brian asked him sometime in the future? Brian hoped he wouldn't have to cross that bridge.

Why would he risk everything that he had in his new life? He had a beautiful wife. No doubt that his kids were beautiful, too. He'd done something only dreamers and fools would consider. He'd made his fortune in a trade that usually leads to one of two endings; long terms in prison or violent death. It was a vicious business, but Pat had known when to pull up stakes, cut his losses, and tally his profits.

As Brian recalled, it wasn't by choice. He thought back to when Mike's new wife was killed. The Orange County Sheriff's office had lost the key piece of evidence. They thought the prosecution was a slam dunk because of a video tape that they'd found at the scene. The district attorney's office had botched the case by not obtaining any additional evidence from the crime scene. Then the tape was lost. The loss of that evidence by the Sheriff's Department caused the charges to be thrown out of court. Shortly after that, Pat and his brothers left town without so much as a good-bye. Pat's parents also moved. The agony of losing a daughter-in-law was too much to bear. They couldn't remain in the town where such a horrible crime was committed and no one was punished. Brian wondered how anyone could manage the heartache of losing such a beautiful, wonderful person, so bright and happy. Brian had only his parents and they were still living at the north end of Skyline Drive in Virginia. Brian called them immediately after Julie Mallernee McKinney died. He wasn't sure why he'd called. He just knew that he had to make that call. He'd found them in good health, his voice sounding scared and apprehensive. Just hearing their voices calmed his heart and from that day forward, he called them at least once a week without fail.

Brian almost decided to pull off the side of the road. He wanted to make sure that Patrick was behind him, leaving the tortuous four walls of the vault behind. He was pretty confident that Pat had done the appropriate soul search and was heading home to bare his soul to his lovely wife. There were many years, many ghosts, and many scars, physical and mental, that had to be re-opened and properly healed with his one and only love. His wife would understand, Brian thought. It would take time for her to fully comprehend the enormity of the past of the man that she loved. But Brian knew from their brief time together that she was extraordinary and loved Pat in an extraordinary way. Then Brian wondered just how much of this mystery *he* knew. How much had Pat withheld from him? *I may never know.* Brian made the turn onto state highway 435 towards Apopka.

Patrick watched as Brian's taillights turned to the south onto Kelly Park Drive. He waited a few minutes and listened for the sound of Brian's mini-van to return. It never did. He made his way back into the vault, moved the heavy oak desk to the side a few feet to expose a section of wood flooring that didn't appear to match the rest of the flooring at the edges. Pat pushed down on the left side of the odd floor panel causing the right side of the panel to pivot up. Pat removed the floor panel to gain access to the door to an underground chamber. Pat inserted the key to the heavy duty lock on the stainless steel door, turned the key to the right, jerked down on the lock and removed it from the heavy, thick hasp. The right side of the climate-controlled, stainless steel chamber contained numerous shelves on which a large assortment of ammunition was stacked. On the left side, a large rack with additional locking mechanisms contained a variety of weapons, from a Heckler and Koch 9MM pistol, a 45 caliber ARN1911and other assorted hand guns to a modified AR15 set to allow fully automatic performance, a Russian-made AK47, and a few others. Pat did a quick inventory of the firearms, checked the climate control system, closed and locked the steel door to the compartment and replaced the wooden floor cover. He'd disposed of the Iver Johnson Sniper rifle immediately after he'd completed the Vallero killing. He did a quick mental review of the coming events and smiled to himself. He was ready.

His mood changed again to one of dread. The emotional roller-coaster ride he was on would not let up. He thought of Diane and the children. What if he was caught in the act? What would happen to them? How would Diane react to finding out she was married to a murderer and a one-time drug peddler? How would Sean face his friends at school? Kids are very cruel to one another when even the slightest weakness shows through. Sean was so young. So was Anna. How could he place his family's wellbeing in jeopardy?

He left the vault, locking the door behind him. As he drove away, his dark mood lifted ever so slightly. He took a deep breath as he headed south on Kelly Park Drive in the first leg of his journey home. His first stop was at Joe's apartment in Pine Hills. Maybe Joe would do him a favor and kill him before Diane had the chance.

Chapter 23

The exercise room at the apartment complex was about 20 feet by 20 feet with just a handful of workout machines: a treadmill, a universal, an exercise bike, and a bench with some free weights. It was nothing to write home about. They weren't top of the line but were commercial grade and kept in good condition by the maintenance manager at the complex. He liked to work out, so he had a vested interest in making sure that they were in working order. The room was painted apartment-complex beige. There were two small windows, a doorway from one hallway that led to the parking lot, and another that led to the laundry room. The laundry room also had a doorway to the opposite hallway. The smell in the room was typical of gym locker rooms. Stale sweat permeated the air like a pile of dirty socks. If you were there to work out, after a few minutes it didn't bother you, but if you were just passing through after taking a shower, it made you feel like you needed another one.

Joe McKinney finished his five mile run on the treadmill. He moved to the universal machine, put the pin in the slot indicating that 220 pounds was selected and started repetitions for his biceps. He was beginning to work up a serious sweat after about ten minutes. He figured about five more minutes of curls, fifteen minutes working on his abs and a ten minute cool-down period and he'd be ready for a swim. What he didn't figure on was Lisa Goddard walking into the exercise room. He couldn't help but allow his eyes to follow her tight body as she made her way around the different pieces of exercise equipment. He watched for just a few seconds and figured that he'd better concentrate on his workout or he'd never finish his routine. He had to avoid distractions, particularly at this crucial time. There were too many things going on right now. Business was at hand, the culmination of planning for years. He closed his eyes and counted the reps as he moved the 220 pound weights with what appeared to be relative ease. He began to focus his thoughts on the next phase of the plan to keep his mind off of the strain of his muscles. The technique worked well. It worked even better for Joe when his focus was anger and hate. He pictured himself grabbing a foe from behind and thrusting...

"Hey, are you okay? You look like your having a heart attack or something."

Lisa's voice startled Joe. He abruptly stopped his reps, opened his eyes, and looked blankly at Lisa for what seemed like a full minute. After the two seconds in real time, he answered, "No...I mean yeah, I'm fine."

"I'm sorry, I didn't mean to interrupt your workout but you really looked like you were in pain, your face was pretty red and strained looking. I saw you had 220 pounds on the machine, I was just a little freaked."

Joe could feel the sweat running down his face. The heat from his body was rising, mostly from the workout but now made worse from coming face to face with this beautiful, young woman. He looked up into her eyes which were still looking at him with concern. Initially the concern was for his health. Now it appeared that she was afraid that she'd interrupted his workout. She thought that he was getting ready to tell her to beat it and not ever do that again.

He said in a calm, but winded voice, "I really am fine. I just wasn't expecting you to...I thought you were getting on the treadmill. It's all warmed up for you. I just got off a few minutes ago."

"Wow, you spend a lot of time down here. I've been in here when you're working out and I'm in and out before you even finish one set. Do you always close your eyes when you work out? That seems like it might not be the safest thing to do. I mean you could lose your balance on the treadmill or a weight could shift on the barbells. You should have someone else here while you work out, too. What if something does happen and you're hurt to the point that you can't help yourself?"

"You're right. I guess you could call it a bad habit. I like to close my eyes because I can think of being in different places. Like just now, I was imagining that I was in the mountains of North Carolina, back-packing up the Appalachian Trail. I used to run up in the mountains along a stretch of the trail when I was stationed at Camp Lejeune."

He really had made the trip several times. He loved the outdoors and the challenge of running in the mountains. "I hope to go back up there someday. It's gorgeous, especially in the fall." He kept talking, not missing a beat. His breathing had returned to normal but his pulse rate was elevated. "Since I got out of the service, I've always worked out alone. I think it's because I really don't have any friends that like to work out and I don't want to spend the money on one of those gyms. They're a ripoff. It's just real convenient to come down here. My apartment's right up the walk. I'm talking too much."

"I know where it is, and no, you're not talking too much." Lisa replied. "I've seen you looking out the window."

Busted!

"May I introduce myself?" Joe asked this in a mock formal voice, partly to hide his embarrassment.

Before he could, Lisa said, "No introduction is necessary. You're Joe McKinney, recently discharged from the United States Marine Corps after six years of active duty. Word gets around, Mr. McKinney. I mean Joe. This apartment complex is like a small town. It doesn't take long for everyone to know your business."

Joe pondered this for just a second or two. Normally this news would have made him analyze things further, and maybe he would later when he was alone, but right now he needed to talk more with Miss Goddard.

"Well, Miss Goddard, I know a bit about you, too." This brought a little smile to Lisa's face. "For instance, I know that you work at the Publix Grocery store in the plaza at the corner of Silver Star and Hiawassee, are 21 years young, and you obviously take good care of yourself. You are not from Florida, originally. I can tell that by your voice, no twang to it at all. So

"I know you better than you think..." The lyrics and tune to the Brian Purcer song jumped out of Joe's mouth before he even realized what he was doing. The smile on his face was wide. Lisa's reaction was a giggle.

"So you're a musician, too. And you know the local talent."

"No, no, no. I just get goofy when I'm relaxed. I saw Brian the other night at the Rock. Great show." He stood and stretched a bit so he wouldn't tighten up while they talked. "What exercises did you have in mind for today? I can help you. Remember the two-man rule you just told me about. I mean two 'person' rule. And, by the way, where is your second person that you were going to work out with? Hmmm? Is your boyfriend on his way down to be your faithful assistant?"

"Okay, I'm busted. I was going to work out alone, but I don't pile on the weights like you. I do what I like to call a light 'aerobic' routine. It's mostly repetition with lighter weights. I don't do heavy duty lifting." Lisa's smile was bright. She had perfect, white teeth and absolutely beautiful eyes. She was, without a doubt, the most gorgeous woman that Joe had ever encountered. And she had a real personality.

"I'm just playing with you anyway. But I am serious. Would you like me to help you with anything in here? We could be workout buddies. You help me by keeping an eye out for me and I can do the same for you. It appears that we both have similar schedules. I can meet you down here whenever you get off work. We can work out and then go for a swim. What do you say? Partners?" Joe's smile was electric as he extended his hand to shake on their agreement. Lisa was melting in front of him.

Hesitantly, she took his hand then gave it a firm shake and said "Okay, sure. But before we get into this routine, we need to get to know each other a little better. I know you're ex-military. Where are you from?"

"Well, I was born in Ohio, in a little town called Port Clinton."

He was just about to talk about his move to Indiana at a very young four years old when Lisa shouted, "You're kidding!!

I'm from Oak Harbor. You know we always kicked your guy's asses in football. Port Clinton sucked."

"Well, lucky for me I didn't go to Port Clinton Schools. My folks moved us to Anderson, Indiana when I was just a little kid. Dad taught at a Christian college called Anderson University so that's where I grew up until I was in high school. Then Dad got an opportunity to move down here to Orlando and teach at University of Central Florida. He moved us out in the country near Apopka. That's where I went to high school. Now that was hard-core culture shock. I don't think he realized what he'd done to us until it was too late." Joe paused here for a few seconds. He had to be a bit cautious about what cats he let out of the bag.

"I know where Apopka is. It isn't that bad."

"It was back then. You have to remember that that area's grown quite a bit over the last eight to ten years. I mean, back then this was Hicksville. Those rednecks were still fightin' the civil war, if you know what I mean." The fake accent widened Lisa's smile again. "My brothers and I were three Yankees from Indiana. We didn't even mind the neegars. Again, Joe threw in the fake, exaggerated accent, this time with finger quotes around the 'N' word. "I have two brothers. Okay. I've thrown you a few nuggets. What about you?"

"Well," Lisa began, "I was born in Oak Harbor, actually at Magruder Hospital in Port Clinton."

"Me too," Joe interjected. "Sorry, continue please. I'll try to not interrupt."

Lisa giggled again. "I went to school in Oak Harbor all the way through high school. I was supposed to go to Bowling Green State University but my brother got into some big trouble. He was dealing dope, mainly to support his Bob Marley-sized dope habit. Well, he got busted with about fifteen pounds of pot. He was set up but it didn't really matter. My folks nearly went broke with his legal fees and trying to keep him out of prison. So they couldn't afford to send me to school. I was so totally pissed that I decided right then and there to get out and do it by myself." Hearing Lisa's story put a sad look on Joe's face. He was doing some instantaneous soul searching. This poor but beautiful creature was cheated out of her dream, at least temporarily, by the same business that caused him so much pain and heartache. His family had suffered, and still suffered. He had so much in common with this young woman. But instead of her reaping the benefits of that world as Joe and his brothers had, she was scraping by and struggling through school. Unlike Joe and Pat, her suffering was working her way through school, not planning to get even.

"Hey, I didn't mean to bum you out. I'm working on getting back into school. I'm smart and I'm driven. I'll finish my degree despite my stupid brother."

Joe's smile returned. He looked Lisa straight in the eyes and said, "I believe you. What do you plan to major in?"

"Criminal Law or Criminal Justice."

Uh-oh. Sleeping with the enemy.

"Maybe business. Then again, maybe architecture. I'm not absolutely sure. I want to get a degree in something that will guarantee lots of income for life. I'm tired of being poor, that's for sure."

"Well, you should scratch Law Enforcement off of your list then. Nobody in Law Enforcement gets rich. It's the lucky ones on the other side of the fence."

"You're right about that one. My brother got caught but before he did, he was rolling in cash. Not rich by any means, but it made him feel rich. It sure put my folks in the poor house."

"Well, you'll have to get your degree, make a ton of money and help them out. When are you going to enroll? And where?"

Lisa gave this one a little thought. Her face became tight, a few wrinkles showing at the edges of her eyes as she squinted. "I think that I'll start this spring. It's too late to get into the fall quarter and besides I'd have to take out a loan. I really want to pay as I go as much as possible. I'm looking at University of Central Florida. I might go to Valencia though."

Joe also gave this some thought. He could pay cash for her school but he couldn't come out and offer this poor girl thousands of dollars in cash. He just met her, for crying out loud. "Listen," Joe said with a smile, "it'll all work out. Trust me. You'll have your degree in whatever you decide within five years if that's what you put your mind to. But for now, let's finish our workout or we'll never get anything done."

"Okay," came her reply with a big smile that seemed to say, '*thanks.*'

They spent the next hour working out together. For Joe, it was barely breaking a sweat but he helped Lisa through her routine. He could see why she was in such great shape. She worked hard, but paced herself, not using weights that were too heavy for her, but enough that challenged her as she progressed along in her repetitions. She was working up a sweat, something that Joe could not ignore. He could barely concentrate on keeping count of her exercises as her beautiful, smooth skin glistened. When they'd finished, Joe asked Lisa if she'd like to take a swim. He told her that he normally did about 50 laps in the apartment pool, but if she'd join him, he'd take it easy and only do forty or so. She replied that she could do fifty laps in the time it'd take him to do his forty.

"Any money on that, young lady?"

"Sure. But instead, loser pays for dinner tonight."

"Now you're talking. I'll take that bet." *This is getting interesting.*

"What's your preference?"

"The winner can decide. That way I'll be sure we won't go cheap."

"Oh boy. Now I'm psyched. You are going down, girl. I hope you ate your *Wheaties* this morning."

"We'll see who needs to change their breakfast cereal and exercise habits. I'll meet you at the pool in about 30 minutes, alright? Don't chicken out on me."

"That's your only chance of winning."

With smiles that were like two junior high school kids, they picked up their towels, tossed final glances at each other and headed towards their own apartments. Joe looked over his shoulder no less than six times as he reached the stairs to his apartment and started bounding up the steps. He stopped short when he noticed Pat's car in the parking lot next to his. This couldn't be good news, he thought to himself. Pat's timing really sucked.

Chapter 24

Ray Krebs and Johnny Poleirmo were interrogating the crack-house bust jailbirds. They were getting the usual smug responses. It appeared that they would finish their questioning without getting anywhere. The next to last loser was on his third arrest for trafficking in crack cocaine and was destined to return to Stark County Prison for some real time. They decided to put a little extra pressure on this dude just to see if he'd break under intense questioning. Good cop, bad cop. That was the game for the afternoon.

It didn't take long. They had a song bird on their hands. It appears that their connection was a white guy from the northeast named Danny Vallero. Unfortunately for Poleirmo and Krebs, Danny Vallero had already been processed by Homicide into the morgue. It had been a long day and Johnny Poleirmo wanted to go home to his wife. She'd been patient with him these past few weeks. Ray was also showing signs of burnout. He and Johnny looked at each other, exchanged tired grins and shook their heads almost in unison.

Johnny said, "Ray, my man, I'm heading home. I'm bushed and I need a full night of relaxation. Besides, Rachael deserves a little Johnny tonight."

"Ray replied, "I know what you mean, man. I'm smoked, too. Head out, I've got a couple of reports back at my desk that I have to review and sign. I'll see you in the morning. Remember to get some rest. I think we've got another apartment bust around 6:30 tomorrow morning. It's going to be a long day."

"We should let homicide know what this clown told us about Danny Vallero. Want me to handle it?" Johnny asked.

"Nope, I got it. Get your ass out of here. You deserve a break. I got you covered."

"Thanks, man. I'll see you in the morning. Have a beer for me tonight. I'm too damned tired."

Johnny left the interrogation room and headed towards his desk. Ray followed close behind and began to shuffle papers on his own desk. He did this until Johnny was out of sight. He picked up the phone and called detective Al Poreczwski, Homicide.

"Hey Al, Ray Krebs, Vice. I've got some info for you. Yeah, you know that stiff, Danny Vallero, who had his brains blown out? We heard through a busted junk head that he was dealing some weight in crack. Sounds like he was going out of town and hauling it in himself. Looks like there's no local connection to pursue."

Al Poreczwski didn't think that Ray Krebs should be making decisions for Homicide, but folks moving drugs were Ray's area of concern. So this news was not of any consequence except now there was a potential motive.

"Thanks for the call, Ray. This is another piece of the puzzle but I don't imagine that we'll be wasting much time on this one. So the druggies and dealers are killing each other off. I wish they'd work faster. Make our load a little lighter."

"Yeah, but it seems like we have more and more trash walking the streets these days. Maybe they're multiplying faster than they knock each other off. You should have seen the house we busted. There were little kids playing on the floor in the same room as grownups smoking and dealing crack. It's a sick world that we live in. You know, you've seen it. Didn't you do a stint in Vice?"

Al's eyes drifted a bit as he thought about his time in Vice. For the most part it was uneventful except one near miss. His partner was shot in the chest not one foot from Al. His partner survived only because of his Kevlar jacket. He suffered a single broken rib. The damn things weren't perfect, but they did work. A broken rib was a small price to pay for continuing to live. "Yep. Nothing like it is today though. You guys have it pretty tough. I guess that's why they keep Vice guys young and move us old timers to Homicide. The path to retirement. I can't wait."

Ray smiled at that and said, "Al, I gotta run. We'll see you. Let me know if you have any questions. I can have a copy of the interrogation sent to you after it's signed. Talk with you later." Ray was done with his 'official' calls from his desk phone. He had one more call to make but it would be from a pay phone on the street. He didn't think that Jason Roberts would appreciate a call that could be traced to a cop's desk.

**

Donnie Lee Lester sat alone in his living room, drinking a beer, watching TV and cleaning his shotgun. He'd been out shooting beer cans off a fence at Jamie Watkin's place in Ocoee. It was always risky business shooting guns with Jamie. He was such a hot-head that you wondered if he'd turn and put one between your eyes. And he was always angry about something. If it wasn't that dope shipments were too slow, it was that they were giving Jason Roberts too much of the take. Or he'd be mad just because he ran out of beer. Donnie Lee wasn't sure if it was his red hair, his being from Texas, or if he sat on a cactus when he was younger and a thorn was still up his ass. He did know that Jamie was loud and obnoxious and was bound to get them both and Bobby Acquino into big trouble. You can only run your mouth so long before it catches up with you and you insult the wrong tough guy.

Donnie was watching the fishing channel on TV. He wasn't sure why, because he didn't fish. He thought about trying it many times, but he was too busy with other things, like making money. He was thinking about the deal that was to go down tonight. He'd just heard about it while he and Jamie were out shooting. Phil Daniels had come out to Jamie's and let them know the details. No big deal, Donnie Lee thought. But Jamie acted as if he were insulted, especially after he'd been called on the carpet the past week.

"How can Jason expect us to make any kind of money with these peewee deals? I mean, we were doing better when we were independents. We were hauling in the dough. We'd never even do a deal this small. I'm about ready to tell ol' Jason he can stick his mule business up his ass. I'm sick of being his hey-boy runner. You tell him to get us some bigger action or we're out on our own. We know all the right folks. We'll put his ass in the poor house."

Phil was a pretty patient guy when it came to dealing with Jamie. It made him a little nervous talking to him while he had a shotgun in his hands but Jamie had never threatened him. They went back a long way to high school. So he usually let Jamie blow off some steam, and then he'd calm down. After that Phil would explain the facts of life to him. 'He was getting the largest deals that Jason had going right now' he'd tell Jamie. 'Things were a bit slow' he'd say. 'When things heated up, Jamie, Donnie Lee, and Bobby would be the top dogs and get the meaty deals'. It was all bullshit to keep Jamie from going off the deep end, but each time Phil explained the facts of life to Jamie he seemed less and less pacified. Phil figured that there would come a time when Jamie would blow up. When that happened, Jason Roberts would pull the plug.

If Jamie was lucky, that's all he'd do. Most likely Buddy would be called in to put a few dents in Jamie's head. And if that didn't work, well Mr. Roberts knew how to handle problems. Jason didn't like trouble and Jamie was a potential source of real trouble.

"Jamie, are you through?"

"Hell no I'm not through. I'm just getting warmed up. I'm telling you right now you better tell that Yankee bastard to free up the goods and start lettin' us handle some weight. This is bullshit, bullshit, bullshit! I'll kick his faggot ass all the way to the north Tennessee State Line if he keeps fuckin' with us."

Patiently, Phil asked again, "Now, are you through?"

"I guess for now."

"Mr. Roberts would like for you guys to handle a twenty five bale move tonight. Your cut is $1200.00 per bale. Cash on delivery. Pick up and drop off points are on the sheet. The cash is in the box in my trunk. Take your cut before you go to the site. Any questions?"

Jamie did the math in his head. Ten grand each for a

nights work.

Not bad except he wanted more. "Next time, I either want a 50 bale load or I want $1500.00 per bale. This is my last deal at slave wages. He can kiss my ass. This is bullshit," he said again, just for emphasis. "I'm pullin' in over a million bucks a year for this asshole and this is the crumbs he throws at me. I can move a hundred bales tomorrow night if he can throw the weight my way. And I can move another fifty the next morning. I can handle it. Can he? That pussy bitch."

Through all of this, Donnie sat quietly. He knew that Jamie was at the end of the line with Mr. Roberts. He thought that after the temper tantrum he threw the other night he wouldn't even be getting this deal. Jamie did bring in big bucks for Mr. Robert's organization, but sometimes money wasn't the most important part of the job. Drawing too much attention to oneself was not a good thing. *Too bad*, he thought to himself. That means that he and Bobby would split the take in two instead of three. *That would be nice.* Well, time would tell if Jamie would take himself out of the picture.

He went back to cleaning his shotgun and watching the fishing channel. A good ol' southern boy had just landed a beautiful large mouthed bass. Donnie Lee had never seen one in real life but it was fun watching these guys on the big screen TV. *Almost like being there*, Donnie thought.

Donnie Lee had no idea that he would not see the day when Jamie was out of the organization.

***

Negotiations went quite well for Brian and the band. They weren't instant millionaires but they were off to a good start. Brian was all set to give his notice at the *Sentinel Star*. He had one more weekend gig at the *Rock*, where his agent and Atlantic Records would announce that Brian and the Hot Licks had signed a major record deal. They would be in the studio recording their first of what would be many albums within the next two weeks. The concert tour would follow immediately after the album's release. Brian and his band members were very excited. Rick Wessler was already talking about what he was buying first. A car, a house, new clothes, almost every sentence out of his mouth was preceded by "I'm gonna buy me a..."

Brian was being a bit more down to earth. He'd been dreaming about this day but he was thinking that he'd hold off on the buying spree. He really needed to think this through so he'd first called his Dad and Mom.

Brian's Dad was supportive but cautioned Brian on not getting into trouble. "You know this rock and roll crowd is all tied up in drugs and sex. Keep your head on straight. This could last for years or it could be short lived. You have to be prepared for the worst and you've got to protect yourself. You'll have all kinds of loonies who claim to be your long lost friends."

His mom was less than enthusiastic. She never did approve of this lifestyle. She never dreamed that Brian would have this opportunity so she never really spoke to Brian about it. Now that he was heading down the road to rock and roll stardom, she had nothing good to say. "Brian, this will ruin your life. I wish you'd walk away from it right now. Working for a living is not all that bad, is it?"

That's when he told them that he might have a steady girlfriend. He told them about Ginny Parks, how they met, where she was from, how beautiful she was, how nice she was, how he was head over heels for her. This news was more to their liking. They never were sure about Brian's love life. He never talked about it with them. He seldom mentioned any girls' names. When he did, he always followed it with "she's just a friend." They were never sure if Brian was interested in girls. He always seemed more interested in *Star Trek*, *Star Wars*, or rock and roll music. He was kind of a skinny, shy kid, not too outgoing in social situations. He tended to hang around his male friends and blushed visibly when talking to any girls. If he had a steady girlfriend this was indeed good news. Maybe he was coming out of his shell. One thing they noticed, even when he was young, when he was performing, he wasn't shy. It's as if he was a totally different person. And he was good at it. If this new girlfriend helped him overcome his introversion, they were all for it. From Brian's description, she sounded like a wonderful girl.

After he hung up the phone, Brian started to plan his financial future. He had two other people with which he wanted to talk finances. He knew that Al Michaels had made a good living in the nursery business and was pretty frugal with his money. When he'd talked to him a few years ago, Al was planning on retiring at 45. That was aggressive. He'd told Brian that he'd have to sock away about 50% of his income to achieve that. When they spoke at the '*Rock*' the other night, Al mentioned that he was a little ahead of schedule, but still planned to keep to the 'retire at 45' goal instead of having a monetary target. Brian was impressed with that. Here he was struggling at the *Sentinel Star* for peanuts and his friends were thinking about their retirement years. With his contract, he could get serious about finances.

The other guy he wanted to speak with might be a little more difficult to talk with right now. He was having a few problems of his own. Pat McKinney probably wouldn't want to hear about Brian's finances while he tried to get back in his wife's good graces. But if things settled down in Pat's life, he knew that Pat made a small fortune and was able to keep a major portion of it. He still didn't understand how he could have kept his life a secret from his wife. What the hell was going through his head? Maybe he was really whacked out of his mind. But if that were the case, how did you start and run your own business? How did you spend six years in the Navy and work on a submarine? Maybe that was it. They're all crazy on subs. *Why else would you get on one of those things?* But if Pat were sane, and he sure seemed that way the other night (though a bit stressed), he'd make an excellent financial advisor. Brian was going to need the advice, he was sure. He'd never seen or handled anything like the kind of money his new contract was about to shower on him. Just the base salary was a lot of dough, but the real money was in the perks; proceeds from record sales, concerts, merchandising, and personal appearances. It was all there for the taking if things went as Brian hoped. He was confident. For the first time in his life he thought he could face anything and anyone. And he was in love. Truly in love with a girl named Ginny Parks.

Chapter 25

Pat and Joe sat down at Joe's living room table. Joe was still covered in sweat from his workout with Lisa. He really wanted to get cleaned up a bit and get to the pool so he didn't keep her waiting, or worse yet, miss her altogether. She'd think that he'd chickened out or just didn't care to see her again. That was the furthest thing from the truth.

"So how're we doing, Pat? I see we're right on schedule."

Pat looked at Joe with a worried, strained look. "I don't want to talk schedule for a minute. I ran into Brian Purcer last night. I was at the vault and he drove right up."

Joe frowned. "What were you doing at the vault? You know we're supposed to stay away from there for now. How the hell did Brian find you there?" Joe said with an edge in his voice that bordered on anger. "What the fuck is going on, Pat?"

"I wrote Brian right when I got out of the Navy. I told him where we were moving and told him I'd like for him to stop by and meet Diane and the kids. He did, only I wasn't there." Pat paused and looked around Joe's apartment, avoiding his stare. "Diane and I had a fight the other night. Actually I blew up at Sean for no good reason. Diane stepped in and I guess we did have a fight. Bottom line is that I walked out and haven't been home since. I went to the vault to gather myself and calm down. I stayed there last night and today. I was sitting there just going over things in my mind when I see headlights on the monitors. It was Brian."

The more Pat talked, the more Joe's face showed his annoyance with what Pat had done. He had to stop himself from leaping right into Pat's face. This was a major blunder on Pat's part and one that Joe would never have believed Pat was capable of making.

"What did Brian have to say? I mean, did he tell you what he and Diane talked about? Why would Diane let him through the door, that crazy looking freak?"

"That's the really bad part."

Joe rolled his eyes at this. "What could be worse than you hanging out at the vault?"

"Brian told Diane about the grove business, the nursery business, that I may have a pretty good stash of cash, and that he couldn't believe that she didn't know. Brian pretty much spilled his guts about everything except the real business. I guess he figured that'd send Diane over the edge. Apparently she was pretty astonished at just what she'd heard." Another pause. "Joe, I don't know what to do. I have to go home and talk to her. She's probably already changed the locks, got a restraining order, and notified the police to be on the lookout for my car. I miss her but I'm more scared to face her than any of these assholes we're dealing with."

"Pat, wake up! She's still in love with you. You're just stressed out. Let's talk for a bit and we'll figure out what we have to do here. First, quit whining. You sound like a school girl. I know you're stressed but, God man, you've got nothing to worry about. We know what we have to do. It's all laid out and if we execute, we're golden. Nothing points to us. Next, slow down on the consulting business. Keep the clients that you have and don't pick up any more. Next is the toughest. You have to go home and talk things through with Diane. You have to tell her everything except, of course, that you were a dope dealer and made the majority of your money that way. You've gotta come clean on the grove, the nursery, even your lifestyle. She'll forgive you for smoking a little dope; even a lot of dope. But you can't hide this stuff from her any longer."

Pat knew that his little brother was right. He sat for a few minutes longer. Then he looked at Joe who was studying his older brother with a calculated look. Pat's slight smile let Joe know that he was getting through but it wasn't a complete victory yet.

Pat said, "Okay. I can do it. I have to take care of the next target. I got the info on Randy."

Joe looked at him in surprise. "You mean Donnie, right?"

"No, I mean Randy. Randy Farley."

Joe was shocked now. "Randy's dead. Killed the other night in his apartment. No details were released except that it was a murder. They had a 'person of interest' but they let her go. I thought it was us."

"Wow!" Pat's first reaction was one of surprise, then confusion. "Coincidence? Randy was up on some dope charges. Maybe he opened his mouth to the wrong folks and they didn't like it."

"Maybe. But I think we better watch developments for a few days. Let's step back for a week or so and let things calm down. Even though Randy isn't really connected to the others too closely, it can't hurt to wait a few days. There's one other thing that you need to know. Jamie, Donnie, and Bobby have been dealing with a guy named Jason Roberts. He's a pretty big time player. It turns out that Danny Vallero worked for him, too. This is another reason that we may want to let things rest for a few days," Joe said.

Pat thought that this was pretty logical. They'd waited for over six years for this. It won't make any difference to wait a few more days.

Joe looked at the kitchen clock and exclaimed, "Oh shit! I'm late. I've gotta run right now!" Joe stood up quickly, pushed his chair in and headed for the door. He didn't have time to clean up now. He'd have to shower real quickly at poolside.

"Late for what?" Pat asked.

"I'm meeting a chick at the pool, if she hasn't already left. I was supposed to be there ten minutes ago. Damn! Let yourself out and lock up. Stay here and think for a while if you need, but think about what I said...about everything. Go home tonight, Pat. You need to go home and make sure everything is right with Diane. I mean it."

"I will. We'll see what happens over the next few days

before we get things back in gear."

It didn't take that long to see what happened next.

***

Donnie Lee had finished cleaning his shotgun and placed it in the gun case in his living room. He left it unlocked in case he needed to access it quickly but there never really seemed to be a need. It wasn't like he was going to shoot it out with the cops. Not many folks knew about his real business except customers and there were few of them, in relative terms. Dealing at this level had real advantages. You dealt with fewer people and you got paid extremely well. You didn't have to fool with the nickel and dime punks who thought that they were hard. Most street punks thought a whole lot of themselves. They dealt with far too many people who they didn't know from Adam. This put them in more danger than they realized. It's amazing how many of these rich, whiny kids squealed when faced with a simple possession charge. They had no problem ratting out the guy who sold it to them. *Punks*, Donnie Lee thought to himself. He was thinking about the deal that he, Bobby, and Jamie were to handle tonight. It was dark at 10:30 pm. The TV was still on with the surround sound going. He'd changed the channel to Great American Country, the country music 24 hours a day channel. A hot new female country singer was on strutting around the stage at the Grand Ole Opry. She looked real good and sang like a pro.

The clank of what sounded like tin cans rattling together startled him. It sounded like it was coming from the back yard. He rose from the couch, rubbed his eyes with the back of his hands, shook his head to get the cob webs out and walked towards the eight foot patio doors. He heard the clanking again and thought that it sounded like a trash can being tipped over, but there were no trash cans in the back yard. He stood in front of the door, looking out onto the lighted grounds around the house. He didn't see anything out of the ordinary. It was a good 250 yards to the grove behind the house. Maybe some kids were having a party back there. He'd have to look in the morning to see if there were any signs of mischief. Lots of kids went parking in groves around central Florida. Donnie thought, *that's how I got my first lay. Kids will be kids.*

And that was Donnie Lee Lester's last coherent thought.

***

The view through the crosshairs was clear and sharp. Donnie Lee's head looked as big as a basketball through the scope. When he stopped in front of the sliding glass door, he might as well have put a gun to his own head. The .338 caliber projectile covered the 280 yards in a fraction of a second. Donnie Lee's brain barely had time to register the muzzle flash before the impact of the bullet pierced his skull. Glass shattered and Donnie Lee's head snapped back. He was down.

Radar released the pressure on the trigger of the powerful Remington SR8 sniper rifle. He released the slight pressure on the trigger, let out a breath of air slowly, and viewed the fallen target through the scope for several seconds. Satisfied that his job was a success, he cleaned up the area and left the grove.

***

Jamie Watkins was heading towards Donnie Lee's house when he saw the lights flashing and the traffic slowing. There was an officer trying to keep people moving and even though Donnie lived on a country road with little traffic, there were at least four cars just idling along, trying to catch a glimpse of something that they could tell their friends and neighbors. Jamie would have laid on his horn in normal circumstances but these were obviously not normal. His mind started to run at a hundred miles an hour trying to determine what could have gone wrong. He was supposed to meet Donnie and Bobby and head for the pickup point. Bobby's car was amongst the half dozen Orange County Sheriff's cars, rescue squad and what, a helicopter in the back?

"What the fuck?" Jamie said out loud, loud enough, in fact that the sheriff directing traffic heard him and asked, "Pardon me, sir?"

"Sorry officer, I've just never seen anything like this out here before. What's going on anyway? Looks pretty bad."

"Sorry, sir, can't say. Can you please keep moving? Don't want to have an accident. We have enough problems here."

***

Al Poreczwski was starting to see a pattern, one that he didn't like; two shootings with a high powered rifle from long range. That was no coincidence. There had to be a connection. This job was nearly identical to the Vallero shooting except in detail: This guy survived, though barely. He'd lain in his own blood for nearly an hour before he was found by a 'friend'. The friend was one Bobby Acquino. He was in tears when the Sheriff got there, holding his friends head in his hands, mumbling something about 'getting out too late.' He was reciting prayers over and over again. The paramedics had to nearly pry his arms from around the victim's neck. He was covered in blood that had started to dry. The sickly copper smell permeated the room where Donnie was found.

During questioning, Bobby had said that he'd come over just to hang out, watch TV and drink. They had no plans to go anywhere but they did sometimes go out to any number of bars. When asked what he meant by his comment 'getting out too late,' Bobby stated that he didn't remember saying that. After that, he wasn't too cooperative.

The crime scene investigative team was combing the grove behind the house. They found an area that appeared to have been recently disturbed but there were no visible foot prints, no gun casing, or real hard evidence. They found that an orange tree branch had been used to wipe out most of the shoe prints though some partial prints were visible. These would be processed but they'd have to piece together numerous partial prints to make anything near a full shoe print. Even that was a long shot. The spot where the orange tree branch was found was where the tire tracks started. Whoever was there had torn out of there, kicking up quite a bit of sand. They had to follow the tracks for about 50 yards until they came across tracks that they could process. Other than that, there was an area that appeared to be kind of a party spot with a fire pit. These were not uncommon in Florida groves. In the pit, which was cold to the touch, about half a dozen cans were tied to the end of several strings. When the investigator picked them up and shook them, they made a heck of a lot of noise. The investigator thought *Is this what lured him to the back door?* That was the only real evidence found at the scene that night. If there was any other forensic evidence to be found, it would have to wait for the light of day.

Donnie Lee was rushed by helicopter to Orlando Regional Medical Center. A neurosurgeon, Dr. R. J. Stein, was called in to assess his chances of survival which were immediately determined to be minimal. He was in critical condition. Activities were limited to those that would help stabilize his vital signs and hopefully keep him from getting any worse. Surgery was out of the question, at least for the time being. Dr. Stein gave the nurses their orders. He was to be informed of any significant changes in his vitals. The next 24 hours would determine if he had a chance to live or not.

Bobby Acquino raced to Orlando Regional as fast as he could. He pulled his car up to the circle and stopped it right in the fire lane, hopped out leaving the car running, and raced into the lobby of the huge hospital. Like all hospitals, Orlando Regional was kept cool and sterile. He asked at the reception desk where he could find Donnie. In turn the desk clerk asked him if he was family. When Bobby said he was the closest thing to family that Donnie had, the clerk told him with no emotion that only family members could see him. He would have to wait until family was notified. Bobby said he needed to speak with the attending doctor. Again the clerk said that he couldn't do that because he wasn't family. Bobby had one last question. "Where is the hospital chapel?"

Finally, a question the clerk could answer. "The chapel is on the second floor to the right after you get off the elevator, then a left. The chapel is just down the hall."

The clerk was about to ask if there was anything else she could do for him, but Bobby was already heading for the chapel, too much in grief and fear for his friend's life. It hadn't even crossed his mind that his life might be in danger as well.

Chapter 26

Ray Krebs' pager beeped. He wasn't expecting to hear from anyone and this annoyed him. He was driving along State Route 441 near Apopka when he read the number on his pager. It was Jason Roberts' number and it had a priority code that he should call Mr. Roberts immediately. This couldn't be good news. Mr. Roberts never contacted Ray directly for any reason. So this came as a big surprise and a source of instant concern. He pulled into the 7-Eleven on the north end of town and dialed the number. Jason Roberts answered the call before the first ring was finished.

"What am I paying you for?" he shouted into Ray's ear. "I got guys getting whacked in their own homes and no arrests? You better get whoever the fuck is poppin' my guys off and fast or you're gonna join 'em. You got that Krebs?"

"Yes sir," Ray said into the handset. But Jason Roberts had already hung up. Ray understood that he had orders to get to the bottom of it and put a stop to whoever was killing Jason Roberts' men. That would be no small task because he had to stick his nose where it didn't belong: Homicide.

***

Lisa was afraid that Joe had stood her up on their first...what...date? This was just a neighborly swim. Can you stand someone up on a swim? Well, he was over fifteen minutes late and she really didn't want to stay by the pool alone at night. The apartment complex was pretty safe by most standards, but there's always a chance that some creep is lurking in the bushes. And there were plenty of bushes to lurk behind by the pool. Also, a number of apartments had patios or balconies that opened right on to the pool area, separated only by a rod iron fence. That wasn't much protection. The good news was that it appeared that lots of folks were home to hear her scream if she needed to get their attention. The pool itself was about fifty feet by twenty-five feet, rectangular; nothing fancy but well kept. The grounds were well maintained, attractively landscaped and stocked with decent pool-side furniture. Several tables had oversized umbrellas meant to provide shade for the fair skinned moms who watched their kids splash and play with their inflatable rings. There was a kiddy pool for the really small children in its own fenced in area and there was a shower at the entrance with cold water. Sometimes in the mid-day Florida heat, the cool water coming out of the shower was scalding hot, but just for a few seconds. You had to be careful though so you didn't get burned with the superheated mist.

There were no kids or moms here tonight. The pool area had been abandoned for the time being. Joe approached the pool's gate, spotted Lisa and immediately began to apologize. "I'm so sorry. My brother Pat was at my apartment when I got there. I had to talk with him for a few minutes. I lost track of time."

Lisa was very gracious. "Don't worry about it. Is he still there?"

"Nope. He left right after me."

"Why didn't you invite him down for a swim? I'd like to meet him. Which brother is it? Didn't you say you had two brothers?" She seemed genuinely interested.

"He has a long drive ahead of him. He's headed back home to Dunnellon tonight. Pat's my older brother. He and his family just bought a house there."

"Isn't that north of Tampa?"

"Yeah. Seems like a nice area. The only thing is it's near the nuclear plant, within about twenty-five or so miles I think." Joe wasn't afraid of nuclear power plants. He just didn't think that property values would hold up well in that area. One accident somewhere in the world and home prices in the vicinity of every power plant in the country would plunge. That's what he believed anyway.

"So he's married? Any children? You have nieces and

nephews?"

"I have one niece, Anna, and one nephew, Sean. Sean's about five, I guess. Anna might be three now. I can't remember her birthday but it's coming up soon." Joe's smile widened as he talked about his niece and nephew. "They're both the cutest kids. They take after their Uncle Joe." Joe and Lisa moved towards one of the lounge chairs and took off their shirts that covered their suits. Joe's was still covered in sweat since he had no time to shower and change. Lisa looked fresh as a morning flower. That didn't get passed Joe. He walked over to the shower, stood aside and turned the handle until the shower sprayed a pretty good volume spray. He jumped under it and did a quick rinse. The water was still warm from being heated earlier in the day. He released the handle shutting off the spray, shook his head and wiped his face with his hands.

Lisa didn't miss a single muscle ripple. They moved into the pool using the steps, following the pool rules of 'No Diving' because there was 'No Lifeguard on Duty' and they would of course 'Swim at *their* own Risk.'

There was an emergency phone station in case someone broke the rules and dove straight into the pool wall and broke their neck. But as careful adults, that didn't happen. The smiles were bright, the conversation cordial. Joe and Lisa chatted a bit then Lisa mentioned the bet. They started at the far wall.

Joe said, "Ready? Go!"

And the race began. It was quite competitive for about the first twenty five laps. Joe was pacing himself for about the first twenty, but Lisa appeared to swim free and easy, with little apparent effort. At lap 32, Lisa was nearly a full lap ahead. Joe started to push himself to catch up. In order to drive himself, he thought about the plan and how he and Pat needed to be very cautious with the out of place killing of Randy Farley. His hate and anger made him push even harder and he began to gain on Lisa, even without knowing it. He was concentrating on other things now. When he was nearly even with her, she kicked it in gear herself. Heading into the last lap, they were neck and neck. Lisa made one final push and reached just before Joe. To her surprise, Joe turned and kicked off the wall and headed back for another lap. She hopped up on the edge of the pool and sat, catching her breath while watching Joe as he made the opposite turn and headed back her way. She saw the expression on his face as he turned for a breath. He was really pushing even though the race was over. As he reached for the wall, Lisa put her hand down so his hand touched hers instead of the wall. He stopped abruptly and stood upright and looked at her with a shocked expression.

"I'm sorry. I didn't mean to startle you."

Joe continued to take deep breaths while he regained his composure.

"Are you okay? You really push yourself too hard when you work out. I promise I won't make you take me anywhere expensive for dinner." She smiled and said, "I won you know."

Joe could do nothing but smile when she told him this. He'd obviously lost count of his laps. She must have won, but it didn't matter to Joe. He'd have flown her to Alaska for Snow Crab if she'd wanted. He was head over heels. His heart was pounding in his chest, partly from the swim in the pool, but mostly from swimming in a sea of love.

Chapter 27

When Pat pulled into his driveway at 11:30 PM, he was exhausted, not from any physical activity, but from a mental workout. His mind had been racing for days, ever since the last time he spoke with his loving wife. *How could I be such an idiot? I have really got to get it together. Diane is going to shoot me as soon as I get out of the car. I just know it.*

He turned off the headlights and engine. He thought about turning the lights off down the block and cutting the engine as he approached his drive but that would never work. His luck, with all the power steering and power brakes off, he'd plow into the house; Diane's new house. If he thought he was in trouble now, he'd really be in deep dung then.

As he got out and closed the car door, the front door of the house opened. Diane started walking towards him but then broke into a trot. They met midway between the car and the house, tears streaming from both of their eyes. The kisses came hard and fast. Pat tried to push her away to say he was sorry, but Diane would have none of it. She only held him tighter and kissed him harder. This went on for over five minutes before they finally came up for air and hard looks into each other's eyes. They each could see deep love for one another. But Pat could see something else in Diane's glossy eyes. He saw the hurt that he'd inflicted. Her eyes showed dark rings where she'd spent many hours crying.

"I will never do this to you and our children again. You have my word."

"Just come in the house, you big jerk. Your kids want to see you." She wiped away tears with the back of her robe sleeve, turned, stood at his side and grabbed him around the waist as they made their way back to the house. Sean met his mom and dad at the door with a big, "Daddy!! You're home!" Anna followed her big brother and yelled, "Daddy!" They both hugged their dad and kissed him with sloppy, wet lips. Pat's eyes welled up again as his kids gave him a hero's welcome, a welcome he knew he didn't deserve.

After Sean and Anna were tucked into their beds, content with the knowledge that their dad was finally home, Pat and Diane sat down in the family room. The moment of reckoning was at hand. Diane didn't know what to expect but she knew something big was coming. Pat took a deep breath, looked around the room, at the rosebud texture of the ceiling. The new wall paper that Diane had put up was just beautiful and matched the curtains perfectly. She had a knack for design that rivaled many professionals. The fireplace looked ready for lighting but in the Florida heat, even at night this time of year, there was no need for a fire. Besides, things were getting pretty hot under Pat's collar already. He was in the hot seat and had a lot of explaining to do.

"Take your time, honey. I know you're nervous but there's nothing to worry about. I love you and we'll get past this...this...whatever it is."

I wish I could tell you everything, Pat thought. *That would make things so much easier on me. But I'm sure it would destroy you. And I can't do that.*

"Well, I know you met Brian. He came to see me at the grove." There. The first truth is out there, and she hasn't killed me yet. But the night was long, and it stretched into morning. Neither of them had to go to work, so no time like the present. Pat spilled his guts about almost everything. He told her about the grove and the nursery. He told her about the money that they made in both and how they skimmed cash and paid far less taxes than they should have. He told her about how their friends started to turn on them. What he didn't do was tell her that he dealt drugs and that's where the 'real money' came from.

"So how much are we really worth?"

"My best guess is about one and three quarters million. Give or take a hundred grand."

Diane's jaw dropped, her eyes were as wide as a cat's on a dark night. "And you bought me this shack?!" Pat didn't know what to say to that. She followed up with, "I'm only kidding, you big dope. I love this house. But almost two million dollars? Where is it?"

"Mostly in stocks, bonds and treasury bills. There is some cash. I've been sending Mom and Dad money for years, about $20,000 per year. Joe and Mike send cash to them too. Their doing well, what with Social Security and that little stipend that we send them. If you'd like we can do that with your folks, too. I mean there's plenty of money. We won't have to worry in our old age."

Diane was still in awe. Pat was smiling a little, but he was still trying to keep his head and keep to the script.

Diane's thoughts turned to Pat's friend, Brian. "He's a pretty crazy looking character. Is he typical of the guys you hung around with back then?"

"Who, Brian? He's a cream puff; a nice guy. He's actually kind of a computer geek. He's been making music since I've known him. Man, can he play a guitar. I've never heard anyone in person or on record that can make the sounds he makes. He's about to land a record deal, he may have signed already as a matter of fact. Brian's pretty wild on stage but he's kind of an introvert in social situations. I think he lets out all of this inner trapped emotion when he's playing in front of a crowd. We should go see him sometime. You'd be impressed."

They sat quietly for a few minutes. Then Diane said, "Sweetie, we have to work on ways to get you to relax. You are so tensed up, and there's no reason for it that I can see. Just tell me what I can do to help."

All sorts of lewd and tawdry scenes went through Pat's brain in an instant but he figured that now was not the time for a crude joke. "You're right. I guess I got all tied up in having to make a living when I got out of the service. I guess I just didn't want to lie around and not do anything for the rest of my life."

Things weren't adding up for Diane. Why would Pat join the Navy if he was a millionaire and why would Joe put himself in harm's way in the Marines? And where was their brother Mike? Diane hadn't even met him yet. She was too curious to hold back any longer. "Pat, why did you join the Navy? You're a rich man. Why would any millionaire join the military? And why did Joe join the Marines? And when can I meet Mike?"

Pat was ready for the first two but he wasn't ready for the last. "I just wanted to give something back to this great country and since I'd come by much of it by evading taxes, I felt that I owed something. I wanted to make amends without facing prison. I think I'm even with Uncle Sam. Joe and I talked about it, and that's what we decided to do." He had to pause and think a moment before he went on. "Mike is another story. He is emotionally crushed. You see, when we lived outside of Apopka, he married a girl from Pennsylvania. Julie Mallernee. She was a great girl, really outgoing and friendly. She smiled all the time." This is where things got a little touchy, because the truth came real close to the big lie about dealing dope. "About two weeks after they were married, Julie went to the grocery store and came home alone. Mike was at the greenhouses. While she was at the store, four guys broke into their house. When she got home, she was putting stuff away and these guys got hold of her. They raped her repeatedly and beat her to death. Part of it was on tape. These bastards took the time to act as if it were a game. They even taunted Mike, Joe and me. You see, we knew these guys. They were supposedly our friends." As Pat was talking about this, his gaze turned towards the fireplace, his face getting red, and his eyes glazing over, teeth clenching. "The tape clearly showed at least one of the bastard's faces and enough of one other to get a description. We knew who the other two were by the voices on the tape. The tape never made it to trial. It was lost or destroyed. All four guys walked. They're still walking free today, except one who was found dead the other day."

"These guys were your friends? Do they live around here?"

"Yep. We haven't seen them in years though," he lied. "They're known to lots of folks in the area though. Mike has never been the same. It's like his heart and soul were ripped from him. I've tried to talk with him about getting on with his life but he's a broken man." The sadness in Pat's eyes was profound. It was as if he were trying to see the world through Mike's eyes.

Diane put her hand on her husband's cheek and turned his face towards hers. "You're not Mike. You can't live his life. If he's to get over this, he has to do it himself. All we can do is pray for him and hope that he can someday find himself. You know his wife wouldn't want him to live his whole life feeling guilty for not being there for her. He couldn't have known and he couldn't possibly have been there 24 hours a day."

"You're right, but I still can't help feeling that we should have done something to help put those guys away or something to prevent it in the first place. That's one reason why we have the alarm system here. I never wanted you to hear this story. Now if you ever meet Mike, this will be the first thing that you think about. I didn't want that."

"Chances are he'll break out of it. I hope I can meet him and I hope the circumstances are better. I can't believe that you've carried this around with you all this time and never told me."

Diane and Pat talked on for a few more hours. They made their way to the bedroom where their lovemaking was steeped in emotion. Their souls were bared to each other, Diane one hundred percent, Pat about eighty-five. The remaining fifteen percent he would take to his grave.

***

Ginny and Brian were on their first real date. They ate at a nice, quiet restaurant in Lakeland. It was a pretty good drive but Brian wanted to get away from Orlando. He also didn't want anyone he knew to interrupt his first real romantic evening with his new woman-friend. The lights were kept low and the background music was quiet, almost inaudible. There were real foliage plants everywhere and the décor was upscale. Brian wore a sport coat and tie with his Dockers. He had to buy them and wash them that morning. They were the first pair of pants that he owned that weren't blue denim. It was also the first sport coat he'd owned since his First Communion back at St. Mary's in Front Royal,

Virginia. When he called he'd asked if a coat and tie were required. His inquiry was followed on the other end by a chuckle and a short "Yes sir." *I guess I've got a lot to learn about class*, he thought to himself.

Ginny was radiant, her smile beaming from ear to ear. Her dark brown hair hung loose round her shoulders. She wore light make-up and a touch of perfume, she said it was Charlie. Brian could care less but he figured he'd better start paying attention to these details if he wanted to impress her. She wore nice slacks and a loose-fitting beige blouse that complimented her eyes. She was dying to hear Brian's news. He'd said he'd tell her over dinner, and they'd just ordered drinks, so she was anxious. She had an idea that he was on his way to stardom.

"Ginny, I have some pretty good news and some pretty great news." She leaned even closer to him across the table. "Yesterday, I signed a contract with Atlantic Records and..." Brian didn't get the next words out because Ginny leapt out of her seat, screaming "yes, yes, yes" and gave him a full deep kiss on the lips. She then alternated with kisses and hugs for over a full minute. The crowd nearest to them started to clap, assuming that he'd just proposed or something equally serious. When she finally gained her composure again, and moved back to her seat, Brian said, "Wow. I hope my other news gets that kind of reaction." He reached in his pocket and pulled out a wrapped box. It looked about the size of a pen and pencil set, but thicker. "This is for you. I want you to know how I feel about you. So, this is just a symbol of...my love. Ginny, I think I'm in love with you."

Ginny's smile grew even wider, but now her eyes filled with tears. She took the box and set it on the table without opening it. She again moved out of her seat to Brian, this time more slowly, deliberately and again kissed him hard on the lips. She didn't linger quite as long this time but looked Brian straight in the eyes and said, "I'm feeling the same way about you, Mr. Purcer. I love you. I think I knew it from the first time we met."

Brian was speechless. After she sat back down, he tried to tell her to open her present, but he had such a frog in his throat, he had to get a drink of water to clear it. Without another word, Ginny unwrapped and opened the box and laid eyes on the most beautiful diamond bracelet that she'd ever seen. It must have cost several thousand dollars. Ginny knew it was part of his signing bonus with the record company. "You didn't have to do this to win my heart. You had it already."

"I'm not taking it back."

"You're damn right you're not," Ginny said with a smile. Brian smiled back and thought to himself that he was one lucky guy these last two days.

After dinner, Brian asked Ginny if she'd like to go dancing or if there was anything else that she'd like to do. And there was. It involved a quiet hotel room and a bottle of wine. So Brian and Ginny checked into the Gaylord Palms on the way back to Orlando and got to know each other much better, well into the next afternoon.

Chapter 28

Jamie went to Jason Roberts' home. He was confused about what to do next for the first time in his professional drug-dealing career. He had to admit to himself that he was scared. Buddy Mahaffey escorted Jamie into a room off the main entrance to his home. It appeared to be an office but was more like an interrogation room. There was a door on the opposite side of the room from where Jamie entered. There was a nice oak table, like a dining table in the middle of the room with four chairs, two on each side. There were no chairs on the ends. It was set up as if there was to be a negotiation of some sort. The only light in the room hung low over the table so that the room itself had dark shadows at eye level when standing. On one wall was a mirror about two feet tall by one foot wide. It had a carved oak frame with unlit candles on each side. He waited in the room for what seemed like an hour, it really was only sixteen minutes. Then, Phil Daniels, Buddy Mahaffey and Jason Roberts entered through the far door. Buddy moved behind Jamie and stood directly in front of the door where Jamie entered. Gone was Jamie's smart mouth and attitude.

"Jamie, why are you here? I thought that you didn't need no faggot-Yankee. I heard that you were the king of this organization."

"I was just..."

Jamie didn't get another word out of his mouth as Jason Roberts was all over Jamie. "You shut your fucking mouth and listen. And I mean keep it shut. Your friends, my employees are being systematically hunted and killed by some lunatic out there and we're going to get to the bottom of it. I can't afford to lose anyone else, even the likes of you. You are going to learn to keep your mouth shut and take orders and work within the organization, not against it. Do you hear and understand me?!"

Jamie stammered for a second too long for Mr. Roberts' liking. He nodded to Buddy who grabbed Jamie by the scruff of the neck, stood him up out of his chair and threw him against the wall to Jamie's left. Before Jamie could react, Buddy had bitch-slapped him with his open palm three quick times in succession. Then he stopped and just stood in front of Jamie with his arms calmly at his side.

The blood from his nose streamed down past his lip onto his chin and started to drip to the floor. Jamie wasn't about to look scared in front of these guys. But he didn't protest or threaten. With the events of the past week, he was starting to feel mortal and vulnerable. He stared back into Buddy's eyes. He sure wasn't going to challenge Buddy and Buddy was between him, Phil Daniels and Jason Roberts. He calmed down and wiped the blood from his nose with the back of his hand. Phil tossed him a hand towel that he pulled from his back pocket. Apparently they'd planned that there would be some blood drawn. At least the floor wasn't covered in plastic where he stood, so he figured that he'd be walking out of here alive.

"Sit down Jamie." Jason's voice was calm now. "We've got people looking into Danny Vallero's and Donnie Lee's shooting. Donnie's in the hospital in critical condition. He's out of commission for some time. We thought that you might have had something to do with it at first, but we know where you were during the shoot."

"I can't believe that you think..." he started to protest loudly, but Jason held up his hand in a gesture to stop. Jamie did so, taking a sideways glance at Buddy, who was sitting next to him now.

"It doesn't matter what you think or I think or what Phil thinks. Danny is dead and Donnie's no good to us. That also means that we have to keep a close eye on Bobby. They are particularly close. If Bobby cracks, he knows too much to be left alone out there. So, we're changing the lineup a little." He said this as if it were a baseball game, the team was in a slump, and changing the lineup would shake up the offense. "You're going to have to bring the new guy, Bill Grimes, up to speed fast. We want you to teach him the ropes on how we run things around here. We want you to teach him the Roberts' way, not the Watkins way. Understand Jamie?"

"Yes sir. I know Bill, not too bright, but he can learn with the right teacher and I'm your guy." Phil and Buddy looked at each other in an expression that begged the question, *Who is this guy? The real Jamie Watkins would have thrown a fit.* "When do we get started?'

"Tonight is still on. Take Bill and get the job done. It's a fifty-fifty split now. You and Bill."

Jamie smiled to himself. It's what he wanted all along. He was growing tired of Donnie Lee and Bobby anyway.

"I'm on it, Mr. Roberts. Sir, I am sorry for the hot-headed remarks. It won't happen again."

"I know that, Jamie. 'Cause if it does, you'll be washing up in Lake Apopka as alligator shit."

***

Brian went in to the *Star* to give his notice and let them know that he didn't plan to return for the remaining two weeks. He decided he'd take his two weeks in vacation time instead. So he planned to walk in, give notice, thank them for the years of experience that he had loading trucks and basically working his ass off for peanuts. He really wanted to tell them that they were a bunch of scum, making folks work that hard for nothing, but he figured it wasn't worth the time. And besides, it really hadn't been all that bad. He'd made a living, been able to pay the bills and actually saved a few thousand bucks, mainly because he lived like a pauper. But that was over now. He'd already made his first big expenditure; a beautiful bracelet for his girl. She'd thanked him in ways he couldn't even talk about without getting flush in the cheeks.

When he walked through the employee's entrance at the *Sentinel Star*, everyone stopped what they were doing and turned to face Brian. Machinery was stopped, forklifts parked and engines shut down. You could smell the propane fumes from the forklifts and the smell of freshly printed papers. One of the guys at the loading dock called out, "Hey boss, look who's here." Danny Mills came out of the foreman's office at the other side of the big loading area where the *Sentinel Star* began its journey all over central Florida.

He said to no one in particular, "Well, well. Looky who's here? Brian Purcer, rock stud of the millennium. Listen Brian, all I got to say to you is..." and he paused. "Con-fricking-gratulations." The entire crew broke out into applause, whistles, and chants of "Brian, Brian, Brian." Danny's administrative assistant, Cindy, rolled out a table with a cake. A couple of the guys carried two boxes, gift wrapped in some loud colors. Brian made his way across the warehouse to the table and got a big hug and kiss from Cindy. He received handshakes and a few loose hugs from his former coworkers. All in all, it was a tough way to end a career. He hadn't expected to receive such a friendly send off. He was grateful and humbled by the experience.

Brian made a point to shake each man and woman's hand and thank them for their kind words. Finally, he met Danny Mills in his office. Danny thanked Brian for his dedication, leadership, loyalty and hard work. He wished Brian well and told him if he ever needed to come back, he was certainly welcome, "but I don't expect to see your face anywhere but on CDs and billboards. Maybe I'll watch *MTV* on occasion just to see you hammering out the tunes." There was an awkward pause, then Danny said, "Good luck and good fortune, Brian. I know you'll make it. You know we'll buy your stuff, if nothing else, just to brag that we know you." His smile broadened.

Brian reached out his hand for one last shake. Smiling, he turned and walked out of the *Sentinel Star* for the last time. When he got to his mini-van, he gave the *Star* building one last look, and drove away. He didn't look into his rear view mirror, not even once.

Chapter 29

Ray Krebs was in early. The Sheriff's office was nearly empty. Most of the night shift was either out on patrol or had gathered in the briefing room for early morning chit chat. Ray made his way to the Homicide section of the office and hung out around Al Poreczwski's desk. He was leafing through the files on Al's desk when Al's voice came out of nowhere. "Hey Ray. Anything I can interest you in? We don't see you Vice guys down this way much."

"Hey Al. I didn't think that you were in yet."

"In yet? I haven't gone home yet. We had a rough night last night. Another shooting with a high powered rifle. Last I heard, the guy was in ICU. Another head shot. What can I do for you?"

Ray thought for a second. He hadn't planned to be caught snooping so he had to think fast. "I was hoping you had that Vallero file on your desk. Remember I told you that one of the guys squealed and gave us Danny's name. Well, we'd been watching Danny off and on for a while. He was apparently getting his stuff from out of state and we wanted to have some information in case the Feds popped in on us. We have a general idea where he was going for his stash but we're not sure. We don't want to look like dunces in front of the fibbies."

"Well we're going to have to hang on to that file. We have a new file now, actually two new ones. You know a guy by the name of Randy Farley was whacked the other night. Drowned in Jack Daniels."

"What? You mean alcohol poisoning?"

"No, I mean drowned. Someone wasted a full bottle of Black Jack on this guy. He was already passed out from a hard night of drinking. Somebody sat on top of him and forced the neck of a JD bottle down his throat. Every time he tried to breath, he sucked in Jack. He did this until he literally drowned. I told you, a waste of a good bottle."

"Vicious. What's the connection to Danny Vallero?"

"Turns out these two guys were at the *Rock* the other night at the same time. There was a scuffle. Danny was involved, Randy wasn't, but they were around the same group of guys. Guy named Brian Purcer, member of the band that was playing that night, and Danny V got into a shoving match over a chick. Her name escapes me, but I have it written down. Anyway Danny boy leaves without his date, the chick they were scuffling over. She and Brian end up together. I guess they knew each other from before that night. We questioned Randy about the scuffle and he admitted he knew Danny and a few others at the bar. He wanted to stay out of the limelight because he's on probation. That may be why he was so cooperative. Turns out that Danny threatened Brian. But he said Danny was a hothead and probably didn't have the gonads to follow through. All mouth, Randy said."

Ray thought for a second then replied, "Someone had the sack. You said there were two new ones. What's the other?"

"Guy named Donnie Lee Lester. He's a quiet guy. No sheet on him but word on the street is that he was dealing in weight. We can't find any employment records on the guy and he was living well. We found a safe full of cash at his home, to the tune of several hundred thousand dollars. That's a lotta coin to have sitting around. He must have been into something big. You guys should check your files on him. See if there was any surveillance history or record of bad guy association. You might get lucky. I gotta tell you, I've got a bad feeling about this. You might also want to check out the guy that found him. Roberto Acquino. He was crying like a baby when we got to Donnie's house. Was mumbling something about 'getting out too late.' He may be our prize. We're gonna try to shake him down a bit, see what falls out."

"When are you planning to bring him in?"

"Sometime this afternoon. Captain wants us to get some

rest first. We have some UC guys watching his movements until we get back in later today. We'll have him hauled in and run him through the wringer. If there's something there, we'll get it out of him. He seemed pretty fragile. By the way, last we heard, Donnie was in a coma. He might be dead by now."

"Let me know if you need any help. We Vice guys like that shit."

Ray smiled the biggest fake smile he could muster. He knew that he had to get to Bobby first and get him out of sight. Jason Roberts couldn't afford to have Bobby Acquino blabbing his mouth to the Orange County Sheriff. Mr. Roberts would be out of business but only after Ray was six feet under. He had to work fast especially if Donnie was dead. Bobby would break down and spill his guts to the first compassionate ear he could find. Then he'd repeat every word to the Orange County Sheriff's Department.

***

Jamie Watkins and Bill Grimes finished supervising the exchange of dope. They'd already received their cash and were pleased at the take, especially Bill. He'd hit the big-time. If this was his only deal, his life was fulfilled. He figured he could flash the cash in front of Karen's nose and she'd be all over him like a cheap suit. He was *the man.*

This was old hat to Jamie. He was aggravated that he had to even be here. He figured that Jason Roberts should just wire his bank account money whenever he wanted it. He also was still stinging from his punishment and he was already formulating a plan to strike back. His remorsefulness didn't last long at all. Working with Bill Grimes was an insult at best. This guy was a blithering idiot and Jamie had just about had enough. Now that the exchange was complete he was ready to get the hell away from Bill.

"Billy boy, let's wrap this up. I've got to get out of here. I'll call you when ole Mr. Roberts needs us again. It won't be long so don't get too comfy. We do this usually two to three times a week."

Jamie thought that Bill was going to wet himself. He

literally jumped up and down with excitement. Jamie was disgusted. He couldn't believe his eyes, a grown man acting like this. He grabbed Bill by the arm and walked him around the back side of his Suburban. When they were out of sight of the other guys he said sternly, "You fucking settle down, you fucking idiot. Do you want to get us killed? This is serious business! You can't think and act like some kind of ten-year-old. You act like that again in front of these guys or any other customer, I'll kick your ass! You got that?"

It was like hitting a puppy with the newspaper. Bill hung his head and apologized. He made some excuse about never having done a deal like this before. He said to Jamie, "The most dope I ever moved before was half a pound back when Pat McKinney and I hung out."

Jamie glared at Bill at the sound of Pat McKinney's name. "You ever talk about that little faggot-punk again, and I'll beat your fucking brains in. When are you and little Bobby Acquino going to get over them McKinney boys? Those chicken-assed punks are gone. We scared them the hell out of town. Now forget them!"

"Well, I talked to Al Michaels last week and he said that Pat might be back in town. He was in the Navy for about six years. He's out now."

"So fucking what? They won't dare come around here. Now take off and don't call me, I'll call you." Without another word, Jamie headed to his Suburban and peeled out of the warehouse. *What a fuckin' moron. And this is what I get for the job that I do.* Jamie was getting more and more pissed as he drove back towards rural Apopka from the back roads around Lake Jem. Well, at least he had a few bucks in his wallet, and a ton of cash in the duffle bag. Even with all his hate for everyone around him, he was feeling pretty good.

***

Donnie Lee Lester was barely alive in intensive care at Orlando Regional Medical Center. Bobby learned where Donnie Lee was and kept watch in the hall outside the ICU. He was praying constantly. He asked God for forgiveness for his sins and the sins of Donnie Lee. He knew that Donnie was not a Christian so he prayed intently for the Lord to forgive him his sins and for his ignorance of God and His religion. Bobby had called his pastor and requested that he say a Mass for Donnie in the morning. He also mentioned that it was worth a $20,000 donation that would show up in the collection tomorrow. Father Keifer had to struggle to contain his excitement at this very generous donation. He promised Bobby that he would be up to see his friend first thing in the morning and that he would pray with Bobby and hear his confession. It was the least he could do.

Nurses were routinely in and out of Donnie's room but they spent little time checking the IV drip and making sure that whatever drugs and chemicals were being fed into his body were in good supply. They marked on his chart and left, heading to the next patient. Bobby was just getting used to seeing the same faces when a shift change occurred. New faces were now making the same rounds, checking the vitals of patients and getting familiar with the names. The head nurse on the floor learned that Bobby was concerned about Donnie Lee. She went to him, put a soft hand on his shoulder, and assured him that they would do everything that they could for him. She recommended that he get some rest and that he might be more comfortable in the lounge. They had couches where he could spread out, since he was the only one left around the ICU. They didn't mind unless security came up and requested that he leave. They were pretty lax with visiting rules for ICU as long as visitors stayed out of the way.

Bobby thanked her but said that he'd stay there in sight of his room, at least when the big entry doors to ICU opened. He must have dozed off because he was startled out of his sleep by nurses running past him through the big doors and into Donnie Lee's room. There was some kind of alarm going off, making a gong sound. At first he thought he was dreaming, but he quickly came to realize that his friend was under duress. The nurses were talking back and forth. One nurse appeared to take charge and was giving very deliberate orders almost in a methodical, mechanical way. She told one nurse to get Dr. Stein on the phone.

What time was it, Bobby thought. 1:12 according to the clock at the nurse's station. Bobby stood and looked into the ICU, listening as they worked to save his friend. The on-duty resident came into the ICU, asked a few questions, and said to the nurses, "Okay, call it 1:14. I'm sorry everyone, you did what you could. Let's get everything in order."

And that was it. Donnie Lee Lester was gone. He didn't know God. He hadn't given a confession to a priest. He hadn't been sorry for his actions. He was knocking on hell's door. Bobby felt sorry for his friend but he made up his mind that he would not be joining his dear friend. He wanted no part of wailing and gnashing of teeth. He would see Father Keifer in the morning and confess everything.

***

Bill Grimes was feeling pretty good. He also had some bucks in his wallet. He had more cash than he'd ever seen before in his life. He was headed to see his woman. Karen had to be impressed with him now. He thought about how much cash they made tonight and started doing the math. He was going to be a millionaire within two years, maybe less. He headed through Apopka to the ABC Lounge on State Route 436 where he used to hang out. He figured that he could share a drink with some of his old buddies. Maybe he'd buy a round just to show them that he was doing great and that he didn't care what they thought about him.

When he got to the bar at 1:30 AM, the fluorescent lights in the package store were blazing, the ABC sign was inviting, and he was in the mood. He parked his car in the back lot and entered the dark, smoke-filled bar. There were about two dozen people in the Lounge this evening, not unusual for this time of night. A few were already well lit, others were just getting started. Bill recognized Bo Williams and Roger Pittman. They were sitting at the bar watching a particularly good looking young lady play pool. She looked good, but she shot terrible pool. She was giggling a lot, too. Bill figured that she'd been here a while and was probably getting free drinks from anyone who thought that they had a chance to get into those tight pants.

"Hey Bo, Roger! How are you guys doing?" Bill was in a good mood, they could see. He had that *I know something that you don't* look on his face. They knew Bill too well and they figured that it would be easy getting the full story out of him. It might not even take a few drinks.

Roger started first. "Bill, how the hell are you? We haven't seen you in ages. What have you been up to?"

"Aw, nothing," Bill replied with his big smile. The bartender came over and took Bill's order, Heineken. Roger and Bo both took note. Bill was a Miller beer drinker. He never strayed because 'foreign beer was too damned expensive.' They both wondered what had changed to where it was now affordable.

"Billy Boy, why are you drinking that stuff? You're so cheap your asshole squeaks when you walk, now you're buying $4.00-a-bottle beer? Did you win the Lotto or something?"

"Nope. I just like this beer." In truth, Bill hated the strong taste of Heineken. He just wanted to look like he had class and money to these guys. "You guys want one? I'm buying."

"Damn straight. This is a night to remember. Billy Grimes is buying someone else a beer." Bo yelled to Eddie, the bartender to send down two more Heini's and put it on Bill's tab. Eddie looked to Bill for approval.

Bill said, "Hell yeah. And I'm buying a round for everyone here."

Everyone in the bar shouted some cheer or shout of approval. All of a sudden, everyone was Bill's friend, everyone except Ray Krebs and one other guy that nobody seemed to know. Ray had been sitting at the bar when Bill commenced to run his mouth. He thought that he was talking in a low voice, but his voice carried. Ray listened to Bill explain every detail of the deal, though the dollar amounts were inflated. He even bragged that he had to take Bobby Acquino's place because Bobby couldn't handle it. "Too much pressure." He said that Bobby was probably at the 'St. Francis I'm a sissy' church down the road right now.

Ray was thinking to himself, *What a loser. Mr. Roberts is going to blow up.* But his immediate job was to gather information. He'd followed Bill into the bar to see if anyone was following him. He shook his head and continued to sip his beer.

The other guy was at the other end of the bar listening, too. He caught one name that grabbed his attention. Jamie Watkins. He turned towards Bill and listened more intently. As he listened, he watched other folks around the bar. Many people were listening. He even noticed one guy walk out of the bar shortly after Bill had announced how much money his take was. He must have figured that the money was still in Bill's car because he hadn't taken it into the bar. He followed the patron out into the parking lot and watched as the guy actually tried to break into Bill's car. He walked over to the guy and simply said, "Looking for a quick score?"

The guy turned and looked into his face and saw that he should just leave, and he did. After the patron was gone, he went back into the bar and ordered another beer. He even had Eddie put it on Bill's tab. When Eddie dropped it off, he shouted down to Bill and said, "Thanks again," and waved the bottle in his direction.

Bill looked his way and replied, "Sure. What's your name?"

"They call me Radar."

Bill simply raised his bottle to Radar and took another long drink of the expensive, awful tasting beer.

Ray took note of Radar. There was something about this guy that didn't fit in here. He was a bit dark skinned, not black, but not white. He may have been mixed or even middle-eastern. But he had Caucasian features and spoke pretty well with a deep southern drawl. Radar had a slightly menacing look. Nothing too obvious. He wasn't looking for a fight. He was just enjoying his free beer.

The gal at the pool table dropped her cue and groaned. She just lost again. The guys at the table were through playing with her, and wanted a real match so they asked if anyone wanted to play. Radar replied that he did. The boys racked them and Radar broke. He let loose a powerful shot and after that, pretty well cleaned their clocks. He played a few more for money and won but bought the losers beers for their troubles. Bill asked if he'd like to play him and Radar turned, and said, "Sure." Bill didn't realize that he was playing for his life. Radar had decided if Bill won, he'd let him live for another day. If Bill lost, well, the plan was in motion. It had to be completed.

Radar said to Bill, "Want to put $500 on this one? Y'all got the big bucks and all."

Bill was always a sucker for a bet and he figured he could make more money tonight. "Sure, man. But let me see your money first."

Radar took out $500 of the money that he lifted from the duffle bag in Bill's car. You want someone to hold it?" Roger Pittman spoke up, "I'll hold it."

Ray headed out of the bar at the beginning of the match. He could care less about the outcome. He was more interested in Bobby Acquino so he headed to St. Francis of Assisi Catholic Church to see if Bobby would show.

Bill lost. Radar shook his head after leaving the bar with Bill's $1000 and a duffle bag full of the rest of his take that night. It didn't matter. He wouldn't need it where he was headed.

Chapter 30

Bobby Acquino headed towards St. Francis of Assisi Catholic Church. He had to get a grip on his emotions. He'd been so distraught that he could hardly drive, crying like a baby off and on for about an hour. He knew that he had to get out of this business or he was a dead man. It was 2:20 AM and he needed to talk. But who could he talk with except God? He wasn't married. His brother was in prison. If he told his parents, what would they think of him? He was their last hope for a good, God fearing child. Hearing all this would crush them and he didn't want to disturb them at this hour. No sense laying this burden on them. That would be so unfair. It was in the scriptures that you should give your burdens to God and he would bear them for you. As he approached the church, he felt like he needed a drink. He drove by the church and headed for the ABC lounge south of Apopka where, unbeknownst to Bobby, a life or death pool match had just completed.

When Bobby pulled into the lot, Bill Grimes was just leaving the bar, as were a number of other patrons. Even in the dim-lighted parking lot Bobby recognized Bill. He pulled up next to him, rolled down his window and asked in a shaken voice, "Hey Bill, is the bar still open?"

Bill looked at Bobby and could see that he was distraught. He replied that they could probably get back inside in time for a drink. He even offered to buy, and they headed back in. Radar saw them enter as he exited. He had business to take care of before his night was done. He went to his car in a dark corner of the lot, fired up his battery powered laptop computer and typed out three notes. He printed all three, folded them into nice, neat squares and set them aside. He next went to the pay phone at the front of the store and called Jamie Watkins' number. Jamie wasn't home yet so he left a message on his answering machine. "Meet me, Bobby and Bill at the vault on Kelly Park Drive at 11:00 AM. We have business. Don't be late." He knew that Jamie didn't recognize his voice because he'd never heard it before. He also knew that Jamie would be there. The vault had some history for Jamie and his buddies. This was where their current business started. This was where the McKinneys helped them establish their clientele. This was also where their friendship started to unravel and hate replaced all of the good times.

Ray Krebs watched Radar's movements from his car. *Who is this guy and what is he up to? He was trying to cover his interest in Billy boy but he couldn't hide it from everyone. He was leaning towards Bill every time he said anything about the deal. Was he DEA? Were the Feds watching Jason and his operation? Man this could get real ugly.* Ray thought that he'd better get on the phone to Mr. Roberts and let him know what was going down here. Just as he was about to leave his car and head for the pay phone, Jamie Watkins pulled up in his oversized suburban, complete with its loud paint job and extra lights on the roll bar. The tires were taller than most grown-ups. *So much for being inconspicuous.* He pulled across two parking spaces at an angle, killed the engine and headed for the Lounge door. Now Ray had a dilemma. Who should he follow, this Radar character or Mr. Roberts' team? He flipped a coin in his mind and tails won. He headed back into the ABC Liquor Lounge and prepared to spy on Jamie, Bill and Bobby. He walked in and sat at a table in the corner of the lounge. The music was loud and the bar was smoke-filled but Ray could see and hear every word. Between Jamie and Bill, there could have been a rock band on stage and he would have still heard the conversation.

Jamie walked right up to Bill where he and Bobby were sitting at the bar. He looked Bill in the eyes. They were just about face to face with Bill sitting on the bar stool and Jamie standing next to him.

"Billy Boy, I thought I told you to keep your big mouth shut. I hear you been spoutin' off about being a big-shot. You tryin' to get yourself arrested or worse yet, me? I'm gonna tell you one more time, you shut the fuck up and we'll get along fine. You'll make lots of money and live to tell your grandkids about it."

Bill stood and got his face closer to Jamie. Only about a foot separated the two and it appeared that they were itching to close that distance.

"You're a fine one to talk, Jamie. You...you get in here and can't stop yapping. I'm surprised the cops ain't in here taping this place all the time. There's probably a cop in here right now just waiting to see if you're going be here like usual, flapping your gums like some little school girl."

"About two more words out of your mouth and I'm gonna seal it with my fist."

Jamie inched ever closer. Finally, Bobby Acquino stood up and tried to get between the two. They both pushed Bobby away while still looking at each other. Eddie the bartender was getting a little nervous at this. He was about to lean over the bar when the bar room door opened and a guy shouted in, "Does anyone own a big suburban about the size of a house?"

"Yeah, that's mine. Who's asking?"

"Some guy just smashed your windshield with a ball bat and hauled ass."

As Jamie and the others were running out of the bar he yelled to the stranger, "Did you see which way he went?"

"Yeah, he was heading into town up 441. I didn't get the make..."

Jamie didn't hear the last words but headed straight for his suburban. It looked fine except the spider-webbed windshield. Jamie was hot. He started to jump in and try to find the chicken punk who did this but when he did, he noticed the note on the wiper blade. He stopped, retrieved the note and read, *Don't bother to follow, just meet me at the vault in the morning at 11:00 AM.* Jamie knew what this was all about. The McKinney brothers were back in town or they sent somebody to do their dirty work.

Bill yelled from his car, "Hey I got a note, too. It says

Don't bother to follow, just meet me at..."

"We know what it says, you fuckin' moron. It says the same thing mine does."

"Mine, too. We're as good as dead," Bobby chimed in.

"Shut up Bobby," Jamie shouted. "Maybe your pussy ass is going to just roll over and die but not me. I'm going to take care of business once and for all. No punk-assed McKinney is going to get to me before I get to them. Both of you get over here. We've got to do some planning. They want to meet tomorrow? We'll show them what they're up against. We're going to talk with Mr. Roberts. We're going to have some fun with those boys, just like we did with Mikey's little bitch. Remember that Bobby?"

Bobby's hair stood on the back of his neck. He hated Jamie worse now than ever, and he wasn't going to be part of any plan that Jamie came up with. His eyes watered from anger and his face was flush with heat. He was glad that the parking lot was dark because he didn't want anyone to see the tears in his eyes. He turned, got into his car and sped off. As he sped away, Jamie hurled insults in the direction of his car. Jamie turned to Bill and said, "Well, are you going to put your panties on and join Bobby, or are you going to stand up and fight like a man?"

"I'm with you, Jamie. Let's do it. What do we do now?"

"Let's take your car to Mr. Roberts place in the morning. You pick me up at 6:30 in the morning. We'll tell ol' Jason what happened here. We'll leave out all the bragging and that shit. He doesn't need to know any of that. Are you with me?"

"We're good, Jamie. We're good." Bill went to his car. Just as he was about to get in the driver's side, he yelled, "Hey, my back-pack's gone! That son-of-a-bitch stole my backpack! It had all my money! Oh shit!"

"Shut up, Bill! You just don't get it, do you? You have to stay cool even if bad shit happens. We'll get your money back and even if we don't there's a hell of a lot more where that came from. Just cool it. We'll see Jason in the morning and get everything back on track."

Hearing Jamie tell someone to keep quiet was the most ironic thing Ray Krebs had ever heard. He could only shake his head in amazement. These two had to be the loudest, most obnoxious people he'd ever heard in his life and now they were a team. He thought to himself that Mr. Roberts would do well to dump these two in the St. Johns River and start from scratch. If they had to go up against this Radar character, they'd probably lose. But who the hell was this guy? *I better get to the station and do a little research.* It would have to be in the morning. This day had already gone on far too long. He went to the pay phone and made his report to Phil Daniels who said he'd relay the information to Mr. Roberts first thing in the morning. When Ray said the name Radar, nothing clicked. But when he said that Jamie was yelling about the McKinney brothers, Phil said he remembered something. The light bulb in Phil's brain went on. *That's what this all is about. The McKinney's are back.*

Phil said to Ray, "Do you remember the Julie McKinney murder?"

At the other end of the phone, Ray cringed. He said, "Yeah, I think I remember it. Is this the same McKinneys?"

Phil confirmed that it was, but he didn't need to say a word. Ray already knew.

Chapter 31

Joe reached for her hand but he just couldn't quite reach her. He kept stretching and straining and he barely had a grip on the rail, he wasn't even sure what the rail was for or where he was. The area around him was misty; a blue haze. The smell in the air was burnt wood, metal and flesh. He couldn't hear her voice but he could read her lips, "help me, please, help me." The look on her face was sheer terror as she reached out trying to grab Joe's outstretched hand. He was looking beyond her now and he saw hands gripping her ankles, dragging her down into what looked like the trap door to a huge furnace. *They were trying to drag her into hell*, Joe thought. *Why can't I reach her?* It was Lisa! Then her face changed to Diane, finally to Mike's wife, Julie. Then Julie let out a blood curdling scream and plunged towards the fire. As she descended, her faced changed again to the other two women, over and over again.

Joe bolted to a sitting position as he awoke from the worst nightmare he'd had in ages. He rubbed his eyes and looked around his bedroom to orient himself. Everything was in order. He could calm down now. Where had he seen this door before? He closed his eyes again and tried hard to concentrate to bring back that image but all he could imagine was fire and the horrified look on his late sister-in-law's face. He hadn't been there for her and Mike, and for this he cursed himself every day. It was 5:25 AM, five minutes before his alarm clock would have sounded.

He was always up before the thing went off, but he normally didn't go through the mental torment of a nightmare first. He'd had bad dreams, but this one caused him to grit his teeth until his jaw was sore. His whole body was tense.

He hopped out of bed, stretched and headed for the

shower to try to wash the demons from his mind. He took a quick shower, dressed in running sweats and shoes, and headed out the door. He ran for ten miles on his usual route. When he got back to the apartment, he stretched, showered again, dressed and headed back out for a nice breakfast at a Crackers Diner. 'Good food at good prices' the sign read. As he entered the diner, he picked up the *Sentinel Star* and leafed through it to the sports. He read as he ate. Nothing too shocking there. But when he got to local law enforcement section, he put his fork down. The story line that caught his eye was 'Man Shot in His Home' with a sub line that read 'Donnie Lester Dead from Gunshot.' No coincidence here. Someone was executing their plan without them. He had to call Pat right away. No, it was too early. Pat had some making up to do. No matter how serious this was, it had to wait.

He had another thought. What if Mike couldn't stand it anymore and decided to do this himself? Did he know the plan? He was at the vault when he and Pat were first walking through the steps. But Mike left before the details were complete. Had they left details of the plan lying around? They couldn't have. They didn't write anything down except some ideas, none of which resembled the final plan. So far, the plan was being executed just as he and Pat detailed. He knew Pat had initiated the plan by hitting Danny, but what about the other two? Well there were only four left. *Maybe we should just sit back and watch the plan execute itself the rest of the way?*

Joe figured that if Mike was the man behind the killings, he had to be close. One way to eliminate him as a suspect was to call him. He couldn't possibly make it all the way in from Vegas, do the deed and get home. He decided to call Mike at 9:00 AM. That way, it wouldn't be too early out there and he could be relatively sure that he couldn't have hopped a flight back. Then Joe wondered if Pat was really implementing the plan, but was just playing dumb. But why would he. This is exactly what they planned to do. He'd have nothing to hide. Besides, about the time of the hit on Donnie Lee, Pat was at his apartment. Joe looked back down at what was left of his scrambled eggs and toast and decided he didn't have any appetite left. He dropped $6.00 on the table for his $3.50 breakfast and headed back to his apartment.

Things were getting weird. Joe didn't like weird.

***

Pat awoke to an empty bed. He looked around the room and didn't see Diane anywhere. But he did catch the smell of coffee coming from the kitchen and he heard her rooting around in the refrigerator. He was home and he felt great. He hopped out of bed, threw on his robe, and headed down the hall towards the kitchen. On the way through, he stopped by Anna's room and looked in at his still sleeping daughter. He opened the door across the hall and peered in at Sean. He was rolling over onto his side, eyes still shut. So Pat continued to the end of the hall and paused. He watched his beautiful wife, hard at work making a great breakfast. She had eggs and bacon, grits, pancakes, coffee and juice. She turned slowly as if she could sense him there.

"Are the kids still asleep?"

"Yes they are."

"Good." With that she walked slowly towards him and undid her robe as she moved closer. When she was within arm's reach, she opened the robe to show Pat a full frontal, eye-popping view. Pat looked her up and down and up again.

"Wow! That is one fine wake up call."

"Take a good look. If you thought last night was good, think about what tonight will bring. Maybe we can take the Redi-Whip to bed with us."

"Oh my! I can't wait for dessert."

Diane heard stirring from the hall and quickly closed and tied her robe. Anna was coming down the hall, rubbing the sleep from her eyes.

"Daddy!"

She ran to his arms and he scooped his daughter up, gave her a big hug and a kiss on the cheek. "How's my little girl doing? I missed you."

"I missed you, too Daddy. You aren't going to leave any

more are you?"

Pat's choked-up response almost got caught in his throat, but he managed to clear his voice and say with a smile, "No sweetheart. I'm not leaving you anymore. When I have to go to work I'll be with you right here in your heart. But I'm always going to come home to my little girl. I promise."

"Don't make promises that you can't keep there, cowboy," Diane whispered in his ear. Pat turned and looked at her and said with conviction, "I can and will keep this promise."

Sean was up now, hearing all the commotion in the kitchen. "Good morning Dad, Good morning Mom." He, too, wiped sleep from his eyes. "I want pancakes for breakfast and lots of bacon."

"Well you're in luck, we have lots of both."

With that, the McKinney family sat down to a normal family breakfast. A few minutes later Pat flipped through the pages of the *Sentinel Star* and came upon a story on page three of the police locals. He nearly choked on a sip of coffee.

"Are you alright, dear? You look pale."

***

Pat finished breakfast, then went to his study and closed the door behind him. The story about Donnie Lee Lester being shot and killed was like a real live ghost story. It's like he planned it, and did it, but didn't remember doing it. It had been done according to plan, but he wasn't executing the plan. This is why Joe had recommended holding off. He had an idea that this was happening. Who knew about it though? Only he and Joe should have had any knowledge of the details. Mike knew some of the early ideas, but none of these killings to date showed signs of those early wild schemes. Had Joe spilled his guts to someone? That just wasn't realistic. Joe was much more private than even Pat. *Could I have slipped up somewhere along the way?* He did do some writing on the boat about the plans, but he shredded all those papers. Could someone have gotten hold of them? If they had, more likely they'd have laughed it off or taken them to the captain to see if he could have this lunatic Electrician's Mate taken off the ship. They didn't like crazies on the sub.

He picked up the phone, had it half way to his ear and stopped. He thought for a moment about what he should say to Joe but his mind was racing, and he couldn't get his thoughts together. He put the receiver back down and sat down in his cushioned office chair. Diane was in the kitchen cleaning up and the kids were in their rooms getting ready for a tough day of playing with their toys. Diane had said that the kids were going over to friends' houses later in the morning so the house was all theirs. Diane had said, 'We can have a warm up session for this evening.' That thought crossed Pat's mind as well, throwing another monkey wrench into the mix. He sat quietly with his eyes closed and imagined that he was in front of the Electric Plant Control Panel on the USS *Alabama*. He imagined that they were steady state, all ahead one third, the ocean calm, the boat cutting through the ocean so smooth that you thought you were on dry land. He had 8000 kilowatts of power at his command, though both generators were never fully loaded at the same time. But he was in control. He knew that he could handle any real or contrived emergency that was thrown his way. What a confidence builder that was, sitting there, almost in a dream-like state. When he opened his eyes, he knew what to do next.

Pat picked up the phone, and instead of calling Joe McKinney, he dialed a number that rang in downtown Orlando. The receiver was picked up and a voice said, "Detective Poleirmo."

Chapter 32

It was 9:00 AM in Pine Hills, Florida. Joe McKinney dialed the number of his younger brother, Mike in Las Vegas, Nevada. He couldn't wait any longer to see if Mike was still in Vegas or if he was roaming the central Florida area in a crazed state, seeking revenge for his wife's murder. He was pretty sure that he knew the answer, but he wanted to be certain. On the third ring, Mike McKinney answered in an unsteady voice, "Hello?"

Joe could tell just by the way Mike answered that he had no part in the killings. The voice was like that of a scared child. Joe figured that Mike probably lived his days and nights in fear of another violation of his life. They did it that easily the first time, why not a second or even a third.

"Hi Mike. It's Joe."

"Joe. Hey."

Nothing further. No, how are you or how's Pat? Nothing. He was a beaten man.

"Mike, I just called to say hi and see how you were doing. Have you talked with Mom and Dad recently?" It was a tough question to ask, because Joe, himself hadn't talked to their parents in quite some time. That was unusual and he felt a twinge of guilt as he asked.

"No. I want to, but I don't know what to say. I want them to know I'm sorry about Julie." Joe could hear Mike start to falter. His heart skipped a beat in his chest and he began to wish that he hadn't called.

"Mike, two of the guys who hurt Julie are dead. Someone killed them. It's getting safer out there for you. Would you like for Pat and me to come see you?"

"Yeah." A few sniffles came across the line. "I'd like that. When can you come?"

"I'm not positive, Mike, but soon. I'll call you again when we make the arrangements. It'll be soon. Okay Mikey?"

"Okay."

"We love you Mike."

The click at the other end of the phone was like a knife to the heart. Joe was nearly brought to tears by his brother's pain and suffering. Not only did the four assailants take away his wife, they took away his life. He was reduced to a shadow of a man. Joe knew without a doubt that Mike McKinney was unable to kill anyone...except maybe himself. The thought hurt Joe even more. He looked around his apartment in frustration and anger. He yelled at God through the ceiling, "Why won't you let us get the revenge that we need?"

God gave no reply.

***

Brian and Ginny were just waking. The room at the Gaylord Palms was fabulous with all the extras any guest would ever want. Brian looked at the clock; 9:45 AM. *What a night.* Ginny was stirring but not opening her eyes yet. She did have a grin on her lovely, but sleepy face. Brian leaned over and gave her a very light kiss on the cheek, then let his lips linger there. He slowly moved down to her neck, then to her left shoulder. Her smile was more pronounced now, as she responded to Brian's teasing. "If you keep doing that, we're never going to get out of bed."

"Then my plan's working. Do we want breakfast this morning, or do we want a steady diet of you and me pancakes with sweet, maple syrup?"

"Umm, that sounds so good."

They stayed in bed for another hour and made love again. Then they got up and showered together. They finally got dressed just before noon. Brian made some wisecrack about skipping breakfast and going right for lunch. "At this rate, we're going to starve to death by next week."

"But we'll die happy," Ginny replied. Then Ginny asked a question out of the blue. "Who are the McKinney brothers?"

"How do you know about the McKinney brothers?"

"I just heard their names from a couple different places,

you for one. When you were talking with that guy, Al, at the *Rock* the other night, I heard you mention Pat McKinney and his brothers. I was just interested." She paused then said, "I also heard Danny talk about them one time. They seem pretty popular, liked and hated kind of guys. Danny hated them, it was clear, but he acted like he hated everybody except women."

"Let me tell you a little story about the brothers, McKinney. Once upon a time, in a land called Apopka, Florida, there were three brothers; Pat, the oldest, Joe, the middle one, and Mike, the youngster. They had an orange grove business. Then they started a nursery business. Then they started another kind of plant business."

Brian went on with his story about the McKinneys, how they were well liked and respected and how they were also very popular. They were just fun to be around and very friendly. They weren't arrogant at all, and they shared lots of things. Well, they got a little greedy, some of their friends got a little jealous, and they got a little careless. They trusted people an awful lot. And in the business they were in, trust is not something to count on. So they had a few problems with others stealing their stuff. They were also finding out that some of the shady stuff that they were doing wasn't right. So they stopped. But it was too little too late for their former friends. That's when big shit hit the fan.

"One day when all three were at the nursery working, some guys, four to be exact, broke into Mike McKinney's house. Supposedly they were looking for dope and cash."

"How do you know what they were looking for?"

"Well, because I know most of them. Or I knew most of them. I haven't seen these guys for almost three years now, at least, maybe four. Anyway, the story doesn't stop here. This is pretty nasty. Are you sure you want to hear the rest?"

Ginny nodded.

"Well, Mike's wife came home from the grocery store and kind of surprised the guys. She tried to run, but couldn't get away. They beat her and raped her, then beat her more. She died in the hospital the next day but she was in a coma when they took her in. Some say she woke up long enough to name names, but that was never brought out in court."

"How did they find out who did it? Aren't they in jail?"

"Well, this is where it gets even worse. One of the assholes taped parts of the rape and beating. They think he stopped because he knew it was getting out of hand. I don't think that he expected it to get that brutal. He also figured out that the tape could send them to the chair. The police found the tape somehow and it was clear as day who two of the guys were. And voices on the tape implicated the other two. They were all former friends and business associates of the brothers. They were arrested and arraigned. But when it came time for a trial, the tape had disappeared. There was no other physical evidence that was recovered because, with the tape, a conviction seemed pretty much a slam dunk. They walked free the day after the arraignment. The Orange County Sheriff's Department tried for years to get the bastards on other charges but no luck."

"God! That makes me sick. How can some pricks get away with that? Others get hammered for such minor stuff. It just doesn't seem fair."

"It isn't, and don't ever let anyone tell you that it is. But what goes around comes around. One of the pricks was killed the other night. Rumor has it he was trying to rape his date. Someone took exception to it and crammed a bottle neck down his throat. Killed him. There are only three of those pricks alive now. Who knows, maybe Julie's ghost is coming back to get them."

Brian went to the door and picked up the complimentary morning paper and brought it back to the table. He and Ginny leafed through different sections, when Brian set his coffee cup down and stared at a news story in the local law enforcement section.

"Remember when I said that there were three alive? Well, we're down to two."

Brian showed Ginny the story about Donnie Lee Lester, how he was gunned down in his home.

"This is getting real bad, Ginny. I hope that Pat doesn't have anything to do with this. I talked with him just a few days ago."

"You talked with Pat? When?"

"I'd gotten a letter from Pat a few months back. He said he was moving to Dunnellon. He wanted to be close to Crystal River Power Plant. He doesn't work there, but he runs a consulting business that specializes in something related to the nuclear business. I don't really know what it is. Anyway, he told me about his wife and kids. Hell, I didn't even know he was married, much less had kids. He invited me up to visit. So I did. When I got there he wasn't home, but his wife, Diane was. She actually let me in and we talked for a couple of hours. I want to tell you, that was one weird conversation."

"How do you mean? Is she some kind of fruit cake?"

"I don't mean that Diane is weird, just the opposite. She's a great woman, not as great as you, Babe, but she didn't know much of anything of Pat's past."

Brian went on to tell Ginny about how Diane had no idea about the orange grove or nursery business. She had no idea about Pat's friends. She wasn't even sure where Pat was at the time. Brian then told Ginny about the vault in the grove and how the brothers used to conduct business from the vault. He told her how he found Pat there mentally torturing himself.

"How did you know he would be there?"

"I didn't. I just had a feeling. Hell, I didn't even think that they still owned the grove where the vault is located. That's a whole other story, about the vault, I mean. But anyway, Pat's there, going over ancient history in his head. I talked to him for hours. I told him to get the hell out of that place. Go home to his wife and make things right. He pulled out behind me, but he went back for some reason. He was only there for about five more minutes, then he left again. I don't know what he went back for, but he must have gotten something that he didn't want me to know about."

"What is it about 'the vault'?" Ginny made a gesture that was exaggerated; kind of making fun of the vault. "I mean, what's the big deal?"

"That's where things really started to fall apart for Pat

and his brothers. They really let things get lax. And they shouldn't have. That vault is like a mini-fortress. If they needed security, they had it in the vault."

Brian again went on to describe the vault and how much steel it was made from, how many cameras surrounded the grove and the area around the vault. He talked about the ventilation system. He even talked about why it was built in the first place. It had nothing to do with the drug trade.

"The thing could probably withstand a nuclear blast," Brian said. "But that's all history. If I were them, I'd tear the damn thing down. It's just a reminder of some pretty shitty times. At the very least, they should sell the grove and get rid of the whole package."

"Wow. This is a bummer of a story. No wonder these guys left town. Whatever happened to Mike? You never said much about him."

"He left for Nevada. He lives somewhere near Vegas. I don't know exactly where because no one talks about him. He's like a lost soul. I've been told that he never speaks about Julie, and really doesn't do much of anything. He's not a vegetable, but you couldn't convince too many people of that. He just dropped out of sight and mind."

"How awful that would be to lose your wife like that. Even worse, to people, no animals, who were supposed to be your friends? It wouldn't surprise me if they were involved these killings."

"Well there's one other thing I need to tell you about. And I'm afraid this one is going to hit a little close to home." Ginny looked at Brian with an odd expression, like 'what do you mean?' "Danny Vallero crossed the McKinneys in a big way, too. It was nothing vicious like the rape and murder but he ripped them off for about fifty grand. He took cash right out from under their noses. He swore to their faces that he didn't do it then he bragged about it to a few of their mutual friends. He wanted to make sure that it got back to them. He joined the 'beat on the McKinney boys' parade."

"Oh my God, you mean there are three murders in the

last week and all of them are people who have crossed the McKinneys? When did all this happen? It had to be years ago."

"I'd guess about six and a half to seven years ago. That's a long time to hold a grudge, don't you think?"

"They had some incentive though. If they are involved, I hope I never cross them," Ginny said.

"Remember, these guys are my friends. Pat is my very best friend, ever in my life. I can't believe that he'd have anything to do with any of the killings, though I don't think that I could blame him if he did. I asked him about Danny by the way. He said, 'good riddance but I didn't do it.' I don't know what to think." Brian thought for a few minutes. He was trying to piece some things together that weren't connecting right. Ginny reached a soft hand over and rubbed his cheek.

"You've got a lot on your mind, don't you sweetheart. I hope you're not too deep in thought to forget about me?"

With that, Ginny walked around the breakfast table and dropped her robe off of her shoulders to the floor. Brian's thoughts changed immediately from a complex human puzzle to basic human instincts. Finishing breakfast was way down on the list of things to do.

***

Buddy stood outside Jason Roberts' office talking with Jamie and Bill. Jamie was his usual loud-mouthed self, even after the tongue lashing he'd taken the night before. Bill was quiet. He looked like a whipped puppy dog. He tried talking with Karen to try to get her to move back in with him. He started to tell her about the cash and the deal and how he was a big dog now. He was about ready to add more bullshit to the description when the phone disconnected. She'd hung up on him. He realized that it might be for the last time. He tried telling himself that he didn't need her, but the fact was he did. He felt like nothing without her and since he felt that way, he was nothing. After the letdown of her hanging up on him, he had his hard-earned cash ripped off. That was really demoralizing. Here he was in the big game and his first payoff was gone, stolen by some petty crook. On the way to Jason Robert's place, Jamie asked him why the long face. When he told Jamie about Karen and the stolen cash, he laughed so loud and long that Bill almost went left of center into the path of a semi. Jamie stopped laughing in time to grab the wheel and pull their car back into the right lane. Jamie made Bill pull over and he took over the driving duties. They made it to Jason Roberts' house without further incident.

"Buddy, some lunatic is trying to lure us to the McKinney grove, to that damn vault. They smashed the fuck out of my windshield last night and ripped off Bill's cash. He left all of us notes to be there today at 11:00. We gotta do something about this before we go settin' targets on our foreheads. I think we need to go out there before 11:00 and scope things out, see what gives. Mr. Roberts got anyone that can help us with this little problem? This guy was a strange bird, too. He had shifty eyes. I wonder where in the hell he's come from. You think he's a hired gun? Maybe ol' Pat McKinney hired someone to do his dirty work. He's too much of a pussy to do it himself."

"Let me ask Mr. Roberts, Jamie. Maybe he knows someone who can help. He knows lots of folks, has lots of resources." He used his fingers to put air quotes around resources.

"When can we talk with him about it?"

"Right now, Jamie." Jason Roberts was standing behind them in the outer office. He looked at Bill and said, "You look like you lost your puppy." His tone was filled with sarcasm. "If you want to remain working for me, you pull your sorry head out of your ass. Forget Karen! She's gone. Forget the stolen money. It's gone. If we recover it, great but for now, pretend that you never had it. After we take care of this little problem this morning, go out and get yourself a whore. Work out your problems on her, but when you come back tomorrow, you had better have your head on straight. Do you understand me?"

Bill looked down at the carpet, and mumbled, "Yes sir."

"Hey!" Jason yelled. "You look into my eyes when I'm talking to you and when you answer me! Stop acting like a little girl. If I wanted a pussy in this organization, I'd have started a cheerleading squad. We've got business to take care of and we don't have time to change your diaper. You got that?"

Bill looked mad now. He looked Jason straight in the eyes as directed and yelled, "Yes sir!"

"That's better. Now, let's talk about our little problem."

Chapter 33

Johnny Poleirmo heard Pat's voice on the receiver and could hardly believe his ears. He hadn't heard from Pat for almost seven years. After all the pleasantries were done, he listened intently as Pat explained his dilemma. As usual, Pat was very calm and direct as he told Detective Poleirmo about what he suspected was happening.

Johnny and Pat had met a number of years ago when Pat had just graduated from high school and Johnny was a young Orange County Deputy Sheriff. They'd come across a car that had flipped in the middle of Interstate 4 near Altamonte Springs. It was a time when traffic on the interstate was outpacing Congress' ability to fund widening projects across the country, particularly in this rapidly growing section of the Sunshine State. It was a dark, cloudy afternoon. It had been raining for an extended period of time and I-4 was slick with puddles. Hydroplaning was a serious risk. A young mother was riding down the interstate heading towards Orlando, when she was cut off by another driver and lost control of her car. Her young infant girl was in a car seat in the back. Pat happened to be a few cars behind the woman and was able to stop his car just before he went off the road himself. He noticed that her car was beginning to burn from the engine compartment.

He raced to the young woman's car and helped her out of her seat. Others came to her aid while Pat went back into the car for her baby girl. He was able to get her out of the car just as the flames were entering the passenger compartment. They spread quickly and engulfed the entire car in less than a minute. As Pat was taking the baby to her mother, Johnny Poleirmo came upon the scene in his Sheriff's car. He started asking questions of bystanders. It became apparent that most thought that Pat had saved the baby's life. Johnny came over and talked to him about what had happened. They hit it off pretty well for a couple of strangers and became friends of sorts. After that chance meeting, they would meet on occasion for lunch or dinner. It turned out that Johnny's dad was in the nursery business just outside of Apopka. Johnny helped out some evenings and on weekends. They'd had a pretty good surplus of Golden and Marble Queen Pothos stock. Pat was in the market for Pothos because he and his brothers wanted to expand their line of plants. So they started a business relationship that lasted for a few years. Things went pretty well between them until Johnny discovered that the brothers' real business was dope. Johnny was shocked at first and he confronted Pat about it. Pat didn't deny it and came right out and told him that he was in the marijuana trade only. No pills, no chemicals, nothing else but pot. He explained that within a few years it would be legal anyway and it really wasn't hurting anyone. He gave Johnny all the usual arguments to try to convince him that it wasn't wrong.

And Johnny gave Pat all the usual arguments that it was. "Pat, it's illegal, for starters. It's like smoking an unfiltered cigarette at best. At worst the stuff is sprayed with God knows what kind of chemicals, insecticides, herbicides, and any other 'cides you can imagine. You know that little kids are getting this stuff and even if the pot isn't killing them, it's exposing them to a host of bad characters. The same crowd that smokes dope also pops pills and some of them even hit the hard stuff. You can't justify your way out of that." Johnny's final argument hit Pat harder than most. "I can't stay in business with you, knowing what I know. And I really can't hang around with you. I work for the Sheriff's office, Pat. It would jeopardize my job. I'm sorry. I love my work and I can't risk it." Pat didn't have much of an argument after that.

When the troubles were coming to a head for the McKinneys, not too long after Pat and Johnny's encounter, Pat called Johnny and told him he'd been right. He let Johnny know who the bad guys were. He hoped Johnny could set up some kind of bust, but that had never materialized. Finally, after Julie's murder and Pat and his brothers were leaving town, Pat called and apologized for being such a loser and for placing Johnny in such an awkward position. He also said that he and his brother Joe were joining the military to pay back their debt to their country. He hoped it meant something. Johnny said he wished things had been different, they could have been friends for life, but the cards were dealt and there was no taking them back to reshuffle. With that, they'd said their goodbyes.

Now Pat was on the phone explaining that he and Joe were as surprised as he was at the murders. He also let Johnny know that Mike was in Vegas and had nothing to do with them either.

"Pat, can I just ask you a few questions?"

"Sure Johnny, shoot."

"Where were you last night at the time Donnie Lee was shot?"

"I was at home with my wife. I'd been at Joe's earlier in the evening but was home by about 11:00 PM. We didn't go out at all. We'd had a disagreement a few nights ago. I'd been away from home for a few days and came home to make up with her."

"Is everything alright now?"

"Yes it is. It's the second time in my life that I've been an absolute idiot. You know about the first."

"Yeah, let's forget about that, okay? Can anyone besides your wife, what is her name..."

"Diane. I'd like for you to meet her, soon. Are you married?"

"Yep. Her name's Rachael. She's a doll. She wants me to get a desk job. Afraid I'm gonna get popped someday and make her a police widow. Anyway, back to you. Anyone besides Diane that can place you at home?"

"My son, Sean. He's five but he can tell you I was home. At least he can tell you that I came home and about the time. I would imagine he could do that with no problem. I promise not to coach him."

"Okay Pat. Don't worry, I believe you. How about Joe? Did he know you were home? And do you know where he was?"

"Joe was entertaining a lady friend after I left. It was his first date in a long time. He appears to be quite taken by this girl. She's a little younger than he is, but she's over 21. He was with her until late. What time did the shooting happen?"

"What time did Joe leave his date?"

"I think that you should talk to him directly. I really don't know those details."

"Look Pat, this is serious stuff. You just keep your eyes and ears open and stay out of trouble. If you see or hear anything suspicious, you call me again. These guys that used to be your dope-headed buddies have developed themselves into some real bad people. They're working for a major dude. His name's Jason Roberts. He runs a lot of dope and not just weed. Many millions per year in revenue. You should be glad you got out when you did."

Amen to that, brother, Pat thought to himself. "Johnny, it was good to talk with you. I wish circumstances were different but, hey, you once told me that you play the hand you're dealt. I just wish I hadn't been dealing from the bottom of the deck. Now I've got a family to protect and my past is riding my bumper. It sucks."

"As long as you're not involved, and I believe that you're not, then you have nothing to worry about. We'll get to the bottom of this. You just stay out of the way."

"Thanks Johnny. I owe you."

"That's where you're wrong buddy. We're good."

***

Jason Roberts had just finished talking to Jamie and Bill. He'd worked out the details with them on how they would go to the grove early in the afternoon and wait for this 'Radar' character to show up. They'd take care of business and leave his body in a shallow grave in the McKinney's grove. 'Nobody will find him for quite a while,' he'd told them. No problem. Jamie and Bill thought that they would get back-up from Mr. Roberts in the form of Buddy and Phil Daniels, but when Jason had said that they were pussies if they couldn't handle this alone, Jamie's pride took over. He wasn't about to take any help from anyone.

He didn't even need Bill there to help. According to Jamie he was just going to get in the way. Mr. Roberts wasn't so sure.

In his office he was now talking with Ray Krebs. Ray was looking around at the handsomely furnished office. *This is what money will buy* he said to himself. He admired the fine art limited edition prints. Then there was the obviously expensive cherry desk and matching library shelves built into the west wall. The large picture window opened to the lake in the back of the property. The yard was landscaped to perfection. It looked like an advertisement for a lawn and garden magazine.

"Ray, I need your attention."

"Yes, sir. I'm sorry, I was just admiring..."

Jason held up his hand. He didn't care about Ray complimenting his yard. He wanted Ray to find out who was killing his people. "What have you got for me?"

"The shooter is a guy who calls himself Radar. I don't have any background on him. All I know is he drives a rental car and has balls. He showed himself to your guys in the bar last night and wasn't the least bit concerned about that. He even challenged Bill to a game of pool and took his money in pool and then took his money from the deal last night. Dumb ass Bill had it in a backpack in the back seat of his car."

"I know all of that. Jamie and Bill told me that much. Tell me something I don't know."

"I think that he's working for the McKinney brothers."

"He's working for who?"

"The McKinney brothers. They used to be friends of Jamie, Bobby, Donnie Lee, Randy Farley, Bill Grimes and Danny Vallero. They used to deal with the McKinneys. They were small time compared to your ops here but they were getting pretty big when shit hit the fan about seven years ago. It's a long story, but in a nut shell, these six did some pretty bad shit to the brothers. They killed Mike McKinney's wife, at least four of the six had a part in it."

Jason shifted uncomfortably in his office chair. He didn't like the sound of this at all. He had dirty guys working for him. But this was a dirty business. It takes a certain amount of brass balls to achieve success in any business; more so in this one. You dealt with scum lower than yourself on a daily basis. He looked back at Ray Krebs and thought to himself *I'm looking at an example right now*. But he needed Ray, because with Ray came inside information from the sheriff's Vice squad. He couldn't afford to lose that connection.

"I want you to make sure that this Radar guy doesn't bother my people again. If Jamie and Bill fail, I want you to finish it. Do you have any qualms about what I just said?"

"No sir. I do expect a sweetened deal though. I'm in this to provide information. If my scope just increased, I expect that there will be a commensurate rise in compensation."

"Yes there will. There's a one-time payout of $100,000. And I'll raise your monthly take by $5,000. Good enough?"

It was a question, but the only right answer was, "Yes sir." Ray gave the right answer.

Chapter 34

It was 7:45 AM. Bobby Acquino sat in the next to the last pew at St. Francis of Assisi. He was oblivious to the beauty of the church that surrounded him. The church was a new facility which held nearly 1200 people at each service. The pews were modern, straight forward, with square backs and light-stained wood. The windows were stained-glass but simple in design. The church was not nearly as ornate as its turn of the century predecessors, but it was quite functional, and best of all, air conditioned. That was the key to getting good attendance in Florida during the summer months. Even in the air-conditioned interior of the church, Bobby was sweating as he poured out his soul.

He was deep in prayer, asking God for forgiveness for all of the horrible things that he'd done over the last years. He was depressed and scared. He was more scared of dying without the Lord's forgiveness than he was of just dying. *How could I have let my life get so out of hand? I've failed my parents, my true friends, and you, God. What do I have to do to be forgiven?* Bobby continued to pray, head down, his mind centered only on his deep sorrow.

A man in black with a white collar was watching Bobby from near the altar. He was a young priest. The priest thought about approaching him, but he didn't want to interrupt his prayer. He could see the intensity in his body language. He felt compelled to ask him about the weight that was on his shoulders.

Bobby felt a presence and looked up to see the priest looking out across the church at him. Their eyes locked for a few moments. Bobby stood and walked towards the front of the church. The priest came off of the altar and approached Bobby.

"You look troubled. Would you like to talk for awhile? I

am Father Keifer."

"Father, I have screwed up my life so badly that I think that I am going to hell."

"My son, everyone, no matter what the sin, has the Lord's forgiveness if only you will ask for it and accept the Lord as your Savior. If you wish for me to hear your confession, I have time now."

Bobby spent the next hour confessing his sins. He broke down in tears a number of times and was clearly troubled not only about what he'd done, but by what might yet happen. Father Keifer listened intently, understanding that this man had done wrong, but nothing that he hadn't heard before. It wasn't that Father Keifer had heard stories of dealing drugs, but he'd listened to stories of infidelity, incest, even a few rapes and a murder. This was something he was used to, and trained to deal with. Many of the stories he'd heard were from people who were not nearly as sorry as Bobby. When it appeared that Bobby was running out of things to confess, he took a moment to collect his thoughts.

"Bobby, you have done wrong and sinned against God. But you have asked God for his forgiveness, and he has given it to you. Do you remember from your youth, the Epistles of Paul? He spoke with such confidence about being forgiven and how he was a servant of God. He turned his life over to God and preached the Word all over the ancient land surrounding Israel. Paul persecuted and killed Christians before he was shown the light of the Word. If Paul was forgiven for killing Christians, surely you are forgiven for your transgressions."

The light came on in Bobby's mind. His face brightened, though his eyes were still bloodshot from his tears. He looked Father Keifer in the eyes and asked, "Do you really think that God has forgiven me?"

"Absolutely, Bobby. All you need do now is go and sin no more. You are always welcome in the house of God, and God will always take you back, regardless of your sins. Talk to God often. If you would like, come back whenever you feel the need and talk with me again. If you feel yourself failing, I am a phone call away, and God is in your mind and your heart. You have a direct connection. Don't be afraid to use the line. It is never busy and the call is free of charge."

Bobby left St. Francis of Assisi Catholic Church at 8:50. Father Keifer had reaffirmed that there was hope for him after all. He still had problems that he knew he would have to resolve, but he determined that he was still salvageable. His soul at least was not lost. He'd prayed for hours asking for God's forgiveness. Now he had to tell his parents the truth, and about his decision to get out of the trade. He would seek their forgiveness for all the pain he'd caused them. His intentions were now on the side of good versus evil. But evil still lurked out there beyond these sacred walls.

**

It was 8:55 AM. The hot Florida sun was already beating down. The humidity hung somewhere around 90% and the glare from the pavement was tough on the eyes. Jamie and Bill sat in Bill's car in the grove across Kelley Park Drive from the entrance to the McKinney grove and the sand road that lead to the vault. They were keeping a watch out for the guy who called himself Radar. They'd been there for several hours already. There was no small talk. Jamie hated the idea that Bill was his only help, and he really wasn't in the mood for any intellectual discussion, though any discussion with Bill could hardly be called intellectual. Jamie thought that Bill was more stupid than anyone he'd ever met. He cursed Jason Roberts for saddling him with this numbskull.

"Jamie, I'm sweating like a pig. Can't we roll the windows up and turn on the AC for a while? I mean I am soaked. I can feel the sweat..."

"Shut up Bill. We can't run the engine, it's too loud. We can't worry about the heat, it's there and there's nothing we're gonna do about it. Just do your job and look out for any car heading to McKinney's vault. Don't you want to get back at this guy? He ripped off your first big payoff."

"Yeah, I do but it's real hot. He isn't supposed to be here until 11:00. Why are we here this early?"

"You're not just acting, are you? You really are this stupid." Bill looked at Jamie with a 'what do you mean?' look. "If we show up right at 11:00, we're sittin' ducks. He could pick us off like we're in a shootin' gallery. We're not gonna be stupid, at least I'm not. Maybe you can go talk him into giving you your money back, but chances are he's gonna want to blow your head off instead. What do you think?"

"I'm not stupid, Jamie."

"Calm down, Einstein. Let's settle back, and take care of this problem. We'll both be richer for the experience, and Mr. Roberts will appreciate it. Now, Billy boy, just concentrate on that drive across the way. When a car enters, we're gonna go across the road and cut off his exit. We'll circle around from either side, and cut him down in the crossfire. This will be easy."

Bill looked across the road for a minute, then back at Jamie, then back at the drive and said quietly, almost too low for Jamie to hear, "But I'm not stupid." Jamie just turned away and smiled. He had to bite his lip to keep from laughing at Bill again.

Chapter 35

Brian dropped Ginny off at her apartment at about 12:10 pm. He had to get ready to enter the studio for recording his first ever album. That meant contacting Rick Wessler and the rest of the band. He wasn't even sure how a recording studio worked when it came to actually recording a song. Sure he knew that there were tracks to record over and over again. He knew nothing of mixing, equalizing, sound quality, pitch control or any of the finer points of creating a CD. He kept calling them albums, and in the industry there were still folks that referred to cutting a sound recording as 'cutting an album.' Brian figured he was about to get an education. He didn't realize that he was about to get an education in criminal justice. He pulled into his apartment and was walking towards his door when he was approached by two official looking men in suits.

"Brian Purcer?"

"Yes."

"I'm Detective Al Porecwzski. This is my partner Detective Richard James. We'd like to ask you a few questions if you don't mind."

"Is this about Danny Vallero?"

"Yes and no. Do you mind if we go inside? It's kind of hot out here."

Brian thought about whether he had any stash visible and apparently the detectives read his mind. "Brian, we're with Homicide. We don't care if you smoke a little grass. And we won't tell Vice unless you've got a couple of pounds lying around your living room. Scouts honor."

Brian was sure he didn't have to worry about that, so he asked the cops to follow him in to his modest apartment. He offered the men a drink, but they declined.

"Brian, do you know a guy named Donnie Lee Lester?"

Brian's heart rate picked up immediately upon hearing Donnie Lee's name. This was definitely not a good thing. "Sure. Or I did. I understand he was killed the other night. Story was in the Sentinel."

"Where were you last night?"

"I was at the Gaylord Palms with a friend. Before that I was at the Cypress Palms Restaurant in Lakeland. We had dinner then went straight to the Gaylord Palms. We arrived at about 8:30 or so."

"I guess you have witnesses?"

"A whole restaurant full. Am I a suspect?"

"Nope. The only reason that we're asking is because of the altercation the other night at the *Rock*. It appears that there's a connection between Donnie Lee Lester and Danny Vallero. Do you know Randy Farley?"

This was getting more and more uncomfortable. Three people that Brian knew were dead. They all had a common thread: the McKinneys. "Yeah, but again, it's past tense. Randy, as I'm sure you know, is dead. That one was also in the papers. He was at the *Rock* the night Danny was killed. Is this going somewhere in particular?"

"Well, yes it is. Do you know a guy named Mike McKinney?"

"Yes." This was getting real weird. He hadn't seen Mike McKinney for a long time. Maybe these guys were just grabbing at straws, or maybe they knew more than he did.

The detectives could see that Brian was getting a bit uncomfortable. "When was the last time you saw Mike?"

"Years. I haven't seen Mike in at least..." Brian had to think for a minute, or at least make the appearance that he was thinking. "Over six and a half years I think. It's been a real long time. Last I heard he was out in Las Vegas." *Come on Brian, don't volunteer too much information. Make them do the work.*

"How about Pat and Joe McKinney?"

They had him on Pat. He needed time to think that one through so he decided to take on the Joe question first. "I haven't seen Joe in about the same time as Mike. They left town on the same day if I recall. I think he went into the Marines." So what lie do I tell about Pat? "Pat, on the other hand is a different story. I saw Pat when he was on leave from the Navy a few years back. His boat docked at Port Canaveral and we met for a drink. Haven't seen him since."

I've got to remember to tell Pat about this. We've got to keep our stories straight.

"Alright, Brian." They went on to ask a few more, seemingly unimportant questions, but they were satisfied that Brian had nothing to do with the murders. Even if he were telling half-truths about the McKinneys, he wasn't a suspect anyway. They left after only twenty minutes and didn't even look back.

Brian realized he was shaking a bit. He had to call Pat, but he wasn't sure if he should do it right away. It was a long distance call from his apartment and he sure didn't want a record of a call to Pat right after the detectives left. He'd wait until he headed out to the studio. He'd stop at a pay phone and talk with Pat about his visitors.

Once back in their unmarked Mercury Marquis, Rich turned to Al, "Do you think he'll make the call?"

"Oh yeah. If the McKinneys are involved, they'll back off. If not, then too bad for the bad guys. We just have more paperwork to process and Ray and Johnny have less dope dealers to watch. Like there's not enough to keep them busy."

***

Bobby Acquino walked towards his Ford Taurus in the church parking lot with conviction. His mind was racing. He had to talk with his parents first. He wanted to get this off his chest while he still had his new found courage. He opened the door to the car, sat in the driver's seat and was buckling his seatbelt when he noticed a note had been placed on his windshield. It was on computer printer paper and was typed out, but signed by Jason Roberts. *Oh damn, what now?* "Meet Jamie and Bill at the McKinney's vault. They need your help. Go there immediately when you leave here." Bobby decided to ignore the note and go straight to his parents' house. Then on the way out to the vault he would get a bite to eat. With any luck he'd be at the vault by 11:00. *I'll let Jamie and Bill know that I'm quitting. It'll kill two birds with one stone.*

Bobby was off by a few birds.

***

Ray Krebs was keeping a close eye on Bill and Jamie from his Jeep. He was in the same grove but a lot deeper than Jamie's suburban. He could barely see their taillights and bumper without his high powered field glasses. He had the engine running and had the air conditioning going just to keep comfortable. The sun was partially blocked by the thick orange trees, but just the small amount of sun that came through heated up the Jeep's interior very quickly when the AC was off. Ray didn't like to sweat. He had his police band radio on. He wanted to know if any sheriff's cars were in the area. Typically, the Orange County Sheriff's office had one or two cars for the entire north Orange County area at any one time.

He also had his cell phone, a relatively new tool in the arsenal of law enforcement. It barely had a signal this far out in the county. It appeared that cell phone towers were being built almost daily and coverage was improving rapidly, but it would be a few years before cell phones would be practical in rural parts of the county.

Ray's cell phone rang, which startled him. He answered, "Hello?"

"Ray, this is Johnny," the crackling sound came through. He could barely hear Johnny's voice on the phone. "Can you come in today?"

"No can do, Johnny. I'm not...area. Is...going on...to know about?"

"Could you repeat that? You were breaking up."

Ray did.

"Well, Lieutenant wants to step up the questioning of anyone associated with the Vallero, Lester,...rley hits. They're Homicide...to be a Vice connection. Are you in tomorrow?"

"Yeah, Johnny, I'll be in."

He could hardly hear Johnny between all the breaking

up. He really wanted Johnny to get off the phone. It was breaking his concentration. He had a more important job to do; one that paid cash money.

"Okay Ray, see...the morning. Can you get here...minutes early?"

"Sure. See you then." He was trying hard to keep the edge out of his voice but it was getting harder to do with each reply.

"Okay. See you." Mercifully, Johnny hung up. Ray went back to his surveillance.

***

"He was in his car somewhere. I don't know where he was though. His cell was breaking up pretty badly. It had to be either in a building or a rural area. You can't hear shit for background noises on those cell phones."

Johnny Poleirmo was talking with Al Porecwzski. They were trying to decide what to do about Ray Krebs. Johnny told Al that he'd received an anonymous call detailing Ray's dealings with one Jason Roberts. The caller told Johnny to ask around the Sheriff's office to see if anyone noticed Ray doing a little snooping where he didn't belong. Johnny hadn't suspected his partner of doing anything illegal up to now. He'd heard other deputies and detectives talking about Ray, but he never really thought that he was on the take. It was time to make sure one way or another.

When Johnny approached Al about his suspicion, Al told him about Ray snooping through his case files on his desk and saying that he was interested in the Vallero case. Said that one of the junkies squealed. The story sounded good, but so what. He could always get a copy of the file if he wanted one. He didn't have to rifle through his paperwork and make a mess of it. One thing that's sacred to cops is their desk.

No one had seen Ray all day into last night when the Lester hit went down. He basically disappeared and hadn't been heard from until Johnny reached him on the cell. *I wonder what he's up to?* Maybe we should swing by his house. Johnny went through his records and found Ray's address. Johnny, Al and

Rich headed out to their cars and headed to Wekiva Gardens, east of Apopka. Nice place for a mid level Vice cop.

Chapter 36

Joe McKinney saw Lisa heading down to the pool out his kitchen window. He opened it and yelled out to her, "Hey, would you like some company?"

"Sure. How soon? I'll only be out there for an hour or so. I have to get to work at 3:00."

"I'll be right down."

Joe grabbed his suit and put it on then grabbed his towel on his way out the door. He was really excited to see Lisa again. As he got to the bottom of his apartment steps, two men in suits stepped out of their parked car. They were looking right at Joe.

"Joe McKinney?"

His first instinct was to run. He realized, of course, that it was a silly idea. Joe stood there for a moment longer until he realized that his feet were beginning to burn on the hot pavement so he moved into a grassy area then he answered, "That's right. What can I do for you?"

"We'd just like to know where you were last night at about 8:00?"

"I was in the weight room until about 8:30, then I was at the pool until much later. What's this about?"

"Can anyone collaborate that?"

"Yes. There's a young lady at the pool right now that I was with for that entire time, except for about twenty minutes while I changed after lifting. I cleaned up to go to the pool. I was up in my apartment in between." He asked again, "Hey, what's this about?"

"Did you know Donnie Lee Lester?"

"Yes I did. I read that he was murdered last evening. What's this have to do with me?"

"Well, if your story checks, it clears you of any

involvement. Was anyone with you during the twenty minutes that you were changing?"

This gave Joe pause. He wasn't exactly sure how to answer this one, but if being here cleared him, he could also help clear Pat if he were here. "Well, my brother Pat was here. He stayed just while I changed then he left."

"Did he say where he was going?"

"Yeah. He said he was going home. He and his wife were having some problems, and he went home to work things out."

"Okay Joe. Thanks. We'll let you know if we need anything else."

That was totally weird. They just asked me and believed me. They must be looking for someone else, but it's clear that they know something. I wonder what's up. Joe knew that he had to get in touch with Pat and see if he really did go home. He and Joe had talked about the possibility that this was going to look like they were involved to anyone who knew about Mike's wife. If the Orange County Sheriff's office was asking questions, then something was known.

After the detectives left, Joe headed for the pool. He watched as Lisa finished up a couple of laps and got out of the pool by the ladder. Her skin glistened as water slid off her perfectly shaped body. Her tan skin was smooth as silk, not a blemish in sight. She smiled at Joe, noticing that he was noticing.

"What took you so long? I thought that you were right behind me?"

"Well, that's an interesting question," he said as he took off his shirt, kicked off his flip-flops, and walked towards her. "Can I tell you something very personal? Can I trust you to keep it to yourself?"

She smiled up at him. "Now's when you tell me that you're with the Secret Service, or is it the CIA, and you can't lift or swim with me anymore."

Joe smiled at the jab. "Okay, that was pretty good. I'm serious though. I'm not sure I should, because it's pretty depressing. I mean, this is about my family, and it has to do with why the two Orange County Sheriff's Detectives were asking me questions a few minutes ago.

Lisa's face turned serious. "You're not kidding, are you?"

"I'm afraid not. Let's get in the pool for a bit."

They both got back into the pool and sat in the water on the shallow end steps. The water was warm from the hot August morning but it felt good as it swirled around their bodies. The sun was glistening off of the ripples on the water's surface, and they had to squint their eyes due to the bright reflection.

"I told you about my brothers, Pat and Mike." Lisa nodded. "Well, we're in business together. We own some greenhouses and a small orange grove. We lease them out to a guy, so we really don't do any of the day-to-day work. Anyway, about seven years ago, Mike got married to a nice girl. They were only married for a couple of weeks when she was raped and killed...brutally." Lisa cringed. "There were four guys that did the killing. Worse, they were supposed to be friends of ours. Worse yet, they were never tried. Evidence disappeared, and there wasn't enough left to get a conviction. They had part of the crime on tape, but that was one of the key pieces of evidence that disappeared."

"God, how awful. Where are these guys now? Are they still out free?"

"Well, that was the reason for the visit a few minutes ago. Two of the four guys are dead. Murdered. One a few nights ago, the other last night."

"Do they think that you had anything to do with it?"

"That's what's odd. They asked me questions in a way that made me think that they knew we, Pat, Mike and I, had nothing to do with it. Which we didn't, by the way, just in case you had any doubts. The one murder happened about the time we were lifting weights or were in the pool. They asked if I had an alibi and you're it."

"I'm thrilled to be your alibi. Do they need to ask me about it? I'll tell them that we spent the night together." She smiled a wicked little, devilish smile.

"Thanks, but I told them you were here at the pool and

they didn't even seem interested in verifying my story."

"Darn. I wanted to brag a little."

"You didn't do anything to brag about."

"There's always tonight. Somebody else might try to pin something on you. You never know, and I want to make sure that you're not implicated." She put her arms around his neck and reached up to kiss him lightly on the lips.

Wow. Now I have my very own alibi. Joe relaxed and put his arms around Lisa and kissed her back. Within five minutes they were in Lisa's apartment in each other's arms, and things were heating up. It was almost 95 degrees outside, but it was getting much hotter in the apartment. Lisa was about thirty minutes late for work. After Joe saw her off, he called Pat's number in Dunnellon. Diane answered on the third ring.

"Hi Diane. Is Pat around?"

"Hi Joe. You sound tired. Everything going alright?"

"Yeah, I just got out of bed."

I'll bet you did. "Pat's in his office. I'm surprised he didn't answer. I'll get him."

Joe heard the receiver clank on the counter and Diane started down the hall. A moment later, Pat said, "Hey Joe. How are you?"

"I'm fine, Pat. How did everything go with Diane last night?"

Diane chimed in from the other receiver, "Just fine, Joe." Then the receiver clicked off.

Pat remained on and said, "She's right. Absolutely wonderful. I told Diane everything about the grove and the nursery. She loves me. I don't know why, but she does. I don't deserve this life."

"You're right. You don't, but I do. I didn't call you to try and convince you what a nice guy you are. I just got a visit from the Orange County Sheriff's Department."

Joe told Pat about the visit and how he might get called on. Pat cut him off. He hadn't wanted to, but he told Joe that he'd called his old buddy, Johnny Poleirmo and told him that he, Joe, and Mike weren't involved in the killings. Joe was speechless. His grip was tightening around the receiver. How could Pat have done this without talking to him first? They were partners in this. They were brothers, for crying out loud! Joe's temper was starting to rise and he had to pull the phone away from his ear for a few seconds to try to regain control. *Think for a second*, Joe, he thought to himself. *He was just trying to do the right thing. Maybe it worked for the best.*

"Joe? Hey Joe, are you still there?"

"Pat, you should have told me that you were pulling this. I didn't know what to say to the cops when they showed up. I guess that's why their questions were so short and to the point. So we're in the clear?"

"Yep. The way it looks, somebody else has a real hard-on for these jokers. There's only two left...well four, if you count..."

***

It was getting close to 1:00 in the afternoon and the sun was really beating down. There was some relief in sight though as central Florida's daily afternoon thunder clouds were beginning to build. The first hints of brief shade were provided by a quickly moving cloud that was working its way up to being a shower maker. The rain, if it happened to fall in the grove where Jamie and Bill were waiting, wouldn't provide much relief. In fact, shortly after the shower, the humidity would climb higher, and the duo would be that much more miserable. They hadn't said more than a handful of words since Bill had declared that he wasn't an idiot. That was about to change.

Chapter 37

Ray Krebs had to alternate between starting his engine and shutting it off. His engine's temperature was climbing as it had to work harder to keep the air conditioning working. The heat of the day was also taking its toll. He was concerned that the starting and stopping would alert Jamie and Bill that they were being watched. He was getting more and more tired of this duty as the day wore on. He'd gotten out of his truck several times to relieve himself, but he was getting hungry now. He hadn't eaten since very early in the morning. That was just a quick Egg McMuffin and coffee, both of which didn't do his stomach any good. He was fighting the urge to abandon this surveillance, but his mind kept going over the things he'd be able to buy with the raise.

He was thinking about Johnny and why he'd called. What was he going to do about that, if he didn't have this problem solved today? He had to be at the office working cases, and he couldn't be babysitting Jason Roberts' army. They were making lots more money than he was. Why should he have to clean up their messes? Who cared if they killed each other off? That wasn't his problem. But the full-time job with the Sheriff's department was his problem. He would have to figure out what to do about tomorrow when he was home tonight. *Just concentrate on one job at a time. It sure is getting hot out here.*

Just then, Ray saw a small puff of exhaust coming from the car he was watching. Were they giving up? Or has something happened and they're on the move? Ray picked up the powerful field binoculars and saw Jamie and Bill rustling around in Bill's car. He couldn't see it clearly, but it looked like Bill was holding a rifle or shotgun. He couldn't tell at this distance. He could only see the barrel. But they were definitely preparing for something.

And then the car was on the move.

***

Bobby Acquino pulled his Ford Taurus into the grove on the sandy road that led to the vault. The car didn't get great traction on the sand, but it was enough that his car tires didn't get buried in the sand and get stuck. He drove the few hundred yards back to where the road made a short turn. He parked near the entrance to the vault. The area in front of the vault could hold about five cars, like a small business. He noticed that the ground hadn't been disturbed in some time, at least several days, maybe longer. He sat for a moment, looking around. No other cars were visible in the grove. The vault looked almost abandoned. There were a few undisturbed spider webs across the entrance. His mind began to race, almost panicking. *Could this be another set up? I'm the next target!* Without a moment's hesitation he threw his car into reverse and floored it. His front tires spun in the sandy ground and started to bury themselves, throwing sand onto a nearby orange tree. He had to stop and calm himself. He knew he had to get his emotions under control, or he'd end up dead. He let all the way off of the accelerator. *So what if I am going to die? If this is it, I'm going to take it like a man.* He calmly started to accelerate again, this time, the sand only gave way slightly and the Taurus backed up out of the ruts it had dug.

Bobby was about to put the car into drive and head back out to Kelly Park Drive when he saw Bill's car barreling down the sandy entrance road to the vault. He didn't recognize the car until it was nearly on top of him. It stopped about fifteen yards in front of his car. He saw both doors open and out jumped Jamie and Bill with rifles in hand.

"What the fuck are you doing here, Bobby?" Jamie's course, Texas drawl still made Bobby's skin crawl. He hated the sound.

"I was told to meet you guys here. The note said it was something important."

"What note? Let me see it."

Bobby headed back to his car to retrieve the note. He was already sweating from the intense heat, high humidity and

244 P. J. Grondin

tension of the situation. The sweat droplets began to run down his face. Bill was looking around, trying to see anything moving. The shadow of a large thunder cloud was over them now. The first lightning crack could be heard in the distance. There was still no rain. Jamie walked around to Bobby's driver side door to look at the note. He was also sweating from the intensity of the meeting. Something wasn't right.

"This ain't Jason Robert's signature. Who gave this to you?" He shouted at Bobby.

"It was on my windshield when I went to my car this morning."

Jamie instantly realized that they were in deep trouble. It was a setup. He looked rapidly around the grove and the area around the vault. He was getting ready to tell Bobby and Bill to get the hell out of the grove when he felt his right leg take an impact that spun him off his feet. He felt a burning sensation in his leg where a bullet penetrated.

Bobby and Bill looked at Jamie wondering what had made him fall. All they heard was a thud when Jamie was hit. Jamie was now holding his leg, which began to bleed through his pant leg and his fingers.

"I've been shot!" Jamie shouted. "Goddamnit. Some motherfucker shot me. Help me get back to the truck!"

Bobby and Bill looked at Jamie like he was crazy for a second. Then they looked at each other. That's when Bill took a fatal shot directly to the chest, piercing his heart. He fell backwards onto the sandy floor of the grove. His rifle was thrown to the side. He died instantly.

Bobby saw Bill fall back and immediately made a move to get into the driver's side of his car. As he opened the car door, a bullet ripped through his head from the rear. It entered just behind his left ear and exited his right temple, taking most of his brain matter and a portion of his skull with it.

Jamie was still writhing around on the ground with his wounded leg. He saw Bill and Bobby get killed, and his stomach was now nauseated, both from his own wound and seeing his partner's bodies. His next thought was that he should play dead.

Maybe the shooter would think he was dead and leave. So he tried. He laid back and closed his eyes but the pain was too much and the bleeding worried him. He tried to think who could be behind this; the McKinney's were in the forefront of his mind. Maybe Mike had come back to take revenge. Maybe the other brothers had done it for him. Could it be some of their customers? They hadn't screwed anyone over too badly. As he lay there in pain, a Jeep rolled up. He kept his eyes closed and tried to keep his breathing to a minimum, but with that much pain it was impossible.

He heard the truck door open. Someone got out and moved to within a few feet. Jamie opened his eyes slightly and gazed up at detective Ray Krebs, down on one knee behind his truck bumper, looking around to determine what was happening. He needed to know where the shots had come from.

***

Johnny Poleirmo and Al Porecwzski were finishing their sweep of the home of Ray Krebs. The judge was a bit hesitant to issue a warrant based on fairly sketchy information, but he relented when they said it could be tied to the murders of Danny Vallero, Donnie Lee Lester and Randy Farley and that there could be other victims. As soon as they walked in the front door, they knew that they'd hit a potential gold mine. Everything in the house was beyond the means of a detective. There were so many adult toys, fine art, gold fixtures, expensive furniture, and a very large safe. It took until past noon to have it cracked, but when they did, they found the mother lode. There was a tremendous amount of cash. They didn't have time to count it all. That would have to be done at the sheriff's office. They also found several guns and one video cassette. Johnny found a VCR in the living room hooked to a big screen TV. They turned both on, plugged in the tape, and watched in amazement as Julie McKinney was raped and beaten. They turned off the tape after a minute or so.

Johnny turned to Al, "The missing McKinney Case evidence. Ray must have been paid off big time to take this. He must have wanted to keep this as his trump card if things got messy."

"Well, let's find our buddy and bring him in. We'll get the crime scene folks in here, so that they can get cracking. Where do we find ex-Detective Krebs?"

"I think I may have an idea. I want to make a couple of phone calls first."

***

Brian called Pat about his and Ginny's questioning. He told Pat that it appeared that they were being eliminated as suspects. As with Joe, Pat told Brian that he was the instigator of the questioning, and that he'd hoped everyone that could have been implicated had an alibi. He figured that Brian had no ax to grind with any of the victims, except Danny Vallero, but he knew Brian was on stage at the *Rock* during that incident. Of his friends and relatives, no one could have been involved in any of the murders so he was confident in calling the Orange County Sheriff's office. He knew Johnny would give everyone a look and come to the same conclusion; none of these folks were at any of the murder scenes.

That left just one big question; who was killing these guys and why. Mike, Pat and Joe had motive. They had air-tight alibis. Pat even had an alibi for the Vallero killing. He was in Jacksonville for a business conference. He was seen there and had several credit card receipts to prove it. Of course no one knew that Joe, acting as his brother, was the one making the charges. That's all Pat needed to be in the clear. The alibis were air tight for direct involvement, but didn't shield them from a possible conspiracy charge. In reality, they could easily be implicated in such a scheme. But there was no conspiracy. The brothers were as much in the dark as anyone. There was only one person out there who knew the real killer. That person had to look in the mirror for the truth.

Brian told Pat that he'd had doubts about his innocence even after their discussion at the vault. He apologized for not believing him. Then they moved on to more pleasant topics, like Brian's upcoming studio session and his night with Ginny. They were getting very close. Ginny made Brian happy and gave him confidence.

He also told Pat how much he enjoyed meeting Diane. He reiterated to Pat how lucky he was to have such a fabulous wife and wonderful kids. Pat replied that he figured that out, and how he and Diane had worked things out. The conversation ended with promises to get together, buying Brian's new CD, attending concerts, having Brian and Ginny over for dinner sometime when he was in town, and assorted other pleasantries. The two best friends hung up, feeling much better than they'd felt in many years.

Chapter 38

Ray looked down at Jamie to make sure he was still alive. He looked pale as a sheet and was losing blood fast. He was also soaked in sweat. His hair was coated in sand from where he rolled his head back and forth.

"Jamie, where did the shots come from?" Ray Krebs whispered.

"I got no idea," Jamie grunted through clenched teeth. "Just get me outta here. I'm bleeding to death lying here."

"Just hang on. I'm going to grab your hand and pull you over behind my truck."

"All right, but hurry. I can't lie here much longer."

The sweat was stinging Ray's eyes. He wiped it away with his wrist as best he could. His body was shaking from tension and fear. *Maybe the shooter's gone. He took out the bad guys. I'm a good guy. I'm the law. This guy won't kill a Sheriff.* After what seemed like a lifetime, he worked up the courage to leap out and grab Jamie. He took several deep breaths, held his final breath and jumped out from behind his truck. He made it almost six feet before the bullet ripped through his right temple and exited his skull. Some of the blood spatter got on Jamie's face.

Ray's body fell across Jamie's mid-section. In a panic, Jamie tried to push Ray's body off of his own. His adrenaline shot up and he was able to roll out from under Ray. He started to pull himself across the sandy floor of the grove when he heard the rustle of leaves from one of the trees. He stopped dragging himself and turned to look up at the figure approaching him. The guy, dressed in green military fatigues, slowly walked over to where Jamie lay.

"Hi Jamie, I don't want to waste any more of what little

time y'all got left, but I just wanted you to know why."

Jamie thought that he must already be dead. But he was still in extreme pain from his leg wound. "Who the fuck are you?"

"Just call me Radar."

"I know that, but why are you doing this? We ain't done nuthin' to you. We don't even know you."

"But y'all know a friend of mine and his brothers. And y'all knew his sister-in-law."

The realization took a moment to register in Jamie's brain. He knew he was a dead man, unless he could get to the gun in the sand that was just beyond his reach. He thought about how he could distract Radar, but he was having a hard time thinking straight at all. Radar saved him the trouble.

"Jamie, is there anything that y'all'd like me to tell Mike McKinney for you?"

"Yeah, you can tell that moth..."

Radar knew that there was no reason to continue the conversation so he raised his Heckler and Koch MP-5N assault rifle and gave Jamie a quick, silenced burst to the head. He looked around to make sure that the others were dead and walked off into the grove.

The rain started to come down, first in a few, heavy drops. Then after several seconds, it started in earnest and the clouds opened up. It promised to be a heavy but brief rain shower, like almost every afternoon shower in central Florida. As he walked away from the scene, he heard sirens in the distance. He picked up his pace to a slow trot and moved deeper into the grove. When he came to the edge of the grove he entered a field that was wooded in areas and grassy in others. He trotted to the second patch of trees and found the horse that he'd tied off earlier. He took a few moments to disassemble his weapon and pack it into saddlebags. He mounted the horse and headed back to the Bar C Ranch about two miles down Kelly Park Drive from the McKinney grove. He returned the soaking wet horse to the stable hand, apologized for the drenched condition of the beast, and thanked him for a fine afternoon ride. He assured the man that he'd be back again to rent one of his fine horses. He took the saddle bag contents and threw them in the back seat of the rented Dodge Sebring. The man who called himself Radar headed out Kelly Park Drive towards *Rock Springs State Park*. Just before he made the entrance to *Rock Springs*, he took a left turn and headed out State Route 435 towards the Lake County Border.

***

Al Michaels was Pat's next call. Al answered on the first ring. He happened to be completing an order for 30 cases of Marble Queen Pothos with a regular customer.

"Pat, how are you?"

"Fine, Al. How about you?"

"I'd be better if the cops weren't coming around asking questions about the McKinney brothers. But it worked out. They seemed more interested in keeping me in the clear than tying me to anything. Sounds like Brian's in the clear for the Vallero thing?"

"Yeah. He was on stage when that happened. They still don't have any clues on who's doing the killing. Pretty scary that three of the four guys are the ones that were involved in Mike's wife's murder. I mean, we're the ones with motive, but we all had nothing to do with it. I still don't get it."

"Well, somebody's doing it. Do you remember anyone that was really pissed, besides you guys? Maybe somebody in the Sheriff's department's pissed that these scum got away with it? Anybody seem...I don't know, psycho about the whole thing?"

Pat thought about this for a moment before answering, but he came up empty. "I can't think of anybody that was totally freaked. You know as well as I do that there were lots of folks that were pissed, but who would be willing to take those clowns on, especially after six years or more? You know, these guys are supposed to be into dealing really big time. Maybe they screwed someone over bad, and the bad guys are just getting even. I'll tell you, I'm not shedding a tear one way or another."

"I'm with you on that one," Al said.

Again the conversation steered towards promises of future meetings and dinner, meeting Pat's wife and kids, and Al's business. As they were about to hang up, Al heard sirens screaming down Kelley Park Drive. About five Orange County Sheriff's cars raced past Al's greenhouses towards the McKinney grove.

"Pat, anything that you know of happening at your grove?"

"No, not at all. Why?"

"Cause half the Orange County Sheriff's department flew past my place heading there." Al heard the sirens turn off, and he knew that they were at the McKinney grove. "I think you may want to get out here. How long will it take you to get here from Dunellon?"

"Maybe an hour and a half, I'd guess. Would you mind taking a drive down there and see if it's anything I need to worry about and call me back?"

"Sure Pat. I'll call you back in about twenty minutes."

Pat cradled his phone and sat back in his office chair. *What the hell is going on now?* It was only then that he remembered the last part of the plan was to lure Jamie, Bill and Bobby to the vault. Someone definitely had the blueprint and that was frightening. It was as if the plan had taken on a life of its own.

"What did you say, honey?" Diane called from the family room. She walked from the family room to Pat's office entrance and looked in at Pat. He cleared his head when he heard Diane call to him. Once again, he had to think in a calm, precise manner. He didn't want it to appear as if he were hiding something from Diane.

"I was just talking with Al Michaels. You haven't met Al yet. Great guy. But he said the Orange County Sheriff's department had several cars at the grove. He didn't know why, but was going down there to check it out. He's going to call me back. He owns a nursery just down the road a few hundred yards from the grove."

Diane gave Pat a worried glance. Pat could see the

tension in her face and knew that he had to allay her fears. He got out from behind his desk, walked to Diane and put his arms around her.

"Listen babe, there's nothing to worry about. I'll find out from Al what's happening and that will be the end of it. It's probably nothing."

Diane gave Pat a light kiss on the lips and turned without saying a word. Pat knew she was still worried. That would have to be addressed later.

***

Al Michaels arrived a few minutes after the Sheriff's deputies and was quickly blocked away from the crime scene. He got close enough to see what he thought were two bodies but he couldn't be sure. The rain had already abated to a slight drizzle. Within about ten minutes, you wouldn't be able to tell that it had rained at all, except that the white sand in the grove would have pock marks where the rain drops hit.

"So what's all the racket about?"

"This is a crime scene sir. You cannot come any closer. Do you live in this area?"

"Yes I do. I live just a couple of hundred yards up the road. I heard the sirens and followed since it was so close."

"Please do everybody a favor, Mr. ...."

"Michaels. Al Michaels".

"Mr. Michaels, I can't say anything so please go home. If there's anything you need to know, you'll hear it on the news or read it in the papers. I'm sorry but that's all I can say."

That was enough for him to get on the phone and let Pat know that the questioning might not be over.

***

"It looked real bad, Pat. I don't know what went on but there were at least two bodies. I didn't hear any shots but I was pretty busy and I keep the music going in the greenhouses, so who knows. I can tell you that the Sheriffs wouldn't talk or let me near the place. There were a couple detectives' cars that pulled in right after I left. I've been watching as more and more official looking folks are heading up there."

"Thanks man. I sure wish I knew what was happening. If you hear anything else, can you call me?"

"Sure, Pat. No problem. Nice talking to you, I wish the conversation hadn't been interrupted."

"Me too, buddy, me too."

Pat hung up the phone and turned to Diane. "That was Al Michaels. He lives down the road from our grove. He said that there was a big commotion there; several Orange County Sheriffs and Detectives. He said he thought he saw a couple of bodies in the grove, but he couldn't get close enough to be sure."

Diane's hands went to cover her mouth as she stifled a gasp, "Oh my God! Someone was shot on our property?"

Pat nodded. "I feel like I should head down there, but I don't know what I'd do or say."

"You don't do anything. You should wait and see if they call you to let you know. If someone calls, we can figure it out then."

That sounded like a good plan. Do nothing.

Chapter 39

The evening news was full of speculation about the killing of an Orange County Sheriff's Vice Detective, Ray Krebs. It hadn't come out yet that Detective Krebs was implicated in evidence tampering from an old case or that he may have been involved with drug trafficking, but that wasn't far behind. The names of the other three victims were listed as Jamie Watkins, Bobby Acquino, and Bill Grimes. Reporters covering the story implied that the murders may have been drug related.

Jason Roberts watched the news in disgust. He couldn't believe that someone was killing off his team. Was it a rival drug gang? If that were the case, he'd have been approached by the group's leaders letting him know their intentions. No such contacts were made. There was no drug war. American teen's thirst for dope, of most any kind, was unquenchable. There was no need for fighting over turf. There was plenty of money to be made. No, this was something else, something different. He couldn't put his finger on it, but there had to be some common thread that Jason just wasn't getting.

He called out to Buddy to get him and Phil into his office as soon as possible. He had a problem and he needed information that he didn't have.

"Phil, Buddy, I know you've seen the news. This is a major blow to our business. I want us to lay low on the sales for a while and do some snooping around. I want you two to talk with anyone that you can about why we're getting hit. Put out some feelers and see if someone is muscling in on our territory. Hell, we don't even have a 'territory' in the way they do in the big cities. This is pretty much wide open. But if I'm stepping on someone's toes, I'd like to know whose toes. We're in the dark here."

"Mr. Roberts, we'll get on it. I have a few ideas on where to start, and we'll let you know what we find out," Phil said.

"If I can speak, sir?"

"Sure Buddy, what's on your mind?"

"Well, sir, I don't think this is business. This is personal. There's been seven people hit, pretty professional-style. But there were no markers, no warnings, no contacts made. Four of the seven were involved in that McKinney girl's murder, and Krebs helped clear our boys. If we can figure out a connection for the other two, then I'd say we have our culprits."

Jason thought about this for a moment. He was wondering if there was something he could do to scare the McKinneys into admitting what they'd done. He could strike back at them. He couldn't let them attack his organization like this. He had to build a good part of his organization back up. As it was, he was at half the men needed to keep his business going uninterrupted. That assumed that he didn't suffer further losses. How could he be sure that the McKinneys, assuming it was them, wouldn't continue to strike?

"All right, I want you to find out all you can about the McKinneys. I want to know everything about their lives, their families, their friends, travel, and what they drive. I want that information early tonight."

Roberts continued with his instructions. He wanted no stone unturned in finding a weakness. He wanted whoever it was that was attacking him to pay, and if it was the McKinneys, too bad for them. They'd be an example of what happened to you if you messed with Jason Roberts.

***

"Pat, I called Mike this morning. He was out of it. He couldn't even hold a conversation. I can't believe that he's still all messed up over Julie. I really think he's done some permanent damage to his brain. I mean he sounded like Rain Man or something. I thought by telling him that some of the guys that killed Julie were dead, he'd snap out of it, but I don't even know if it registered."

Pat and Joe were sitting in Joe's apartment talking over

the events of the last few days. They were baffled about how their plan could have gotten into someone else's hands. Why would anyone carry out these executions for them? Pat was going over every detail that he could think of, where someone could have found the plan. It had to be written down somewhere in a place that was accessible to some tough bastards. Joe was in the Marines. Maybe he had a copy and some of his jarhead buddies got hold of it and carried it out for Joe; some kind of Semper Fi brotherhood thing. But Joe had said that he never had a written copy anywhere, not even a scribble. He had it all committed to memory. It was all he thought about while in boot camp, when he wasn't learning the details of how to be a proficient killing machine.

Pat's face was stone cold. He was deep in thought about the whole turn of events. Here, they'd laid out an entire plan for revenge, and they couldn't even carry out a fraction of it before someone stole their fire. These bastards stole their lives, at least for a while, and now they were supposed to pay for their sins at their hands, not some unknown person. Now this other person stole their rightful vengeance. How were they ever going to be made whole? At least Pat was able to take out Danny. One small victory, but that was just to make sure that he had the balls to carry out the real executions. The four murderers were the primary targets. How else could they satisfy their need for justice?

"Who were these guys working for? I mean who is the real supplier?" Pat asked Joe. "You mentioned his name once; Robert Jess, Rob Jason, something like that."

"Jason Roberts. He runs a load of grass and more recently, some coke and crack. He's been expanding his operations this summer. He was recruiting new faces to be mules. Bill Grimes was one of them. His career was short lived, in more ways than one. Why do you ask?"

"Well, we can't get the dead guys, so who's left?"

"Pat, we can't go around killing everyone that knew these guys. What do you want to do, go find their parents, old girlfriends, anyone they slept with? Where do you draw the line?

We're not vigilantes."

Pat looked at Joe. "Where did they draw the line? They killed an innocent girl. She had nothing to do with our business. Those bastards destroyed so many lives when they took hers. Why shouldn't we destroy the guy who helped them?"

"Because we're better than they are. We can't stoop to their level. Look, they're dead. That's what we wanted. It's over, Pat. You've got to get over this need to get revenge. We got it, or it was handed to us. Even better than that, we don't have to worry about ever being blamed for this. We were nowhere near the scenes. We're clean as far as the law is concerned. Let it go, man! Go home to your beautiful wife and kids and love them with all your might. Spend your energy there. Protect them from things like this."

Pat thought about his little brother's words. There was genuine wisdom in them.

"You're right you know. I do have my outlet. What are you going to do with your energy?"

Just then, the doorbell rang. Joe opened the door to Lisa Goddard and said, "My alibi. Come on in."

She smiled that beautiful smile of hers and took a few steps into Joe's apartment. She was dressed in a long shirt and had a beach towel thrown over her shoulder. Pat couldn't tell if she had anything on underneath, but he assumed there was a bathing suit under the shirt.

"Oh, I'm sorry," she said to Joe. "I didn't know you had company." She looked over at Pat, then back at Joe and said, "Wow, you two could pass for twins. This must be Pat."

"Yes, it is. Pat, Lisa Goddard, Lisa, Pat McKinney." They shook hands, Pat smiled. Lisa smiled back. "Pat was just leaving."

"Oh, yes I was. Are you two headed for the pool?"

"Yes, we are. I have a bet with Lisa that I can beat her this time in a fifty lap swim. She won by a hair last time."

"Last time?" Pat asked.

"Last time was the first time, and I owe her a dinner. I want to win a dinner back. Maybe we'll bet a movie this time."

Lisa laughed and said, "Or maybe a real night out on the town. How about a Brian Purcer concert? He's supposed to be touring starting next month after they cut their CD."

Pat chimed in and said, "That won't be too expensive. I can get you free tickets to one of Brian's concerts. I think I can even get you backstage passes if you like."

"No way!" Lisa exclaimed. "How do you pull that off?"

"Brian and I are best friends. I'll bet that Joe can probably get you into the recording studio to listen to him record a few sets."

Pat looked at Joe who was smiling. Lisa looked up at Joe with her excited face and asked, "Can you really do that?"

"I'll sure try. I think that if we end our swim early, I can contact Brian and make the arrangements. If we're going to do that, we need to get our swim in soon. I want to talk with Pat for a few minutes. Why don't you head down to the pool, and I'll be right down."

"Alright, but don't be long."

Lisa made her way down the steps and angled towards the pool. Joe turned to Pat and said, "There's where my energy is going. She is the most gorgeous creature on earth. And she is so wonderful to talk to and swim with and lift..."

"Alright, already. I get it, she's great," Pat said. "I'm happy for you, Joe. It looks like you're happy, too. Take it slow, brother. I've got to head home. I'll call you tomorrow. Are you going to call Brian or do you want me to call?"

"Why don't you call? He's really your friend. I just know him through you."

"I'll do that. Later, man."

The brothers shook hands and Pat headed down the steps towards his car. He didn't see the car slowly driving by, rolling down the two windows facing Joe's apartment. As he was about to get to the bottom step, two men leaned out the car windows and unloaded two 9mm pistols in Pat's direction. Pat dove from the steps behind a car near the base of the steps. His heart raced as he hugged the bumper. As quickly as the firing started, it stopped and the car sped away, turning left at Silver Star Road.

Pat didn't have time to see anyone, only a plain dark-colored car. He scraped his elbows and his right knee. He also hit his head on the bumper, but his head just bounced off the rubberized plastic.

Joe raced down from his apartment with his Glock 9mm in his hand, but he wasn't able to get a shot off. The car was already out of sight. Joe's neighbors started to peer out of their apartments to see what all the commotion was about.

Lisa heard the shots and headed back to Joe's apartment from the pool area. She'd just taken her shirt off and was getting ready to jump into the pool when the shots were fired. She saw Pat sprawled out on the sidewalk and Joe at the foot of the steps with a gun in his hand at his side. She screamed as she ran towards Joe, "What happened? Oh my God, is your brother alright?"

The wood railings on the steps were splintered in several places. The car that Pat jumped behind had several bullet holes and a shattered back window. The smell of cordite hung in the humid air. There were streaks in the parking lot where the car accelerated when it left the scene. The crowd was getting bigger as more neighbors came out to see what all the commotion was about. Pat tried to get up, but he was sore and still shaken from the ordeal.

Joe came over and grabbed Pat by the hand, "Let's get up. We can get cleaned up in my apartment."

Pat slowly got to his feet while Joe helped steady him for a bit. He looked at his knees and elbows and felt his head. It was already starting to swell. "Got any ice?" Pat asked his little brother.

"You bet." Joe turned to Lisa, "Can I get a rain check on the swim?"

"You can but I'm going with you. I think you're going to need another alibi," she said and tried to smile. She was looking around nervously, as if she was afraid that the shooters would be back any second.

"Are you sure? We aren't going to be much company."

"Oh yes you are. You've got some tough questions to

answer. First one is 'who the hell is shooting at you and your brother?"

"Lisa, for once I can honestly say that I don't know."

Lisa, Joe, and Pat headed up the stairs to Joe's apartment. Joe had already told Lisa about Mike's wife. He explained that he didn't know who the shooters were, because their enemies were all supposedly dead. While Joe was talking with Lisa, Pat called Diane and told her he'd be late. When she asked why, he'd said that he'd scraped his knee after falling down Joe's apartment stairs. It was just a stretch of the truth.

A few minutes later, a knock on the door made them jump a bit. Joe looked out the kitchen window before approaching the door. Just as he thought, the Orange County Sheriff's Office sent a couple of deputies over to question Pat and Joe and anyone else who was willing to talk. After about twenty-five minutes of questions and answers that really answered nothing, the deputies left. They said a crime lab team would look the scene over, but would probably only find bullet fragments in the wood. Maybe they'd get lucky and find an intact bullet somewhere in one of the cars. Not real likely. The guy who owned the car that was shot up the worst was pissed, but there was really nothing to be done, except call his insurance company in the morning.

Pat cleaned and taped his knees up and borrowed a pair of jeans from Joe. They were a bit tight and a bit long but they'd do in a pinch.

Pat said his goodbyes to Joe and Lisa and headed out the door. This time he looked around a bit nervously for any strange cars or goofy looking characters. There were none. He hopped in his car and headed for Dunnellon.

Back in Joe's apartment, Lisa was hugging Joe tightly. She was scared for him and Pat and she wanted to know why.

"Joe, why are people shooting at you and your brother?"

"I wish I knew. I thought that our problems were over this afternoon when the last of the creeps were killed. Now I have a feeling that all the creeps aren't dead. I mean, the guys that killed my sister-in-law are, but apparently there's more lurking out there."

"What are you going to do? You can't just stand by and be targets for someone that you don't even know. Do you have any ideas about who these guys are?"

Joe thought about whether to tell Lisa about the Jason Roberts connection. He figured that he and Pat would have to do something about it, and soon. Just then he had a terrible thought. *Diane and the kids. They're back in Dunnellon unprotected.* Joe's face turned red and tightened with worry.

"What is it, honey?"

"Pat's family. I have to call Diane right now. Pat just left and I can't reach him. Listen, go down to the pool and get your things together. I'll call Diane and tell her...I don't know what I'll tell her, but we're going to Dunnellon as soon as I get off the phone. Maybe we can catch up with Pat."

"Alright. I'll be right back." She grabbed Joe's face, turned it to her and kissed him deep and hard. She headed out the door and down to the pool. She was back in less than two minutes. But would it be two minutes too late?

Chapter 40

Diane hung up the phone from Brian Purcer. Brian was planning to bring Ginny by to meet Diane, Pat, and their two kids. He'd just finished another day in the recording studio and was feeling pretty good. It took a while to get used to playing partial songs, stopping, starting in the middle of a song, then adding overlays onto already recorded material. By the end of the day, the songs sounded better than he could have dreamed. Diane had told Brian to stop by. Pat was on his way home and would be there in about an hour.

When Diane hung up the phone it rang almost immediately. It was Joe. He sounded a bit tense. "Diane, this is Joe."

"Yes I know, Joe. You sound worried. Is everything alright?"

"Not really. I need you to lock up the house and close the curtains. Keep the kids away from the windows. Pat's on his way, but it's gonna be about an hour or so. I'm coming, too. I hope to catch up with him. We should both be there at the same time. Pat didn't want to tell you earlier when he called, but somebody tried to kill Pat. They drove by my apartment and shot at him as he was leaving. He's okay. He didn't want you to be concerned."

Diane felt like panicking. Her head was spinning with this news. What was going on with this husband of hers? Was his past going to destroy their family?

"Is Pat all right? Is he hurt?"

"No, he's fine. He really did scrape up his knees when he hit the sidewalk, but he wasn't hit. But you've got to stay in the house and away from the windows. Don't let anyone in. Try to call Brian back and ask him to wait for a little while. Pat can call him when he gets to the house. If anyone you don't know comes to the door, do not answer it. Look out one of the bedroom windows that have a clear view to the front door to make sure you know who's there. Did Pat teach you how to use a gun?"

This sent Diane's nerves into overdrive. She hated to even have guns around the kids but she knew how to use one, if it were necessary. She knew where Pat kept his 9mm and the ammunition. And she knew where the key was kept just in case. The kids were in the family room which had an eight foot sliding glass door.

"This may be nothing. It could be random, but with everything going on right now, I doubt it. Get going Diane. I have to get on the road. Don't worry, this is just a precaution."

Right. She was frightened and tense.

"Okay."

She hung up the phone, then she tried to reach Brian and Ginny but couldn't. So she went on with making preparations like Joe instructed.

Diane went to the sliding glass door first and closed the curtains. Then she went to each room and closed the shades. The windows were already locked.

Diane said to her kids, "How about if we play back in Sean's bedroom for a while? Dad's going to be home soon. Let's make something for him."

"Alright," Anna yelled.

"Okay. What should we make?"

Diane hadn't thought that far ahead so she said, "How about if we talk about some ideas and we can decide together."

That seemed to satisfy the kids. So they started to toss around ideas on what to make for Daddy. *How about a bullet proof vest.* Diane's thoughts were distracted but she kept her cool for the kids' sake.

After they decided on a picture, they set about coloring the picture. It was a beautiful mountain scene that Diane started and the children filled in with fall colors. They also cut out some shapes that they pasted on the picture for birds, clouds and the sun. It was taking shape when Diane thought that she heard a car door shut, then a second car door. Her heart rate quickened. She put her finger up to her mouth in a 'quiet' gesture. The kids didn't understand so she whispered, "Let's be real quiet so we surprise Daddy. You stay here and keep working on his present. Okay?"

They both nodded. Diane stepped out of Sean's room and went to her and Pat's room where she had a good view of the front of the house.

She carefully looked through a slit in the curtains. There was a truck across the street. Two men were approaching the house. One of the men was a big guy, probably six feet five inches and well built. He looked like a linebacker for a pro football team. The other was not as big, maybe six feet tall, and less muscular. Diane couldn't see their facial features, but they were dressed in jeans and T-shirts. They both had hunting vests on, but the vests looked new. They walked directly towards the front door. Diane went to Pat's office, opened the desk drawer, and reached in to get the key box. She took out Pat's keys and fumbled for the key to his gun drawer. She was very nervous now and dropped the keys once. She finally got the right key and opened the drawer. She picked up Pat's 9mm, and shoved in the clip. She looked the gun over, made sure that both safeties were in the safe position, and walked towards the office door to the hall. When she reached the hall, a loud knock at the front door startled her. She kept her cool. Then Sean asked from his room, "Is Daddy home?"

She whispered back to him, just loud enough for him to hear, "No Sean. You keep your sister in the bedroom."

Then another knock, this one a little louder. Diane was petrified. Her breathing was deep and her fear grew with each passing second. She felt she had to do something, but what? The walls in the hallway seemed to be closing in on her. She moved closer to the doorway where the children played and decided that was the best place to stay. At least she'd try to protect her children.

***

Outside, Phil Daniels and Buddy Mahaffey were looking around the neighborhood for signs of anyone looking their way. The sky was darkening as the sun started to set below the tree tops to the west. The air was still and humid. The neighborhood was an odd mix of elderly retirees and young families. It seemed that most folks were inside eating dinner, or were out for an early evening. The houses were spread out at a pretty good distance as most of the lots in this subdivision were one acre plots. Finally satisfied that no one was around, Phil turned to Buddy and nodded. Buddy turned square to the door and prepared to kick it in when they heard the sound of glass shattering from behind them. They both looked at Phil's truck and saw fragments of the shattered driver's side window fall to the ground. "What the...?" Phil asked perplexed at what he saw.

A moment later, while they watched, the back window splintered into a million pieces, most of which landed in the bed of the truck.

"My truck," Phil yelled. "What the fuck is happening to my truck?"

They both ran towards Phil's truck. Phil walked through the chips of glass in the street while Buddy went around back. As Phil looked around at his truck, he heard a series of loud thuds. He looked down and saw three fresh bullet holes within a foot of his arm. He quickly realized that they were being fired upon.

"Get in the truck! Get in the truck now!" he yelled at Buddy. Buddy heard him and understood that they were in danger if they didn't react quickly. They got in and Phil started the truck in a big hurry. They heard two more distinct thuds on the side panel of the truck bed and felt a slight vibration as the bullets penetrated the metal skin. As soon as the engine fired, he floored it and burned rubber all the way down the street. They left Dunnellon without looking back.

***

Diane heard the racket as they left her house, away from danger. She sensed that they were safe and moved into the master bedroom to look out the window. All she saw was the smoke from the burning rubber of the big four wheel drive truck.

Sean asked, "What's all that noise from, Mom?"

"It was just a big truck going down the road sweetie. Go back and finish Daddy's drawing with your sister."

"Okay Mom."

Diane walked away from the front window and went to the side window just to see if anyone was still outside of her house. Initially, she didn't see anyone. Then she noticed movement from a stand of trees to the side of their property. A man jumped down from one of the tree branches and walked casually away from their house. He was carrying something, but Diane couldn't see what it was. *That's odd, she thought. I wonder if he saw the guys who were at the door. What was he doing in that tree?*

She walked back in Pat's office, removed the clip from Pat's gun, made sure no rounds were chambered, and locked the gun back in its place. She made sure everything was locked and went back in to stay with the kids. She had just settled down when the doorbell rang. It startled her a bit so that even Sean asked her if she was okay. She assured her inquisitive son that she was, and she headed back to the master bedroom to peer out the window. It was Brian and a young woman that she supposed was Ginny Parks. She took a series of deep breaths and went to the front door to welcome her guests.

When she opened the door, Brian asked, "Who's been drag racing in your street? There's a line of tire burns for about fifty yards. Somebody was in a hurry."

Diane wasn't sure just what to say, so she told her guests about the truck and the guys that were at her front door. She left the part out about Joe's phone call and the gun. No sense running Brian and Ginny off before Pat and Joe arrived.

Pat arrived about twenty-five minutes later. Joe and Lisa arrived shortly after that. Pat hugged his wife fiercely for several moments, then hugged his children with just as much intensity. Brian introduced Ginny to everyone. Joe likewise introduced Lisa. Lisa confessed to Brian that she was a big fan and was thrilled to meet him in person. Brian's face flushed with embarrassment. He still wasn't used to being a rock star. Even the kids were introduced before they were escorted off to bed. Sean tried to put up a fight to stay with the grownups, but mom and dad won that argument.

After the kids were safely tucked into bed, Diane told her husband and her guests exactly what had happened earlier in the evening. When she told the part about the guy from out back, Pat and Joe looked at each other as if to say, 'that's the guy with our plan.' Pat asked Diane, "Exactly which tree was he in?" Diane pointed out the tree, though it was very dark by now. Pat grabbed a flashlight from a kitchen drawer and motioned to Joe to follow him. Pat told everyone to sit tight that they'd be back in a jiffy. He and Joe headed for the tree.

When they arrived, it was easy to see where the mystery man had jumped down from the tree. In the light of the flashlight, they could also see where he'd picked up several items from the dirt under the tree. "Shell casings. I can still smell the cordite. He was shooting from here. Did you see all the glass in the street where their windows were blown out?"

"Yeah. But what gives? He could have easily killed them from here. It looks like he just wanted to scare them off. He's already killed what, six guys? Why not a couple more? This whole thing is just weird."

They headed back to the house agreeing that they didn't find anything of interest, just some footprints. The rest of the evening was actually very enjoyable as both Ginny and Lisa got along quite well. Diane, as usual, was a great hostess and made everyone feel at home and very relaxed, despite the events of the evening. They stayed up late and were disappointed when Brian said he had to leave. He had to get back in the studio for another grueling day of recording music. Lisa asked for his autograph before he could get out the door. His cheeks again flushed.

"I'll do one better than that," Brian said. "You and Joe, Pat and Diane get the first copies of our CD. I'll sign those. My signature really isn't worth much, but the CD hopefully will be. Keep your fingers crossed."

"Thanks so much, and it was a thrill meeting you. You too, Ginny and Diane."

Joe said, "We better hit the road, too. You guys be sure to lock up. You get the alarm system working?" he asked Pat.

"Yep. I just hope I can remember how to arm the thing."

Everyone said their goodbyes with hugs all around. Once the crowd was gone, Pat and Diane headed for the kitchen to clean up.

Diane leaned against Pat and said, "So what are you keeping from me? You don't get shot at for something that happened over seven years ago."

"It's nothing, really. Nothing that can't be handled," he said coolly. But on the inside he was wrestling with what to do next. He thought that he knew, but it wasn't going to be easy. It could even be deadly. There was also the unknown assailant.

"I can see those wheels turning. You know something. Fess up now or you're sleeping in the dog house."

"But we don't have a dog house."

"I'll build one. Start talking."

Over the next hour, Pat told Diane about the guy named Jason Roberts and how he was a business partner to the guys that were killed.

"This Roberts character must think we have something to do with it, because of Mike's wife and all."

"What's the 'and all' part?" Diane asked.

Pat figured it was time to come totally clean. If he kept lying to Diane, even little lies, he'd get caught. He just wasn't good at it anyway. So he gave it to her straight. "I am going to tell you everything I can remember about my life that may have anything to do with this. Can you handle it?"

Diane took a deep breath, then Pat started talking. He told her about the drugs, the betrayal, the fighting, and the real business. He reaffirmed the bit about the legal business. He could tell this was a bit much to lay on her all at once. She'd suspected that he was involved in drugs somehow, but not to this extent. She was shocked and scared and confused.

"Pat, I need a drink and make it a stiff one."

After Pat mixed their drinks and sat back down in the living room, Pat asked, "Is there anything else that you'd like to know?"

"Surely there's not more."

"Not that I can remember right now, but some things…I just can't remember."

Diane's expression became stone cold serious. "Pat, promise me that you'll never again get involved in that lifestyle. And I mean on your heart. If it happens, we, me and the kids, will leave you faster than you can bat an eye."

"You have my word. That Pat is gone for good. I know it's hard for you to trust me at my word right now, but you have nothing to fear...at least not about that."

They hugged for a long time after that. They didn't say another word, and they both dozed off to sleep for a time before they woke up and made it to bed. They stayed awake another forty-five minutes to make passionate, emotional love. Then they slept for a full nine hours.

They'd have slept longer, but the kids came in complaining that they were hungry.

Chapter 41

Jason Roberts had lost his appetite. He sent out his best guys to do a job, and they'd botched it. What was he going to do now? He had to rebuild his organization from the ground up. That would take time especially since the team he had left would have to work extra hard to keep up with the flow of weed coming in. He wasn't sure his suppliers would understand if he couldn't handle the weight. He had to contact them and explain that his situation had changed a bit and that he'd like to slow down the flow for a short while. He'd explain that it would actually be good for business. With less dope on the street, it would be harder to get and the price would be forced up; simple supply and demand. They'd go for it, he thought. Or they'd tell him they'd get another dealer to handle it. Lots of folks were looking to move up in this business. *Well, it was worth a try*, Jason thought to himself. He definitely couldn't keep up the pace with the crews he still had. It was just too few bodies to handle the volume. He was in a tight spot, and he knew it. Then he had another idea. *If you can't beat 'em, join 'em. Or in this case, have 'em join me.*

"Phil, Buddy, get in here. I have an idea and I need you to tell me if I'm just going nuts here."

Phil and Buddy listened. They weren't the smartest guys in their classes, but they thought that Jason's plan might work. It wasn't going to be easy getting the McKinneys to join forces, but it was in both of their mutual interests. The way Mr. Roberts explained it they could either join them or die trying not to join. It was up to them.

The other issue that had to be dealt with was the mystery man. Maybe the McKinneys knew who he was. Maybe they hired this guy to do their dirty work, so they could keep their hands clean. Could Jamie have been right about this? Was this guy working for a rival dealer? Not likely. Why would he camp out at Pat McKinney's house?

"How close to either of you did the shots get tonight?"

"Real close," Phil said. "I mean, when the bullets hit the truck, they had to be right next to my left arm."

"Did any of the bullets hit on your right side? And how many bullets hit the truck on your left?"

"Well, none hit on the right. There were about three shots, and they all hit within a few inches of each other. What are you getting at, sir?"

"You should be dead right now...if he wanted you dead. He was just trying to scare you guys off. We're dealing with a real pro here. I think this guy is paid protection. His first assignment was to even the score, you know, cause of the one brother's wife. Now he's just protecting them. We have to find this guy and take him out, and then we can get back to either dealing with or doing away with the McKinneys."

Buddy and Phil looked at each other, then at Mr. Roberts and nodded in agreement.

Roberts said, "I know a few guys that can handle this. You guys have a load to manage tonight. The details are on my desk. It shouldn't take more than a couple of hours. Report back to me when you're done."

"Yes sir," they both answered in unison, and left his office.

He went for the phone and dialed a number of an old acquaintance from the northeast. "Hello Antonio. Yes, it's been a long time. How have you been? Are you still doing business? How would you like to help out an old friend? It'll be worth your while to take a vacation to Florida, trust me."

***

It was 2:42 AM on the digital alarm clock when the phone rang. Pat stared at the red LCD readout as the numbers seemed to come in and out of focus. The phone rang a second time, and Pat leapt from his side of the bed. He and Diane kept the phone on the dresser so that they had to get out of bed to answer it. That way they were somewhat awake by the time they had to talk with someone.

"Hello," Pat mumbled groggily into the phone.

"Pat, is that you?"

The unsteady voice on the other end of the line sounded weak and shaky. He thought for a moment then recognized the voice of his youngest brother, Mike. "Yeah Mike, it's me. You sound tired Mike. Are you alright?"

There was silence on the line for a few seconds, then Mike answered, "Pat...I can't take it anymore...I...I really can't. I miss her, Pat."

He could hear Mike begin to sob on the other end of the line. It was breaking his heart to hear his brother in such emotional turmoil.

"Mike, you're going to be alright. You know that all the creeps are dead, right? They've paid for what they did. Come on, Mike, you don't have to suffer anymore. You don't have to be afraid of anything. Julie wouldn't want you to suffer like this."

"I know...she wouldn't, Pat. But I just can't stand it anymore. I love you and Joe. I love Mom and Dad. Tell them that. You tell them that," he repeated.

"Mike, I'm right here for you. You don't do anything stupid, you hear me. Joe and I will come out and get you."

"No...No Pat. It's too late for that....It's too late." There was a silence on the line that seemed to last forever. Then Mike said, "I'm going to see Julie." And the line went dead.

Pat raced over and flipped on the light switch. Diane woke up hearing Pat moving about the room and asked, "What are you doing? What's wrong?"

"It's Mike. I think he's going to kill himself. That was him on the phone. He said he was going to join Julie. He was really on the edge. I've got to call the Vegas Police and see if they can get over there and stop him."

Forty-five minutes later, Pat's phone rang again. "Pat McKinney?"

"Yes."

"This is Sergeant Perez with the Las Vegas Police. I'm sorry sir, we found your brother. It appears that he took his own life. There was an empty bottle of alcohol and some kind of pill bottle on the bedroom table. We were too late. I'm sorry sir."

Pat's eyes flooded with tears. He couldn't believe that Mike was gone. "Thanks for calling, Officer." Pat hung up the phone. He sobbed for several minutes while Diane tried to comfort him with hugs and kind words, but it was no help. He had feared that this day would come. Joe and Pat both knew that Mike was devastated by his wife's murder and worse that the murderers got off without so much as a slap on the wrist. Pat's pain was intensified by the fact that they couldn't exact revenge on the bastards by their own hands. He hoped that he would meet the person who did this someday. Somehow, he felt that he would. He wanted to shake his hand, but he also wanted to find out what motivation they had to carry out their rightful act of vengeance. After several minutes, Pat gained control again. He hugged his wife hard and thanked her for being there with him.

"I will never let this happen to you."

"I know, darling, I know."

"I have to call Mom and Dad...and Joe."

The call to his mom and dad was very emotional. They both had feared that Mike would not recover from his loss. Pat's mom sobbed as Pat had done. Pat's dad simply spoke in solemn tones about how he was so sorry. He said that he would take care of their mother. He also offered to take care of getting Mike's body back to Florida. He knew that Mike wanted to be with Julie so he would make sure of that. He would let Pat and Joe know when the arrangements were set.

"Pat, your brother loved you and Joe. He just couldn't see a life without Julie. He felt so guilty that he wasn't there to protect her. There wasn't anything that you or Joe or your Mother or I could have done to save him. Those bastards might as well have killed him when they killed her. They really did, it just took Mike longer to die."

"Dad, I'm not sure I can handle this right now. I really do appreciate it."

"Call Joe, Son. He needs to know."

"Bye Dad. Give Mom our love. The kids can't wait to see you and Mom again. A funeral wasn't what I had in mind."

"Son, why don't you and Diane let Sean and Anna come with us for a week or so. You both probably could use a break."

You don't know the half of it, Dad, Pat thought to himself. "I'll talk it over with Diane and we'll let you know. Love you."

The line went dead.

The call to Joe went as expected. Joe shed no tears, but Pat could hear the shattering of drywall in Joe's apartment. After a few minutes, Joe and Pat agreed that they needed to meet to make some new plans. It was time to pay a visit to one Jason Roberts.

Chapter 42

Al Porecwzski couldn't believe his eyes as they looked at the Crime Scene Investigation Unit's pictures of the carnage at the grove on Kelly Park Drive. He and his partner, Rich, and Johnny Poleirmo were sipping coffee, going over every little bit of evidence that they could, to try and piece together what had gone on with Johnny's partner. They had a story board with three by five cards plastered all over it. Each card contained little bits of information. They were trying to group the cards into logical groupings but they were coming up empty. Nothing made sense. No pattern, no real information from any source that pointed to Ray Krebs as a good cop gone bad. It appeared that his standard of living was about four times his means. There were no credit card records. Everything apparently was paid for in cash.

Johnny was beside himself. How could he not have seen what Ray was up to? He worked side by side with the guy for years. He knew that an Internal Affairs investigation was coming, and he'd have to answer some really tough questions; questions for which he had no answers. He also knew that his wife, Rachel would not appreciate his own department going over every inch of their home looking for signs of a co-conspiracy. He had nothing to hide, of that he was confident, but his reputation around the department would be tarnished regardless of the outcome. That was a simple fact of life. It would be years before he'd feel that his fellow deputies and detectives weren't staring at him. Their confidence in him would always be shaken. How could they go out on raids with him, when there was doubt about which side of the law his loyalties rested? Johnny was finding it difficult to concentrate on the case. He kept going over and over in his mind if there were signs that he missed. Why hadn't he known what Ray was doing? Maybe he'd never know.

"Johnny, Captain wants to see you."

"On my way."

"Are you ready for this?" Al asked.

"I'm as ready as I'm ever gonna be. All I can say is that I didn't see it and from what we see here, we still don't." He headed for Captain Frank Sterns's office.

"Johnny, shut the door behind you, please." Johnny did as instructed and looked around the office. It was a totally enclosed office with only one window that looked out onto Colonial Drive in Orlando. The office walls were beige and had a number of 'I love me' certificates hung on the walls in various places. A picture of the captain's wife and three children was on his desk, which was clear of any paperwork except two manila folders. He could see his name on the tab of one. He expected that the other bore the name of his ex-partner, Ray Krebs.

"Johnny, I don't know quite how to start this discussion. You've been with the Sheriff's department for over eleven years. You've done well throughout your career. There's nothing I can find wrong in this folder. But in a few minutes, Internal Affairs is going to walk through that door," pointing to the door behind Johnny, "and recommend that you be removed from Vice, lose your detective status and get reassigned to traffic detail. That means you'll be on a motorcycle covering parades, and crap like the Zellwood Corn Festival and the Winter Park Art Show. You don't want that at this stage in your career, do you?"

"No Sir." Johnny was staring straight at his captain, stone faced. He stood with his feet spread at shoulder width, hands folded in front of his belt. He wasn't sure what was going to be said, but he was sure that it wasn't going to be good.

"We need you to come clean on this, Johnny. We need you to tell us everything you know about Ray, and we also need to know what your involvement was in all this."

The captain's southern drawl was starting to get on Johnny's nerves. Since he'd been in Florida for quite some time, he'd picked up a slight southern touch to his speech, but not the long, drawn out, deep southern twang of the captain's voice. "Captain, I'm going to tell you and the IA guys this. I don't know anything about Detective Kreb's activities that were outside the limits of department policy or the law. I don't know how he got away with what he apparently did for so long, and I absolutely was not involved in anything that is against department policy or the laws of any governmental body. I have thought about this until my head hurts and I come up empty." Johnny made a small gesture with his hands as if showing the captain that there was nothing there. He refolded them and resumed his stance.

"Very well, Johnny. Hold tight here for a moment, please." Captain Sterns punched his phone and said, "Sandy, send in Detectives Sanders and Dempsey."

The tinny electronic sound of Sandy's voice came back, "Yes Captain."

Moments later, the two detectives entered the captain's office, said hi to Johnny since they all knew each other, and stood next to the captain's desk.

"Johnny, please sit."

For more than two hours, Internal Affairs Detectives Sanders and Dempsey grilled Johnny with tough questions about details of many of the busts that Johnny and Ray went on together. Questions were asked about potentially missing money and drugs, and meetings outside of normal department hours. Johnny recalled most incidents and answered the questions without missing a beat. Then came a question about a traffic stop a number of years ago involving a young woman and her baby. During that accident, he became friends with a young man named Patrick McKinney. "Johnny, did you know that Pat McKinney was under investigation for drugs sales?"

"No sir. That was before I was in Vice. I found out that he may have been doing some things that were unlawful, and I ended our friendship. I didn't pursue investigations because I wasn't in Vice, and I had no evidence of a crime."

"Do you know a gentleman by the name of Jason Roberts?" Detective Dempsey asked.

"I know the name, yes sir." He looked at Captain Sterns for a moment. Then he told the IA detectives, "There is an ongoing investigation and beyond that I am not at liberty to say anything. After our investigation is complete, I will provide whatever details you wish. I cannot jeopardize the integrity of the investigation."

Captain Sterns' face twisted into an angry stare. "Who the hell do you think you're talking to here, Johnny? I want you to answer the question! You're under investigation here and we want answers!"

Johnny returned his captain's angry stare and simply stated that he could not answer the question for the reason already stated. "What evidence do you have that would cause you to investigate me for any reason? Because my partner was a crook? I'll give you that, but what have you found or do you suspect that I've done that gives you cause to investigate me?"

"I can't answer that question. It's an ongoing investigation," his captain shot back. He rose from his seat and leaned towards Johnny in an aggressive position. He moved around his desk and stood only inches from Johnny's face. "But if we find anything, you'll be out of the sheriff's department faster than you can spit." He placed emphasis on 'spit' so that a bit of spray went in Johnny's face, which turned red with anger. It was all Johnny could do to restrain himself. He wanted to bring his fist into Captain Sterns' jaw but held his position.

"Is that all, Captain? I have work to do."

"You're confined to your desk until further notice. You will not carry a firearm while under investigation."

"Sure," Johnny said with adequate indignation. He turned and left the office without closing the door behind him.

Chapter 43

Antonio Scalletti got off a private jet at the Orlando Business Airport. The sun was bright and caused a glare as it reflected off the light colored concrete of the approach to the small building housing BusClas Aviation. The temperature was standing at 91 degrees and the humidity was over 80 percent. Antonio was a healthy looking 52, with dark olive skin and dark eyes. He wore a neat sport coat and slacks made of light fabric, loafers, and a white Izod golf shirt. He carried a small suitcase and a golf bag carrier. He looked like he was ready to hit the links. He was greeted by Jason Roberts and Buddy Mahaffey in a dark sedan. Buddy offered to take his bags, but Antonio declined and placed the bags in the trunk.

When they were safely in the back seat of the car, Jason described the job that Antonio was to perform. It all sounded pretty easy. Not much of a challenge.

"Where would you like this tragic event to occur?"

"We'll let you know. I just want to return a favor."

"I believe I can help you, my friend. Here is my account number. Let me know when you've completed the arrangements. You'll know when the job is done."

"Thank you. Now, where would you like us to take you?"

"I think I'll stay in Lake Buena Vista. There are a couple of nice courses out there. They're pretty challenging from what I've heard. I may even play one of the Disney courses. I've always liked the Mickey Mouse-shaped sand-traps."

***

The telephone call to Pat came from Phil Daniels. It was 1:40 in the afternoon. Jason Roberts wanted to meet with Pat and his brother Joe to talk about a business proposition. He felt a business arrangement with the brothers would remove any problems between them. Phil explained to Pat that Mr. Roberts understood the issues that they had with Jamie and the boys, and that he wanted to remove that stigma between them. He wanted to talk strictly about business. Pat told Phil that he would agree to the meeting on the condition that only Pat, Joe, Jason and Phil were present. Pat said he wanted the meeting to take place at Trimble Park, north of Zellwood. Pat and Joe would be there at the northern– most shelter at 9:30 PM. Phil agreed.

***

Trimble Park was a pie shaped wedge of land that stuck out into Lake Beauclair on the north and west and Lake Carlton on the south. There was only one road into the park. The only other access was by boat or a very long swim.

At 7:30 PM, Joe and Pat drove around the area leading to Trimble Park. They found nothing suspicious but continued to drive the back roads for a time before leaving the area completely. They drove around Lake Beuaclair several times before heading back towards the park entrance. They talked about Mike, asking each other how such a horrible thing could have happened. Joe told Pat a few Marine horror stories, about young men who were barely out of high school. They'd joined the service to get an education, a job and some career experience. They entered boot camp at Paris Island as cocky, smart-assed little kids. They left after thirteen weeks of intense training on how to show respect for your drill sergeant, your parents, your country, and your God. They left as men with a mission. Protect this great country with your heart, body, and soul. They left as killing machines, but only killing if necessary. They were taught that this country was free, but that freedom came at a cost. It was paid for in blood, the blood of their fellow Marines and other servicemen and women. Mike's death was horrible, but not because death was horrible. It was because the circumstances behind his death were horrible.

It was one of the reasons that Pat and Joe had joined the service in the first place. They had a debt to pay. They didn't want to repay that debt rotting in a prison, so they'd signed up for six year hitches each. It also gave them the training and discipline that they needed to carry out the plan, the plan that appeared to be executing on its own. They talked awhile about who could be doing this, and again they got nowhere. They now knew for certain that it wasn't Mike. "God rest his soul," Joe said.

They came back an hour later after driving US Route 441 to Leesburg to speculate what business arrangement Jason Roberts might have in mind. They agreed that it didn't matter, they weren't interested.

At 9:20 PM, they returned to the park in northern Orange County, near the Lake County line. They made their way to the northernmost shelter and found that a black sedan was already parked at the shelter. Their headlights were pointed right at the sedan, but they couldn't see anyone in the car or at the shelter. Pat stopped the car a good distance from the sedan and put the gear shifter in park. They stayed in the car for a few minutes and looked in all directions for anyone. All they saw were the silhouettes of palmetto bushes next to the car. The park looked eerie in the dark. The tall trees created a large canopy, blocking out the stars from view. The Spanish moss hung in long streamers from the tree branches adding a spooky aura to the park. There was no one else in sight. No other vehicles could be seen on any roads that passed in the vicinity of the park.

"I don't like this at all. Should we get out or wait?" Pat asked his brother who was better trained in tactical situations.

"My gut says to stay put for a few minutes. Let's see if these guys show their faces. Just keep looking around. I'll take a look through the night glasses and see if anyone's out there. Shut off the car and kill the lights."

Pat did as instructed and Joe fired up the night scope. He scanned the car and could see two heads in the front seat. No other people were visible in the car. They didn't appear to be in any hurry to get out so Joe continued to scan the area around the shelter and the trees beyond. He thought he saw another body in the distance, but he couldn't be sure. He continued to scan the horizon then came back to the spot where he thought he saw something. There was no movement and no clear image. The green image in the glasses looked almost like that of an early, primitive video game. But this was no game they were playing. Caution was a matter of life and death.

"There are two guys in the car. I thought that I saw another guy in the trees about fifty yards to the front left of the car at maybe 11:00 o'clock. You won't be able to see anything without night vision, so don't bother trying. It's almost 9:30, so things should happen within the next few minutes. Are we ready?"

Pat reached to his side and felt the Glock 9mm and the modified AR15. It was adjusted to go to a full automatic, just like an M16. It held thirty rounds. Joe checked his 9mm and TEK 9. They both hoped that they would not have to use any weapons, but this was a messy business.

The doors to the sedan opened. The interior lights were set to stay off, so the brothers couldn't see the faces of the men that emerged from the sedan. They also opened their doors and stepped out. All car doors closed at about the same time. Tension was high and all four stood still for a few seconds.

***

In the distance, Antonio Scalletti raised his silenced M16A2 and took aim at Pat's head. The night vision scope provided a clear, close-up picture of his target with a set of crosshairs that was directly on Pat's nose. He raised the barrel of his weapon slightly so that he was aiming for the top of Pat's forehead. He steadied his arm against the tree where he stood, took a deep breath and...

***

Radar pulled lightly on the trigger of his silenced Heckler and Koch MP-5N. He felt the slight recoil as three rounds were released. The flash was visible to all four men at the cars, though the sound of air rustling the leaves of the trees drowned out any sound made by the weapon.

Antonio Scalletti felt the impact for only an instant. The bullets entered his left temple in a tight pattern, but exited the right side of his head in a gaping hole left by the projectiles as they turned his brain matter to mush. He died instantly.

Pat and Joe dove back towards the doors of their car. Pat

scraped his already scabbed knees on the parking lot pavement as he did, tearing a fresh layer of tissue from his kneecap. They jumped in and Pat started the car, slammed it into reverse, and swung the car towards the park entrance. The two guys in the other car did the same.

**

In the other car, Phil Daniels and Buddy Mahaffey started to follow Pat and Joe towards the park entrance.

Radar took a bead on the car's right front tire and shot it out. As the car slowed and lost control, he shot out the right back tire, causing the car to bog down in the sand on the side of the road just past the shelter.

Phil and Buddy opened the car doors and dove behind it for cover. They didn't hear a single shot. All they saw were muzzle flashes. But they knew that this guy, whoever he was, knew how to shoot. They stayed behind the car for a long time before they even dared to look up to see if their assailant was still out there. After half an hour of waiting, they started the two mile trek to US 441 and another several miles south to the Texaco station and a pay phone. The call to Mr. Roberts was not going to be pleasant, but they were too scared to care. He was safe in his house. They were out here exposed to some psychopathic killer, walking down an isolated road in rural Orange County.

**

Al Porecwzski and his partner were running into nothing but dead ends. The rental car used in the Farley killing had been rented to a hooker. The hooker swore that she was paid a thousand bucks to rent the car by a guy she never saw. She and a john rented the car using a fake ID. She made a thousand bucks. The john got laid for free. The other dead end was the rented house across from Danny Vallero. Again, rented by a known hooker, again she made a handsome sum for a few hours' work. Never saw the guy. But there were fewer dead ends than there were dead bodies. There were even fewer clues. The case was going nowhere.

Then in walked Johnny Poleirmo with a smiling face.

"Guess what, guys. I'm chained to my desk."

The forced smile twisted into a red, angry set of gritted teeth. Johnny brushed his hand across his desk and knocked a stack of files to the floor. The entire room of deputies, clerks, and 'clients' looked his way.

Al said, "Johnny, are you getting paid?" Johnny nodded. "Then don't sweat it. Take your paycheck, wait till this blows over and enjoy the fact that you don't have a boat load of stress twisting your gut. It'll pass man."

"You're right, it will." Johnny leaned down to pick up the files, because no one was going to do it for him. A few of the files were mixed up in his file toss. He picked up two forms from different cases and looked at both. Jason Roberts was the subject of one. Danny Vallero was the other. Johnny paused to think for a minute. What is the relationship here? Did all these guys work for Roberts? Just then his desk phone rang. "Johnny Poleirmo."

The voice at the other end said, "Have I got a deal for you."

"I'm listening."

When Johnny hung up the phone, he was smiling, and this smile wasn't forced.

***

It was nearly 1:00 AM when Phil Daniels and Buddy Mahaffey reported to Jason Roberts what had happened. They'd taken the body of Antonio Scalletti to Lake Beauclair and dumped it in a marshy spot on the lake's edge. They had no desire to be caught trying to recover a dead body and bring it back to get a proper burial. They figured that the alligators would drag the body into the lake and take care of the evidence. That was proper enough for a man of his caliber. They tossed his gun about thirty feet into the lake.

"Did you see the shooter?"

"No. We didn't even hear a shot. All we saw was flash. He shot out the tires on the car. This guy, whoever he is, can shoot. He could've killed us, no sweat. I'm convinced that he just wanted to keep us from getting to the McKinney's. Hell, a tire is hard as hell to hit, especially on a moving car. He has some serious hardware, too. This gun let out a triple burst. You could see the separate flashes, but they were quick, real close together. You could hardly see that they were separate bursts. This guy ain't no novice, boss."

"Buddy, do you agree?"

"Yes sir, Mr. R. This guy is good. Wish he was on our side."

"We can try one more time to get the McKinneys and this shooter on our side. They must have hired him. Why else would he be doing this, and why would he just want to scare you two. If he could have, and he had good reason, you'd be dead, again, right?"

"Yeah," was their answer in unison.

"I think I'm going to give Mr. Pat McKinney a courtesy call."

Chapter 44

Pat and Joe were at Pat and Diane's house talking in the office with the door closed. They wanted to go over the events of the past week and see if they could make sense of all that had happened. There were too many people shooting around them and not at them. They came to the same conclusion that whoever was doing the shooting was definitely not after them. Joe mentioned that he saw the guy at Trimble Park who was in the trees, but the flashes didn't come from that direction. They came from a different area of the park, maybe fifty to sixty yards away. It didn't make sense. It had to be this same mystery guy, though. Who else would get involved in something like this?

"Maybe the cops have a new vigilante group, like in that one Dirty Harry movie," Pat said. "That's pretty far-fetched, I know, but what other explanation is there?"

Joe wasn't buying it. In the Marines they learned that things don't happen by coincidence. Things are done with a purpose. "We need to lay low for a few days. What do you say we take a trip out of state? Your kids aren't in school. I'll see if Lisa can join us for a few days."

"I've got a better idea, why don't you take the vacation, and I'll stay here with Diane and the kids. We can take a shorter trip and go down to see Mom and Dad. They probably could use the company right now.

Diane said that Mom called her with the details of Mike's service." Joe's head sank a little. He hadn't given much thought to Mike's suicide over the last day. "His ashes will be delivered to Mom and Dad this Friday. They'll be placed in the mausoleum vault with Julie in Pennsylvania. We need to be there."

Joe agreed and said that no matter where he and Lisa

went, he would be at the services. "So it's settled. We're lying low at least until next Monday. That gives us five days to think this through. Do you have any great ideas?"

"Yeah, I do. Here's what I think we should do."

For the next half hour, Pat laid out his plan to Joe. Joe nodded his head in approval for the most part. When he'd heard the majority of the plan, Joe reviewed it with Pat and they made some minor changes. Much depended on some outside activities that were beyond their control, but they figured if they could pull this off, it would solve their problems for good.

It was getting late and Joe still had to drive back to Orlando, so they wrapped up a final review of the plan. Since they were the only ones around to discuss it, if this plan took off on its own, they had to figure that God was the shooter. That was unlikely.

***

Johnny Poleirmo looked at the receiver like he'd just had a conversation with an alien. He held it for several seconds before returning it to its cradle. He stared at the phone a while longer.

"Who was that?" Al Porecwzski asked Johnny.

"You won't believe this. Some guy just said that there is a dead body at Trimble Park by the boat dock. Said the guy was killed by some guys working for Jason Roberts. I asked him how he knew this and he said he saw it. Said it happened late last night. This whole McKinney/Roberts thing is starting to really stink." He motioned to Al to come closer and whispered, "This guy said that Roberts is the one who ordered hits on Donnie Lee Lester, Bobby Acquino, Jamie, Bill, and Danny. Oh, and Randy Farley. I asked him what relation they had to Jason Roberts. He said they worked for him. But that they stole a boat load of money from him over the last few months, and he wanted to teach them a lesson. I asked him how he knew all this, and he said he's inside the organization."

Al's eyes were wide, listening to Johnny walk through the details of what he allegedly knew of Jason Robert's organization. "Is he supposed to call you back?" Al asked.

"He says yes. He wants us to check out the facts. Said

that a light military infantry gun was used in the hit last night. Said the gun's in Lake Beauclair about thirty feet offshore by the dock. I guess we can check it out. Trimble's about forty minutes away. Do we need divers?"

***

It was an absolutely gruesome find. The body had been a midnight snack for a couple of hungry gators. They'd fought over the remains and there wasn't much left. This was going to be the Orange County Coroner's greatest challenge ever. They didn't know the man's identity. They only had the word of an anonymous tip. So far, the tip was on the money. They also found the gun where it had been purported to be. So far, the guy was on the level.

"What do you think?" Al asked Johnny and Rich.

"It all fits with what he said. Body was right where he said it would be. Same for the gun. Maybe he's the trigger man. Maybe he's got it in for Mr. Roberts. Sure would be nice to find out who the dead guy is, where he's from, and what business he had here."

"Well he couldn't have been all that good. He got snuffed and eaten. I hope he gave those gators indigestion, because I sure got it after seeing that carcass. Man, they tore him up. Anything on the gun?"

"We're just starting to check it out. Standard military issue M16A2 except that it was modified with a silencer. Never fired a round, magazine was full. He came here for business. I wonder who he was gunning for? He came out here loaded for bear but got beat to the punch. Are the crime scene guys here yet?"

"Yep. They just started. We're trying to keep everyone out of the park until they get through. They already determined that there were two cars in the park that were really squealing out of here. One had its tires blown out. It looks like they may have been shot out. The other made it out of here without a problem. They found where the guy had been when he took the taps to the head. He was about forty yards from the shelter. They noticed a pattern from where the guy's brains splattered. They figured out which direction the bullets came from. Found a freshly broken tree limb about seventy yards away from where the victim was squatted down. They also found matted leaves and a little disturbed sand. No shoe prints or anything. The shooter didn't come into the middle of the park. He apparently had a boat. Who knows where he went from here. He could have accessed miles of shore in the Dora Canal System. Hell, there's dozens of lakes just within a five mile radius. Plus, he goes 500 yards to the west and he's in Lake County."

Johnny asked Al if he'd contacted the Lake County Sheriffs yet. He nodded yes.

"Too many killings. The Sheriff is going to want results fast. This is getting too public, and the Sentinel is having a field day. Sales must be up with this much mayhem."

"Let's just hope it ends real soon." Johnny was not confident that it would, but he knew some things that his new temporary partner didn't know. Maybe they were closer than they even knew.

***

The memorial service for Mike McKinney was small and solemn. Only family members were allowed. Mike had few friends left in the world. Mike's mother was dressed in a black dress and wore a black veil hung low over her face. She'd been crying for some time before the service, but maintained her composure during the service. She'd expected this day would come sooner than later. She knew of Mike's drinking and that he just wasn't taking care of himself. She also knew he was consumed by grief after losing Julie. Most people get over tragedy over time, but she'd told her husband that Mike would never get over his despair.

Mike's maids had sent flowers and a poem about Mike, and what a beautiful person he was inside. It's too bad that the beautiful person was held prisoner by ugly guards called guilt and remorse. He was deeply in love with his new bride. She was taken from him in the most heinous way at a time when their lives should have been the most joyous. The feeling that he should have been there to protect her never left him. When he died, he had less than $120,000 left of a significant fortune. When he got to Vegas, he started to gamble to hide his sorrow, but he stopped that when he'd get so drunk at the dollar slots that he'd pass out and fall off of the stool. He was not welcome in most casinos, so ended up staying home to drink most of the time.

He left the remainder of his money to his maids who took care of him for years. They approached his mom and dad to try to return the money, but they would hear none of it. Mike's parents assured them that Mike would want his caretakers to have the money. They were grateful and assured them that they would take care of readying the house for sale. Mike's parents were very gracious in return. The service ended. The funeral home took charge of Mike's ashes and assured the family that they were in good hands. The ashes would be shipped to the same funeral home that handled Julie's service. They would then be placed in the mausoleum with Julie's remains. They would be joined again, this time for eternity.

Pat and Joe said their goodbyes to their parents. The afternoon clouds were starting to gather in preparation for the daily shower. It had been a bright, sunny day until the last half hour. It seemed appropriate that some amount of gloomy weather would move in. But, like the clouds of the Florida afternoon, these dark clouds of Mike's death would pass.

Joe spoke to Pat as they got into Pat's Taurus, "Finally, Mike's at peace. I wish there'd been a way we could have helped him."

"We had a plan, Joe. We tried to do what we thought was right. Even if we'd have succeeded, I'm not sure that it would have helped. I'm not sure we'd feel any more satisfaction than we feel right now." He paused and looked around the church parking lot. "We can't dwell on this. We have work to do. Tomorrow, we've got a house call. Are you ready?"

"Oh yeah."

They drove back to Orlando in silence. Joe fell asleep while Pat drove.

Oh yeah, Pat thought to himself. *We're not through yet.*

Chapter 45

Brian Purcer and the Hot Licks' fifth day in the studio was by far their most productive. They'd completed recording nine of the eleven tracks slated for their first album. They had two more to finish tomorrow and then they'd break for a day or two. Two sound engineers would review the tracks to see where overdubs were necessary. The studio owner and lead sound engineer told Brian that there wouldn't be much overdubbing. His gut feeling was that they could get away with minimal changes, and that they should only need to add a few lead guitar spots. The rest would be ready for mass production. The band's agent had already called asking how the studio work was going and was pleased to hear about the band's progress.

Steve Foreman, Brian, Rick, and the other band members were in the lounge area in the studio. The room was sound-proofed so that the noise from the studio area was muffled and not annoying. That was important now, because a loud, horrible sounding band was in studio number two. They sucked but the lead singer's daddy was paying the bill, so they let them record whatever they wanted. Steve was thirty-four years old and had owned the studio since he was twenty-two. He had long, light brown hair and light blue eyes. He played a number of instruments and on occasion played back up for bands that needed a bass player or rhythm guitar. He'd even tried back-up vocals one time, but the band decided that it didn't work for their piece. He never tried that again. Steve got several beers out of the refrigerator, since they were done for the day. They each popped the tops, clinked necks together, and took a long pull.

"You guys should be on tour in less than a month. Are you ready for this?" Steve asked Brian and Rick. "You know, once you start on the road, there are few breaks. It's a money train, but it can be grueling. One thing for sure, you won't have any competition from those guys." He made a gesture at the wall towards the other studio.

"God, I hope we don't sound that bad. I guess we're as ready as we're ever gonna be, man. We've got the energy. I just hope we can keep it up." Brian said. "Steve, give it to me straight. How do we sound compared to other bands you've produced?"

"I'm not going to lie to you. You've got about the best tunes that I've heard in a long time. I've had a lot of good bands in here. You guys are right there at the top. Don't let it go to your head, man. As fast as it comes, it can go faster. My advice is ride the wave while it's cresting. Your wave is cresting right now. It could stay for a long time or it could fizzle. Either way, don't sweat it. You're going be rich. What you do with it, that's up to you."

"Thanks, man. You've been a great coach for us."

"It doesn't matter if you're a great coach, if you haven't got the players. You guys are the players."

"Hey guys, I've got to hit the road. I'm picking up Ginny in about thirty-five minutes. We're going to grab a light bite to eat and turn in early. We have to be back here at what time?"

"8:00 AM and be fresh. Don't be up all night. I know you rock stars think you'll live forever, but you get old fast." Steve pointed a finger at the band members.

"Yes, Mom," came the sarcastic chorus in near unison.

Steve just shook his head and went back to the control counsel for studio number two.

***

Pat was up at 5:30 drinking coffee and eating Frosted Flakes, his favorite breakfast cereal. He sat at Joe's counter reading the previous day's sports section about the Florida Marlins and the start of the Buccaneer's pre-season. As usual, there was some speculation that the Bucs would have a decent team and there were the usual outspoken critics saying that they'd screw it up yet another year.

Pat heard the door to Joe's room open and light footsteps

went into the bathroom. Lisa had spent the night and was just using the facilities. She and Joe were getting serious. She'd spent the evening even with Pat in the other bedroom. Joe really appeared to be falling hard for her. They got along so well and shared so many interests. He envied Joe that. He and Diane loved each other deeply, but they really had very little in common. Pat liked sports. Diane was more of a homebody, enjoying making crafts and changing the home décor almost as often as the changing seasons. But they were a good match. Life with each other was never boring. Pat hoped and prayed that his remaining brother would find peace and happiness with the right soul mate. It appeared that Lisa might just be the one.

While Lisa was still in the bathroom, Joe strolled into the kitchen in his boxers. "Why are you up so early? You need your rest."

"I couldn't sleep any longer. I was thinking about you and Lisa."

"You pervert."

"No, you dork. I was thinking that you should make sure that you never let her out of your sight. She's a real doll. Protect her."

"Pat, just because bad things happened to Mike, doesn't mean..." Joe stopped, then continued, "You need to take care of your family, too. Maybe you should have gone home last night. Have you called Diane since the service?"

"Yeah. I called her last night. She's fine. She said that she keeps the doors locked and the alarm on, but she feels better now that all these bastards are dead. Her words, not mine."

"We'll see what today brings. I'm headed back to bed. We've got a few hours before we need to hit the road. You should, too."

"I'm going to finish breakfast and go down for an early swim. Then I'm going to call Diane." Pat said.

"See you in a couple hours."

The door to the bathroom opened and Lisa's footsteps could be heard heading back to Joe's room. *Lucky Bastard*, Pat thought to himself.

***

Brian and Ginny did go to bed early, and they did get to sleep early, but not before they made love for over an hour. They were passionately in love now. Brian was concerned that things were going too fast in both his career and his love life, but he couldn't stop either one. So at 7:50 in the morning from the studio he called his friend, Pat McKinney, to talk about money and love and music. Diane told him that Pat wasn't there and that he didn't come home last night. Brian quickly asked Diane if their problems had surfaced again, and she just as quickly put his fears to rest. He'd just come back from Mike's funeral service down in Ft. Myers and rather than drive home, he stayed with Joe overnight.

Brian grimaced when he heard Diane mention Mike's service. Pat had called with the news about Mike the day before. It was truly a sad story. Brian had forgotten to tell Ginny about Mike. He'd tell her tonight for certain.

Then Steve called Brian: "We're ready for you. I want you to listen to these first three songs before we start to record the first take on the new track. I think we need to add some lead guitar...."

***

Jason Roberts was also up early. He didn't sleep much at all. He had a hooker over for the night and at $1500 per night, she was supposed to relieve him of all his worries. It didn't work. The sex was great, but he still had big problems with business. He needed replacements for his lost team and he needed them fast. He drank coffee and tried to figure out what to eat for breakfast.

"Do you like pancakes?" Sheila asked from behind him. It surprised him to hear her voice. He figured that she was still in bed.

"Why, you want to cook some for me?"

"Sure, for what you pay me, I can do a little domestic work. I won't even charge you extra. It'll be a bonus."

"You're on." His lips turned up in a little smile. It was the first time in days that he'd had occasion to smile even a little. He stared at Sheila's ass while she bent over to get out the griddle. *That was an extra bonus,* he thought.

"Right after breakfast, you've got to shower and get on out of here. I'll arrange for Buddy to take you home. I'll be on the patio when you get the pancakes ready. And bring more coffee when you come out."

Jason took his coffee and headed outside. He sat at the patio table and looked through the morning paper. Sheila moved around the kitchen working on the flapjacks and bacon, pouring orange juice, putting silverware and linen napkins on a serving tray. She glanced out to make sure that he was seated comfortably and concentrating on the paper. She looked through the doorways from the kitchen into adjoining rooms to check for Buddy, Phil, and the rest of Jason's help. No one was around that she could see. She reached into the pocket on her robe, pulled out a tiny microphone and stuck it under the edge of the countertop. She finished cooking Jason's breakfast, loaded them onto the plate and took the serving tray out to the patio.

"Breakfast is served," she said with a million dollar smile. "Is there anything else that I can get for you before I take a shower?"

"No, go ahead. Be sure to let Buddy know when you're done. You need to be out of here by 9:00. Thanks for breakfast. Buddy will make sure you're paid. You were a lot of fun."

Jason went back to his paper. Sheila turned and headed to the shower but she had a few places to stop on the way. She planted three more microphones as she made her way through the house; one in the living room, one in the entrance to Jason's office and one in the dining room. She tried to get inside his office but the door was locked. Satisfied that her work was done, she took her shower, dressed, did a little makeup work, and dialed the number Jason had given her for Buddy.

Within forty minutes of serving breakfast, Sheila was out the door. Not a bad night for a hooker. $1500 for services rendered and $1000 to plant some illegal listening devices for someone she didn't even know. It was all pretty exciting. Her adrenaline was pumping as she thanked Buddy for the ride to her apartment in Clermont. She couldn't wait to tell her friends about her adventure.

Chapter 46

It was 9:40 AM by the time Buddy made it back to Jason's. As he took up his position at the entrance to Jason's office, Phil Daniels came in to check on schedules for the day.

"There's nothing going down until 8:30 tonight. We have to oversee a drop at the Albertson farm. We got a big move going on; a hundred and forty." That meant one hundred and forty bales of marijuana. Phil raised an eyebrow. That was an unusually large move. He guessed that Jason was trying to make up for a few lost deals in the last few days.

"I guess we're going to be busy tonight. That will take some time. Is everything set to go?"

"Yeah. There's nothing unusual about the deal, just size. Jason's a bit tense after the botched move on the McKinneys. He thought that his dude from Boston would just do it and head home. What a mess. We don't have Ray to know what the cops are doing. We really need another inside guy there. That's going to hurt."

As Pat and Joe listened to the conversation, they were making adjustments to the signal to make sure everything was being recorded clearly. The signal from the office was strong and clear. They really had all the information that they needed now, with the knowledge of a big deal going down, and the fact that Jason had set up the hit on them. They knew that Sheila was gone and that Phil, Buddy, and Jason were the only people in the large house. No one else was expected. If they could just get the three of them together...

Jason had finished his breakfast, showered and dressed and was ready for a day of serious planning. He needed to resolve the issue of retooling his organization. Buddy and Phil were loyal and they'd make good leaders, if he could find the right people to fill in behind them. That was going to be the order of the day. Phil and Buddy needed to get out this morning and start recruiting new, young talent to take over for the likes of Donnie Lee, Bobby, Jamie, and Danny. He also knew that there was a big hole in intelligence. Ray had kept them informed if they were getting any attention. *This won't be so bad though. It'll be tough at first, but it will be like starting fresh but with significant experience and knowledge of the business. Not to mention the contacts.* But he had to act quickly. In this business 'what have you done for me lately?' was a key element. If you lost a contact, it was difficult to get it back.

Jason entered his office from the bedroom and looked over his schedule. There was little going on today so he buzzed Phil and Buddy, "Come on in, guys. We've got work to do."

***

With the three gathered in Jason's office, the monitors were left unattended in the office entry. This was Pat and Joe's moment of opportunity. They were parked in a rented utility van in a wooded area behind Jason's property. They wore surveyor uniforms. They knew that Jason's neighbors to the south were gone on a cruise, so they took the opportunity to act like they were surveying their property line. Pat set up a tripod and Joe took the long red and white poll with him along the edge of Jason's property. They acted casual and carried clipboards and jotted down figures which meant absolutely nothing. They met at a spot adjacent to Jason's garage where there were no windows facing his neighbor's property.

"See anything?" Pat asked as the two looked around the neighborhood.

"Nope, we're clear. Nothing over the house wire either." Together they moved towards Jason's house and worked their way around to the patio. The office was on the opposite side of the house. Pat and Joe found the patio door open, just as Sheila had said. He never locked the patio door except at night. They shed their surveyor's gear on the patio and drew their guns. They both had MP5 silenced automatics; very menacing looking when they're being pointed in your direction. They were amazed at how easy it was to conceal them in their fake gear. Pat and Joe wasted no time making their way through the elegant house. The plush carpeting everywhere made it easy to move through the house without a sound. When they got to the office vestibule, they stopped, listened, and determined that all three were still in Jason's office. Joe held up his fingers for the countdown. Three, two, one...

Jason, Phil and Buddy had no time to react. Pat and Joe were through the door and had their guns trained on the three before they could bat an eye.

"Don't move a muscle!" Joe yelled. And they didn't. Buddy was the guy that they were most concerned about, with his history of barroom brawls. Guns didn't seem to scare him much. But he was a pretty smart guy, and in this situation, must have figured that it wasn't worth getting blown away. He just sat back in his easy chair and tried to relax. Phil Daniels appeared tense, with his eyebrows furled in a frown. He was sitting forward in his chair and appeared ready to take a chance.

After a few seconds, Jason spoke. "Phil, just relax. If they were going to kill us, the deed would be done. Am I right guys?"

"We'll see," Pat said. "We have a little score to settle. You see, we really don't like the idea of someone running around trying to kill us. You know we had a personal score with Jamie and the others. We have no beef with you. So why try to kill us?"

"Well, you put one hell of a dent in my organization. You wiped out about a million and a half bucks a year out of my cash flow. That hurts. It's going to take time to replace that. I wanted you to pay."

"What if we told you that it wasn't us, that we don't know who it was, and that we'd like to know that as much as you." Pat said.

"Well, I'd be real surprised. So what are you saying? Maybe we could team up to figure this out? After that, what should we do? I've heard you guys have some experience in this business. It sounded like you did okay until all of the personal stuff happened. What would you say to a partnership?"

"Partners don't go around putting out contracts on each other." Pat replied.

Jason thought for a moment before he spoke. "Partners also don't break into each other's houses and hold automatic weapons to their heads. How about if we introduce each other and clear the air? You know, if we're keeping score, we're really even. You took out my guys, I tried to retaliate. If you're willing, we can call a truce and discuss the future. There's a whole lot of money to be made."

They were in. Pat and Joe realized at that moment that they had the upper hand.

Chapter 47

Pat and Joe agreed to terms with Jason Roberts. After thirty minutes of tense negotiations where guns were raised more than once, they agreed that Pat and Joe would be equal partners with Jason. At first, Jason had suggested that he get 50% of the profits and Pat and Joe would get to split 50%. After showing Jason that they had the upper hand, Jason agreed to a 30% split for each with 10% being distributed to the senior support guys. That meant Phil, Buddy and a few others would get paid a flat rate and split 10% as an incentive to expand the business. In theory, the working stiffs could make nearly as much as Jason, Pat and Joe. That seemed like a good plan and a good recruitment tool. The new business would take off and grow. The hardest part was keeping control of the growth and hand selecting recruits. Lots of people would want a slice of the pie. Pat and Joe explained that they had to make sure that the pie remained under control and didn't outgrow their ability to manage it. Jason was impressed with the brothers' negotiating skills and was equally impressed by the plan itself. He wanted to get the details on how to keep records and administer the new business. They explained that they could make the whole business look legitimate with help from Pat's legal advisor and accountant. He was already handling the brother's current business affairs. It would be an adjustment to take the books to the next level but it was manageable.

After all was said and done, the parties nervously shook hands. The deal was done. The new partnership would start tonight with the Albertson deal. Jason gave the details to Pat and Joe. They would all meet at Albertson's warehouse. Phil, Buddy, and Joe would stay at the warehouse and supervise loading the bales into delivery vans. Jason and Pat would be at the farm house handling the finances. They would leave in two cars, Pat and Jason in Pat's, the others in Phil's SUV.

Jason wanted to get this off on the right foot so he proposed a toast to the new partnership. "To making lots of money!"

"I'll drink to that," Pat raised his glass and took a swig. And heads nodded all around. They were all actually smiling when Pat and Joe left the house and headed back to Joe's apartment. They had to be back at Jason's place by 7:00 pm for the drive to Umatilla.

***

Radar drove north along US Route 441 to State Route 19 in Eustis. The route used to be through sparsely populated country where all one would see were citrus stands and flea markets where old hub caps were sold. Now the strip of roadway was ripe with commercial businesses; strip malls anchored by Publix supermarkets, and new housing developments. The driving was stop and go for most of the trip until Radar made it through the town of Eustis. Then the scenery turned more agricultural. There were still a few active citrus groves, several foliage nurseries, and the occasional tomato field. In the town of Umatilla Radar turned west on County Road 452. About three miles outside Umatilla was the Albertson farm. The 325 acre farm was mostly for dairy cows, but some of the land was planted with tomato plants and a small section of citrus trees. The citrus trees were survivors of the deep freeze in the late 1970s. The farm appeared to be a thriving business. The buildings were well kept, including a barn, the main house, a warehouse with loading dock, and a greenhouse for tomato seedlings. The farm was located on Lake Yale Road, to the south of County Road 450. Lake Yale was on the southwest border of the property. There was a stand of pine trees to the south of the lake.

Radar drove by the property, then back onto County Road 450. He then took Route 42 east back to Altoona, then south on Route 19 and back onto County Road 450 past the property a second time. Approximately three and a half miles west on County Road 450 he turned south onto Thomas Boat

Landing Road. Several marinas with boat rentals were on the western shore of Lake Yale. He parked his rented SUV at one of the marinas and rented a small motor boat. He also bought some bait, a package of hooks and other assorted fishing supplies. He figured that he could boat across the lake to a point within about a mile of the property and hike the remaining two miles to the farm and warehouse. He went back to his SUV and gathered his hiking gear. He loaded the boat and headed out into the lake.

It was early evening. There were a few other boaters on the lake, but none came close. He found a spot to anchor the boat near shore in a secluded area hidden by trees along the shore. He put his backpack on and made his way to shore. In this part of Florida, people owned large tracts of property, but rarely saw most of what they owned. As he made his way through a wide, marshy area of land he could smell the decaying vegetation. He was sweating profusely in the early evening heat. Even the shade of the trees hiding the low sun where he jogged couldn't stifle the heat and humidity. He was used to this type of trek, though. He practiced runs like this frequently in the swampy area where he lived. This was a walk in the park by comparison.

Radar made good time initially jogging through the forest land, through marshy areas where gators and water moccasins sat waiting for the right meal to come along. He was familiar with this type of terrain though. He wasn't concerned with these fellow predators. He was hunting two legged animals. He wanted to make sure the McKinneys were protected and that the slime that was trying to seduce them wouldn't get away with murder. He was a man on a mission and nothing was going to stop him from carrying out that mission.

Radar didn't encounter any gators or snakes in his path. There were plenty of cubby holes for them to hide, but none came out to greet him. He just kept cruising at a pretty decent clip, only stopping twice to catch his breath and take a quick swig of water. He washed the water around in his mouth then spit it out. *No sense getting cramps.*

It was 8:20 PM when he took up his position in the pine tree stand just to the southwest of the Albertson property. It was about 1500 yards to the warehouse. By 9:15 it would be dark enough for him to make the sprint across the property to the warehouse and see first-hand the transaction that was going down tonight. The tomato field was at full height to provide some cover for his advance. Now it was time to sit and watch. He would see what he could learn from this vantage point. Maybe it wouldn't be much, but he already knew what he needed to know. He had just under an hour to wait. But that was nothing compared to a lifetime of misery, or a lifetime of regret for not using his skills to the best of his ability. If he died during one of his adventures, then he would die knowing he did his best to make the world a better place.

***

Sonny Albertson was a mean bastard. He had no time for nonsense and he had no time for joking around. When Jason had called him and said that there were new players in the game, he told Jason that the deal was off and slammed the phone down. Jason called him back and tried to calm him down. He assured Albertson that there would be no trouble and that these guys were good. Jason gave him his word that he would never jeopardize their business relationship. After fifteen minutes of arguing back and forth, Jason was finally able to soothe Sonny's ruffled feathers.

"You know I've had some difficulties with my help recently. I had to recruit some new blood. These guys are good. You'll meet them tonight. It'll go as smooth as silk, I promise you."

The deal was still on.

Jason hung up the phone and rubbed his hands together. He was making calls to his other contacts, reassuring them that everything was on track. He was arranging deals, one after another. The new partnership was going to be great. After the past week and a half of setbacks, he was flying high, in a manner of speaking. Jason had over a million dollars' worth of deals arranged. He hung up the phone and it rang immediately. It was Phil.

"Mr. Roberts, we're ready to go whenever the

McKinneys get here."

"Great, Phil." The excitement in Jason's voice was evident. Phil didn't share that excitement. He felt like he'd been passed over. Why should these Johnny-come-latelies get the profits? He and Buddy had been with Jason for years, working hard and taking the risks for him. It just wasn't fair. Maybe he and Buddy should strike out on their own, make a little competition for old Mr. Roberts. Could it be that Jamie had been right all along? Maybe Jason was taking advantage of them. He'd go along with this arrangement for now but he figured it wouldn't be too long before he was fed up. This partnership couldn't last.

Jason continued, "Phil, you and Buddy are a key part of this organization. Don't worry about this. I can guarantee you both that this arrangement will benefit all of us. Trust me on this."

The tone of his voice led Phil to believe that Jason was already plotting a way to get the McKinneys back for the damage that they'd done to his organization. He was probably just biding time.

"Yes sir, Mr. Roberts. I understand."

"Phil, call me Jason."

"Yes sir...I mean Jason." Phil hung up the phone and smiled.

***

Diane was upset and scared. Pat wouldn't tell her why he wasn't going to be home until late that night. All he would say is that she should trust his judgment and hug the kids for him. He would try to be home by a little after midnight and that he and Joe would be together.

"You're not going to do anything stupid, are you?"

"Of course not, babe. You know me."

Diane smiled and said, "Yes, I do and that's why I'm worried." Her smile faded and she said, "Whatever it is that you're doing, you be damned careful. If you don't come home to me safe and sound, I'll kill you myself."

"I love you." Pat hung up the phone.

"I love you, too," she whispered to the dial tone.

Chapter 48

At 9:20 PM, the semi truck pulled into the warehouse at Albertson's farm. The large bay-sized door closed behind it. Radar told himself to remain cool and wait. He'd made the run across the 1500 yards from where he'd been watching the farm and was now just seventy-five yards from the warehouse. It wouldn't take any time at all to cross the field behind the white slatted fence to get to the warehouse. There were several entrances to the building. The warehouse was about two hundred feet long by eighty-four feet wide and had two high bay doors. The building siding was steel painted light beige with dark brown trim. It looked like it was painted every two weeks as clean and fresh as the paint job looked.

After another fifteen minutes, two vehicles approached. The cars parked around the back side of the warehouse so that they weren't visible from the road. Two men got out of each car. One had a briefcase. He couldn't tell from that distance what they were carrying, but this was drug business. You had to assume that everyone was carrying some kind of heat. Two more men exited the farm house and went to the warehouse from the front and entered the front service door. The men who'd arrived in the cars headed for the back service door to the building and went inside.

The sun had set to the west and visibility was getting bad. Radar got out his night vision scope and put it over his head. He watched the road for other vehicles, expecting at least two more. He noticed a dark van go by the property twice. That was of interest, though nothing to be concerned about. Then he noticed a dark sedan go past the property. The car looked a bit too 'official'. *Just something else to keep in mind.* There was very little traffic on County Road 450 and none on Lake Yale Road.

It would be easy to keep track of any cars that might approach the warehouse. *This is a great location for an operation like this.* Time was passing slowly now, as he became more attentive to every detail that came to his senses. There, two more cars approaching. These two also went to the back of the warehouse. Three men got out of the first vehicle, an SUV of some type. Two got out of the second sedan. They also went to the back service door and disappeared.

Radar looked at his watch. 9:45 PM. *Showtime.* He started to make his way to the warehouse along the fence line of the pasture. It was an easy path and he knew he had plenty of time to get to the action. As he moved, he took a magazine of 24 rounds and plugged it into the MP5 Carbine. He had plenty of spares should the need arise. It was his hope that all he needed to do was observe.

***

Inside the warehouse, a police band radio was crackling. Jason was introducing Pat and Joe to Sonny Albertson. Buddy and Phil were standing behind the group looking on. Sonny was not pleasant and not really interested in meeting the new partners, especially since this deal was particularly large. The tension was already higher than with a normal deal.

"I ain't pleased about this little twist, Jase."

"Sonny, my man, relax. This is going to work out just fine. These boys know the business real well, and they're real good with their guns. They both got some military background. Have I ever steered you wrong?"

"No, but I still ain't happy." He turned to Pat and Joe and said with a surly grunt, "I'm going to be watching you both real close, you understand?"

Pat's eyes locked on Albertson's. "Likewise," was all he said. That didn't appear to make Sonny Albertson happy. Joe shifted a little from one foot to another. He and Pat were packing Heckler and Koch 9mm semi automatics, but they didn't have the firepower to stand up to an assault by these hoods. They were carrying a couple of shotguns that appeared to be more suited for hunting than guarding a large load of dope. But Buddy and

Phil were loaded for bear with M16 A2s. All in all, there were seven Albertsons and associates, Jason, Buddy, Phil, Pat and Joe in the warehouse. The tension was pretty high, but was broken when one of the Albertson boys said, "Are we gonna do this or what?"

Sonny Albertson gave the word with a mere nod of his head. He remained staring at Pat except when his eyes shifted to Joe. The man with the briefcase tossed it up on a table, opened it and stood back. Jason approached, picked a seemingly random bundle of bills and flipped through them. He didn't bother to count because that would literally take hours. Apparently they'd done enough business together that there was trust or an understanding that the amount would be correct.

Pat said to Jason, "I thought that business was conducted in the farm house? I really don't like it when things happen unexpectedly. I think that you, me and Sonny here ought to take this part of the business in the house."

Sonny simply barked at Pat, "We'll do business where I say, and we're doing it here."

"Okay, but next time when I'm told something, I expect that it goes that way. Either of you have a problem with that?"

Sonny looked at Jason then back to Pat and said almost in a growl, "You'll do business how I say. If you don't like it..."

Jason stepped in. "Sonny, cool off. I told him that's how we do it and he's right. If we say we're doing something a certain way, we should do it that way. Pat, if you don't mind, we'll do it here this time. Look, we're all going to make lots of money. We can work on details next time. Okay?"

Tempers eased slightly but the tension was still high.

The inside of the warehouse had a gantry crane that was large enough to ride over the semi's trailer. As they were talking, the Albertson boys, Seth and Will were making preparations to move the crane to a position where they could remove the contents of the trailer. Beside the trailer were several vans with their doors open, ready to load. The first pallet of bales was being lifted and moved to the first van near one set of roll up doors. By Pat's calculation, it would take about 45 minutes for the vans to be loaded. It was no wonder why men took the risk to deal in drugs. It was a multimillion dollar profit every year, and you only had to do this a half dozen times a year. Dealing was risky, but the risks were minimized when you had an efficient operation like this one.

***

Radar was standing beside the service door near the back of the warehouse. He listened for any activity inside the warehouse, then cracked the door open ever so slowly, listening for any squeaky hinges. He had the door open just enough to peer inside. It looked like everything was going smoothly. He counted heads to make sure that everyone was accounted for and slipped inside the door. He moved behind a set of shelves that held farming equipment parts. His movements were slow and stealthy and he maintained visual contact with every person in the warehouse. He listened to the conversations going on, but there was little in the way of small talk. These guys were all concentrating on the business at hand.

The only thing he noticed was a bit of tension between Pat and Sonny Albertson. He decided that there would be no ambush in here so he moved back to a position closer to the door. He was settling in to a surveillance position. This would be a short night. No problems. Once the deal was done and the warehouse cleared out, he could leave without anyone knowing that he was there at all.

***

Back in the City of Umatilla, the Lake County Drug Task Force was getting their gear ready. Several members of the Orange County Drug Task force were there as well. Johnny Poleirmo headed up the Orange County Unit. He'd been reinstated. Internal Affairs turned up evidence that his captain had conspired with Ray Krebs to protect one Jason Roberts and his organization.

Sheriff Henry 'Hank' Franklin was the lead for this operation. They had six sheriff's cars, one surveillance van, and a spotter car involved in the bust. The brief was over, and they were ready to move on Hank's signal. The plan was to go in silent from both ends of Lake Yale Road so that there was no escape path for any vehicles at the farm. They would approach without lights until they were at the warehouse, then make a loud speaker announcement that the place was surrounded. Hank hoped to have this wrapped up peacefully.

He'd had suspicions about Sonny Albertson's kids, but he had no idea that the old man was involved. Hell, they went to church together.

"Alright, men, let's ride."

It sounded like a posse in a western. The cars moved out, one by one, each with their assignments. No lights, no alarms, no warning until everyone was in place. No radio contact either. It would take about five minutes to get to the Albertson's farm. The ride was tense. Johnny rode with Hank in the lead car.

"How'd you find out about this deal, detective?" Hank asked Johnny.

"I've got two guys on the inside. I've known the one for a long time. We were friends for a while, but then his life got screwed up a bit. He straightened himself out though. Spent some time in the military. His brother, too. Marine Special Forces. They're a couple of fine men now."

"Well let's hope that this goes off without a hitch, and we'll see where we go from here. If these fellas are as good as you say, I'd like to thank them when this is over."

They rode the rest of the way in silence. When they were about 200 yards from the farmhouse on Lake Yale Road, they heard a siren off in the distance. It sounded like an ambulance but they couldn't be sure.

"Oh shit!" was Hank's only comment.

***

Inside the warehouse, Sonny Albertson heard the siren, too. He signaled for his boys to stop the crane. They listened as the siren appeared to get closer to the Albertson Farm.

Sonny pointed to two men and said, "You two, out the front service door and see if that cop's coming here. If you see him approaching, get your asses back in here.

Radar tensed as he listened to the siren get closer. He

wasn't watching for police, though. His eyes were darting from man to man to see if anyone was freaking out, or if they were keeping their cool. One of the Albertson boys on the crane was beginning to fidget around a bit. He reached to the floor of the crane and picked up his shotgun and gave it a once over. He appeared to be ready for a fight. *That might be my first target*, Radar thought.

The two men went outside the warehouse door and looked down the road in the direction of the siren and saw nothing. They stood there for a moment longer and were just about ready to step back in when they saw the cars approaching the warehouse. Then they saw the mounted flashers on top of the cars. They were only about one hundred fifty yards up the road and closing fast.

The two ran back inside the warehouse and shouted, "Cops! Right up the road!"

Sonny turned to Jason with an angry look on his face. "You told me that these two were clean."

He glared at Jason a moment longer then raised his 9mm and pointed it at Jason, then shifted it towards Pat. Before he could get a bead on Pat, Radar let loose with a short, silenced burst from his MP5. The whispering sound of the rounds could be heard, but was merely confusing to the crowd in the warehouse. Joe was the only one who recognized the sweet sound of silenced death.

Sonny Albertson was knocked back by the impact. Radar wasted no time re-sighting on the Albertson boy on the crane. Another quick burst and he was dead, falling to the bed of the semi truck. Two of the men ran to the vans and started to open the high bay doors. They started the vans and squealed the tires in an attempt to get out before the sheriff's cars arrived. One van tried to make it through the doors before they were open. The roof of the van caught the bottom of the door, making a loud scraping noise. Once the door was clear, the van sped off around the back of the warehouse. Their escape from the warehouse was cut off by several Sheriff's cars. The second van had a similar fate. Both drivers got out and raised their hands, knowing that they had no chance of escape.

Inside the warehouse, Jason Roberts looked at his fallen business associate and ran to the east side service door. Phil and Buddy followed. Pat and Joe retreated behind a work bench at the west side of the warehouse. They went down on one knee behind the bench on the same side of the warehouse as Radar. Pat and Joe were looking around the warehouse for any threats. Joe spotted Radar, and was confused by the figure in military style uniform, sporting a night scope on top of his head. He thought that this guy was really out of place. Where did he come from? He didn't remember seeing him enter the warehouse. He tapped Pat on the shoulder and pointed in Radar's direction. Pat gave a similar look of confusion. Joe recognized the MP5 Carbine with attached silencer and figured he must be on their side. He'd taken out Sonny Albertson before he could shoot Pat.

Their attention was drawn to gunfire that was coming in their direction. It was M16 fire from Buddy and Phil. Jason Roberts also had a pistol firing in their direction.

"I guess the partnership is over," Pat said to Joe.

"Looks that way. I guess they aren't happy with the arrangements anymore."

They both raised their 9mm pistols to return fire, but couldn't get much of a view from behind the shelves. They sat with guns in hand and hoped that they weren't rushed or they'd be dead men. Then another silenced burst headed in the direction of the west service door.

They heard a groan and someone shout, "I'm hit, motherfucker, I'm hit!"

They heard the service door open and close and there was silence inside the warehouse. They heard car doors open and close and lots of yelling outside. There were no more shots fired. It sounded like the Lake County Sheriff's department had things in hand. Pat and Joe cautiously stood and looked around the warehouse. There appeared to be no threat left inside, so they laid their guns on the floor and stood. They looked over to where the uniformed gunman had been, but he was nowhere to be seen. They walked out away from the shelves, continued to scan the empty warehouse, and kept their empty hands in front of them. The doors to the warehouse flew open, startling the brothers momentarily. The Sheriff's deputies ordered them to lay face down on the ground, hands spread. They did so gladly.

Johnny Poleirmo and Sheriff Hank Franklin entered the warehouse and saw Joe and Pat face down, being cuffed. Detective Poleirmo went over to where Pat lay and said, "Hey Pat, I'd like you to meet Sheriff Hank Franklin."

"Hey Johnny, can I get up first?" Pat asked.

"I guess that'd be alright."

Chapter 49

Pat and Joe met Hank Franklin and shook his hand. They swapped war stories briefly. It turned out that Hank was also a former Marine and had been stationed at Camp Lejeune briefly. Another of the Sheriff's Deputies had been in the Navy on the Carrier Nimitz. He was an MP, not a nuke like Pat.

Pat introduced his brother Joe to Detective Poleirmo. The detective gave them praise for their part in this major bust. He said that he'd like to talk with them about possible work in the future. Pat asked the detective if he and his wife would be interested in coming to a barbeque in Dunnellon some time. He assured Pat that he would.

Joe and Pat gave their statements to the Lake County Sheriff's department and promised to testify whenever the trial was scheduled. They had no pressing matters on their schedules, unless Lisa managed to set the hook. Then Joe might have a wedding to attend. It was 12:15 AM when Pat and Joe left the Lake County Sheriff's office and headed for Pine Hills. They thought about stopping for a beer, but decided that it could wait. On the way home, Joe asked Pat again who in the hell he thought that this mystery guy was. And again, Pat answered that he had no idea. They both agreed on one thing, they wanted to thank him.

Joe got to his apartment at just after 1:00 AM. He offered to have Pat stay the night, but Pat refused. He had to get home and see Diane. "I want to look in on my kids and see them sleeping soundly. I want to kiss my wife. I want to sleep in my own bed. I'll call you tomorrow sometime."

Pat looked at Joe and said, "It's finally over. We didn't get to do the honors, but it's really over."

"Those kind of honors aren't all they're cracked up to be.

You should know."

"You're right. At first, I thought that I'd feel some relief. I thought that killing Danny would make me happy. It wasn't like that at all. It was like dread. I think I'll be going to church next Sunday."

Joe headed upstairs to his apartment and was met halfway by Lisa. She threw her arms around Joe and kissed him hard on the lips, then hugged him again. They headed up the rest of the stairs together.

Pat headed for Dunnellon. He was dead tired from the strain of the evening, but he had no trouble making the drive. When he pulled into his drive, Diane ran out to the car and gave Pat the same routine as Lisa gave Joe.

"Don't you ever do this to me again," she said and kissed him hard again. They went inside to their bedroom, made love for an hour, and then slept until 8:00 the next morning. They were hauled from their bed by two very excited kids.

"Hi Daddy. We're starving," they shouted, smiled, and laughed.

"Okay you two. We're coming."

Diane whispered in Pat's ear, "And we'll be coming again later tonight," and she licked his ear.

Anna said, "Yuck. Mommy licked Daddy's ear."

"Yuck," Sean repeated after his little sister.

***

It was the Thursday morning after Brian Purcer and the Hot Licks opening concert. Brian had invited Pat, Diane, Joe, Lisa, Al Michaels, and his girlfriend to the show as his backstage guests. It was a sold-out show at the Orange County Convention Center. Brian had three more shows around Florida over the next week. One was in Tampa so he had time to spend the day in Dunnellon at Pat and Diane's. The whole group came to the barbeque for a late lunch and an afternoon of relaxation. Johnny and Rachael Poleirmo were there, too. Pat had barbeque ribs and chicken on the grill and cold beer and wine in the refrigerator. They were out on the patio enjoying the view of trees behind the house. The six of them were talking about Brian's concert and how he was really enjoying the early success of the band's CD. Brian was cautioning everyone that success was fleeting in this business. "It's too easy to get caught up in the excitement and blow it. Lots of stars die without a dime to their names," Brian said.

"But we're not going to let that happen to you, my friend. Have you talked to my financial friend yet?"

"Yes I did. I have an appointment next week. We'll be swinging back through here to do a show at the Lakeland Civic Center. Remember when we saw the Stones there? You left the nursery in the middle of the afternoon, when they announced that tickets were on sale. The show sold out in four hours, man. That was unbelievable."

"It was a blast." Diane gave Pat another look like, *there's another story that you never told me*. Pat looked back at her like, *there'll be plenty more where that one came from. What can I say?*

Sean came out to the patio yelling, "Dad, the mail's here." He handed the small stack of mail to Pat and headed back inside. Pat leafed through the stack of mostly junk mail, a charge bill, which he handed to Diane.

"This one's for you."

Then he came across an envelope with no return address. It was postmarked Jacksonville, Florida. Their address was handwritten in black ink and was neat, but not distinctive. It was addressed to Pat. The others were back talking about the show with Brian. Then they started in on Joe and Lisa, asking about plans. They both turned a bit red with embarrassment. They were non-committal.

Pat opened the envelope and pulled out two newspaper articles that had been cut from the Florida Times-Union out of Jacksonville. The heading on the first said 'Couple, Daughter Slain'. Pat read the article all the way through. It described the brutal murder of a couple from Moniac, Georgia and the murder/rape of their daughter. It went on to say that the Sheriff's office had no suspects. The victims were William Eugene Hatcher, Sr. and his wife Darlene, and their fourteen year old daughter. Their son, a member of the United States Navy, was at sea when the murders took place. Pat's head was swimming, and his face must have shown the pain he was experiencing.

Diane looked over and said, "What is it, sweetie?"

"Nothing. Anybody else need a beer or a glass of wine?" Joe and Brian both nodded and Pat headed into the kitchen, purportedly to get beer.

Pat read the second article. This heading read, Brothers Slain.' The story told of the brutal slaying of the Henson brothers. They were out on bail from a molestation charge when they were shot and killed. The shooting was with a .38 caliber hand gun. They were both bound and gagged and shot in the genitals. They were left to bleed to death in that condition. The final pieces of the puzzle were in place. Pat shook his head in disbelief. He turned the second article over and read a handwritten note, "I'll catch up with you soon." It was signed 'Radar'.

Pat was subdued for the rest of the afternoon. He enjoyed everyone's company, and they vowed to do it again real soon or as soon as Brian could get off the road.

When everyone left that evening, Diane and Pat relaxed in their living room on the rug in front of the fireplace. Diane asked Pat about the letter. He told her it was from a friend from the Navy. He then asked her if she really wanted to know everything about him. He told her that she might not like the whole story. She replied that she could live without knowing, but that she would always wonder. She also said that she was picking up bits and pieces along the way.

Pat looked into her eyes and asked as seriously as he could, "Is that going to be enough for you? I mean, I'm not sure you really want to know. I'll make you a deal though. If you ever decide that you want to know everything, you just ask. Fair enough?"

"Fair enough."

"I have one more thing to do before I can rest easy. I have to go to the grove tomorrow. It may take a few days but I'll be home every night."

"What do you plan to do?"

Pat's lips curled up slightly at the corners. He leaned over and kissed his wife on the cheek then laid back and stared at the fire light reflecting off of the ceiling.

***

Johnny Poleirmo was back at the Orange County Sheriff's office finishing up his paperwork on the case when Al Porecwzski came over from homicide.

"Hey Johnny, nice job with the Lake County boys. Sounds like a real haul; a hundred and forty bales? Street value must be pretty high, no pun intended."

They both chuckled a bit.

"We were pretty much just along for the ride, but you know what scares me? Some of the hardware they had was definitely military grade. Where are these guys getting this stuff? It's some pretty scary duty out there right now."

Al nodded his head in agreement. "Worse, it's for what, pot? We wiped out that shipment and there's already a dozen other dealers scrambling to get the open action. Why are we wasting our time on that stuff? We have some serious crap out there. Crack, Crank, Heroine? All those date rape drugs? And we're risking our lives on grass. I don't know, Al. Is it worth it?

"You got me partner. I just want to make it to fifty-five so I can retire up north. Hell, my folks want to move down here. I can't wait to get back to New York. Crazy, ain't it?"

Johnny just smiled and signed the last page of his report. *I guess this is what we're calling success these days.*

Chapter 50

Pat was at the grove at 7:15 AM. The trees were full of oranges ready to be picked. He pulled one from a tree, pulled out a pocket knife and peeled the outer skin by making four longitudinal cuts at quarter distance apart. He ate the sweet plugs of orange as he waited for his guests to arrive. He'd called a number of people to meet him there throughout the day. His first visitor was a scrawny-looking man from a scrap yard. He had dark, rough looking skin and was slightly hunched over from his shoulders up to the base of his skull. He looked to be about sixty years old, but Pat guessed at closer to fifty. He reckoned the extra ten years of wear and tear was courtesy of hard work and harder drinking. He told the man what he wanted and asked when he could get started. The man said that he'd be back in less than an hour.

His second guest was Al Michaels. He tossed Al an orange whose skin was already cut, ready to peel and eat. He asked Al if he would be interested in buying the nursery for $150,000. Al told him that it was worth well over $500,000. Pat said he knew. He told Al if he wanted to buy it and resell it that was up to him. Al agreed and they shook hands. Pat assured him that he'd stop by his house for a beer before he headed back to Dunellon. They shook hands and agreed to get the paperwork together in the next few days.

The third visitor was from a real estate company that specialized in commercial sales such as orange groves. Except for the asking price, Jimmy Pitman had the contract all filled in and ready to sign. He looked around the property and said, "Hey, I remember this grove. This used to belong to Mr. and Mrs. Hammerick. You're one of the brothers that bought it back about ten years ago."

"That's right. You were Mrs. Hammerick's agent back

then."

"Old Mrs. Hammerick is still alive and enjoying life up in North Carolina. She sends a postcard once in a while. Why are you selling?"

"Well, this grove is haunted. There are ghosts everywhere. You see over there by the vault? Four guys were killed there just about a week ago." Pat pointed to the remnants of the yellow crime scene tape that had been tied to the trees.

"I read about that in the papers. One was a Sheriff. He must've been a bad egg. They said he was involved in drug protection and some other bad shit. Pardon my language."

"No problem. That's why we're selling, though."

As they talked, a large flatbed truck pulled into the drive approaching the vault. The guys from the scrap metal company were back. They parked and started to unload equipment with a fork lift made for riding in sandy areas like orange groves and beaches.

Jimmy Pitman asked, "What are they doing here?"

"One thing I forgot to tell you is that the vault doesn't come with the grove. These fellows are removing it. I'll have sand brought in to fill in the hole."

"Are you serious? It'll cost you a ton to remove that thing."

"It's already cost me a ton. Anything else I spend is an investment in my sanity."

Jimmy Pitman shook Pat's hand, took his copy of the agreement and headed back to his car. As he was pulling out, another car pulled in. William Hatcher, Jr. walked up to Pat and held out his hand. He didn't smile or show any emotion at all.

"I got your note," Pat said. "How did you figure all this out?"

"Y'all talk in your sleep for starters. I was afraid that some of our shipmates on the *Alabama* would think that y'all was loony. I'm surprised the Navy let ya stay in, yackin' it up like that. Hell, y'all kept me awake many-a-night. Then when ya wrote out a few bits and pieces on that notepad in your bunk, and we had a battle stations missile drill, I saw the notes showing from under your bunk. I started to do a little investigative work on my own. It pissed me off. Y'all don't know what I went through when my little sister was killed." Hatch paused and looked around the grove. He took a deep breath, popped a slice of orange in his mouth, and savored the taste for a few moments. Then he continued, "It was bad enough that they killed my folks. But my innocent, baby sister...I still have nightmares. I figured out who they were, gave the information to the cops, and they said they couldn't do anything about it. After I caught up with 'em, well, y'all read the article. The cops knew it was me, but they left me alone. Didn't even question me. Guess they figured justice was served."

"Why'd you take on my problems?"

"I already have blood on my hands. I've got no one left. Y'all's got a wife and kids. A real life to live."

"How'd you get out of that warehouse in Umatilla?"

"There's a trap door in the floor. It goes to the house. I went into the house and out the side door. I ran along the pasture fence to the road. It took me two hours to make it through that swampy area. I had a boat out on Lake Yale. They were pissed that I was out on the lake so late. I gave them an extra hundred bucks for their trouble and they were happy."

"One last question. What's up with this 'Radar' shit? Where'd you come up with that name? Sounds a little 'secret mission-ish, don't you think?"

"My sister used to call me that, you know, after the guy on MASH. I did it in her honor. I guess it was kind of corny."

They stood in silence for a few minutes, watching the guys prepare to tear down the vault, thinking about their own ghosts.

Finally Hatch broke the silence. "Ya know, I'll never get over losing my parents and my sister. It hasn't destroyed my life, but it sure has changed it. It's gotta be the same for y'all. True?"

Pat thought about this for a minute before answering. "It has definitely changed my life. Mike let it destroy his. It consumed him. Joe and I, well...we'll survive. We're going to exorcise our demons. It starts right here."

Another car pulled into the grove. Joe got out and came over to Pat and Hatch.

Pat turned to greet Joe and said, "I'd like you to meet Hatch, code name Radar."

Joe took Hatch's hand and shook it. He smiled and said, "I admire your work. But what's with the 'Radar' thing?"

Hatch just shook his head and smiled. "I'll let Pat tell y'all that one."

The three of them stood and watched as the men lit their torches and started to disassemble the vault, one piece at a time. As the walls came down, Pat could feel the ghosts of his past fly away. He felt free for the first time in years.

###

McKinney Brothers Mystery Suspense Novels

A Lifetime of Vengeance
A Lifetime of Deception
A Lifetime of Exposure
A Lifetime of Terror
A Lifetime of Betrayal

Peden Savage Suspense Novel

Drug Wars
Flash Drive

Non-Series Novel

Under the Blood Tree

Pete 'P.J.' Grondin, born the seventh of twelve children, moved around a number of times when he was young; from Sandusky, Ohio to Bay City, Michigan, then to Maitland and Zellwood, Florida before returning to Sandusky, OH. It was there that he met his future bride.

After his service in the US Navy in the Nuclear Power Program, serving on the ballistic missile submarine, USS *John Adams*, Pete returned to his hometown of Sandusky, OH where he was elected to the Sandusky City Commission, serving a single term. He worked as an Application Process Specialist in the IT department of a major electric utility until his retirement in 2015.

His current novels in the McKinney Brothers series are *A Lifetime of Vengeance, A Lifetime of Deception, A Lifetime of Exposure, A Lifetime of Terror, and A Lifetime of Betrayal*.

His first two novels in the Peden Savage series are *Drug Wars* and *Flash Drive*. His first non-series suspense novel is *Under the Blood Tree*.